BOOK THREE OF
THE DARKWOLF SAGA

# THE
# SCARLET
# QUEEN

## MITCH REINHARDT

# THE SCARLET QUEEN

For Sue

# Acknowledgements

Developmental/Copy Editor – Alice McVeigh
Cover Design – James Egan at Bookfly Design
Interior Design – Marina & Jason Anderson at Polgarus Studio
Beta Readers – Scott McDonald, Danny Hay, Sue Call,
                    Stacey Call
Proof Reader – Alexis Whitney at Sweetheart Author Services

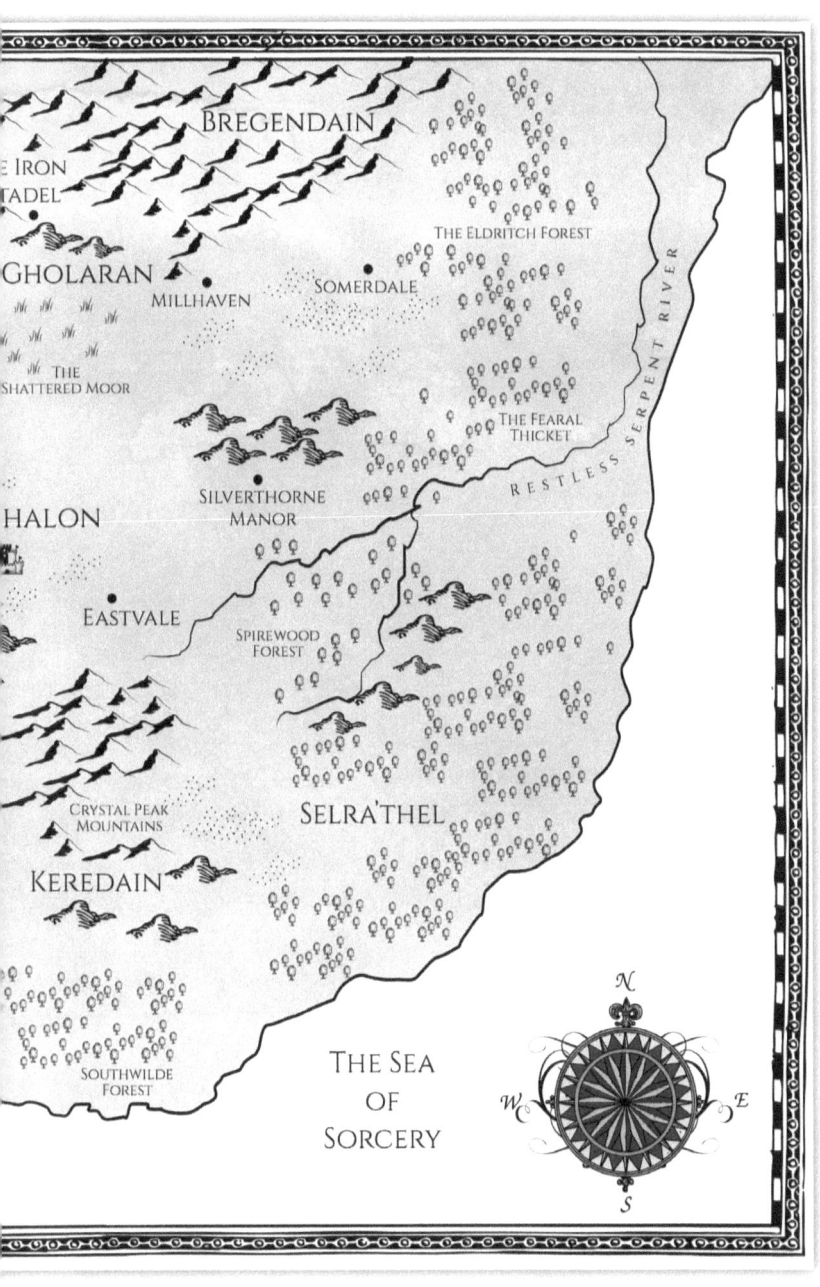

BREGENDAIN

THE IRON
CITADEL

GHOLARAN

MILLHAVEN

SOMERDALE

THE ELDRITCH FOREST

THE
SHATTERED MOOR

THE FEARAL
THICKET

SILVERTHORNE
MANOR

RESTLESS SERPENT RIVER

HALON

EASTVALE

SPIREWOOD
FOREST

CRYSTAL PEAK
MOUNTAINS

SELRA'THEL

KEREDAIN

SOUTHWILDE
FOREST

THE SEA
OF
SORCERY

N
W   E
S

# CHAPTER ONE
## JANE'S ESCAPE

*How had she gotten here?* Biting her lower lip, Jane tried to remember. There had been some kind of an argument, she knew. The others had tried to force her to go with them. She thought she'd known who they were but still she had resisted. At least, she recalled resisting, even fighting. She had the bruises to prove it.

Though obviously she must have lost, having awoken at the garrison of Troll Fang Pass. Brushing back her shoulder-length brown hair, she pulled on the sheepskin cloak she had stolen from the unconscious midwife, hoping, rather guiltily, that the blow to her head hadn't hurt her much.

Jane slipped down the wooden stairs and into the chilly courtyard, heart racing. Outside, everyone appeared to be in a hurry. Heavily armored men and elves were bustling about, packing supplies and making preparations for their march toward the great walled city of Chalon, the trade center of Alluria. The tramping of boots on cobbles mingled with creaking wagons, yelled orders and horses' whinnying. Keeping her head down and her cloak wrapped tightly around her, Jane slipped unnoticed through the heavy wooden gates of the battered garrison.

Rain must have fallen overnight, leaving a soggy, uneven path. Jane glanced over her shoulder. Nobody was in pursuit, at least, or at least no one that she could detect. Eventually, of course, they would be after her, but this was her only chance and she had to take it. She took a deep breath and bounded down the rocky hillside toward Troll Fang Pass. A few minutes later, she darted across the pass before disappearing into the remnants of a forest.

Many of the trees had been damaged by barbarians and ogres during the attack on the garrison. It seemed like a long time ago, but perhaps it hadn't been. Her memory felt shaky – now and then she even felt dizzy. *There had been a huge battle and...*she shuddered as a grotesquely misshapen, glaring ogre surged up from the depths of her memory. *Something* had happened after the ogre had dragged down the garrison wall, but she couldn't quite remember what.

But this was no time to become distracted. Pulling herself together, she started running again. Her breaths lingered in the chilly air for only a moment before dissipating. Her legs soon began to ache, but she knew that she had to put as much distance between herself and the garrison as possible. To the north, where the trees gradually thinned, a snow-capped mountain range emerged into view. By then, she simply had to stop, her chest hurt there were still no pursuers behind her.

She closed her eyes and stood for a moment, breathing heavily, trying to remember someone. Yet, each time, just as the face started to form, it slipped teasingly away. Suddenly, she raised her head and smiled in sheer relief. She had forgotten his name. Even his face and the outline of his strong form was only partly clear. However, she was suddenly sure – as sure as if she'd heard his voice. She was heading in the right direction and that *he* was there, high in the mountains, waiting for her.

But then another shudder of nerves ran through her. What if she was captured on the way? What if she never saw him again? What was his name? Zane? Zach?

The thought was unbearable. Grasping her cloak tighter still around her shoulders, she resumed her course north. And whenever the sensation that she might be making some fundamental error nagged at her, she pushed the thought away. She had to get back to the one who truly mattered.

Nearly a mile further on, Jane suddenly froze. In the distance, almost a hundred yards away, she had spotted the unmistakable shapes of two armored sentries. They were standing on a hillside, their horses, cropping grass, tethered to a nearby tree. If she could only divert the sentries' attention, she just might stand a chance of stealing one of the horses. How much easier her task would be if only she could ride. Jane moved closer, shielding herself within the dense undergrowth. Yet as she crept near enough to see the sentries, her hopes sank. They were unmistakably elven warriors, casual, graceful, symmetrically featured.

Jane frowned. Elvish ears could detect almost anything. She would have to get much closer than felt safe to distract them, or even to use a spell to entangle them with the surrounding trees or plants. With a sigh of frustration, Jane retraced her steps, as quietly as she could, back into the woods. Once there, she picked up her pace, leaping over fallen branches, weaving between bushes and trees.

An unexpected rumble of thunder caused her to pause and glance upwards, where roiling wreaths of clouds foreshadowed a wet night. As the first few raindrops landed on her face, Jane closed her eyes and tilted her head back.

"Jane!"

Someone was calling her. Jane's eyes widened, her hand rushing to her throat. She tensed, conscious of a tingling on the surface of her skin and a heavy weight in her stomach. She crouched, poised to run.

"Jane!"

*It was a familiar voice,* she thought, just as the rain began to fall harder. She also caught a brief glimpse of movement through the trees. Panicking, Jane whirled and sprinted away. *Why hadn't she remembered to cast the spell that masked her tracks? How stupid she had been!*

As she ran, she distinguished several different voices behind her, some male, and some female. They were getting closer and closer. Suddenly she recognized the one of the voices. Sawyer, someone called Sawyer. He sounded almost frantic.

*Perhaps she should try to hide…no, they were too many and they would certainly find her.* Instead, she had to keep running. There really was no going back.

"There she is!" cried a female voice.

Glancing over her shoulder, Jane saw four shapes running toward her. Two beautiful female elves skimmed, with enviable effortlessness, through the forest, easily outdistancing two human males.

The taller elf, whose skin was a golden bronze, had dark blonde hair and leather armor. Jane gasped. She had such presence that the trees and shrubs leaned away from her, enabling her to pass without hindrance.

The smaller, younger female, who was similarly clad,

carried a bow and sprinted in her wake while the two humans crashed through branches and stumbled over rocks in a determined effort to keep up. The taller dark-haired male, whom Jane secretly acknowledged to be well-built and good-looking, wore intricate armor with a sword and scabbard flung across his back.

Her last pursuer was less intimidating. He was blond, thinner, and smaller, wearing a simple tunic and breeches which seemed a little too large for him. He kept getting snagged on branches and losing his footing. She was sure she could outrun him.

Still, she couldn't possibly outrun them all, especially the elves.

Jane swiftly scoured the area for acorns, slipping several tightly into her palm.

*If she could just give herself time to get away, she'd be able to mask her trail and she might still be able to find a place to hide.* They were closing on her, but she had to try. Briefly pausing, she pointed toward the ground, summoning up the druidic words.

"*Bar'athel envora*," she said.

The grasses instantly lengthened, whipping the air like vibrant snakes, while the trees stretched their limbs in effort to ensnare her pursuers. Sawyer hadn't noticed what was happening until he was wrapped in a grassy cocoon, as was the smaller, lighter human.

*Geoff,* she remembered. *Geoff, of course…*

But the two elves were far nimbler, especially the one carrying a bow. Her fourth pursuer, however, the taller elf, had only to hold up her hand for the treacherous grasses to shrink back into themselves, overruling Jane's spell.

Blinking in disbelief, Jane realized that the tall elf was incredibly, shockingly, powerful. No matter how furiously she concentrated, the surrounding flora ignored her. Instead, she watched, in a near-panic, as Sawyer and Geoff were released by the grassy tendrils that she had summoned to hold them.

*Ariel.* Jane groaned, as her memory retrieved the name. Then a flash of movement to her left caught Jane's attention. The elven archer was also rapidly closing in.

"*Ana'thel,*" Jane shouted as she threw an acorn. However, she had misjudged the distance and the projectile struck a tree behind her target, though its green explosion still rocked the delicate elf off-balance. Sawyer and Geoff were closing in on her, yet Ariel was almost upon her.

Without another thought Jane threw another acorn, this one straight at Ariel.

"*Ana'thel,*" she yelled, anticipating another explosion.

Instead, Ariel neatly caught the acorn between two slim fingers.

No explosion. Nothing.

Jane's jaw dropped as she watched Ariel drop the acorn beside her, having neutralized Jane's attack. Jane gritted her teeth and glared.

"Okay, then," she said. "Fine. Give this a try."

Jane slung the remaining acorns at Ariel and the others with all her might.

"*Ana'thel!*"

She flicked her fingers, expertly dispersing the remaining acorns in several directions. Ariel, who had been sprinting toward her, stopped, spun around and ordered, "Get back, all of you!"

"Look out, Geoff!" Sawyer shouted as he pushed the smaller teen to the ground.

The resulting mass of explosions sent chunks of soil and bits of trees flying. Briefly, a thick, smoky haze filled the air and lingered. Jane spun and dashed away.

"Sawyer! Geoff!" Ariel called.

"We're okay," Sawyer coughed back. "Don't worry about us. Keep going!"

Jane frowned. How could she possibly outrun Ariel? Digging into her reserves of strength, Jane pushed deeper and deeper into the woods. From her left, Jane heard something whistling through the air followed by a distinct *thwack* as an arrow impacted the base of a tree just ahead.

*So close!* Shaken, she tried to avoid the arrow as she ran, but her foot tripped on the shaft, sending her tumbling to the ground and knocking the breath out of her. She scrambled to her knees, gasping for air.

Glancing around, she saw that the elven archer had already nocked another arrow and was taking careful aim, eyes narrowing. *Ishara. Her name was Ishara.* At least there were a few acorns within reach. Jane grabbed a handful of acorns, gritty with grass and dirt. Just as she was about to hurl them, she became distracted by a flash of movement at the top of the hill just ahead of her.

Confused and exhausted as she was, she still half-recognized the man in tattered animal skins. Her momentary hesitation gave Ariel just enough time to close the distance between them. As Jane wheeled around, she found herself face to face with Ariel.

Her emerald green eyes held Jane motionless. Before she could react, Ariel waved a slender hand over her face.

*"Sol'nara."*

"Sleep, Jane," Ariel said. "Sleep."

As she collapsed into Ariel's arms, the elf regarded the human teenager for a moment. Then she directed a sharp glance toward the tree line at the top of the hill. A couple of branches still swung back and forth. *Someone, or something, had been there and had distracted Jane.*

Ishara appeared beside Ariel, with bow and arrows.

"Her power grows."

Ariel nodded but remained silent. She shifted Jane's body in her arms and lifted her up. They turned and started walking back toward the others.

"But did you see?" Ishara persisted, keeping her eyes forward. "Her aura has dimmed. She no longer shines like Geoff and Sawyer."

"Yes," Ariel said with a frown as she looked down at the two red scars on Jane's neck. "I too am troubled. Evil has taken root in Jane."

# Chapter Two

## A Beautiful Nightmare

Geoff coughed and held his aching right arm as he scrambled behind Sawyer. Occasionally he glanced down at his blood-soaked hand and winced. He'd been nailed by some flying debris, perhaps a rock or a chunk of tree, loosed by one of Jane's explosions, and he'd also inhaled dust and smoke. He was relieved to see Ariel and Ishara emerge from the thick woods about a hundred yards away.

The second Sawyer spotted them he began to run. Geoff tried to keep pace, but fell behind, still coughing.

"Jane!" Sawyer called. "Is she okay? What happened to her?"

"She is fine," Ariel said, handing Jane to Sawyer. "She needs rest."

"What's happening to her, Ariel?" Sawyer said. "Why'd she try to kill us?"

"I am not convinced that was her intention," Ariel told him flatly. "I believe she merely wanted to escape."

"Escape?" Sawyer said. "I don't get it, I thought she'd be herself again once we got her away from the Shadowlord. Why would she want to escape from us?"

*Good point,* Geoff thought as he trotted up to the others. He'd also hoped the old Jane would return once they'd rescued her.

"Geoff, you are injured," Ishara said as she took Geoff's arm and examined it.

"A little," he said. "I think it's okay. One of Jane's exploding acorns got me."

Ariel took his arm and gently rolled up the sleeve to his tunic, revealing a large cut on his forearm. She removed a small brown leather pouch from her belt and sprinkled some crushed leaves over the wound. Geoff had seen this spell before. It was one of the first spells Jane had learned from Ariel.

"The cut is deep," Ariel observed, as she placed her palm over the wound. "*Ilinara tae ullnara taethos.*"

Geoff's arm tingled and he felt a warming sensation radiating from his arm to his shoulder, into his chest, and then all through the rest of his body.

"Better?" Ariel inquired, with a slight smile.

"Yeah, thanks," Geoff said. The pain had disappeared, and he felt refreshed, almost renewed. He raised his eyes to Ariel. "So what happens now? What do we do with Jane?"

"We must hurry back to the garrison," Ariel said. "Trelane and Commander Renfry will wait, but not for long. The Shadowlord's great northern army has already been sighted near the pass. We must pack our things and prepare to leave."

"But what about Jane?" Sawyer insisted. "She's not herself. She's different, somehow. We gotta help her."

"We will. I promise," Ariel said. "First, we need to get Jane as far away from the Shadowlord and his army as possible."

Ariel glanced over her shoulder to the north. Geoff was

sure he saw a hint of worry in her expression. Anything that could give Ariel cause to worry came under the heading of bad news. She was the High Druid of Alluria. She could do the most amazing things. She could cast spells, heal, and she was the greatest warrior he'd ever seen. She reminded Geoff of the superheroes he'd read about back at home. So, if Ariel was worried, then they were really in trouble.

"What is it, Ariel?" he asked. "What's wrong?"

Ariel turned back to Geoff and the others. "Nothing. We have lost time we could ill afford to lose. As I said, we must hurry back."

"But she blew up half the forest with a handful of acorns," Sawyer said, turning to Ariel. "How's that even possible? I don't remember you teaching her how to do that."

"I did not," Ariel countered, her face became expressionless as they marched back the way they had come.

Geoff kept an eye on Sawyer. He would glance down at Jane from time to time with a pained look in his eyes. He looked worried and angry. If vampire lore in Alluria was anything like it was back home, a vampire's bite would have made Jane the vampire's servant, even his slave. For Jane, that would be worse than death. Geoff bit his lower lip as he thought. Maybe they could make some wooden stakes and put an end to the Shadowlord? He felt sure Ariel would know what to do, she always did.

He noticed Ishara walking, tight-lipped and eyes lowered, although occasionally she would cast a glance at Ariel. Apparently, she knew something he and Sawyer didn't. All he knew was that something felt wrong.

"So how're we going be able to travel with Jane always trying to escape?" Geoff asked, directing his question at

Ariel's back as they walked. "Sawyer's right. She tried to kill us and she did blow up half the forest. How do we defend ourselves against that?"

Ariel didn't answer. Geoff looked at Sawyer, who shook his head as he carried Jane.

"Ariel?"

"Geoff, we must first return to the garrison," Ariel said. "We will have time to decide once we have consulted with the others and are safely on our way to the city of Chalon."

"But we gotta help her," Sawyer said. "Isn't there some spell that can make Jane herself again?"

"The Shadowlord's hold over her is stronger than I had realized," Ariel admitted as she turned around and exhaled loudly. "Remain hopeful, Sawyer."

"In movies back home," Geoff began then paused to swallow. "The only way to save someone from a vampire's bite is to kill the vampire who bit them."

"Another reason why we should've killed the Shadowlord when we rescued Jane," Sawyer said in a terse tone. "Look, let's go find him and put an end to all this. Let's win the war and release Jane at the same time. What's wrong with that?"

"Nothing," Ariel said, picking up her pace. "I am sure he will be here soon. Do you wish to wait for him…and his army of thousands?"

Sawyer didn't answer. He just looked at Jane again. His grim, tight-lipped face was all Geoff needed to see to know he was hurting and confused. Sawyer and Jane really liked each other, it was obvious to everyone else even though they had tried to keep it a secret. On more than one occasion Geoff noticed them sneaking a kiss when they'd thought no one else was paying attention.

"I would gladly face the Shadowlord again if it meant we could save Jane," Ariel said. "But now we know he is not our final enemy. It is Lysis, the Scarlet Queen."

"We gotta do something," Geoff said. "How're we gonna travel to Chalon with Jane if she's always trying to get back to the Shadowlord?"

"And," Ishara said. "Though I am not well versed in vampire lore, I believe time is not Jane's friend."

"What?" Sawyer said as he abruptly stopped and faced Ishara. "What's that mean?"

"It means," Ariel said quietly, "that if we do not help Jane soon, she will be lost to the darkness forever."

"Whoa, whoa, whoa," Sawyer said. "What exactly are you saying? Jane's gonna die?" He glared at Ariel. "We can't let that happen. Whatever it takes, just tell us what to do, Ariel."

"Sawyer," Ariel said, holding up a hand for calm, "we are already doing everything we can. Jane must be kept as far away from the Shadowlord as possible if we are to undo the evil that has infected her. So, we must hurry back."

"Ariel," Geoff said, locking his eyes on hers. "Are we going to lose Jane?"

Ariel regarded him for a few seconds before responding, a few seconds that struck Geoff like a blow to the stomach.

"Of course not," Ariel said finally. "Not, at least, as long as I live."

No one said another word the rest of the way back as they struggled with their own concerns, for Jane and for themselves. The falling rain and thunder further dampened everyone's mood. Geoff's thoughts drifted back to the old horror movies he used to watch on TV. They never ended well for the vampire, and their slaves always seemed to meet with a gruesome end.

When they arrived at the garrison, they were met by the handsome, imposing figure of Trelane, commander of the elven forces sent by Selra'thel's king, Andurys. Not a single dark blond hair on Trelane's head was out of place. He approached them as they emerged from the battered forest on the other side of the pass from the garrison.

"*Hal'inari*," he said, looking at Ariel and Ishara, who returned his greeting. Then he regarded Jane, still sleeping in Sawyer's arms.

"How is your friend?" he asked.

"Not sure," Sawyer said, shaking his head. "She's okay for now, I guess."

Trelane nodded and looked at Ariel. "I have sent a scouting party north. The Shadowlord's army is rapidly approaching. By this time tomorrow they will be here. We should leave for Chalon at first light."

"Have you sent word to Chalon? Lionel must be warned."

"I have," Trelane said. "So has the garrison commander. His name is Renfry, and I believe him to be trustworthy."

Ariel lifted a single inquisitive eyebrow.

"I thought, since King Lionel does not trust elves," Trelane said, "that perhaps he would trust the word of his commander. Renfry seems to be an honorable human."

Ariel nodded. Geoff wiped the rain from his eyes. He turned to Ishara, who was standing a few feet away. Judging by somber her expression, she wasn't enjoying standing around in the rain either, but it was Sawyer who said, "Hey, we need to get Jane somewhere dry; also, my arms are killing me."

He shifted the weight of Jane's body in his arms and walked through the front gate of the garrison. Geoff and Ishara followed him. Looking over his shoulder, Geoff noticed Ariel and Trelane had remained and were speaking to each other in their elvish language.

"I don't suppose," Geoff whispered to Ishara, "that you'd care to tell me what they're talking about?"

Ishara kept her gaze forward. "They are talking about you."

"Really?"

"No, silly," Ishara said. "They are talking about when and where to best face the Shadowlord."

"You've got amazing hearing," Geoff said. "I can't even hear their voices anymore."

Ishara stopped and stared back at Ariel and Trelane. Geoff paused too, curious.

"What is it?" Geoff said. "Now what're they saying?"

"He is telling her that scouts have reported seeing a man in frayed animal skins nearby."

"You mean that Alex guy? The one who helped us with the bandits?"

"Ariel seems to think so," Ishara said with a nod.

"Caught between the Shadowlord and a werewolf…this isn't looking good."

"Yo!" Sawyer called from the doorway to the keep. "You coming or not?"

Geoff and Ishara followed Sawyer into the small keep where they were met by Commander Renfry. He stroked his graying dark beard and smiled at them. His large, scarred arms folded across his chest. Geoff noticed that he also sported a fresh scar on his cheek from the battle at Troll Fang Pass.

"I was beginning to worry about you," Renfry said. "I'm glad you found your friend. How is she?"

"She's okay," Sawyer said. "She just needs to rest for a while."

Renfry nodded and motioned up the stairs behind him. "Very well, you know the way to my quarters. I've cleared out the rest of my belongings. The room is yours. Remember, we leave at dawn."

"Thanks," Sawyer said. He climbed the uneven wooden stairs to one of the few rooms in the keep left intact after the siege.

"The midwife that Jane injured," Ishara said, stopping in front of Renfry. "Is she better now?"

"She took a good knock on the head," Renfry said. "But yes, she'll be fine. If Ariel has time, perhaps she can examine her."

"Of course," Ariel said as she walked up. "Where is she?"

"In the kitchen with the other two midwives from Chalon," Renfry said. "Last I heard, the bleeding has been staunched but she's still in pain. Imagine what would've happened if your friend had got hold of a real weapon instead of a piece of firewood."

"I would rather not," Ariel said. She looked at Geoff and Ishara. "Go. I will be along as soon as I have tended to the midwife."

Geoff and Ishara ascended the stairs. The room at the top contained only a single bed, a few rickety wooden chairs around a table, and a rough stone fireplace. Jane was lying on the bed with Sawyer beside her.

"Looks like we gotta clear out tomorrow morning," Geoff said, pulling up a chair and having a seat.

"Yeah, I heard," Sawyer said. "Renfry's voice carries."

"Ariel will be here soon," Ishara said, leaning her bow against the stone wall as she walked over to the bed and caressed Jane's cheek. "She is so brave to chance the wilds of Alluria."

"I don't think she had anything to worry about," Geoff said. "She almost took us all out with her spells. She can take care of herself."

"So how do we get Jane back?" Sawyer said, looking up at Geoff and Ishara.

Geoff shook his head and glanced at Ishara. She remained silent as well.

A brusque rap on the door announced the arrival of two ruddy-faced midwives, wearing long dresses and aprons. The first was carrying bedding and a pillow, while the second had a pitcher and a bowl with a washing cloth.

A booming crash of thunder rattled the lone window in the room, startling the midwives and Geoff.

"Oh my, my," said the second midwife as she set the pitcher on the table. "If this crumbling keep and the Shadowlord won't be the death of us, then this awful weather will."

"Up, dears," said the other, plopping the bedding down by Jane's feet. "We need to see to your poor friend's comfort. Move now, give us some room."

Sawyer looked at Jane for a moment before he was shooed off the bed. The steady tapping of the rain against the window drew Geoff's attention. Peering through the thick glass he noticed that it had suddenly grown darker outside, much darker. It didn't seem like a natural darkness. There was something eerie about it.

"Come," Ariel said. She had appeared at the door and

motioned for everyone to leave the room while the midwives began their work. "Jane will be well-attended. We have much to discuss."

Ishara grabbed her bow and followed. Geoff noticed that Sawyer glanced back at Jane one last time before shutting the door.

"All these elves," said the first midwife, the moment the door closed. "I only hope Commander Renfry knows what he's doing. Why would any normal person want to trust elves?"

"And there's are so many of them," said the second midwife, adjusting her wimple disapprovingly. She leaned forward and whispered, "I say they're secret allies of that Shadowlord. I wouldn't trust them, always strutting about pretending they're better than everyone else."

"Elves better than us? Stuff and nonsense," the first midwife said. Nodding at the sleeping Jane, she added, "As for that poor sweet creature, you want my opinion, she's been bewitched and I say it was that tall yellow-haired elf druid that did it."

"Well, *I* heard that she was kidnapped by the Shadowlord, and held a prisoner in his castle. Can you imagine the horror?"

"Oh my, that must've been a nightmare."

The midwives quickly finished their work and left. Jane opened her eyes when she heard the door shut behind them. Her gaze fell upon the window. For a long moment, she watched the rain streaking down the glass. Then she got out of bed, and crossed over to the window, peering into the dark torrential downpour.

Running her fingers down the glass's cool surface, she sighed. "A beautiful nightmare."

# CHAPTER THREE

## STORMS

Geoff followed the others down the rickety stairs. Ariel walked to the rough stone fireplace situated in the center of the far wall. She took a few pieces of firewood that had been neatly stacked beside it and tossed them in.

"*Ignara.*"

As soon as Ariel finished uttering her spell, a small burst of fire danced sideways along the length of each log. Sawyer stretched out his hands to let the warmth of the fire heat his fingers. Geoff did likewise.

"So Ariel, you still haven't really answered my questions. How do we get Jane back? Why'd she run away in the first place?"

"The truth is…I do not know," Ariel said. "I am as surprised as you by Jane's actions. She seriously injured that midwife who was cleaning her room. She must have been compelled to do it because our Jane would never harm another. She is a healer."

"So what're you saying? Why *did* she run away? And why did she fight us? Is she possessed or something?"

"Or could she be under the spell of the Shadowlord?" Geoff suggested.

"Not yet," Ariel said. "At least not fully. I believe Jane's mind is still her own and she has a strong will. I think within Jane a battle rages between good and evil. She may be utterly confused. As Ishara suggested, time is against us."

"But she fought us. Twice," Geoff added. "She almost killed us, Ariel."

Ariel turned her gaze to the smoky fire in front of them and sighed.

"She did, and, for that reason, we must all be vigilant and keep an eye on Jane. She needs us and we must not fail her."

As Geoff stared into the fireplace, watching the flames lick the blackened stone, another troubling thought popped into his head. "But what if we lose her? What if she does go bad? Could she become a vampire, too?"

Sawyer shot an irritated glance at Geoff.

"Look, I don't want that to happen," Geoff continued, "But it's not a dumb question. I'm just asking what might happen to Jane if, you know, she gets away and the dark side wins and all."

"That would be up to the Shadowlord," Ariel said. "However, the answer to your question is 'yes.' Almost certainly, Jane would be lost to us forever and become a malicious creature, preying on others."

"Oh, great," Sawyer said moodily as he tossed a pebble into the fireplace. "I can just see us trying to explain *that* to her parents. 'So sorry, Mr. and Mrs. Harvest, but we went to fantasy land and now your daughter's a vampire. Hope you have a nice day, anyway!'"

"Yeah, tell me about it," Geoff said heavily, then he added, "But what could we do to break the vampire's bond? Drive a stake through his heart? Maybe drag him into a sunrise and watch him burst into flames?"

Ariel tilted her head and looked at Geoff with wide eyes.

"Wherever did you hear that? Let me dispel some of your misconceptions about vampires," Ariel said. "I do not know how you came to believe vampires burst into flames in sunlight or die from a wooden stake driven through the heart. Ridiculous."

"Movies," Geoff muttered, "And books, too."

"I do not know anything about movies," Ariel said. "But it seems your books are little better than fairy tales full of wild assertions written by madmen."

"So how do we kill a vampire here?" Sawyer said.

"In daylight, a vampire is as normal as any man," Ariel said. "But at night, a vampire's strength and agility rise to impossible levels and they gain dark powers of hypnosis and suggestion, enabling them to manipulate their victims. However, it takes an enchanted weapon piercing its heart to kill a vampire."

"Like your scimitars," Geoff said. "And Sawyer's sword."

"Hold on a minute," Sawyer said holding up a hand. "It was daytime when you fought the Shadowlord in the grasslands. He put up a good fight and almost killed you. How could he do that in daylight?"

"True," Ariel agreed. "He was stronger and faster than any human could ever be, but I am not sure how he maintained most of his vampiric abilities even during the day."

Several moments of silence passed, then Sawyer cleared his throat and asked, "So what's our next move?"

"We go south to Chalon. We regroup and prepare to face the Shadowlord's northern army."

Geoff swallowed but kept his gaze on the fire dancing in

the fireplace. A moment later they heard the two midwives leave Jane's room and come down the stairs. They were complaining about how much work needed to be done before they left and worried if they were going to be able to sleep with thunder booming all around. Geoff was pretty sure he wasn't going to get any sleep. He was worried about Jane. Ariel's answer to his question wasn't what he hoped to hear.

"Sawyer, you and Geoff remain with Jane," Ariel said as she got to her feet. "Ishara and I will keep watch. Never let her out of your sight, do you understand?"

"Yeah, got it," Sawyer said with a grunt as he climbed to his feet.

Geoff followed Sawyer up to Jane's room, feeling chilly the moment he stepped away from the fireplace. When Sawyer opened the door, they stood in place, shocked to see Jane out of bed. She was standing at the window. She turned toward them. The first thing Geoff noticed was her blue eyes were rimmed red and her face was moist. Her hands trembled uncontrollably at her sides.

"Help me."

"Ariel!" Geoff shouted over his shoulder as Sawyer went to Jane and wrapped his arms around her.

"It's okay, babe," he said. "I got you. It's okay."

Jane sobbed and hugged Sawyer. As she did, Geoff noticed her arms and shoulders quivered.

"Something's wrong, Sawyer," Jane said. "I can feel it. Help me."

Ariel and Ishara appeared at the doorway. Geoff stepped aside as they brushed past. For a moment, they blocked his view of Jane and Sawyer. Jane's sobs filled the room.

Outside, the combined sounds of the rain beating against the window and thunder created a melancholy harmony. Geoff swallowed and walked toward the others. Sawyer still held Jane in his arms while Ariel and caressed her shoulders.

"We are here, Jane," Ariel said quietly. "You are safe."

Geoff touched Jane's forearm. Her muscles were rigid and he saw the goosebumps on her skin. Geoff frowned. He'd never seen Jane in such despair and he wanted to help her. He looked at Ariel, half hoping and half expecting to see her cast a spell to take away Jane's suffering and make her smile again. Ariel's face, however, was as stoic as ever. Jane released Sawyer and turned to Ariel, tears streaming down her cheeks.

"I don't feel well," Jane said between sobs. "I feel like I'm drifting away or something. I'm scared."

Ariel brushed a strand of hair out of Jane's eyes. "We will watch over you and keep you safe."

Geoff's eyes became misty. He blinked a few times to clear his vision. His heart sank like a heavy weight had been placed in his chest. Jane was the one who wanted to help Ariel save Alluria the most when Ariel had asked for their assistance. Geoff looked away and wiped a tear away with his hand. Jane didn't deserve to suffer like this. No one did.

Ariel led Jane back to her bed as Ishara hastily fluffed up a large, rough-sewn pillow and Sawyer hovered. Jane grasped his hand as Ariel pulled the covers up around her neck.

"Sawyer," Jane said. "Don't let me go."

"I won't, I promise. Not gonna happen."

Geoff went to the other side of the bed and touched Jane's hand, which felt a little too warm. He also noticed tiny beads of sweat on her forehead and her neck was moist.

"Ariel, she's burning up," Geoff said.

Ishara wet a cloth beside the basin and handed it to Ariel. Once the cool, wet cloth was pressed against her forehead, Jane closed her eyes and seemed to relax. Sawyer took a step backward, his gaze never leaving her.

Suddenly, her eyes flew open and she sat up and screamed.

"He's coming! I can feel him," Jane's eyes darted about the room. "He's furious and he's coming to kill us!"

"*Sol'nara*," Ariel said with a swift caress of Jane's cheek. Jane immediately fell asleep. Ariel stood up and placed her hands on her hips.

"What was that?" Sawyer demanded. "What'd you do to her?"

"A harmless sleeping charm," Ariel said. "She will sleep until roused. Tonight we stay together, in this room with Jane."

"What was she talking about, Ariel?" Geoff asked, remembering the panic-stricken expression on Jane's face. "What did she mean by 'I can feel him'?"

Ariel looked at Geoff. He blinked under her scrutiny, but held her gaze until distracted by a bright white flash from the window, which was followed by a deafening crash of thunder. The rain pounded heavier than ever against the glass, and the wind picked up.

"The Shadowlord has entered Jane's mind," Ariel said. "He's coming closer."

"He's coming now?" Sawyer asked. "In this storm?"

"How close is he?" Geoff wanted to know.

"Close enough that Jane can sense him," Ariel said. "And close enough that, through Jane, he can sense us as well."

"How's that work?" Sawyer questioned, putting a hand on his sword.

"He can see what Jane sees, can't he?" Geoff said. "He knows where we are and what we're saying now. Right?"

Ariel looked at Geoff and nodded. "It seems that some vampire lore in your world is correct, after all. A vampire as powerful as Zorn can control the mind of his servant."

"Jane's not his servant," Sawyer said grimly. "And she never will be."

"Agreed. Jane's mind is still her own," Ariel said. "We must make sure it stays that way."

"How will we travel if the Shadowlord can spy on us though Jane?" Ishara asked. "Surely he will seek to attack us at the first opportunity."

"Good," Sawyer said. "Bring it on, let's finish the fight."

"You are correct, Ishara," Ariel said. "The Shadowlord would attack us if he knew our location." She turned to Sawyer. "Perhaps we can use this to our advantage. If we can lure him into a battle at a location of our own choosing, we may be able to defeat him if we fight together."

"Let's do it," Sawyer said. "Just pick the time and place, I'm in."

"Me too," Geoff added.

"Let me consider our options," Ariel said. "For now, you should all try to get at least a little rest."

Geoff and Sawyer bedded down on the floor, bundled up in their blankets while Ariel and Ishara stood watch. But Geoff was unable to sleep. Instead, he watched as the fire in the little fireplace dwindled and died until all that was left was a pile of glowing orange embers. He was relieved when the storm outside finally subsided. Normally, he liked to listen to rainstorms, but this one made him feel uneasy, like it was an omen or a harbinger of approaching evil.

From time to time he thought he heard Ariel and Ishara whispering, but no matter how hard he tried, he couldn't make out the words. Sawyer's snoring was partly to blame. Still, he wasn't snoring as loudly as usual. If Geoff hadn't been worried that the Shadowlord might kick down the door at any moment, he'd probably have dozed off much earlier than he did.

A gentle shake of his shoulder woke him, and Ishara's quick smile let him know that things were still okay. As Geoff rubbed the sleep from his eyes, he realized that he could have used another couple of hours curled up under his blanket. There were voices from the courtyard below, a sense of action and activity. He turned to where the gray light of early morning filtered through the window, and saw Ariel observing the scene.

"Morning," Geoff said as he sat up. His hair was standing nearly straight up. Ishara smiled and smoothed it down with her slender hand.

"Good morning to you," Ishara said. "Did you manage any sleep?"

"Not much. Can I sleep a little longer?"

"Unfortunately no," Ariel said, maintaining her gaze on the courtyard. "We need depart for Chalon now. You can rest when we arrive."

"We aren't taking gryphons again, are we?" Sawyer asked, propping himself up on his elbow. Geoff recalled how frightened Sawyer had been when they flew by gryphon to the garrison at Troll Fang Pass. The gryphons had soared to incredible heights at amazing speed.

"Not today," Ariel said. "It will be safer if we travel with Trelane and Commander Renfry. Get up, we must make ready to leave."

Sawyer groaned and rolled to his knees, his legs were tangled in his blanket, which made it difficult for him to get to his feet. Ishara must've sensed this because she offered her hands to Geoff and Sawyer and helped them to their feet.

Geoff glanced over at Jane, who still seemed to be wrapped in a peaceful slumber. Normally, Jane was one of the first in the group to wake. Ariel's sleep spell must've placed Jane in a deep slumber.

"Hey, Jane," Sawyer said, "Time to get up." When Jane still didn't stir. Sawyer gave her shoulder a gentle nudge. "Jane, we gotta get up."

This time she stirred and moaned. Her dark, tousled locks fell across her face as she rolled over.

"Hey," Sawyer said. "Get up, sleepy."

"Mmmmmmmm," Jane purred. "Can I have five more minutes?"

"No," Ariel said. "Time to go. Get up, Jane."

Jane opened her eyes and brushed her hair away from her face. As soon as she sat up, she cringed and placed a hand on the back of her head.

"You okay?" Sawyer asked.

"Ugh…I think so. Something hurts."

"What hurts?"

"I'm not sure," Jane said. "All of a sudden I felt a sharp pain. It's probably just another migraine coming on."

Everyone looked at Ariel. Instead of responding, she closed her eyes and turned away. Geoff noticed that Ishara was very quiet as she bundled her things together.

Sawyer helped Jane out of bed, gave her a cup of water and even helped her pack for the journey south to Chalon. Once everyone was ready, Ariel led them downstairs.

Commander Renfry and Trelane, standing just inside the door to the courtyard, were waiting for them.

"*Hal'inari,*" Trelane said, placing a hand over his heart. "We have grave news. Our scouts report that a second dark army approaches. This one is located just east of here."

"It must be the army that attacked Bregendain," Ariel said, frowning. "If they join with the oncoming northern army, there will be no stopping them until they reach the city of Chalon."

"Aye, true enough," Commander Renfry agreed. "But the dwarves at Bregendain exacted a heavy toll on the Shadowlord's eastern army. They now number no more than five thousand."

"Indeed," Ariel said. "It was a mistake for the Shadowlord to attack the dwarves in their northern mountain kingdom."

"A battle-weary army would be…an excellent opportunity," Trelane said with a slight turn of his head as he raised an eyebrow.

"Our numbers match theirs," Ariel said with a quick nod. "We should not let this chance slip away. It may never come again."

# CHAPTER FOUR

## EASTWARD

"So, we're in agreement then," Commander Renfry said, stroking his graying beard. "We attack and annihilate the Shadowlord's eastern army, then turn south to Chalon."

"Word must be sent to Chalon," Ariel added. "Lionel and Maelord will need to be warned." Hearing his father's name mentioned so prominently gave Geoff a sudden swell of pride. His father wasn't just a wizard, he was also a respected leader.

"Agreed. I'll send a messenger at once," Commander Renfry said. He turned and left the room, his armored boots clomping loudly as he strode away.

"And I will send word to King Andurys," Trelane said. "We will need reinforcements if we are to defend Chalon."

He bowed his head and turned around. Before he reached the door to the courtyard, Ariel spoke.

"Trelane," she called. He turned back around and looked at her. "I am glad you are here. It will be an honor to fight by your side again."

He placed a hand over his heart and departed. Watching them, Geoff wondered how many battles they had fought together. That must've been a sight. Trelane appeared to be every bit as capable as Ariel in battle, and she was the best fighter he'd ever seen. He glanced over at Sawyer, who was holding Jane's hand. Geoff's heart lifted at the sight. With Jane and Sawyer back together, everything seemed to be heading in the right direction.

Ariel turned and faced them.

"This will be a difficult battle. The dark army to the east is like a wounded animal," she said. "Keep an eye on each other and remain vigilant."

"We will," Ishara said. She had appeared at Geoff's side and brushed against his shoulder. He caught her characteristic scent of honeysuckle, mixed with lilacs. Ishara always smelled like she'd just rolled in a flowerbed, which never failed to raise Geoff's spirits. In fact, despite Ariel's warnings, Geoff was feeling more hopeful. Sure, his palms were a little moist, but with the combined might of an elven army and the troops from the Troll Fang Pass garrison, they had a good chance of winning.

"Come," Ariel said. She led them out of the room and the busy courtyard. Outside, the sky was a dingy gray and there was still a slight chill in the air. The rain from the previous night, coupled with the imprints of a multitude of horses, men and wagons had transformed the courtyard into a soggy mud pit.

They moved from wagon to wagon until Ariel found one that was only half-filled with bags of grain and salt. They climbed in the wagon and waited. About an hour later, the combined forces of Trelane's elven army and Commander Renfry's troops rolled, wagon by wagon, out of the battered garrison at Troll Fang Pass.

Geoff glanced up the pass to the north as their wagon was pulled along. They'd seen the size of the army that approached from the bleak wastelands of Gholaran. In size, it dwarfed the five thousand fighters to the east. Worse still, the Shadowlord himself was leading it. Geoff noticed that Ariel, sitting tight-lipped across from him in the wagon, was also looking north. Her tight-lipped expression unsettled him.

Even with her gifts, abilities and magic, Ariel seemed thoughtful and worried. And anything capable of concerning Ariel was something to be reckoned with and feared. Every now and then she would stand and look toward the head of the column.

Ishara, by contrast, kept her attention focused on the surrounding countryside, which was gradually transforming into a lush and hilly landscape. Geoff opened his mouth to ask what she was looking for but then he shut it. He already knew. She was scouring their surroundings for any sign of the enemy.

Jane rested her head on Sawyer's shoulder as they rode. She had closed her eyes and appeared to be napping. The rough bouncing of the wagon didn't seem to bother her much. Sawyer ran his index finger over the large sapphire in the pommel of his sword, the Stormblade, a restless expression in his eyes. Of course, Sawyer had saved them from the ogre, and had almost singlehandedly beaten back the siege at the Troll Fang Pass garrison. But Geoff feared that the coming battle was going to be very different. He'd read many histories about two armies facing each other on open ground.

They traveled for the rest of the morning and late into

the afternoon. Their only encounter that day was with a two-hundred man militia mostly sporting chainmail armor from the town of Eastvale, well to the south. The militia had been marching to help defend Chalon, but joined their caravan after a discussion with Commander Renfry.

Then, without warning, the entire column halted.

"Stay here, all of you," Ariel ordered, as she slipped off the wagon. "I will return shortly."

At the head of the column, Trelane, mounted and in battle armor, waited. As Geoff watched, Trelane turned and gestured toward a row of forested hills to their right. Beyond the hills a line of mountains rose steeply into the mist, a line which seemed to be vaguely familiar to Geoff.

"Silverthorne Keep and the village of Silverthorne lie beyond those trees," Ishara said, as if she were reading his thoughts. "Higher ground," Ishara said with a nod. "If we fight here, we will have the advantage."

"So we're really doing this," Geoff said. "Seriously? Army against army, hacking and stabbing at each other and all that?"

"We have no choice," Ishara said as she glanced at Geoff and raised an eyebrow. "Unless you know a spell that will vanquish our enemies from a distance?"

"No, of course not. Dad might, though."

"He might. Your father is a great and powerful wizard."

"Maybe you can tell me about him one day. He didn't have time to tell me much. We left for Troll Fang Pass so soon."

"Even among the elves your father's deeds are legendary," she assured him.

"Really? That's cool," Geoff said.

"I wonder if we'll be able to visit Silverthorne again," Sawyer said thoughtfully. "You know, just to see what happened after we escaped the werewolf."

"Silverthorne," Jane said with a groan. Don't remind me, those catacombs were disgusting."

"Yeah, and if Geoff hadn't fried those big, ugly carrion mites with that magic fireball, I don't think any of us would've gotten out alive."

Geoff shook his head. "I wish I could remember. I'm still not sure I did that."

"Of course you did," Sawyer said. "None of the rest of us could've done it. Like that dragon in the swamp, remember?" Geoff turned his attention to the head of the column of troops. Some of the leaders at the front had already dismounted, and were starting to unload supplies.

"Hey, looks like we're stopping."

"Yep," he said, half-rising. "They're getting ready to set up camp."

"When the battle comes, I will more than likely be in the trees with the rest of the archers," Ishara said, pointing in the direction of the small, woodsy area. "We will have excellent cover there."

"What about the rest of us?" Sawyer asked. "Where're we gonna be?"

Ishara pursed her lips and glanced at Jane for a moment.

"I am sure Ariel will let you know," she said. "I do not think she will want any of you involved with this battle."

"Why not?" Sawyer asked. "We did good at the garrison, right?"

"You did," Ariel said, appearing next to the wagon, "However, Ishara is right. This battle will be too dangerous for other reasons."

"Yeah, it's different from a siege," Geoff said, getting to his feet in the wagon. "Different type of battle."

"What do you know about battles?" Sawyer said.

"Geoff is right," Ariel said. "You will be needed for other tasks during this combat. Tasks of arguably greater importance."

"Okay," Sawyer said as he rolled his eyes. He stood and took Jane's elbow and helped her to her feet. Everyone hopped out of the wagon.

"We will camp at the far edge of the trees," Ariel said, indicating the area Ishara had already noticed. "I will assist Trelane and Commander Renfry. Ishara, as you said, you will be based in the trees with the rest of the archers. Geoff, stay close to Ishara."

Ishara nodded and looked at Geoff with a smug, self-assured smile. Geoff mimicked her smile.

"Know-it-all," Geoff whispered.

The rest of the day was spent assembling tents, along with helping the soldiers unload supplies and fortify their positions. The sun was beginning to set when an elven scout returned, sooner than expected. Geoff watched from a distance as the scout reported his findings to Trelane, Ariel, and Commander Renfry. From the scout's animated gestures, Geoff guessed the enemy was close.

"That looks kinda bad. Wonder what he saw?"

"Duh," Sawyer said. "A big army, maybe?"

"Yes," Ishara agreed, "They are close, just over the next horizon."

"Now I get it," Jane said. "You're reading his lips, aren't you?"

"I am."

"In that case, how long have we got before the battle?" Sawyer asked.

"I do not know. I missed that part. Perhaps tomorrow morning…" Ishara's voice trailed off as she took a step forward, her gaze locked on the conversation. "He is describing something else." They waited for her to explain, but she remained focused on the scout.

"What? What's he describing?" Sawyer demanded.

"A dark shape…flying high overhead," Ishara murmured. "Darting in and out of the clouds."

"A dark shape? What kind of dark shape? Shaped like what?"

"I am not sure. The scout caught only a brief glimpse before it disappeared."

"A dragon, maybe?" Sawyer looked at Geoff. "Good thing we have our resident dragon slayer then."

Geoff swallowed and glanced up at the early evening sky. What could they do if a dragon swooped down on them? He could imagine any number of ways a flying dragon could wreak havoc. He hoped Ariel would know what to do if there really was a dragon.

Ariel returned a few minutes later. Before she could say anything, Sawyer said loudly, "So what about the dragon?" His voice carried and several soldiers from Chalon stopped what they were doing and looked their way.

Ariel's eyes widened as she looked at Sawyer. She stepped closer.

"Hush. Do you want to panic everyone here? What makes you think there is a dragon?"

"That's what the scout said, right?" Sawyer motioned toward Ishara, who had self-consciously begun to count every arrow in her quiver.

Ariel looked at Ishara.

"I observed the scout while he was speaking," Ishara admitted. "Though I never mentioned the word 'dragon'." She shot Sawyer a sharp glance.

"Well what else could it be?" Sawyer said.

"Many things," Ariel said. "And do not be foolish enough to start rumors before a battle. Such nonsense will only damage the morale of the men. Now, will you please start unloading the wagon?"

Without a word, Sawyer climbed back onto the wagon and picked up a large sack of flour. Geoff stepped to the edge of the wagon and Sawyer deposited it in his arms. Geoff was just pivoting to put it on the ground when he noticed that Ariel was returning to the front of the column.

"Hey, where're you going?"

Ariel spun around and started to walk backward as she answered.

"To confer with Lord Trelane and Commander Renfry, of course."

She waved and turned back around, walking at a brisk pace. Geoff watched her go. He was glad she was on their side and, in a way, he felt sorry for the enemies who would face her soon.

"Yo, Geoff," Sawyer said, handing a small, dark wooden cask to Jane. "You gonna hug that sack the rest of the day or help us?"

"Oh, sorry," Geoff said, dumping the burlap sack on the ground.

He looked up just in time to see a smaller sack flying toward him. Ishara had accepted it from Sawyer and tossed it in his direction. It hit him squarely in the chest.

He barely had time to wrap his arms around it and secure it next to his body. Jane had taken a position a few feet away from him and she was also receiving tossed supplies from Ishara. Their makeshift assembly line worked well with Geoff and Jane catching whatever Ishara lobbed toward them.

Once the wagon was empty, Ishara picked up her bow and quiver and then glanced significantly at Geoff. His eyes met hers and she quickly looked at Jane and then back to him. The unspoken command to keep an eye on Jane was clear and Geoff gave Ishara a small nod.

"I will return soon," Ishara said. "I must join the other archers while our battle plan is being formed."

She turned and trotted toward the small tree line. Geoff watched her. Her strides were effortless, like the strides of a track and field athlete.

"Okay," Sawyer said. "I guess we hang out and wait for further instructions while the army of darkness approaches."

He sat on a cask and looked at Jane.

"Have a seat," Sawyer said, slapping the top of an adjacent cask. "I'm pretty sure Ariel will come and tell us to find a safe place to hide."

Jane sat beside Sawyer and surveyed the preparations of the troops. Some were still wrestling with their tents, while others unloaded barrels full of arrows.

"This looks really bad," Jane said, rubbing the side of her head and wincing. "Ariel and Trelane don't seem to be as confident as before."

"Yeah," Sawyer said. "Seems like a lot hangs on the outcome of this battle."

"What happens if we lose?" Jane asked. "What then?"

"I don't know," Geoff said, plopping down on a large sack. "I suppose we'd need to run away as fast as we can if the battle goes bad for us."

"Well hey, that's one thing we're good at," said Sawyer sourly. "We've been running for our lives ever since we got here."

The three of them sat in silence for a while. No one knew how to break the gloomy mood and the cold reality which had descended on them. Geoff remembered some of the famous medieval battles he'd read about. Before every battle, there had always seemed to be a nervousness, an unspoken anxiety that everyone had to deal with individually. After all, nobody was immune to the fear of dying. Geoff was opening his mouth to suggest that maybe it wasn't such a great idea to sit around dwelling on what might happen, when Jane suddenly sprang to her feet.

"Hmmm? Yes?" Jane said, looking directly north.

"Jane," Sawyer said. "Are you okay?"

She didn't answer. Jane began walking north, toward the direction of the Shadowlord's army.

"I hear you," she said, and a surge of fear crawled up Geoff's spine at the empty tone in her voice.

He leapt up, but Jane was now moving with a brisk, determined pace. Sawyer bounded past her and turned around, grabbing both of her arms.

"Jane," Sawyer said. "What're you doing? Where're you going?" Geoff ran up behind Jane and took hold of one of her arms. Jane was trembling. He felt her pushing, trying to get past Sawyer.

"Jane?" Geoff said. "We have to stay here."

"Hey," Sawyer said in a loud voice as he gave her a quick shake. "Stop it."

Suddenly Geoff felt the tension in Jane's arms ease and she took a deep breath. She looked at them. The confusion in her eyes was evident as she began to survey her surroundings.

"Wha...what happened?" Jane said as she stopped and placed a hand on the side of her head.

"You just jumped up and started walking north," Sawyer said, his voice full of concern. "What're you doing, Jane?"

"Didn't you hear it?" Jane said. "Someone called my name."

# Chapter Five

## Reunion

Geoff looked at Sawyer, who was shaking his head as his gaze centered on Jane. His furrowed brow indicated he was worried as he slowly turned Jane around.

"No," Jane said, pushing one of his arms away. "Seriously, didn't you hear? You must've. Someone called to me."

"Okay, okay. C'mon Jane," Sawyer said. "Let's sit down for a while and rest. I got you."

Geoff started to turn and follow them when he spotted Ariel in the distance. She was standing in the tall grass apart from the troops. From the angle of her body, it appeared that she was moving on a path to intercept Jane. Her usual staunch expression had been replaced by a look of worry. At least that's the best way Geoff could describe it. He shrugged and held his hands up, trying to make the gesture big enough so Ariel would notice.

Geoff hurried back to Sawyer and Jane. Seated back on their casks, Sawyer had his arm around Jane's shoulders and Jane was still rubbing her head. Sawyer pulled a small flask from his belt, uncorked it and handed it to Jane.

"Here," he said. "Drink this. It's water."

Jane took the flask and drank, her hands quivered as she tilted her head back. She kept her eyes closed and almost emptied the flask.

"Jane," Geoff said. "Are you alright?"

Jane coughed on the last bit of water. Covering her mouth as she dealt with the spasms, it took her a second before she could speak. After she regained her composure, she looked at them.

"You guys must've heard it," she said. "Right?"

"Not a thing," Sawyer said.

"Yeah, we were sitting around and then you suddenly jumped up and started walking away. It was kinda weird."

"Look," Jane said, firming up her voice. "I'm not crazy. I know I heard it. Just as plain as I hear you now. Someone was calling my name."

"Okay," Sawyer said. "We believe you. We didn't hear it, that's all. Who was calling you?"

Jane blinked and thought for a moment.

"I…I can't remember," she said. "That's strange."

Sawyer frowned at Geoff, who persisted, "Can you remember anything about the voice? Anything at all?"

Jane bowed her head. "No," she said shaking her head. "Only…I had a feeling. I felt like something was…stalking me. Something with a deep hunger. Something sinister."

"We better tell Ariel," Geoff said to Sawyer. "I think she already knows, but this Jedi mind trick stuff is scaring me."

"Yeah. It's like in the woods when she fought us." Taking Jane's hand, Sawyer said, "Jane, listen. You have to fight whatever this is. Do you understand? You *have* to. Promise me you'll fight it."

Jane let out a long shuddering sigh and met Sawyer's gaze.

"I will," she said. "I promise. Don't let it take me, Sawyer. I feel...I feel like something is creeping into my veins."

"Not gonna happen, Jane," Sawyer said with a tight smile. "I promise."

Jane closed her eyes and leaned into Sawyer's chest. He wrapped both arms around her and held her close. Geoff felt awkward standing there while Jane and Sawyer shared a tender moment. He glanced around for a distraction. Pretending that the large quarter horses were also in need of comfort, he walked around the wagon and began to caress their strong necks. He was rewarded with a few loud snorts.

"Tell me what happened to Jane."

Startled by the voice behind him, Geoff spun around. Ariel was standing there looking past him toward Jane and Sawyer.

"It was kinda like before, when she fought us," Geoff said. "Jane said she heard someone calling her name. Then, she just got up and started walking north."

Ariel observed Jane and Sawyer for a minute. Geoff kept his eyes on Ariel and wondered what she was thinking. After an uncomfortable minute watching her, he had to say something.

"Ariel," he said. "Is this what you were worried about? Jane trying to get back to the Shadowlord?"

Ariel didn't answer. Instead, she turned away and walked back to Commander Renfry and Trelane. As Geoff watched her go, a chill of dread washed over him. Something bad was going to happen. Jane was losing it. With a dangerous army bearing down on them from the north, it wasn't hard to connect the dots.

As for the other two, they were still snuggled together, Sawyer holding Jane protectively.

Geoff took a deep breath and exhaled. "I hope nothing bad happens to them," he said under his breath.

Alex pulled his tattered animal skins closer about him, picking up his pace. He had to get as far north as he could before nightfall. He hadn't expected to run into Ariel and the three outlanders.

It had been the young druid girl that he'd noticed first. Seeing him had startled her as she tried to make her way north and given Ariel time to catch her. He'd watched the fight between the girl and her pursuers. It surprised him and made his heart ache. The girl was so young, so full of life, boundless energy and power. However, there was something troubling about her too. She was different. She was changing, becoming darker. His jaw tightened at the memory and he tried to push the girl from his mind. Whatever happened to her, it was up to Ariel to handle. He wanted to help, but he could do nothing.

A rumble of thunder overhead announced a coming downpour. Glancing up, he saw the gloomy clouds twisting in the dimming sky. A sudden snap of a twig came from the trees in front of him. He crouched and sniffed the air. Mingled with the smells of rain, earth, and heavy, smoky oak trees was the unmistakable musty scent of men.

Ahead, not more than a hundred feet away, three figures came into view. They were clad in leather armor and black fur cloaks. Their rough faces were painted with strange symbols and their eyes traced with black, giving them the skull-like appearance characteristic of their tribe, the Skullsworn. Alex knew, these were elite warriors, advance scouts for the Shadowlord's army. As they moved closer, he saw they carried forged steel weapons bearing the seal of Chalon.

When the last barbarian passed, he rose. The closest barbarian heard him and spun around, but before he could reach his sword, he took a crushing right hook to the chin, which sent him sprawling to the ground. Alerted by his heavy grunt on landing, his two comrades raised their swords and charged. He dodged the first thrust from the next assailant, grabbed his wrist, and twisted the sword from his hand.

Maintaining a firm grip on the second barbarian's wrist, he faced the last. He ducked away from the overhead attack and brought the sword he'd captured into the midsection of the last barbarian, who crumpled to the dark, mossy ground. There was a strong jerk on Alex's arm as the remaining barbarian wrenched free and lunged at him. A quick thrust of his sword ended the last barbarian's attack as a heavy rain began to fall.

Alex looked at the bloodied sword in his hand. It was indeed a fine forged steel weapon made by the smiths of Chalon and meant for soldiers and guards. They were a common sight in the city and a far better blade than barbarians could fashion for themselves. How did barbarians manage to get these weapons?

A series of loud flapping noises made by something large and followed by a coldblooded hiss echoed in the rainy forest. Alex whirled in time to see a black dragon-like beast land in a small clearing twenty yards away. Atop the flying beast was a dark-haired warrior in black and silver plate mail. He wasn't wearing a helmet and even if he was, Alex would have recognized who had just dropped in on him. It was his old friend, Zorn, the Shadowlord.

"At last," Zorn said. "The predator has caught his prey."

A heavy feeling settled in Alex's chest as he watched Zorn slide from his saddle to the ground. The rain began falling harder, tapping out an ensemble on the leaves and trees.

"It's been a long time."

"It has," Alex said, gripping the barbarian's sword tighter.

"Remove your hood."

Alex pulled his tattered hood back, revealing a weathered face in dire need of a shave.

"You've looked better," Zorn said, raising his eyebrows.

"So have you."

"Perhaps so," Zorn said dryly.

"And you smell like an open grave," Alex said.

"You don't want to know what you smell like."

"How did you find me?"

"It was luck," Zorn said as he took a few steps toward Alex holding his arms out from his sides. "I was looking for someone else, instead I found you, scurrying like a rodent through the trees."

Alex smirked. "Who were you looking for? A girl? Have to capture them these days, do you? Can't keep their interest any other way?" Alex tensed, as he thought the scowling Zorn might attack. Then he said, with deliberation, "So what happens now?"

"I kill you."

"Even as a man, I'm not so easy to kill," Alex said.

"No, of course not. You were a great warrior; one who was destined to rule. Now look at you; nothing more than a forlorn prince. An exile."

"And you? What happened to you?"

Zorn unsheathed his sword. Immediately the intricate runes carved into its black surface began to glow red.

"You," Zorn said, walking toward Alex. "You're the reason for all this. If you hadn't saved that coward Lionel from the werewolf, none of this would've ever happened."

"He was our friend," Alex reminded him.

"And what about me? Was I not your friend?"

"You were my best friend," Alex breathed.

"I haven't forgotten. Now look at us. I lost my soul for you! We are cursed! Damned!"

Alex winced and blinked a couple times and looked down as he nodded. "Aye," he said. "We are."

"I tried to help you. I searched for the one who created the werewolf that attacked you. And I found him. A dark druid who had invaded and poisoned the Eldritch Forest. I was going to make him release you from your curse or kill him."

"Ariel finished the task," Alex said. "The dark druid was her beloved mentor, Bhael."

"I know. Nonetheless, as I hunted him, something else hunted me."

"What hunted you?"

Zorn gazed into the distance. Alex saw a pensive, melancholy expression wash over Zorn's face, something he recognized from the days when they'd been close. There had been a deep trust between them, a sure and tested bond. Yet now Alex realized that he was looking at a stranger.

"The Scarlet Queen," Zorn said at last.

"The Scarlet Queen? In Eldritch Forest? A long way from her throne in Uln."

"Aye," Zorn said bitterly. "A long way."

"Why is she waging this war against us?"

"Because she can," Zorn snarled. "It is her destiny to rule. There is no one stronger. She intends to rip Alluria apart and make it bleed. You, however, are comparatively fortunate. She merely wants you dead."

A deep feeling of despair tightened Alex's chest. Such a conflict would assuredly turn Alluria to ruins. He'd not only lost his friend, he'd also lost his father's kingdom. Whether wittingly or not, they had all seemed to have done the Scarlet Queen's bidding. If true, then all was lost.

Perhaps he wouldn't live to see it. Alex knew he stood no chance against a fit, fully-equipped and armored Shadowlord, but if he was going to die, then he was going to die like a warrior.

"If you're here to kill me," Alex said, raising his sword. "You best get on with it."

# CHAPTER SIX
## BATTLE'S EVE

Geoff was secretly amazed at the efficiency displayed by the troops of Chalon and Selra'thel. Before night fell, troop positions had been set, armor readied, food prepared and supplies dispersed where they would be of most use. Elves and men worked together to create barricades and to assemble the ballistae dismantled at the garrison and conveyed by wagon.

Looking up, Geoff noticed the night sky sparkled with stars. It was a beautiful night, but Geoff still felt tense.

The sound of someone jumping up and down behind him made Geoff turn around. Sawyer was performing his usual ritual of loosening up. After a few quick jumps he rapidly rotated his head in a circular motion, then began twisting from side to side.

"Sawyer," Jane said sitting by a small camp fire. "What are you doing?"

"Just getting loose. I don't want to pull a muscle, you know."

"You keep jumping and twisting like that and you'll probably do just that – pull a muscle."

"I need to be ready," Sawyer said. "What if there's a sneak attack or something?"

"You don't see any of the other soldiers doing that, do you?" Jane said, motioning to the army spread out in front of them. Geoff glanced around and had to admit that Jane was right. After a long day's travel and work, the soldiers all seemed to be relaxing by the fire, sharpening weapons or chatting among themselves. Every now and then a patrol would walk past. Otherwise, the camp had a subdued feel to it. Sawyer stopped his calisthenics and joined Jane by the fire.

"Yeah, okay, I guess you're right. Don't think I'm gonna get much sleep, though."

"No one does, in these kinds of situations," Geoff offered, moving to the opposite side of the fire. "More than likely, everybody's thinking about the coming battle, or maybe their loved ones and if they'll ever see them again, stuff like that."

Two figures emerged from the darkness and stood in the firelight. Ariel and Ishara. Their elven features appearing even more angular in the shadows. Ishara tossed several extra logs on the fire while Ariel spoke.

"I do not want any of you to fight tomorrow. This battle will be decided by the combined forces of Chalon and Selra'thel."

"Why not?" Sawyer asked with an annoyed tone.

Ariel went over to the fire and took a place beside Ishara. "Because I cannot guarantee your safety."

"When did that ever stop us?" Jane said. "We can help."

"Yes," Ariel said. "Each of you have already helped and will continue to do so. Sawyer, do you remember how the troops at the garrison reacted when you killed the ogre?"

"They cheered," Sawyer said. "They fought harder after that."

"They did," Ariel said with a quick nod. "Tomorrow, they need to know the Stormlord is with them."

"Seems like the best way to do that is for me to be on the front line with them. I don't get it. Why can't we fight?"

"Because if anything happened to you," Ariel said. "If you should fall…the morale of the troops would collapse and the battle would almost certainly be lost."

"Hasn't he proven himself yet?" Jane said.

"Indeed, he has. Several times over."

"So then why can't we help?" Geoff said, crouching beside Ariel at the fire.

"I have already answered that question," Ariel said. "I know each of you want to help. I suspect one day soon your help will be sorely needed. However, until we are sure of what we face, I must ask you to remain here and not join the battle. Not this time."

Geoff looked at Ishara. She did not return his gaze this time. Instead, she remained focused on the sticks in the campfire.

"Jane," Ariel said. "Will you please help with our wounded tomorrow? I fear your healing skills may be pushed to their limits."

"Of course."

"Thank you," Ariel said as she plucked a darkened stick from the fire and blew red embers from the tip. "Sawyer, Geoff, I need your help with something else. Ishara, please stay with Jane."

Geoff and Sawyer followed Ariel to the far edge of the camp. She stopped and broke off the tip of the stick in one hand, crushing the charred remains as she handed the stick to Sawyer. She observed them for some seconds in the near dark before speaking to Geoff and Sawyer in a hushed tone.

"While it is true that I cannot protect you tomorrow," Ariel said, leaning close. "The real reason why you cannot join the battle tomorrow is because I cannot fight effectively and keep an eye on Jane. I need both of you to watch Jane and keep her safe. Will you do this?"

"Yeah," Sawyer said, straightening. "You know we will."

Ariel looked at Geoff, waiting for his answer as she began to smear the blackened powder from the charred stick over her face, neck, and arms.

"We won't let anything happen to her."

"Ariel," Sawyer said. "What're you doing?"

"Ishara and I are joining a small scouting party. We will determine our enemy's strength and then harass them, creating as much chaos for them as possible tonight."

Geoff glanced back at their camp. Ishara had enlisted Jane's aid in applying the charred ash on her face, arms, and legs. "Will you and Ishara be okay?"

Even in the dark with thick, diagonal streaks of black soot across her face, her emerald green eyes shone clearly.

"Yes," Ariel said. "Do not worry. We will return soon. Take turns at watch and remember what I said."

Ariel turned and walked back to Ishara and Jane. She and Ishara inspected each other in the flickering firelight.

"So you're concealing yourselves," Geoff said. "Making it harder to be spotted when you go scouting tonight."

"Isn't that obvious?" Sawyer said, giving Geoff a nudge.

The sound of someone clearing their throat behind them made Geoff and Sawyer turn around. Standing at the edge of the camp, also streaked in black was the imposing figure of Trelane. He had swapped his elven battle armor in favor of brown leather. He looked like a dark giant to Geoff. His well-defined muscles, no longer hidden, suggested he was a warrior to be reckoned with in battle. Several more camouflaged elven warriors stood behind him.

"We are ready," Trelane said. His set jaw and somber expression relayed the seriousness of the task to be done. Ariel and Ishara gave themselves one last, quick inspection then joined Trelane. As Ariel walked past Geoff and Sawyer, she made eye contact with them. Geoff nodded. He understood what Ariel was signaling to him and Sawyer. Ishara impulsively kissed Geoff on the cheek and gave him a reassuring smile.

"Do not worry," Ishara said.

"Be careful," Jane blurted out. Her eyes were wide. Ariel turned around and regarded Jane for a second.

"Stay together," she said. "Stay with Sawyer and Geoff. We shall return soon."

With that, Ariel and Ishara disappeared into the darkness with Trelane and the others. It was a small scouting party, Geoff thought. No more than a dozen warriors or so. Watching Ishara and Ariel walk into the dark night unsettled him, he felt as if he wouldn't see them again. He shook his head to clear his mind of such gloomy notions. The earthy smell of smoke from many campfires filled the air. Geoff took a deep breath. Somehow, he found the smoky aroma calming. If this hadn't been the eve of a battle, he would've thought it was a pleasant night to camp out.

"I hope they'll be okay," Jane said, settling down beside the campfire.

"C'mon. It's Ariel and Ishara," said Sawyer lightly. "They can handle anything, you know that."

"I know," Jane said, peering into the darkness after them. "Still, I wish they hadn't gone. Something doesn't seem right."

"What d'you mean?" Sawyer said, giving Jane his full attention. Geoff also looked at Jane. He hadn't expected her melancholy mood.

"I don't know," Jane said, tossing a stick into the fire. "Something seems…I don't know, strange."

"What're you talking about, Jane?" Geoff said.

Sawyer took Jane's hand and held it up to his lips and kissed it.

"Don't worry," he said. "If anything happens, we got this. Nothing's gonna get past me and Geoff tonight."

Geoff shot Sawyer a quick glance. Ariel hadn't intended for Jane to know they were charged with keeping watch over her. He saw a strange look on Jane's face, she opened her mouth to say something, but frowned instead.

"Yeah," Geoff blurted out. "Why don't you and Sawyer try to get some rest? I'll take first watch, then you and Sawyer can have second watch."

"Good idea," Sawyer said, acknowledging Geoff's redirection of the conversation. "Let's try and get some shut-eye, Jane."

"I really don't think I can," Jane said with a shiver. "Who could possibly sleep tonight?"

"Ariel said you need rest, remember?" Geoff said, thankful for the way his ruse went off. "She said you might need to heal a lot of injured soldiers tomorrow, so you should probably try to catch a little sleep."

While Sawyer spread a couple of thick blankets on the ground, Jane scanned the darkness, already backlit by multitude of army campfires, and said, "I wonder why we're camping on the very edge, and away from all the soldiers?"

"Probably because it's quieter." Sawyer patted the space beside him. "C'mon, Jane. Let's snuggle."

"Thanks, but I think I'll stay here, if that's Okay."

Jane curled up beside the fire, while Sawyer looked at Geoff and shrugged. It was unusual for Jane to be standoffish, but she *had* been acting a little weird for a while. When Sawyer covered Jane with another blanket, she smiled at him and closed her eyes. Sawyer tucked himself into his own blankets near Jane and lay looking up at the night sky. A minute later he lifted his head and looked at Geoff.

"Make sure you don't fall asleep," Sawyer cautioned, giving a quick nod in Jane's direction. "And wake me up when it's my turn, okay? Night, Jane."

"Goodnight," she murmured.

Geoff, seated on a stump, tugged his own blanket closer. It was already a pretty chilly night, in his opinion, but he might as well try to stay warm. The hazy orange glow from the campfire extended in a radius of about twenty feet. It was the darkness beyond which worried him. Sawyer and Jane also worried him. Normally, they'd have been nestled together with Sawyer's arm wrapped around Jane.

Geoff paced to the edge of the light, keeping himself moving. Every now and then he peered into the darkness, stopping to study any perceived movement, occasionally aware of soldiers who were equally wakeful. As the night wore on, Geoff found himself thinking about Ishara and Ariel and what dangers they might be facing.

He imagined an army of barbarians chasing them, the black-furred ferocious werewolf leaping at them from the darkness, even the tall figure of the Shadowlord swinging his dark blade with glowing red runes. Geoff wished he had kissed Ishara one more time before she left. What if she didn't come back? What if none of the small scouting party returned? Geoff grasped the Wizard's Key through his tunic, partly to make sure it was still there, strung around his neck, and partly because it was their way back home.

It wasn't all that cold, but he still felt chilly. If only his dad, the wizard Maelord, had been around, he'd have felt more at ease. Geoff wondered what he was up to at that moment. Was he attending some war council in Chalon, or maybe in his tower, perfecting some new spell that might help to bring this war to an end? Whatever he was doing, Geoff hoped his dad was safe.

For the next couple hours, Geoff thought about the coming battle and what, if anything, he could do to help. He wasn't sure he could use his magic to kill a person. It hadn't bothered him to defend himself and kill the bog drake, or even the carrion mites, but killing someone else was another matter. He hoped he wouldn't have to make that decision. By the time Geoff checked on Jane and Sawyer, they were both asleep.

Still, something made him a little uneasy. The campfire was starting to ebb and die. He placed another couple logs on the fire, keeping quiet so he wouldn't disturb them. The glow from the fire brightened and expanded, revealing a slight movement beyond the others that caught his eye.

He squinted. Something was moving on the ground. No. *Something was below ground pushing its way up from below.* The earth began to rise a little at first, then Geoff heard distinct scraping and clawing below the burgeoning mound. The digging sounds became faster and more frantic.

"Hey! Sawyer! Jane!" Geoff called. "Wake up! Something's coming up from the ground!"

"Huh?" Jane murmured. "Geoff? What's going on?"

Sawyer shot up, eyes wide open and looked at Geoff.

"Geoff," he said with a hint of grogginess in his voice. "What is it?"

Geoff pointed behind them and shouted, "Look!"

Emerging from the soil was a grayish-yellow near-skeletal hand, its elongated fingers ending in curled and jagged claws.

# CHAPTER SEVEN
## NIGHT ATTACK

Sawyer leapt to his feet and drew the Stormblade from its scabbard. The sword began to glow as tiny, bluish-white arcs of electricity scintillated along the length of the blade.

"What the hell is that?" Sawyer breathed. "Jane, get behind me!"

Instead, she grabbed his arm and squeezed it, pointing toward the army tents nearby.

"Look, we're *all* under attack! What *are* these things?"

All around them there were hoarse shouts of warning from the troops, and unearthly screeches from the invaders. He spun and saw pitched battles with men and elves fighting off grotesquely skeletal, human-like creatures. The creatures attacked with wild abandon, ripping and tearing with sharp claws and jagged, broken teeth. A rancid, putrid stench washed over Geoff, causing him to crouch and cover his nose and mouth.

"Here it comes!" shouted Sawyer.

The creature digging its way out had finally emerged, its form emaciated, almost shriveled. The smell of decay intensified as it stretched its clawed fingers and tilted its head left and right, its bones and muscles cracking and popping with every movement.

It gazed around with empty eye sockets. Then it opened its mouth, revealing rotting, uneven fangs and let out a piercing screech. Geoff, who was closest, covered his ears.

He took a step toward Sawyer and Jane. The creature whirled and looked at Geoff.

"Geoff! Get over here!" Sawyer shouted. "Hurry!"

Geoff spun and ran toward Sawyer and Jane just as the creature tried to grab him. Its claws raked and ripped the blanket he had thrown on for warmth. He caught a glimpse of Jane, who looked repulsed. Geoff heard footsteps closing in on him. It was only a few steps away. Sawyer stepped forward.

"Duck!" Sawyer ordered as he swung his sword at the creature. Geoff dove to the ground, skidding and rolling past Sawyer. The Stormblade sliced deep into the shoulder of the creature, who uttered another unearthly shriek as it bent all its attention on the sword-wielder. Crouching over, it snarled and leapt high in the air at Sawyer. Sawyer ducked the long claws as they reached for him and swung again. This time, he struck the creature in the side as it sailed past.

It clutched its side and landed hard, clawing and kicking wildly at the air. Jane removed a tree limb from the campfire then struck the foul creature several times with the end that was ablaze. It burst into flames and the stench of burning, rotting flesh permeated the air. The creature shrieked one last, agonizing scream and then crumpled into a burning heap.

"Way to go, Jane!" Sawyer shouted. He looked over at Geoff, who was getting to his feet. "You okay, Geoff?"

Geoff felt a stinging pain in his knees. Looking down, Geoff saw his knees bleeding through new holes in his trousers.

"Yeah," Geoff said. "I'm okay. That was good thinking with the fire, Jane."

"I didn't have anything else to hit it with, but I didn't know it would burn like that."

Suddenly, another two grotesque shapes rushed at them from opposite sides of the camp, each screeching as loudly as the first. Their matted hair dangled like seaweed from their eyeless heads. Geoff was closest to the first creature. It sprang at him with surprising speed, its claws open and ready to rend him to pieces.

"Geoff!" Jane shouted.

Falling back, Geoff threw up his hands to fend off the attack. A shimmering golden translucent shield appeared between him and the creature. Geoff was breathing so fast it felt like he was gasping for air as he watched the creature claw and tear at his shield, which was the largest he'd ever cast. He felt a tingling, thrilling sense of power deep in his chest as he realized that he could manipulate the shield. His father hadn't taught him that. He elongated the shield and heightened its glowing surface so the creature couldn't leap over it or easily run around it.

"Sawyer, look out!" Jane screamed.

Geoff glanced over in time to see Sawyer swinging the Stormblade at the third creature, which backed away. Its face wrinkled with rage as it screamed at Sawyer. It continuously opened and closed its serrated claws. This gave Geoff an idea. He touched his hands together then separated them, moving one toward Sawyer while maintaining the shield between himself and his own attacker with the other.

As he moved his hand, the golden shimmer enveloped Sawyer and Jane, encasing the three of them in the magical gold-tinged glassy bubble. Sawyer lowered his sword and touched Jane on the shoulder.

"You okay?"

"I'm fine," Jane said, then she turned to Geoff. "That's amazing! How're you doing that?"

"Dunno," Geoff said. "It just kind of came to me, like it was automatic or something. Dad never told me I could shape it."

"How long can you keep the spell up, Geoff?" Jane asked, eyeing the two frenzied, angry creatures claw and bite at the shield.

"I'm not sure," Geoff said. "I don't think for much longer."

"We better get ready then," Sawyer said, raising his sword again and taking a deep breath.

Jane picked up another burning limb from the camp fire.

"Whatever these things are, they burn really fast," Jane said.

"What are they, anyway?" Sawyer said.

"I don't know," Jane said. "They look like they're already dead."

"They stink like they're dead too."

The ghoulish creatures circled and leapt at and on the shield, attempting to scratch or claw their way inside. As he watched, Geoff began to notice a dull throbbing rising from the back of his head.

"Guys," Geoff said. "What's the plan? I can't hold the shield for much longer. I never created one this big before and it's starting to hurt."

"What do you have, Jane?" Sawyer asked. "Got any cool druid spells to get us out of this?"

"Maybe I could try to entangle them. That would give us a little time."

"Sounds good," Sawyer said with a nod. "When Geoff drops his shield, hit 'em with that spell. I can finish them once they're entangled."

"Wait," Jane said, "We need to get them closer together for a better chance of this working."

"Jane, go stand by Geoff," Sawyer said. "I'll try to lure 'em to the other side of Geoff's magical shield."

"Sawyer, you can't be near them when I cast my spell or you'll be entangled too," Jane said. "You'll need to get out of the way in a hurry."

"Got it," Sawyer said. "Just don't miss with that spell."

Sawyer walked to the far side of the shimmering shield. The creatures followed him, gnashing their teeth and clawing at the shield. He took a defensive stance, one that Ariel had taught him, and prepared himself.

"Okay Geoff," Sawyer said, keeping his eyes on the screeching creatures. "Drop it."

Geoff stopped concentrating and the shield dissipated. With a howl, the creatures bounded toward Sawyer.

"*Bar'athel envora*," Jane said, pointing at the ground between Sawyer and the creatures. The grass and shrubbery rose up and writhed like snakes. Sawyer turned and ran, luring the creatures closer to Jane's entangle spell. In a matter of a few steps, the creatures found their bony limbs tightly wrapped by animated grass, weeds, and other plants. Furiously, they started trying to tear and rip at the greenery holding them fast.

As soon as they would come close to freeing a leg or an arm, thicker, leafier plants would twine themselves around the appendage and immobilize it. Soon, both creatures were reduced to muffled cries within their green cocoons. Sawyer tried to work his way close enough to finish them with his sword, but the snaking foliage was too powerful.

"So far, so good," Geoff said, "Now what?"

"I need to get closer," Sawyer said, trying to gauge where he could safely step. Geoff did likewise. However, the writhing patch around the creatures was much too large for Sawyer to get close enough to finish them with his sword. Suddenly, two loud *snaps* rang out. They sounded like brittle tree limbs cracking.

"Geoff," Sawyer said, with a hint of awe in his voice. "Look!"

Geoff glanced to where Sawyer was pointing, just as several more snaps filled the air. The shapes of the cocoons encasing the creatures had begun to change, as did their bodies. The tone of their shrieks changed from rage to pain and fear. Geoff's jaw dropped. They were being crushed and twisted grotesquely, bones parting. They were being *tortured*.

"Jane?" Geoff asked, "What're you doing?"

Jane had not stirred from her spot at the edge of the encampment. She was no longer chanting her spell. Instead, she held one hand, fingers spread outwards, toward her prisoners. It was the malicious look in her eyes and the sneer on her face that chilled Geoff to his core. As he and Sawyer watched, Jane slowly closed her hand into a fist, an expression of dark exaltation on her face. All the while the cocooned creatures howled, but by the time Jane had closed her fist, the crumpled and crushed forms had stopped making any sounds.

"Oh Jane…" Geoff said, shaking his head. He turned back to look at the misshapen cocoons.

"I didn't know she could do that," Sawyer said.

"Me neither," Geoff said. "I don't think Ariel would teach her how to crush entangled enemies."

"No."

"It's like she enjoyed it."

"Whatever," Sawyer said. "They were trying to kill us anyway."

"Hey Jane, great jo…" Sawyer said, his voice trailing off suddenly.

Geoff also turned toward Jane and froze. A horrified look fell over his face.

"Those two won't be bothering us anymore." Jane said, stopping as she noticed the look in Sawyer's eyes.

"What?" She asked. "What is it?"

"Jane!" Sawyer shouted. "Look out!"

Jane looked at Sawyer and Geoff, her brows furrowed in bewilderment. Then she realized they were looking past her. *Behind her.* Jane whirled around to see the sunken and empty eye sockets of another creature only inches away.

# CHAPTER EIGHT
## FOREST BATTLE

Sharp sounds of steel on steel rang out and echoed throughout the otherwise tranquil forest. Both combatants, one in black plate mail armor and the other wearing ragged animal skins, were locked in a fatal struggle.

Alex stepped back just in time to avoid a slash aimed at his neck. Zorn's blade whistled past, crimson runes hissing. Alex countered with an attack which struck Zorn's thigh. His blade failed to penetrate the black armor, but the force of the blow extracted a loud grunt from Zorn, who retaliated with a backhand to the side of Alex's head. The impact of the blow was strong enough to cave in the side of a normal man's face.

Alex, however, was not normal. Neither was Zorn. They were unnatural creatures doomed to an eternity of solitary agony and darkness. Yet their afflictions had enhanced their physical prowess. Each was able to strike with uncanny speed and accuracy while withstanding attacks that would kill any other human.

Alex staggered backward, pain shooting through his right cheek and a trickle of warm blood running down to his chin.

"The blood of a werewolf," Zorn sneered. "I can't imagine anything more revolting."

"I can," Alex said with a wolfish smile. He stepped forward with a loping gait, he aimed his sword at Zorn's chest.

His attack was parried with ease. Zorn spun completely around and followed with a strike at Alex's legs. Alex jumped, bringing his knees up to his chest. As he landed, Alex brought his sword down with an overhead strike at Zorn's head. This attack was parried as well.

Both Zorn and Alex stepped back, an understood moment of respite and respect.

"You're faster and stronger than I remembered," Zorn admitted. "It seems some of the wolf inside has…enhanced you. But it matters not. We both know how this will end."

"Even if you kill me now," Alex said, sword at the ready. "You and your queen will fail."

"How so?" Zorn sneered, feinting and thrusting his sword at Alex.

"Evil may have its time," Alex said, dodging the attack. "But destiny will always side with the good and the brave."

"Ha," Zorn scoffed, snarling and swinging his black blade at Alex's neck. "Whoever controls magic controls destiny. And there is none stronger than Queen Lysis. Her power is absolute. The arch of her neck, the twist of her brow, she can shrivel any creature with a glance."

"And do you think she'll keep you around when she is done with the rest of us?" Alex asked, ducking Zorn's strike. "You're nothing to her, like the rest of us. Something to be crushed beneath her feet."

"What could *you* possibly know of the Scarlet Queen?"

Zorn said, swinging his sword furiously at Alex. "You're an animal, no more than a wild beast roaming the forests. She is beyond your comprehension."

Alex backed away, dodging and parrying Zorn's attacks. Though he was able to defend himself, he was increasingly aware that he was tiring. Zorn was right. He could not win this fight.

"I understand her perfectly. Every night I hear her laugh," Alex said. "She mocks me. She delights in tormenting me. Tall, sinister, forbidding. Her dark red hair and burning red eyes are seared into my mind. She is evil incarnate."

"At least we have that in common," Zorn said through clenched teeth, lunging at Alex.

Alex again backed away, bringing his sword up to parry the attack just in time.

"I should've ripped you to pieces on your desolate mountain," Alex said. "The young druid girl saved you."

"Aye, she did. Her power grows each day. She'll make an excellent dark druid."

Shocked, Alex lowered his sword. "What do you mean?"

"Precisely what I said," Zorn smiled, revealing a set of fangs. "Jane cannot escape her fate. I've seen to that. The suggestive powers of a vampire's bite are inescapable."

Suddenly the confrontation in the woods he witnessed between Jane and the others made sense. She was changing. Her aura had diminished. When he last saw her, Jane's aura had shone as bright as the sun. He was the wolf then, in a pitched battle with Zorn. Something happened that prevented him from finishing Zorn. His memory was only flashes of bits and pieces of what happened that night. It was always like that.

In addition to his enhanced strength and agility, Alex was able to see one's aura, or their spirit. The best way he could describe it was a glow that surrounded everyone. He wasn't sure, but those who were good at heart shimmered like a star in the night sky while those who were not had a darker, almost gloomy aura. Zorn's aura was sinister and black as pitch.

Alex stepped forward and attacked with a double slash to Zorn's body which was easily evaded. Zorn wasn't tiring. Even though Zorn wore plate mail armor, he was energetic and incredibly strong. Alex leapt at Zorn again. This time they closed together, with each grasping the other's sword hand. Alex seized Zorn's throat with his other hand and squeezed. Wincing, Zorn gripped Alex's in return. The stinging cold metal of Zorn's mail gauntlet startled Alex at first, then Zorn's grip tightened. Alex gasped for air through clenched teeth as he continued to squeeze Zorn's neck.

Suddenly, Zorn's eyes opened wide and the grimace on his face faded. A low growl emanated from Alex's throat and his eyes remained focused on Zorn's neck. Alex's hand had grown larger and become covered with coarse, black fur. He felt his fingers dig deeper, his nails became claws. A surge of adrenaline coursed through Alex as his breathing became rapid. Zorn released Alex's throat and gripped his wrist.

"How…" Zorn said, eyes wide in a look of disbelief etched across Zorn's face as he struggled against the fur covered vice wrapped around his neck. Another surge of adrenaline pulsed through Alex as he slammed Zorn to the ground. The beast stirred within Alex. An eruption of hate and fury overcame Alex. Even though Zorn was inhumanly strong, he kept his grip on Zorn's wrist, immobilizing his sword hand.

A ravenous hunger welled up within Alex, a singular, blood drunk obsession overtook him. Part of the wolf that had always lain dormant during daylight was emerging. The scent of this particular prey was too strong to resist. It was something much older and deeper, like an eternal blood feud. The abhorrence between werewolves and vampires through the ages ran deep. The instinct to destroy the other was innate. It was a command of the blood that must be obeyed.

Zorn released his sword and wriggled his hand free from Alex's grasp. Gripping the claw wrapped around his throat with both hands, he began to exert his vampiric strength. With a snarl, Alex reimposed his own will and wrenched Zorn's wrist away. As he did, he felt Zorn's strength began to waver. His victory was near. Then, as Alex was beginning to dig his claws deep into Zorn's neck, something dark and smoky wrapped itself around his hand and his neck.

The black cloak Zorn wore had come alive. It became a writhing mass of tentacles that engulfed Alex and lifted him off the ground and off Zorn. Alex twisted and tried to grasp the vaporous tendrils, but his hands merely passed through them. He snarled again and glared at Zorn. More snake-like appendages wrapped themselves around his arms and legs, leaving Alex suspended three feet off the ground and completely at Zorn's mercy.

"There, there, beastie," Zorn said, retrieving his sword. "Time to put you down."

Zorn rubbed his neck and looked at the blood on his gauntlet.

"You will pay for that," Zorn sneered. "That's twice you nearly killed me. You'll never have another chance. Queen

Lysis wishes you dead. So be it."

Zorn slashed Alex's right side with his blade. Alex screamed. His entire side seemed to explode, as if his body had been set on fire. Never had he felt pain like this. He couldn't move, he was paralyzed. Then he caught a glimpse of Zorn's sword. The runes carved into the black blade had begun to smoke and glow red. Zorn slowly dragged the edge of his sword across Alex's chest. Again Alex screamed.

It wasn't only the wounds Zorn inflicted on him, there was something sinister about Zorn's sword. It possessed a malicious presence, like it was alive and reveling in his pain. It was feeding on him. Alex's vision became a blur of red and black. He felt himself weakening and he was powerless to stop his tormentor.

*At least it would be over soon,* he thought. His nightmare would finally end. In a way, he was grateful. He had suffered long enough under the spell of the beast. Alex began to feel like he was drifting, floating away. He saw the faces of his father and mother.

He was back in Chalon and he was young. How he loved roaming the halls when he was a child. His castle explorations were the highlight of his younger days. As he grew older, he began to explore the city of Chalon, then the surrounding countryside. He was free and happy.

"Why are you smiling?" Zorn snapped, lifting his sword to strike the killing blow. "I'll rip you apart! I will…"

Alex thought he heard loud thumping noises coupled with the clang of metal. Alex heard other sounds. They were muffled, deep, husky voices. Then something struck Zorn in the side. Actually, it was several somethings, many even. Alex's vision faded further until he saw nothing but a gray blur filled with movement. He felt the smoky tendrils release him and he dropped to the ground. He felt only the burning sensations of his wounds, nothing else. Something bright and orange flashed nearby. What could that be? Fire?

Many shapes moved around him now. Everything was a whirlwind of movement filled with the same muffled voices, except now there was shouting and was that the sound of battle? Alex tried to open his eyes but couldn't. He was too weak. He heard the thumping sound again. It was running, the sound of armored boots running past. He thought he heard a screech and hiss, and then cheers.

Alex lay in the grass fading in and out of consciousness for several long moments before he became aware that a shape stood over him, blocking out what light remained of the day. It was watching him, perhaps trying to determine if he was too far gone to try and save. Then the shape bent closer and Alex saw the outline of a wide nose and long, pale yellow beard.

"Damn, how many times have I saved your life now?"

# CHAPTER NINE
## THE DWARVES OF KEREDAIN

It wasn't the aromatic smell of sausage cooking over open fires, nor was it the stout smell of mead in the air that awakened Alex. It was a rough nudge and a familiar, loud, gravelly, voice that roused him.

"Wake up, you flat-footed, surface-dwelling elf lover." The rough voice was nearly a shout. "We need to talk."

Alex opened his eyes. At first, his vision was blurry, which matched the way his head ached and swam. The wounds he had received from his encounter with Zorn burned like a thousand hot needles were searing his flesh. Alex moved a hand to rub the cut across his chest but a heavy boot pinned his arm to his side, preventing him from touching it.

"Best not touch that. We've just dressed your wounds."

Alex gazed up at his benefactor and a faint smile crossed his lips. Sitting beside him was what looked like a large barrel with muscled arms and legs protruding from it. His blond hair was streaked gray, as was his ample beard. It was Baldon Stonemaster, dwarven king of Keredain. His sunken blue eyes scanned Alex for a moment. The metal plate he held in his large, gnarled hands looked too small for him, but his pewter mug was easily twice the size of a normal drinking mug.

"I always said you were a few whiskers short of a full beard," Baldon said, taking another long gulp from his mug. "But only in jest. I didn't believe it till now."

Alex raised himself up on an elbow, grunting at the pain. Glancing around, he saw what must've been thousands of dwarves, all armored and ready for battle. They too were eating and drinking as they sat in circles near caches of neatly stacked weapons.

"Do you want to tell me when it happened?" Baldon said.

"When what happened?"

"When you bumped your head," Baldon growled. "Whatever possessed you to attack a fully armored knight of Zorn's caliber? Especially since he became all dark and evil and such."

"I didn't," Alex said as he sat upright, again grunting in pain. "He hunted me down, attacked me."

"Hrmph," Baldon said as he shoveled more sausage and bread into his mouth.

"And why do you call me 'elf lover' like it's an insult? I thought dwarves liked elves."

"We do," Baldon said raising his bushy eyebrows. "Dwarves and elves have had amicable dealings long before humans showed up. We trust elves a lot more than we trust your kind, that's for sure."

Alex felt a nudge on his right shoulder. He turned his head and saw another dwarf standing over him holding out a plate of greasy sausage, cheese, and bread as well as a smaller brown clay mug. This dwarf had deep red hair and a crooked nose. His beard was thick and wild. Alex nodded in thanks as he took the plate and mug.

"So," Baldon said as he laid his plate down and focused his gaze on Alex. "You going to tell me why the Shadowlord is hunting you? I assume it has to do with your…affliction."

"Aye," Alex said, taking a sip from his mug. Dwarven mead, strong and bitter. The muddy brown drink burned as he swallowed it. "It does. I'm pretty sure the beast has been attacking his troops at night."

"Ha!" Baldon said with a smile. "That'll do it. Zorn is the type to take that sort of thing personally."

"I don't think it was his idea," Alex said. "He said the Scarlet Queen commanded him to hunt and kill me. She seems to command him in everything."

The smile disappeared from Baldon's face. He leaned forward, eyes shining.

"Alex," Baldon said in a low serious tone. "If she's after you, then you have a serious dilemma, my friend. Of all the rulers in Alluria, she should be avoided at all costs. She may look human but she isn't. I don't know what she is, but her sorceress powers can lay waste to entire cities. She can burn an army of thousands to ashes. Best you stay away from her. She enjoys killing, that one."

Alex focused his attention on Baldon as he spoke. The King of Keredain wasn't afraid of anything, nor was any dwarf for that matter, but something about the scarlet-haired queen gave him pause.

"I've heard similar stories," Alex said. "Each ending in death and carnage."

"Believe them," Baldon said. "She isn't one to bargain and she isn't merciful."

"She sent armies to siege Keredain and Bregendain to the

north. If you're here then you must've defeated her. How did you do it?"

Baldon sat in silence for a moment. He took another drink from his mug and sighed heavily.

"We didn't defeat the Scarlet Queen, she drove us from our mountain homes. What you see before you are all the menfolk to survive."

"I'm sorry," Alex said. "Can you not regain your homeland? Surely King Andurys will send help. And Lionel—"

"She attacked us with the dead," Baldon said, smashing a gnarled fist into a hand. "She sent two armies. We were able to beat back the army of barbarians she sent against us, but every barbarian we killed rose again as an undead warrior. They now stalk the dwarven halls. Shambling around, no minds, no words, only frightening wails that freeze you to the core. Perhaps King Andurys may send help. He's a good and just king, but Lionel is a gutless, scheming, worthless liar. What good can he be against the Scarlet Queen?"

"She can control the dead, too? Incredible."

"Aye, can anyone defeat her?" Baldon tossed his empty mug on the ground in disgust. "How do you kill an enemy that's already dead? An enemy that keeps hacking at you when you're down, feeding on you while you still breathe?"

"Then it's worse than I thought," Alex said.

"It is," Baldon said. "Queen Lysis is determined to bring us all under her heel and crush us. We need a leader to stand against her."

Alex leaned back again and exhaled. He thought for a moment.

"Well, that isn't me," he said. "No one will follow a werewolf."

"Well it damn sure isn't Lionel. Do you think that fool would help us? He won't even save his own people," Baldon said bitterly. "Why the hell is he sitting on the throne of Chalon?"

Alex shook his head.

"I told you long ago he was weak and worthless. You should've chosen someone else."

"I didn't choose Lionel," Alex snapped. "I didn't choose anyone. And I damn sure didn't choose to be a monster."

"Well, it happened," Baldon said, standing up. "The question is; what're you going do about it?"

Alex didn't answer. He laid in the grass staring at the dark sky overhead. Baldon grunted and started to walk back to his troops. His dissatisfaction of Alex's non-answer was obvious. He stopped and looked over his shoulder.

"We go to battle the barbarians that attacked Bregendain. They're marching to Chalon. We intend to stop them. We can't defeat the dead, but we can exact some measure of revenge. If you weren't so damn beat up, I'd ask you to join us. But then I'd have to worry about keeping you alive again and you'd get in the way."

Alex let out a short chuckle.

"We can't have that now, can we?"

Then Baldon turned around and faced Alex.

"Wouldn't it be something to see," he said, raising both bushy eyebrows. "If Chalon had a leader the people could count on in dark times? Someone who would bring them together with dwarves and elves and rebuild this world?" Baldon nodded at Alex. "Their true king, perhaps?"

Baldon turned and strode back to his troops, barking orders. Alex sighed and slowly shook his head.

"Aye," he said under his breath. "Wouldn't that be something? Their true king, the werewolf."

He closed his eyes. His confrontation with Zorn left Alex wounded and exhausted. Soon, the moon would rise and his nightmare would begin again. The nightmare that had haunted him every night for years. For now, he needed rest before the nightmare overtook him again. He felt a tingling in his wounds. His rest would be short.

He had always been healed by the dark curse that had claimed him just before his transformation. Whatever wounds he had suffered during the day were healed when he became a werewolf. The tingling sensation was only the beginning of the healing process. Alex winced as he rolled to his side and painfully pulled himself to his feet. Yet as he glanced around he felt heartened. Thousands of dwarves, armed and ready for battle were assembling and making ready to march. They would march all night if Baldon commanded it. Dwarves were strong, hearty, and had more stamina than any other folk in Alluria.

He had to put as much distance between himself and Baldon's army as possible. He caught Baldon's gaze and nodded. The look on Baldon's face said it all. He knew what Alex was doing. The dwarven king returned the nod and went back to preparing his men for a long march. Alex staggered for the first few steps, but then found his balance and made his way into the dark forest. As he disappeared into darkness, he heard Baldon's conversation with the red haired dwarf who had brought him food and drink.

"So that's Alex. The one you spoke of so often," the red haired dwarf said. "The dark wolf. Seems like a formidable warrior. If he wasn't hurt, we could use him in battle. How far do you think he'll get with those wounds? He needs rest."

"Aye. That's him," Baldon said. "You'll not find a braver man...nor one more tormented. He saved my life many times during our younger adventuring days. I'd fight by his side against any foe. To answer your question, he'll go as far as he needs to save us. Unfortunately, he won't find any rest this night."

"He's heading toward the barbarian army of the Shadowlord," Fralic said.

"He is," Baldon replied. "Better to unleash the beast on one's enemies than one's friends."

Alex made his way deeper into the forest. He'd noticed certain physical changes in him since he'd been cursed with lycanthropy. In addition to being able to heal faster, he possessed excellent night vision, increased strength, speed, along with a heightened sense of smell and hearing. He didn't consider these attributes to be bonuses, though. They merely reminded him of his curse. What bothered him most was the memory of the nameless faces of those he had killed the previous night. There were so many. Too many.

# Chapter Ten
## Darkness Rising

Jane screamed and fell backward, hitting the ground hard. The creature stood over her for a few seconds, sniffing at her. Geoff was sure Jane was a goner. He thought if Jane could cast a spell, or he could try something like a lightning bolt, but there was a chance he'd hit Jane too. Plus, Sawyer had charged the awful creature that loomed over her, sword high overhead. In doing so, he placed himself directly in front of Geoff, cutting off any line of sight Geoff may have had to cast a spell.

"Sawyer! You're in the way!"

Even as Geoff finished his words, the creature looked up and noticed Sawyer. It let out another ear piercing screech and leapt over Jane to meet Sawyer's charge.

"Jane, get out of the way!" Geoff called.

Jane didn't move. She lay motionless on the ground. *Oh no! Did it kill her? Was she hurt?* It looked like the creature had ignored Jane, but everything happened so fast that Geoff wasn't sure. The flurry of activity between Sawyer and the creature drew Geoff's attention as the two engaged each other.

The creature attacked and slashed with its claws. Sawyer was able to dodge most of the frenzied attacks, but one or two got past his defenses, raking harmlessly across his elven battle armor.

Sawyer swung the Stormblade at the creature's torso, barely missing. It yowled and stepped back, flexing its claws and snarling.

"Geoff," Sawyer said, keeping his gaze on the creature in front of him. "Go check on Jane. I got this."

Sawyer positioned himself between Geoff and the creature, providing a blocker for Geoff. Dashing to her side, Geoff dropped to both knees and shook her shoulder. He didn't see any injuries.

"Jane? Are you okay? Get up!"

She didn't move. Geoff took her hand and placed two fingers on the underside of her wrist. There. A pulse. It was fast and strong.

Behind him, he heard Sawyer's blade singing as it sliced through the air. The foul-smelling creature continued to rip at Sawyer with its claws.

"She's okay, Sawyer!" Geoff called. "I think she just fainted."

"Great," Sawyer said through clenched teeth. "Now we just gotta deal with this thing."

Sawyer stepped forward and stabbed at the creature's chest, forcing it to back away. Geoff rose and took a position behind Sawyer, his mind racing for the appropriate spell. He needed to get a clear line of sight with Sawyer was safely out of the way. Just then, the creature leapt high into the air. Geoff froze. It was going to spring over Sawyer and attack him! But Sawyer was too quick. He leaped, thrust his blade upward and impaled the creature.

However, it didn't die. Shrieking, it began to flail its limbs wildly, as arcs of electricity from the Stormblade roiled over its body. The creature's weight and awkward movements at the end of the sword caused Sawyer to lose his balance and fall on his back. As he did, the creature became further impaled. It let out a final screech as it reached for Sawyer's neck and face before dying. Its grayish body convulsed with electrical energy.

"Sawyer!" Geoff marveled. "That was amazing! You looked like one of those superheroes in the comics."

Then Geoff realized Sawyer was struggling to get out from under the creature's corpse. He ran to Sawyer and grabbed his arm and helped Sawyer to his feet. Sawyer was covered in a blackish fluid that smelled like rotten eggs. He held his nose and stepped back from Sawyer.

"Ugh, Sawyer, you're gonna need a bath."

"Yeah yeah," Sawyer said as he turned to go check on Jane. Geoff looked down at the desiccated looking thing that had attacked them. Its sharp claws were half as long as Geoff's arm. Its human-like features were distorted, elongated arms and hands. Its legs were also a bit longer than they should be.

"Sawyer, I think this thing's been dead for a long time," Geoff said. "Maybe it was once human, but why is it shaped funny?"

"Who cares? It's finally dead. Hey, Jane's coming around."

Geoff spun around and ran to Jane and Sawyer. Jane clutched at the back of her head as Sawyer helped her sit up.

"What happened?" Jane said.

"You were attacked by one of those sick creatures," Sawyer

said. "I think you banged your head. Can you stand?"

"I…I think so," Jane grunted in pain as Sawyer helped her stand.

"Hey Geoff, could you get her some water?"

Without a word, Geoff ran to their supplies and grabbed a small flask of water.

*Whack.*

The sudden impact of a heavy blow startled him. Geoff whirled. He dropped the flask and his mouth fell open.

"Jane!" he yelled.

Standing over Sawyer, who was lying on the ground with blood gushing from over his right eye, was Jane. She was holding a thick branch with both hands. Before Geoff could do anything, Jane brought it down on Sawyer's head with another loud *whack.*

"Jane, no!" Geoff ran toward her. "What're you doing?"

*He had to do something or she was going to kill Sawyer! If he could wrestle that club away from her, maybe call for help.* Geoff's mind raced. He didn't want to harm her with a spell, but if he could place a shield over Sawyer…

Jane turned and faced Geoff, still clutching the bloody club. He froze in place. Geoff felt as if he'd been punched in the stomach. His body shivered. Her expression was cold and empty.

"Oh no," Geoff muttered as Jane's gaze met his. "Jane?"

Her soft blue eyes had turned pitch black. He was unable to tear his gaze from the black pools of hatred that had been Jane's eyes. A contemptuous sneer slowly crept across Jane's face. The stark fear that gripped Geoff made it difficult for him to breathe.

Jane dropped her club, raised her hand and pointed at

him. Geoff felt himself being grappled and entwined by the nearest tree. The branches tightened so much that Geoff felt like his ribs were being crushed. He gasped for air. His eyes saw red and the pain in his sides was excruciating. Then Jane quickly flicked her wrist as if to dismiss him.

Geoff was violently whipped away by the tree and thrown through the air with fantastic speed. His body crashed through limbs and shrubs before he struck the base of another tree. For a second, everything went black. When he opened his eyes, something warm and wet flowed into his left eye and obscured his vision. He tried to lift his left hand to wipe his eye but his arm didn't respond. He raised his right hand. It was covered with lacerations and scrapes. He wiped his eye. When he pulled his hand away it was covered in blood.

He didn't feel any pain, though. Instead, his whole body was numb. From where Geoff had come to rest, he could see their camp through the trees. Sawyer lay where Jane had attacked him, half his face was bright red in the firelight. Jane stood motionless, surveying the army of men and elves nearby. They had dispatched the other creatures that had attacked them and were tending to their wounded.

Jane's solid black eyes observed them for a moment. Then she turned and stepped over Sawyer as she walked into the forest. The trees parted and moved out of her way as she disappeared into the darkness.

"J…Jane," Geoff choked before everything faded to black for him.

# CHAPTER ELEVEN
## AFTER

W as it getting lighter? Did he smell smoke? Where was he? Someone squeezed his hand. No. Someone was holding his hand. Slender, soft fingers tightened their warm grip on his while another set of soft fingers caressed his forehead. Honeysuckle. That's what he smelled. Honeysuckle and wild flowers.

"Geoff?"

The voice was kind and gentle. His lips curled up at the edges, a feeling of contentment washed over him. He didn't know if he was in heaven or not, but the state of bliss he found himself in made him think he was elsewhere.

"Geoff?"

He felt someone rest their hand on his chest. A glimmer of light slid through his eye lids. If this was a dream, he didn't want to wake up.

"Geoff? *Nu Tel'mor?*"

The angelic voice was that of a girl. He knew that voice, he was sure of it. Something stirred in Geoff's memory and he opened his eyes as he inhaled. It was too bright. He closed his eyes again and turned his head.

"Wake up, Geoff."

Those words, someone had called him that before. Ishara. Geoff opened his eyes again and blinked several times. He saw grass and trees. He felt a soft caress on his cheek and someone gently turned his head. Ishara was kneeling over him with a wide smile on her beautiful face. She shimmered with a gold and white gleam about her.

Geoff smiled.

"Hey," he said.

"Hey yourself," Ishara said, running a thumb back and forth along his jawline. She leaned closer and kissed his lips several times. Then she whispered into his ear.

"Welcome back, *Nu Tel'mor.*"

"Thanks," Geoff said.

He lay there looking into Ishara's green eyes. He took her hand and kissed it. Ishara smiled. Suddenly Geoff remembered what had happened. His eyes opened wide and a feeling of gloom and fear overtook him.

"Oh no! Jane!" Geoff said as he struggled to sit up. "She's gone evil, Ishara. We're in big trouble. She tried to kill us. Wait! Sawyer! Is he okay?"

"Shhhhhhhhh," Ishara said, gently placing two slender fingers across his lips. "Sawyer will be fine. He is resting."

Ishara looked to her right. Geoff followed her gaze and saw Sawyer lying on a blanket. Ariel was leaning over him. She was examining his forehead where Jane had struck him. Geoff let out a sigh of relief and looked at Ishara.

"Jane attacked us," he said. "I've never seen her like that before. Her eyes, they were all black, like—"

"Like pools of pure evil," Ariel said as she stood and crossed over to Geoff. "I have seen them before."

Geoff looked at Ariel and blinked a few times, trying to put together what that meant.

"Yeah. Your mentor, Bhael. You had to kill him, right?" Geoff said.

Ariel nodded.

"But we can get Jane back, can't we? We rescued her from the Iron Citadel and fought off the Shadowlord. What do we do? We gotta get her back. Can you can track her?"

"Geoff, please rest," Ariel said. "Morning is fast approaching and there is a battle to fight. I need you to watch over Sawyer while we engage the enemy."

Geoff nodded. Though she smiled when she spoke to him, the tone in Ariel's voice was somber. Geoff swallowed and calmed himself.

"It was horrible, Ariel," he said. "First, these awful, stinking things came out of the ground and attacked us, then—"

"Wights," Ariel said.

"Huh?

Wights?" Geoff said.

"Yes," Ishara said. "Wights are dead things raised by dark magic. You and Sawyer did well to slay three of them."

"Dark magic?" Geoff said. "But I don't think Jane raised them. Well, I didn't hear her cast any spells."

"She did not summon the wights," Ariel said. "Someone else did that. Someone infinitely more evil than Jane could ever be."

"Ariel," Geoff said, "Jane is so powerful now. I think she can do everything you can. She can make trees move out of her way and she doesn't need to speak to cast spells. She walked away in that direction." Geoff pointed north. "The forest does her bidding, but in a twisted way. She crushed two wights to death and it looked like she enjoyed it. Then she made a tree toss me away like nothing."

"Geoff," Ariel said, her eyes falling to the ground. "I know. I will do everything I can for Jane. If what you tell me is true, then it is horrific news and my heart is broken, for Jane has become a dark druid."

"So how do we get her back?" Geoff said.

Ariel looked at him but said nothing.

"Ariel?" Geoff said, his voice rising. "How do we get Jane back? We have to go after her."

"I do not know," Ariel said. "The Shadowlord's bite has made Jane…susceptible to evil. She has fallen away from the light."

"So Jane is gone?" Geoff said, shaking his head in disbelief. "You have to do something, Ariel. Please."

"I will try," Ariel said. "For now, though, you must rest."

Ariel stood and exhaled. She looked north, gazing far into the distance. Geoff wondered what she was thinking. Ishara caressed his forehead, pushing his blond hair back.

"Do not worry," she said. Then she leaned forward and kissed him again. Geoff smiled. He'd never been kissed so much, especially by a beautiful girl. He thought it was amazing how she could make him smile, even with an army approaching and Jane gone.

"We must prepare for battle," Ariel said. "Keep safe. Keep Sawyer safe."

Ishara grabbed her bow and stood. She looked down at him and smiled one more time.

With that, Ishara and Ariel turned and walked toward the gathering troops nearby. Geoff watched them leave.

"How did everything get so messed up?" Geoff said under his breath.

Ariel marched toward the small gathering of men and elves standing outside a large tent. Trelane's tall, muscular shape stood out among them. Ishara walked beside Ariel, glancing at her now and then. Ariel did not return her look. After a while Ariel spoke.

"You are concerned for Jane, as am I. But I have no answers."

"If Jane has become a dark druid," Ishara said. "What can we do? She nearly killed Sawyer and Geoff. Imagine that much power in the hands of a human who has been corrupted by evil. She would be—"

"Unstoppable."

"Then what shall be done?"

Ariel said nothing. She continued her determined stride. Ishara frowned. She was younger than Ariel, but she was an elf, not any elf, she too was highborn and she would not allow herself to be ignored. She quickened her pace and then planted herself directly in front of Ariel, locking gazes with her.

"What," Ishara said. "Shall be done with Jane?"

Ariel's jaw clenched. She was breathing harder than usual. Ariel returned Ishara's stare and for a moment Ishara sensed Ariel's anger and pain, if that was the right word. Ariel blinked and raised her head. She looked around, as if trying to etch every tree, every blade of grass, every stone into her memory.

"I do not know," Ariel said finally. "As I said, I do not have any answers."

"Can Jane be redeemed? Can she be saved?"

"Again, I do not know, Ishara," Ariel snapped. "I cannot overcome every evil minion the Scarlet Queen throws at us! I do not have the strength to keep killing those who are dear to me. My heart is breaking. Jane's power already rivals mine. Every day, every minute, she grows stronger. I do not know if I can withstand such power...nor do I wish to face Jane in battle." Ariel looked at Ishara. "I may not win such a confrontation."

Ishara was taken aback by Ariel's outburst. She had never spoken to her in such manner. The thought of standing against Jane weighed heavily on Ariel, as did the dread of what must be done if such a battle took place. The old legends told of battles between high druids and dark druids that lasted for weeks and destroyed leagues of forests, mountains, and even entire cities. Ariel was as powerful a high druid as there ever was, Ishara was sure of that. Yet, if Jane *already* rivaled Ariel's power...the thought made Ishara shiver.

"If Jane must die," Ishara said softly, looking down. "I do not know if I can be a part of that."

"Nor I," Ariel said. "Yet again the Scarlet Queen has succeeded in dividing us, and this time she has claimed one of our dearest and brightest."

Ishara raised her head and looked at Ariel. Her eyes were moist.

"I am sorry," Ishara said. "Please forgive me. I did not mean to upset you."

"There is nothing to forgive," Ariel said, placing a hand on Ishara's shoulder. "You are concerned for Jane, as am I."

Ishara smiled and placed her hand over her heart. Ariel

returned the gesture and smiled.

"Come," Ariel said. "Let us learn what our enemy is planning."

They walked to the gathering of commanders in front of the tent. Ishara observed Trelane and Commander Renfry, they seemed to have become friends since the siege of the garrison at Troll Fang Pass. Trelane greeted them as they approached, placing a hand over his heart, "*Hal'inari*," he said with a slight bow of his head. Ishara and Ariel did the same in unison.

"Welcome back," Renfry said. "Trelane has been telling me about your scouting party last night. Over one hundred barbarians dead. Well done."

"How many did we lose to the wights?" Ariel said, ignoring Renfry's compliment.

"So far almost two hundred," Trelane said. "Some of them are trying to recover from their infected wounds."

"Horrible damned things," Renfry said.

"Undead," Ariel said. "Only a necromancer of great power could raise so many at once."

"The Scarlet Queen," Renfry said, nodding.

"I am not sure she has such power over the dead," Ariel said. "Perhaps the troubling development signals the arrival of a new enemy."

"Wait, you said the Scarlet Queen was our true enemy," Renfry said. "Now you say it is someone else. Exactly how many enemies are we facing?"

"Perhaps our enemy has allies," Ariel said. "Queen Lysis has marshalled her forces against us. It would be folly to think she only has barbarians and orcs at her command. She is a sorceress, not a necromancer."

"She has lived for a thousand years," Trelane said. "Is it possible she has learned the ways of the necromancer in that time?"

Ariel raised her eye brows.

"Perhaps," she admitted. "But if our foe possesses the vast capabilities of a sorcerer and a necromancer…"

"Then we're doomed," Renfry said.

No one said a word. A feeling of gloom descended on Ishara. *How can they hope to stand against such a foe?*

"However, I do not believe Queen Lysis is both sorceress and necromancer. She would have had to be nearby to summon the wights. We have seen no signs of her. Not here, nor in the barbarian's camp."

"And the Shadowlord?" Renfry asked. "Was he there last night? In their camp?"

"Briefly," Trelane said. "While we watched and waited, he mounted his black beast and flew away."

"Which direction?" Renfry asked.

"Northwest," Trelane said, pointing in that direction. "But we do not know if he returned after we left."

"It matters not," Ariel said. "Are we prepared?"

"Aye," Renfry said.

"If we win the day," Ariel said, raising her chin. "Then we will have proven the Scarlet Queen can be defeated and hopefully more will rally to us and join the fight."

"King Andurys has pledged the entire might of Selra'thel," Trelane said, looking at Ariel and Ishara. "But that will not be enough."

Everyone stood there, looking at each other. Ishara knew King Andurys would honor his word. All elves kept their promises.

"And Chalon?" Ariel said. "Will Lionel send help?"

Commander Renfry said nothing, he only pursed his lips and looked away.

"Then it appears we are on our own," Trelane said.

"The sun is rising," Ariel said. "We must assemble our forces. Our enemy will be here before we know it."

Commander Renfry held out his hand to Trelane.

"Fight well," Renfry said.

"And you," Trelane said as he took Renfry's hand and shook it.

A horn sounded in the distance to the north. The deep blast was a signal to prepare for battle.

"Assemble the men," Trelane said. Then he looked at Ariel and Ishara. "You two know your posts. Let the enemy come, we are ready."

# CHAPTER TWELVE
## THE BATTLE OF THE RED STEPPES

Geoff sat up. The horn in the distance was ominous. His ribs were still a little tender, but he felt much better. Ariel must've healed him and Sawyer.

He tried to push himself to his feet, but he was too weak. He wobbled for a minute and fell back. Instead, he crawled nearer to Sawyer, who was still asleep, and still recovering.

Another horn sounded, this one much closer. All around the camp, Geoff saw troops rushing to ready their ranks for battle. Trelane and Commander Renfry were riding horses, shouting orders and overseeing final preparations. Geoff sighed.

"I wish we could help," he said.

He looked down at Sawyer. His wound had been healed, but he needed rest too. If Sawyer were healthy, Geoff was sure he'd make a difference in the battle, just like he had at Troll Fang Pass. Geoff glanced in the direction Jane taken the night before. The cool gray light of morning filtered through the trees, making it easy for Geoff to see the exact spot he'd last seen her.

"I hope our side wins," he sighed. "I hope Ariel and Ishara don't get hurt."

"Geoff?"

Sawyer's voice was barely above a whisper. Geoff looked at Sawyer again. He was blinking his eyes as he tried to wake up.

"Hey Sawyer," Geoff said. "How're you feeling?"

"Like crap," Sawyer said wearily. "What happened?"

"Ariel said you need to stay here and rest," Geoff said. "They're about to start the battle. We better stay put."

"Geoff," Sawyer said, his eyes closed. "What happened last night?"

"Don't you remember?" Geoff said. "We were attacked by wights."

"What's a wight?" Sawyer said, becoming more lucid.

"Those smelly dead things that came out of the ground and attacked us," Geoff said. "They attacked the whole camp, but I think we killed all of them."

"Where's Jane?" Sawyer said, clearing his throat. "Someone sucker punched me last night."

Geoff fidgeted. He wasn't sure how Sawyer would react to being told that Jane had almost killed him.

"Geoff?" Sawyer said. "Where's Jane?"

Geoff bit his lip before letting out a long sigh. There was no getting around it. He took a deep breath. Best to just say what needed to be said and be done.

"Gone."

Sawyer opened his eyes and looked at Geoff. "Gone where?"

"I don't know. After she whacked you good a couple of times with a tree branch, she tried to kill me. Then, she just left."

"What?" Sawyer said, narrowing his eyes and shaking his head. "Bullsh—"

"It's true."

"Wait. What?" Sawyer shoved himself up on an elbow. "Are you telling me *Jane* tried to kill us? Jane?"

Geoff nodded.

"I think she succeeded, or would've succeeded if Ariel hadn't healed us.

"So she hit me with a tree branch and knocked me out, then went after you, too?"

"Yeah," Geoff said. "Well, she didn't club me over the head. She just kinda had a tree sling me into the woods. I felt like I was dying."

"Me too," Sawyer said. "She really cracked my head good, didn't she?"

"Yeah. Twice."

"I never saw it coming," Sawyer said. "Why would she do that?"

"Sawyer," Geoff said. "She isn't the same person. She's changed."

"What?" Sawyer said, rubbing his forehead. "What're you talking about? She's back. We rescued her. She just needs time."

"Maybe, but I don't think that's what Ariel believes," Geoff said. "Jane might be as powerful as Ariel, which makes her a major threat to everyone."

"So what's next?" Sawyer said. "How do we bring Jane back?"

"Dunno," Geoff said. "Ariel and Ishara were really worried."

"If she can't come back then…" Sawyer's voice trailed off and his eyes grew wider as he realized the alternative. "Oh hell no."

Sawyer forced himself to his feet, holding his head the whole way.

"Geoff, help me get my armor on," Sawyer said, looking around for it. "We gotta find Jane. Then we'll help Ariel win this battle."

"Ariel said for us to stay here," Geoff said. "I'm supposed to keep an eye on you. Plus, you're crazy. Jane will turn us into mincemeat again. I saw her, Sawyer. I know. We don't stand a chance against her. She's dark and evil now. You have to listen to me."

"Maybe if we can talk to her," Sawyer said, slipping the breastplate on. "You know, reason with her and appeal to the good in her."

"No, Sawyer," Geoff said. "She's gone bad and we can't do anything."

"Damn it, Geoff! We just can't..." Sawyer sat down with a thud and ran a hand through his dark brown hair. "We can't let her go. I won't..."

"I know," Geoff said. "I don't want to lose her either. I think only Ariel can help her now. But..."

Sawyer studied Geoff for a moment.

"But what?"

"But I'm not sure it's possible," Geoff said, licking his lips. "I mean, what if the best way to help Jane is to...kill her? You know Jane wouldn't want to be evil. Never. What if there's no other way?"

"There has to be," Sawyer said flatly. "This is Jane we're talking about, not a rabid dog. She's out there, all alone."

"You're right," Geoff said. "Believe me, if Jane ran into anything that meant her harm, she'd—"

"Bust it up," Sawyer said, finishing Geoff's sentence.

"Yeah, she would."

"Okay, then help me with this armor," Sawyer said.

"Let's go do something to help our side win this battle."

Geoff knew this wasn't what Ariel wanted, but he wasn't going to stop Sawyer from getting involved, either. So, he helped Sawyer into his armor and handed him his sword. More than once Geoff had to take Sawyer's arm and steady him, he was on the verge of losing his balance and falling over. Sawyer closed his eyes and took a deep breath. Then he looked at Geoff, "Let's go help our friends."

Ariel stood beside Trelane and Commander Renfry and inspected the lines of troops massed before them. Despite losses from the wights the previous night, they appeared to be ready for battle. Tense, but their morale was intact. The morning was gray, the sun struggled to peep through the clouds. The ground began to vibrate beneath her feet. Ariel was the first to feel it. After a minute, the troops began to look down at their feet and murmur amongst themselves.

"Steady, men," Renfry said. "It's no concern."

Renfry leaned close to Trelane and whispered, "I wish we had more men to shore up our left flank. We're weakest there."

Trelane nodded, glancing at Ariel. While Ishara had taken position with the other archers further behind the lines, Ariel had been tasked with 'filling in' wherever a potential breach threatened the outcome of the battle.

Then the enemy appeared over the horizon. A dark army of barbarians and orcs approached them. Behind them, catapults rolled into position.

Several minutes of uncomfortable silence passed, the armies faced each other across the wide, sweeping meadow.

Ariel counted twenty catapults, far outnumbering their eight.

"There," Trelane said, pointing near the back of their lines. "Beside their catapults. Their commander, the Shadowlord himself."

Commander Renfry squinted to see at such a distance but failed to see Lord Zorn in the sea of darkness that faced them.

"I'll take your word," Renfry said, shaking his head. "If only I had the eyes of an elf."

Ariel and Trelane exchanged looks. It wasn't the first time they'd heard those words. But with the Shadowlord leading the army arrayed before them, the outcome of the battle was far from certain.

Then Ariel heard something in the distance, past their weak left flank. Singing? *No, it was chanting, a cadence.* Specifically, it was a dwarven cadence! Ariel's heart leapt as she saw the dwarven army marching toward them. *The dwarves of Keredain have arrived!* Ariel looked over her shoulder at Trelane. He was smiling and nodding his head at the welcomed sight.

"Dwarves?" Renfry said. "They're so short."

"You have never seen dwarves in battle before," Trelane said, clasping a hand over Renfry's shoulder. "I assure you, our left flank is no longer a concern."

Ariel ran to the dwarves, who had taken a position in front of the human troops on the left. She looked for the horned helmet and the axe of her friend. As she neared the left flank, she saw the distinct shape of Baldon Stonemaster, King of Keredain. He was shouting orders at the humans, telling them to move because they'd only get in the way.

"Baldon!" Ariel said, raising a scimitar overhead and placing a hand over her heart.

The stout dwarf in the horned helm looked her way and did the same. Seeing Baldon again after so many years warmed her heart. Ariel returned to her position beside Trelane and Commander Renfry.

"I see Baldon still likes to make a grand entrance," Trelane said. "He and his warriors are most welcome."

"Aye," Renfry said. "If only they weren't so short."

"If I were you," Ariel said. "I would not repeat that in their presence."

Renfry opened his mouth to respond, but then a horn sounded, its low, rolling tone rumbled over the battlefield. Immediately the morning sky was interrupted by fiery missiles launched from the dark army's catapults. Most of them landed either too short or overshot their mark. A few, however, landed with devastating explosive effect, all but annihilating those unlucky enough to be struck.

"Catapults! Archers!" Renfry shouted, waving toward the enemy ranks. "Away!"

They returned fire with catapults manned by elves, who were experts at judging distance. Each of their meager eight catapults scored successful hits, including destroying no less than four enemy catapults. The archers, however, let loose a massive volley of arrows that felled hundreds.

Another volley of arrows followed with equal effectiveness. Ariel, Renfry, and Trelane watched as the Shadowlord's army returned fire with their archers. The range of their bows was far shorter, though, and none found their mark. There was another exchange of catapult fire with the same results. The Shadowlord lost more troops and more catapults. Two more volleys of arrows from the archers had started to thin the ranks of the enemy's right flank. This was their weakness. But even with such dreadful losses the Shadowlord still had an army of thousands.

"We've got them!" Renfry said, clenching his fist in the air. "There's no way they can match our archers. Do you see? Nearly every arrow kills an enemy."

"The Shadowlord has not moved," Trelane said. "It is as if he is waiting."

"The Shadowlord is no fool," Ariel said, a frown falling over her face. "Zorn is one of the best tacticians I have seen. He has a plan. Be on your guard!"

"What could he possibly be waiting for?" Renfry growled.

To their right, a great upheaval in the ground sent many archers flying. Their screams rang over the battle. Ariel saw Ishara land on her backside, but she sprang to her feet, nocked an arrow, and fired into the ranks of the Shadowlord's army.

A horrible feeling filled Ariel's heart. A dread and a fear that made her shiver. Rising from the upheaval were dozens of large, twisted, gnarled tree roots. Each the size of a tree and they swayed and writhed all about like great earthen tentacles. A few picked up soldiers and tossed them away. They were flung in random directions, but they all stopped screaming when they landed. Others were crushed under thunderous slams.

"Ariel," Trelane said turning to her. His eyes wide with worry.

"By the powers!" Renfry shouted, unsheathing his sword. "What is that?"

Ariel's heart felt like it was in an icy grip. For a moment, her feet wouldn't obey her. She stood in place, shaking her head.

"Here they come!" Renfry shouted. The dark army charged across the field, eager to shed blood.

"No," Ariel said in a pleading voice. The writhing tree roots had formed a protective circle around a solitary figure.

"Jane!" Ariel shouted. She drew her twin scimitars and rushed toward the dark druid.

# CHAPTER THIRTEEN
## THE NEXT DARK DRUID

"Sawyer, did you see that?" Geoff said, pointing at the edge of the battle. "The ground just exploded!"

"Yeah," Sawyer said. "Looks like the bad guys have a secret weapon."

Geoff and Sawyer made their way closer, edging their way downhill, careful to stay concealed by trees and undergrowth. The pungent smell of burning pitch hurt their and throats. A gray smoky haze had formed over the battlefield.

"Ugh," Sawyer coughing, "I can't breathe."

"Crouch lower. It'll get worse as we get closer."

"Stop," Sawyer said. "The Stormblade. It's trying to tell me something." Sawyer unsheathed his sword, which was already glowing with a blueish white hue. "We're in serious danger, Geoff. Be on the lookout."

Geoff glanced around. Being on the fringe of a battle was by its nature hazardous, but Geoff knew Sawyer meant something else. Geoff saw movement below them, near the tree line. He rubbed his smoke-filled, irritated eyes. The trees were moving! Their branches waved about and their roots struck out at men and elves as they retreated.

Another massive explosion of earth and rocked the battlefield. This time several catapults and their crews were strewn across the field.

"Holy crap!" Geoff said. "What did *that*? Look at the size of that crater."

He felt Sawyer grip his shoulder and squeeze. Geoff looked at Sawyer. He was pointing at the writhing trees. Their roots had grown into large, gnarled appendages protruding from the ground.

"Not what," Sawyer said. "*Who*."

Geoff's gaze followed Sawyer's finger. There, in the middle of the writhing, whipping appendages was Jane. She was crouching on all fours, her fingers dug deeply into the ground. Geoff saw her lips were moving too, but he was too far away to hear. Many archers fired arrows at Jane, but they were blocked by the tree roots that swayed around her.

"Those trees are protecting her." Sawyer said.

"I'm guessing they're following her commands. She's gonna wreck the whole battle."

"C'mon," Sawyer said as he moved past Geoff. "Let's get closer."

"Sawyer, are you suicidal? No way!"

Geoff didn't argue with Sawyer often, but this time it felt appropriate. Sawyer was being foolhardy. Jane's pet trees would flatten them in a heartbeat.

"Yeah," Sawyer said, turning around to urge Geoff on. "She isn't looking this way. She's only interested in the battle. Let's go."

Sawyer got on his stomach and began to crawl toward Jane.

"Sawyer!" Geoff said in a half-whisper. "What're you gonna do when you get down there?"

Sawyer looked over his shoulder at Geoff and raised his chin quickly toward Jane. Geoff slithered after him. *Bad idea. This was a bad idea. We're gonna die.*

As they crept closer, Geoff paused to take in what was happening with the battle. The barbarians and orcs had charged across the field and fighting was now at close quarters.

Across the field, on the far left, thousands of short, sturdy looking soldiers first fired their crossbows, each firing a drum of bolts like a machine gun.

"Dwarves," Geoff said under his breath. He'd never seen a dwarf like this, much less a whole army. When they ran out of bolts, they drew various swords, axes, spears, and hammers. They waded into battle, pushing the enemy back.

Trelane and Commander Renfry were holding the middle ground. Geoff blinked a few times and focused on Trelane. The tall elven commander was an imposing, figure, using his sword with both hands. Every swing of his sword felled another enemy. The bodies around Trelane were piling up, making it difficult for him to maneuver. He left a wake of dead bodies behind him. It didn't matter, orcs or barbarians, he sliced through them with ease. *Whatever he hits he kills. He's a great warrior.* Commander Renfry was busy shouting orders as he fought.

Then he saw the one he was looking for, Ishara. She was rapid firing arrows and moving. She was amazing. Her targets fell like blades of grass. Running out of arrows was the only thing that slowed her down, but once she found a fresh supply she continued firing away.

Ariel was the next one Geoff noticed. She was running

their way! She motioned for Ishara to follow her. Ishara did so, but she made a wide circle as Ariel ran directly at Jane.

"Geoff," Sawyer whispered. "Get over here. C'mon."

While Geoff was watching the battle, Sawyer had managed to inch within a stone's throw of Jane. Geoff joined Sawyer. They were partially concealed behind a small hill and a few large rocks. Jane was chanting something Geoff had never heard before as she kept her fingers dug into the ground.

"*Talos neygada annara, talos neygada eyrael.*" Jane said over and over.

Geoff wasn't able to see her face because they were to her left, so he only saw her profile. He guessed her chanting was what made the trees do her bidding, but he wasn't sure. He and Sawyer watched as Ariel weaved and dodged her way through Jane's protective circle of snake-like tree roots. When they tried to smash her into the ground, she jumped away. They also tried to sweep or slap at her, but she either dove out of their path or hurdled them, each time landing closer to Jane. If Ariel hadn't been fast and dexterous, she'd have been crushed.

"Sawyer," Geoff whispered. "How's Ariel going to stop Jane?"

Sawyer only shook his head.

Geoff's heart was pounding. This was shaping up to be an epic battle and Sawyer's instinct was right. They needed to get involved.

"So what do we do?" Geoff said, keeping his eyes on Jane and Ariel.

Sawyer ignored Geoff. He maintained a tight grip on his sword, watching intently as the two druids battled.

"Sawyer," Geoff said, giving his shoulder a shake. Sawyer turned his head to Geoff.

"What, Geoff?"

"What're we gonna do?"

"I don't know," Sawyer said, turning back to the battle. "Let's see what Ariel does."

Geoff noticed something when he returned to watching Jane and Ariel. She was no longer immune to Jane's spells. Twice, she had to either cut her way out of an entangling trap, or use a counter spell to free herself. Finally, Ariel made her way to Jane, who stood to meet her.

"*Solnara*," Ariel said, passing a hand over Jane's face.

Nothing happened. Geoff noticed the look of surprise and alarm on Ariel's face as she was rocked back with shock. The moment of hesitation was all Jane needed. Jane locked her gaze on Ariel, holding her fast. Then Jane lifted her arm and made a movement of contemptuous dismissal with her hand. Geoff and Sawyer heard Ariel grunt in pain as she was launched with amazing velocity into the gray sky, her form getting smaller until it disappeared in the distance.

"Ariel!" Geoff shouted, rising to his knees. "Sawyer, did you see that?"

"Yeah I saw that," Sawyer said angrily, pulling Geoff back. "Get down!"

It was too late.

Jane's head whipped around and her gaze fell on them. Her eyes were solid black, just like the night before.

"Uh oh," Geoff said. "Sawyer, we gotta go! Run!"

Geoff pulled Sawyer to his feet and they turned to flee, but they took a few steps before the ground erupted beneath them, flinging Sawyer and Geoff through the air in different directions. Sawyer landed near the main battle while Geoff tumbled and rolled down a hill until he felt a pair of hands stop his roll. He came to a rest on his stomach near the bottom of a grassy hill.

"Geoff!" Ishara said, turning him over so he could see her. "What are you doing here?"

"We thought…" Geoff started, then shook his head. "I don't know what we thought. We just wanted to help."

Ishara stared, her green eyes wide.

"You both have lost your minds," she said. "Ariel told you to stay in camp."

"Exactly," Geoff agreed. "That's what I said to Sawyer."

"I did not see him drag you downhill to the battle," Ishara said. "You followed him."

"Yeah," Geoff said, "But I didn't want to."

"Sometimes I do not know if you humans are brave or simply foolish," Ishara said, pulling the last arrow from her quiver. "Are you injured?"

"Just a little dizzy," Geoff said. "Ishara, Ariel's gone. Jane sent her flying, just like Ariel did to the Shadowlord a while back."

Ishara turned her gaze to the smoke-filled sky over the battle. Geoff followed her gaze, but didn't see anything. Ishara climbed up the hill and peered over. Geoff followed her. Jane was sending the tentacle-like tree roots out into the battle. They were ravaging what was left of the entire right flank of humans and elves.

"What do we do now?" Geoff said.

Ishara didn't answer. She raised up on one knee and lifted her bow. Geoff realized she had Jane in her sights, but she didn't fire. She seemed to be waiting for something.

"What're you doing?"

Ishara didn't answer. She looked up every now and then, but kept her aim.

"You can't kill her," Geoff said, his heart hammering in his chest. "It's Jane, Ishara."

"Geoff," Ishara said. "When I look at Jane, her aura is now black. She is evil and she is costing us this battle."

Something overhead caught Ishara's eye. Geoff looked up. A great hawk with golden brown feathers circled above the trees. Ishara took a breath and aimed at Jane. She pulled the bowstring back, her arrow ready to end Jane's life. Ishara glanced upward one more time. Geoff did the same. The golden hawk stopped circling and flew straight up with amazing speed. Ishara lowered her gaze on Jane. Her eyes fixed. She was about to kill Jane!

"Wait!" Geoff shouted, grabbing her arm. "Don't kill her! She can be saved, I know it!"

Ishara shrugged him off.

"Geoff, please!" Ishara hissed through clenched teeth, looking at him with wide green eyes. "You must trust me."

Geoff and Ishara maintained eye contact for a few seconds, then Geoff blinked and nodded. He felt a pang deep in his heart. "I trust you."

Ishara turned to Jane and focused her aim again. Jane was seconds away from dying. Geoff winced as he watched Ishara fire her arrow at Jane. His heart stopped as it sailed through the writhing, gnarled tree roots and grazed Jane's arm, causing her to cry out in pain and grab her wound. Jane lifted her gaze and looked directly at Ishara and Geoff. A horrible, twisted grimace fell across her face.

Jane pointed at them. A small black orb with green

flashes within it appeared in Jane's hand. She flung it at them. Ishara grabbed Geoff and dove down the hill. They tumbled together, coming to a stop near the bottom of the slope. Above them, the hill where they had been hiding exploded. Ishara and Geoff were covered with dirt and debris.

"Geoff," Ishara said. "Get up, we must…"

Geoff brushed himself off and stood. Ishara was standing still looking behind him, near what was left of the hill. Her voice had trailed off. Her tight-lipped expression and her eyes signaled something dreadful was behind him. Geoff whirled around. Jane was standing above them, her hands stretched out before her. Her fingers elongated and grew, whipping about as they approached Geoff and Ishara, finally ending in the head of a grotesque snake. Each of the snake heads dripped a milky white venom from its fangs.

"Jane, no!" Geoff shouted as he jumped in front of Ishara and put his hands up. He felt a surge of magical energy from deep down rise up and exit through his hands, creating a shimmering, translucent shield around them. Its golden hue was a barrier of protective magic. The next instant the snakes struck the shield.

Their impact jarred Geoff and Ishara, knocking them off balance while sending them several yards back. It felt like a truck had collided with the shield. The snake heads slithered around, trying to find an opening, then Jane retracted them.

"Ishara, are you okay?"

"Yes," she replied. She pointed at Jane through the golden shield. "Geoff, look out!"

A black missile struck the shield, this one much more powerful than the first Jane had thrown. It shook the ground and Geoff's spell faltered, but he managed to conjure up another shield. He was beginning to weaken. Geoff wasn't sure if he could keep the shield up through another black orb. Jane pointed at them again, this time she seemed determined to end their lives.

Then the golden hawk appeared, diving straight down toward Jane. With her attention on Geoff and Ishara, Jane failed to notice the hawk land behind her. In another moment, Ariel's form appeared and she stood directly behind Jane. Alerted to movement behind her, Jane swirled around and met a left hook from Ariel. She was unconscious before she hit the ground.

Ariel looked at Geoff, raised her eyebrows, and let out a loud sigh.

"Geoff, you were amazing," Ariel said. "Your shield drew Jane's attention long enough for me to strike. Well done, good wizard."

"Those black globes," Geoff said, referring to Jane's attack spell. "You were only just in time. I wouldn't have been able to keep the shield up anymore."

"But you saved our lives," Ishara said as she wrapped her arms around Geoff, whispering, "And you trusted me. Thank you."

"You're welcome," Geoff said, smiling.

A great roar of cheers erupted from the battlefield.

"Oh no! Sawyer!" Geoff said. "Where's Sawyer?"

# CHAPTER FOURTEEN
## THE KNIGHTS OF CALADAR

Jane's spell caused the earth beneath him to violently erupt, sending Sawyer nearly thirty yards away. He landed in one of the craters Jane had created earlier with her explosive spells. The fresh, loose dark earth made for a soft landing. Sawyer rolled down it until coming to a stop at the bottom of the large earthy depression.

Sawyer stood up and promptly fell back. Dizzy from the flight and tumble, Sawyer closed his eyes and lay still, waiting for his head to clear. The shouts and sounds of battle were all around. After a few moments, Sawyer opened his eyes. The Stormblade was lying half way up the side of the crater. Sawyer rolled to his knees and crawled toward the shining sword. He was almost within reach when two combatants appeared just above him at the crest of the basin.

A thick, snaggle-toothed orc ran his jagged blade through the body of a soldier from Chalon. Then the orc lifted him off the ground and tossed him over Sawyer's head. The soldier's body tumbled and rolled to a stop in the spot where Sawyer had landed. The hair on the back of Sawyer's neck stood up and his heart began to race. He looked at the orc.

It was looking down at him with wild hatred in its eyes.

The orc threw his head back and let out a bloodcurdling battle cry. Then jumped into the crater, his bloody sword still dripping as he bore down on Sawyer.

"Oh hell," Sawyer said as he quickly crawled the rest of the way to the Stormblade. The orc was huge, it thundered toward Sawyer like a gorilla. Sawyer gripped his sword, spun around, and blocked the orc's first attack, which was an overhead slash. The force of the blow rattled Sawyer to the core. The orc followed with a swift kick to Sawyer's chest, sending him tumbling, head over heels, to the bottom of the crater again. As soon as he came to a stop, he raised his sword in a defensive manner, which he had learned from Ariel.

The move saved him as the orc tried to run Sawyer through. He just managed to parry the attack. Enraged by Sawyer's defensive skills, the orc began to swing his jagged sword with wild abandon. His mouth was frothy with blood-lust. Sawyer managed to get to his feet as he parried the orc's wild attacks. Every attack left him open for a counter attack, yet Sawyer hesitated. He'd never been in a battle for his life, he was terrified. However, if the orc would finally tire, perhaps he could knock it out. As Sawyer considered the possibility, he blocked another overhead slash. This time, the orc grabbed Sawyer's other arm. The orc's grip was like a giant vice.

"Aaargh!" Sawyer yelled as the orc squeezed.

Sawyer dropped to his knees. The orc held Sawyer's captured arm up and lifted his sword. The thought of losing his arm, not to mention his life, fortified Sawyer's resolve. He plunged the Stormblade deep into the orc's side and kept pushing. The orc gasped and shook, its eyes flew wide open and then it crumpled, lifeless, to the ground. Relieved and gasping for air, Sawyer began flexing his fingers until the numbness abated. He tried not to look at the orc, forcing himself to recall how Ariel had said to show them no mercy because they would never show mercy themselves.

Sawyer noticed a foul smell. He looked down. He had indeed soiled himself during his fight with the orc. There wasn't anything he could do about it at the moment, though. He had to get back and try to help Jane. He scrambled up the side of the basin and was greeted with far more disgusting sights and odors, for dead men, elves, dwarves, orcs, and barbarians lay everywhere. The stench of burning tar mixed with blood and other foulness lingered over the smoky battle field.

The fighting had shifted to the left. The barbarians and orcs had driven the forces of Chalon and Selra'thel to the edge of the open field. Trelane was drenched in blood, but his sword continued to cut huge swaths through his enemies. Berserking barbarians and enraged orcs were no match for the elven champion. It occurred to Sawyer as he watched Trelane in action that he had utilized the same attacks and moves that Ariel had taught him.

He turned to run back toward Jane. Several large explosions in the woods made Sawyer stop. They were in the area he had last seen Jane. Had Geoff unleashed his magic on her? Was Jane throwing exploding acorns again? Movement to the left caught Sawyer's attention. In the distance, the Shadowlord was walking his horse toward him, sword drawn with glowing red runes. But the immediate threat was about a thousand barbarians that had been held in reserve charging from the outer fringe of the forest, just in front of the Shadowlord. They were coming his way.

He looked back in the woods and bit his lower lip. He didn't dare lead all those barbarians to Jane or Geoff. Sawyer whirled and dashed back toward the battle. The troops from Chalon and Selra'thel had held and were in the process of pushing the orc and barbarian hordes back with a counter attack. Sawyer noticed a contingent of smaller, stockier forms armed with spears and axes had broken the enemy charge and were close to outflanking them.

Another group of the stocky warriors let loose with crossbows that fired bolts in rapid succession. They reminded Sawyer of machine gunners from old war movies. Whole ranks of orcs fell under their withering barrage. *If the reinforcements joined the battle before Trelane and Renfry could turn the tide, it would be over – especially once the Shadowlord joined the fray. What could he do? He was stuck in the middle, but he had to try and give them time, he had to try something.*

The large sapphire in the pommel of the Stormblade flashed. Sawyer looked down at his sword and then he realized what must be done. He planted himself firmly in front of the oncoming barbarians and drove the blade of his sword into the ground in front of him. Kneeling, he grasped the pommel with both hands and focused. In his mind, he imagined arcs of lightning creeping across the field toward the charging barbarians.

Then he realized it was real. *He was doing it. He was holding them back!* He smiled with elation. He may as well have been a wizard.

Seeing the glittering arcs of strange light heading their way, many barbarians hesitated in their headlong plunge into battle, but several of the wildest ones with painted faces continued forward. The lightning from the Stormblade crept across the field, like the legs of a spider. Each leg of the spider branched out and became two or three additional legs.

The painted barbarians who charged into the creeping lightning were immediately struck and dropped to the ground. Some were thrown backward, their muscles trapped in uncontrollable spasms. Sawyer looked at the Shadowlord. He had paused his advance as well.

"Come on," Sawyer said under his breath. "Come get some."

There was a huge commotion to the left of the battlefield. Shouts and screams rose and the ground trembled. Sawyer saw what seemed like an endless silver river of mounted knights in shining armor riding down the barbarians and orcs. He couldn't take his eyes off them. They were amazing. Every knight swinging his weapon left and right, their slivery armor shone in the day light. They overwhelmed and rode through the enemy horde which had pushed the forces of Chalon and Selra'thel to the edge of the meadow.

Glancing back, Sawyer saw the barbarians had turned and fled. The Shadowlord had also turned his horse around and rode away. The shining knights, however, charged after the fleeing barbarians and their master. Sawyer stood transfixed as they rode by, his insides rattled with every hoof beat. They were like rolling thunder across the field. Their leader, a knight wielding a large war hammer, stopped in front of Sawyer while he urged the other knights forward.

Sawyer's mouth dropped as the leader's gaze fell upon him. Sawyer raised a hand in greeting. The knight regarded him for a moment and then raised the visor of his helmet. The face was that of a man approaching middle age. His neatly trimmed black beard was streaked with gray. His brown eyes bore wrinkles around them and his face was tanned. He smiled at Sawyer and clasp his right arm across his chest.

"I'd heard rumors the Stormlord had returned," he said. "I'm glad they were true. It is an honor."

He bowed his head. All Sawyer managed was a loud swallow. He didn't know what to say.

"I admire your bravery," the knight continued. "I'm Lord Shaun Hammerfel, commander of the Knights of Caladar."

Shaun looked around the battlefield and then settled his gaze back on Sawyer.

"I'm sorry we're late," he said. "We've been dogged by the Scarlet Queen ever since we left Caladar."

"Thanks," Sawyer said, trying to regain himself. "Thanks for saving us. If you hadn't shown up when you did, we would've bit the dust."

Shaun raised his eyebrows at Sawyer's description of the battle.

"From what I saw," Shaun said. "This battle was already on the verge of being won."

Sawyer smiled. He hadn't done much, but now that the battle was over, he was glad to have taken part. His small contribution was stopping the barbarian reinforcements from entering the battle, which probably helped. Suddenly he realized Jane and Geoff were missing.

"Jane!" he shouted. Sawyer turned and began running back to the last spot he'd seen her and Geoff. He sheathed his sword as he ran, trying not to look at the bodies of the fallen. Then an armored white horse appeared beside him.

"Give me your arm," Shaun said, holding out his hand.

Sawyer reached up. Shaun took hold of Sawyer and easily swung him up onto his horse.

"Point the way, Stormlord," Shaun said, looking over his shoulder.

Sawyer pointed to the forest just beyond where the elven and human archers had been. Two deep craters now dotted the landscape. Fresh earth and rocks lay everywhere. The horse they rode was both powerful and surefooted, it navigated the debris with little or no instruction from Shaun. Entering the forest, Sawyer noticed the smoke had begun to clear. Then three figures emerged from the trees.

Geoff and Ishara were walking, a few paces behind Ariel. In her arms, she carried Jane.

# CHAPTER FIFTEEN
## TO SAVE WHAT WE LOVE

At the same moment, Ishara took Geoff's hand in hers. Pulling him to her, she whispered, "Once again you saved me. How many times?"

"Hey, you saved me too," Geoff said, his cheeks growing warm. He tried to think of something cool or romantic to say, but nothing came to mind. "That was kind of scary, huh"

The sound of hoof beats approaching caught their attention. Looking up, Geoff saw a knight in shining armor atop a gleaming white warhorse galloping their way. Sitting behind the knight was Sawyer.

"Caladar," Ishara said, smiling. "The Knights of Caladar are here."

"Cool," Geoff managed to say as he watched them.

The white horse stopped in front of Ariel and Sawyer slid off. Ariel knelt and lay Jane in the grass as Sawyer dropped to his knees and looked at Jane.

"How is she?" Sawyer said. "Is she okay?"

"She is fine," Ariel said. "As well as she can be for the moment."

Sawyer brushed Jane's hair out of her face, revealing a bruise on her cheek. Geoff noticed he frowned. Ariel ignored Sawyer's frown and stood up. Looking at the knight on the white horse, she placed a hand over her heart and greeted him.

"*Hal'inari*," Ariel said smiling. "It is good to see you again, Shaun."

"And you," Shaun said, bowing his head. "You'll have to tell me what happened here. I've never seen such destruction."

"I shall," Ariel said. "And the battle? From the cheers across the field I trust we have won the day."

"We have," Shaun said. Then he nodded toward Sawyer. "Thanks to the Stormlord. He played an important part. He's a brave warrior."

Ariel looked at Sawyer, who hadn't looked up from Jane. She nodded.

"Of course," Ariel said. "Of course he won the battle for us. It is what he does. He *is* brave...very brave."

They went to the battlefield. Sawyer carried Jane the whole way. Trelane and Commander Renfry, flanked by their officers, greeted them.

"I'll say this," Renfry said. "You knights from Caladar know the precise moment to show up."

"*Hal'inari*," Trelane said with the customary hand over his heart.

Shaun responded with his arm across his chest.

"Looks like we missed most of the battle," he said. "How many did we lose?"

"Too many. We're still counting," Renfry said. He looked at Ariel. "We could use your help with the wounded, if you don't mind."

"Of course not," Ariel said.

"After we have sorted our wounded and dead," Trelane said. "I propose a meeting. We have much to discuss."

"Indeed we do," Shaun said. "The Scarlet Queen herself marches toward Chalon, burning everything in her path."

No one said anything. The moment of silence punctuating the fear and dread they all felt.

"Go, begin your counsels without me," Ariel said. "I will be along after I have tended the wounded."

The three warriors obeyed and returned to their troops. The knights who had chased the barbarians had returned. Their arrival met with cheers from both elves and men. Ariel went to Jane and Sawyer.

"Did you have to hit her?" Sawyer asked bitterly, "Wasn't there another way?"

"There was no other way."

"Seriously, Sawyer. Jane was trying to kill us. After she blew you and me up, she went after us." Geoff indicated Ishara and himself with a thumb. "Snakes came out of her fingers, it was gross."

Sawyer noticed the cut on Jane's arm that Ishara's arrow had made. He looked at Ariel again.

"What can we do?" Sawyer muttered.

Ariel looked down at Jane but didn't answer his question. Placing her hand over the wound on Jane's arm, Ariel took a breath.

"*Ehlia sa maros*," Ariel said. The cut on Jane's arm closed and the bruise on her face faded.

"Thanks. She always liked that spell," Sawyer said.

"Sawyer, Jane is still dangerous," Ariel said, placing a hand on his arm. "Her power is devastating."

"Yeah," Geoff said shaking his head. "You should've seen her, Sawyer. The things she did."

Sawyer looked at Ariel.

"So what happens now?"

Ariel closed her eyes and let out a long sigh.

"Sawyer, Jane is—"

"Still here," Sawyer insisted, pointing at Jane. "Ariel, she's still here. I know it. She isn't so far gone that she can't come back."

"Perhaps not. But you must know the darkness inside her grows every minute."

Geoff cleared his throat, "So what happens next?"

"First she must be restrained," Ariel said. "Both physically and magically. I need time to decide what is to be done with her."

Ariel undid leather straps from her boots and used them to bind Jane's hands and feet. Then she gagged Jane with a strip of cloth from inside her belt.

"Is all that really necessary?" Sawyer muttered. "She's out cold. She isn't going anywhere."

"Yes, it is necessary," Ariel said.

She reached for a small black leather pouch inside her tunic and opened it. She pulled out a single oak leaf and crumpled it in her fist.

"*Te'renar ulran valnos te'renar,*" Ariel said, holding her fist above Jane and letting the leaf bits fall onto her. When they landed on Jane they sparkled for a second and then disappeared.

"What was that?" Geoff asked, unable to remember Ariel or Jane ever using such a spell before.

"A spell of confining," Ariel said. "Jane will not remain

unconscious forever. This spell ensures she will not awaken and begin casting dark spells."

"So it put her in sort of a stasis?" Geoff said. "She's safe, right?"

"Precisely," Ariel said. "She is safe and will not harm anyone. Now, I must go and tend to the wounded."

Ariel turned and looked at the three of them.

"Be alert," she said. "And be safe. Ishara, your help would be most welcome."

Ariel and Ishara walked away, leaving them standing in the blood-stained field looking at Jane.

"What a day," Sawyer said. He sat beside Jane and crossed his legs. Geoff sat on the other side of Jane, also crossing his legs.

"So what did you do?" Geoff asked. "In the battle, how did you do that turned the tide?"

"Nothing," Sawyer said. "I just made some barbarian reinforcements hesitate, that's all. Those guys, the knights, they showed up and did all the work."

"Whatever you did must've made a difference."

"Did Jane really make snakes come out of her fingers?"

"Oh yeah. They shot out of her finger tips and would've killed us. They just couldn't get through my shield spell. Then, she started throwing hand grenades."

"Hand grenades?" Sawyer asked.

"Yeah, well, I don't know what they were exactly, but they packed a wallop. I couldn't keep the shield spell up much longer and then Ariel flew in as a hawk and knocked Jane out."

Sawyer didn't say anything. He looked at Jane. Geoff knew Ariel's rough treatment of Jane didn't sit well with

Sawyer, but Sawyer didn't see what happened.

"Sawyer," Geoff said quietly. "It was the best way to stop Jane. Really, it was. She was about to kill everyone."

"Yeah, I guess,"

They sat in silence for a while before Geoff spoke. "I better get some firewood before it gets dark. You gonna to be okay, Sawyer?"

"Yeah, I'm good."

Geoff headed back to the woods from which they emerged with Jane, mainly because there wasn't as many dead bodies that way, but also because the forest was closer. He picked up a few sticks and moved a little further into the trees. He looked back. Sawyer was still sitting with Jane. There was a lot of movement and shouting on the far side of the field. He hoped most of the wounded could be saved, but he knew it would take a miracle for that to happen. It was a day he'd never forget.

Sawyer, Ishara, him, everyone almost died today. *Sawyer was right. What a day it was.* Geoff yawned. He didn't sleep much the night before with the wights attacking and then Jane turning evil. Geoff stopped. He heard voices over the next hill leading into the forest. His heart began to beat faster. Who was there? He crouched and quietly laid his armful of firewood on the ground. The voices were female. There was an argument or something happening. Geoff got on his stomach and low crawled up the hill. He began to hear more the closer he got to the top of the hill.

"She is our friend, have you forgotten?" Ishara said.

"Of course not," Ariel said. "Jane is dear to me, as are Geoff and Sawyer."

"Yet you speak of killing her," Ishara said, her voice

growing in volume and agitation. "This is not the act of a friend."

"Jane would rather die than become an evil creature," Ariel said firmly. "It is an act of kindness, a mercy. No one would miss her more than me."

"And Sawyer?" Ishara said. "Do you think he would let you kill Jane? You know he and Geoff would oppose you."

There was a moment of silence.

"Yes," Ariel said. "They would fight for Jane. We both know this. Ishara, you saw for yourself what she is capable of doing. We nearly lost this battle because of her. Trelane and Renfry have already spoken with me. They will no longer allow Jane to travel with them."

"Then we travel as before," Ishara said. "We have done well to survive on our own."

"Travel *where*, Ishara?" Ariel snapped. "Do you think Jane would be welcome in Chalon? In Selra'thel? No, she must be dealt with while we still have the power to do it."

"She is our friend," Ishara said quietly.

"So was Bhael," Ariel said. "Jane's power has grown faster than I ever could have imagined. What sort of use do you think the Scarlet Queen would have for her? If Jane is allowed to continue, she could destroy all of Alluria."

"So this is what must be done?" Ishara said. Is there nothing else? Anything else? If there is any other way at all then we must try. Jane deserves that much."

"She does," Ariel said. "But any attempt to release Jane from the vampire's curse will more than likely cause her to suffer and perhaps kill her."

Geoff's hands were trembling and his mouth was dry. He peered over the hill just enough to make sure he had truly heard Ariel and Ishara discuss Jane's fate. Geoff winced. The sinking feeling in his chest felt like a gaping hole where his heart beat. It really was them. *Oh no! He had to get back to Jane and Sawyer. They were going to kill Jane!*

Geoff slid back down the hill as quietly as he could, keeping his eyes on the hilltop. So long as Ariel and Ishara were talking, he had a chance of getting away unnoticed. Then his left foot kicked the small pile of sticks he had gathered, breaking one with a sharp *snap*.

Geoff's heart skipped a beat. He was sure Ariel and Ishara heard it. Their elven ears didn't miss much. Geoff jumped up. *Oh no! Oh no!* He said to himself over and over as he ran back to Sawyer and Jane. Behind him, he heard Ishara call his name. They were so fast too, how could he outrun them? Geoff's chest ached as he ran faster than he had ever run in his life.

Sawyer was still sitting beside Jane when Geoff appeared, stumbling and almost out of breath.

"Saw…Sawyer…Help," Geoff said. "They…they…want to…kill Jane!"

"Huh? What're you talking about?" Sawyer stood up and placed a hand on the pommel of his sword. "Slow down, Geoff. Who wants to kill Jane?"

"Ar…Ariel and Ishara," Geoff said, pointing back toward the forest he had just fled.

"Have you gone crazy? Why would they want to kill her? That doesn't make sense."

"Sawyer," Geoff said, regaining a bit of his composure. "I heard them. They say Jane is too dangerous and the only way to deal with her is to kill her now…while they can."

Sawyer looked at Geoff and frowned. Geoff nodded. Sawyer looked past Geoff.

"Is that true?" He asked.

"Sawyer," the sound of Ariel's voice so near startled Geoff and he spun around. Ariel and Ishara were standing directly behind him, grim faced. "We do not want to kill Jane. Please believe that. She is all but lost already. You yourself saw what she is capable of, she is a threat."

"I…I can't believe what I'm hearing," Sawyer said, shaking his head. "She's here because of *you*. We all are. And now you say she needs to die?"

"Sawyer, I cannot defeat her if we battle again," Ariel said. "She now derives her power from darkness. Her power is boundless. I can feel it growing inside her even now. I am so very, very sorry."

Sawyer and Ariel stood in place, staring at each other. Geoff looked at Ishara. Her eyes were moist.

"Ariel, Jane wanted to come here and help you," Sawyer said, his voice quivering a little. "I'm only here because of her."

"I know," Ariel said. "This is not something any of us want."

"I can't let you do it," Sawyer said. "You'll have to kill me first."

Ariel's face wrinkled and she clutched her stomach. She looked as if she had been kicked by a mule. The pain in her eyes reflected her heart breaking.

"I know I'm no match for you," Sawyer said as he unsheathed the Stormblade. "But if I stood by and let you kill her, then part of me would be dead anyway."

"Me too," Geoff added, stepping forward. "Please don't do this."

Ariel looked down at her feet. She was breathing heavy.

Geoff tensed. He had no idea what was going to happen in the next moment. The thought of fighting Ariel and Ishara was nothing short of suicidal as far as he was concerned. Geoff's leg was starting to shake uncontrollably.

"Sawyer," Ariel said, looking up quickly.

Sawyer assumed a defensive stance, his sword at the ready. Following his lead, Geoff held up his hands and a shimmering shield appeared between them. Standing there, facing each other, Ariel locked eyes with Sawyer. Geoff looked at Ishara.

"Please help us, Ishara," he said. "I know you're against killing Jane."

Ishara maintained a tight-lipped expression. She slowly closed her eyes.

"I cannot be a part of this," Ishara said to Ariel. "I will not fight those of whom I am fond."

"Nor I," Ariel said. She unbuckled her sword belt, letting her scimitars fall to the ground. "Sawyer, walk with me. Please."

Sawyer began to lower his sword, but raised it again.

"Have I completely lost your trust? Please walk with me."

Sawyer thought for a moment, then lowered his sword. "No tricks?"

"No tricks," Ariel said. "You have my word. I hope that still means something to you."

Sawyer exhaled. He put a hand on Geoff's shoulder. Geoff let his shield down.

Ariel motioned for Sawyer to follow her as she walked away.

"Would you have attacked me, Geoff?" Ishara asked, her voice soft yet full of concern. "Would you have cast a spell at me?"

A rush of guilt overtook Geoff. He thought he was going to be sick. He looked down and shook his head. "No," he said. "I could never do that. I'm sorry."

"You were protecting your friend," Ishara said. "You were protecting Jane. I understand."

Ariel walked beside Sawyer, her head lowered and elegant shoulders bent. Sawyer had never seen her like this before and didn't know what to say. They walked maybe a long way from the others before she turned to face him.

"Please forgive me," she said. "I never meant for this to happen."

"So what happens now?"

"Jane is in such pain, Sawyer," Ariel said. "You know this. I thought that if I were able to help her pass…I would be doing her a favor and save Alluria at the same time."

"Jane is your friend, Ariel," Sawyer said. "She thinks the world of you."

"And I think the world of her. Tell me, Sawyer. Would you sacrifice one friend to save your world?"

"No," Sawyer answered flatly. "Not Jane. No way. The world needs more people like her. Every world needs more Janes in them."

"And if that friend was beyond help? Beyond saving?"

Sawyer looked away.

"You're telling me there is no way to save her? You don't have any spells or herbs or whatever to get Jane back? There's absolutely *nothing* we can do?"

Ariel was silent. Sawyer saw it in her eyes. There *was* a possibility.

"What? What is it, Ariel? What do we have to do to help Jane?"

"You have to let her go," Ariel said with a sigh.

"I don't understand."

Ariel touched his arm. Sawyer looked into her moist, emerald green eyes.

"There is a way. One way," Ariel said. "But it is dangerous and the likelihood of Jane surviving is minimal."

"We have to try."

"No," Ariel said. "*I* have to try. Deep in the Spirewood Forest is a sacred grove with a pool of the purest water. Pure enough to cleanse any curse, any disease, and refresh one's spirit. Only the High Druid may enter and perform the ritual of cleansing. It is a dangerous ritual."

"We'll go with you," Sawyer said. "We can at least go part of the way, right?"

"No," Ariel said. "It is a journey I alone must take. I will care for Jane and protect her. But Sawyer, cleansing this, cleansing vampirism has never been done. A dark druid in the sacred waters may have unexpected and terrible consequences. I do not know what will happen. You must prepare yourself because Jane may die."

Sawyer maintained eye contact with Ariel.

"There's no other way?"

"Sometimes," Ariel said, placing a hand on his cheek. "In order to save what we love, we must risk losing it."

# CHAPTER SIXTEEN
## SEPARATE WAYS

Geoff took a step toward Ishara. She flew into his arms, hugging him tightly about the neck.

"What has become of us?" She whispered into his ear.

Geoff sniffled and wiped a tear from his eye.

"Everything's gone wrong," he said. "How did that happen?"

"The Scarlet Queen," Ishara said. She released Geoff and stepped back. "It is her doing. She sets us against each other."

"We have to stop her," Geoff said.

"We will," Ishara said, taking his hand in hers. "Together."

Then she kissed Geoff, her lips were soft and warm. For the moment, Geoff felt at ease. Being with Ishara was comforting. Perhaps in some way he comforted her, too. He squeezed her hand. Ishara looked at him.

"You are still an excellent sneak thief," Ishara said, her eyes lighting up and a little smile sweeping across her face. "Not many humans are able to sneak up on an elf, let alone two elves."

"Yeah, well you two were talking so loud," Geoff teased. "I thought elves were quiet."

"We have our loud moments, too," Ishara said, maintaining her smile.

They looked at each other for a few moments, then Ishara's face and tone became serious.

"Geoff," Ishara said. "I am not sure if Jane can ever come back to us. Ariel is right. If Jane were unleashed upon Alluria the devastation she would wreak would be terrible."

"I was hoping Ariel could cast another cool spell and fix Jane," Geoff said. "Sawyer and I wouldn't know what to do without her. If there is anything, I mean *anything* that we can try to bring Jane back then we have to give it a go."

"Only Ariel knows that," Ishara said. "Believe me when I say we want our Jane back, too."

"I believe you. I'll always believe you."

Ariel and Sawyer returned from their walk. Geoff thought it looked like a truce had been established.

"It is settled," Ariel said. "Tomorrow Jane and I will depart for the Spirewood Forest while the rest of you accompany Trelane and Commander Renfry to Chalon."

"What?" Geoff said. "You're going to the Spirewood Forest? We'll come too. That's where we first met."

"It is," Ariel said. "But this time Jane and I must go alone. There is a ritual I can attempt which may rid Jane of her dark affliction, but it may not succeed and Jane may not survive." She looked at Geoff. "You must prepare yourself in case that is the result."

Geoff looked at Sawyer, who nodded.

"Why can't we come with you?" Geoff asked.

"Because," Ariel said. "Only the High Druid may enter the scared grove and perform the ritual of cleansing."

"Are you sure about this course?" Ishara said, a hint of

worry in her voice. "That ritual is attempted only under the direst of circumstances."

"And this is a dire circumstance," Ariel said. "Perhaps more so than any other time in the history of Alluria."

Ishara frowned, but said nothing more.

"I still think we should come with you," Geoff said. "At least we could go to the Spirewood forest and stop while you and Jane go in, right?"

"Hey Geoff," Sawyer said. "It's okay, we have to let her try this by herself."

"Ariel," Geoff said. "What are Jane's chances?"

Ariel took a moment before answering, "As I said, you should prepare yourself for the worst."

Geoff stared at Ariel as he considered what he had heard. He knew if Ariel could use softer words to make a hopeless situation sound not-so-hopeless, she would do it. However, this time she was telling them a hard truth.

"This is the only way," Ariel said. "I promise you I will do my best to help Jane."

"It's just…she's our friend," Geoff said. "We need her back."

"I know," Ariel said softly as she looked down at Jane. "We all do."

Ariel walked toward the soldier's camp at a slower pace than Geoff had seen before, like she was trudging through deep mud in a rainstorm.

"What you need to understand," Ishara said, addressing both Geoff and Sawyer, "Is the cleansing ritual is just as dangerous to the High Druid as the one being cleansed. Ariel may die too."

Geoff groaned. *How could he have been so stupid? How*

*did he not grasp this himself?* The realization of the importance of the cleansing ritual being successfully performed was nothing short of a last ditch effort. If it failed, not only would both Jane and Ariel die, but Alluria would more than likely fall to the Scarlet Queen. Sawyer's voice snapped Geoff out of his contemplations.

"She said we go to Chalon," Sawyer said. "I'm to train with that Shaun Hammerfel guy while you train with your dad. Oh, and Ishara too." Sawyer pointed his head in her direction.

Sawyer sat down beside Jane. For several moments he studied her as if he was memorizing every aspect of Jane's appearance. Sawyer's gaze went from Jane to staring into the distance. *He was too quiet.*

"What do we do if they don't come back?" Geoff asked.

Neither Ishara nor Sawyer offered any answers. Their silence annoyed Geoff, but he didn't have any answers either. Then it occurred to him that maybe they hadn't really rescued Jane when they took her from the Iron Citadel. Maybe she was already gone. The Shadowlord's vampiric bite had taken her away, made her a creature of darkness and turned her into a weapon for the Scarlet Queen.

"All we can do is wait...and hope," Ishara finally said.

Geoff sat down beside Sawyer and glanced at Jane. She appeared to be the same old Jane, but in a deep sleep. She looked content. He studied her face, like this was the last time he'd ever see her. He hated the idea of saying good-bye to her. It was way too soon for that. Ishara sat on the other side of Geoff. As she took out an apple, his stomach growled. It was loud enough that he felt embarrassed. He shifted his weight and tried to hold his stomach in. He had found this method seemed to help when he was hungry while taking a test in school.

Without a word, Ishara offered him the apple while she reached into her small sack and pulled out another.

"Thanks," Geoff said.

Ariel went among the wounded soldiers, healing their wounds and comforting them as best she could. Helping them served to take Ariel's mind off Jane, at least for the time being. But no matter how many humans and elves she helped, Jane was never far from her thoughts. She worked the rest of the afternoon casting her druidic spells until she was exhausted. She began to walk back to her companions, but Shaun Hammerfel and Baldon Stonemaster appeared. They were in much better spirits than Ariel.

"There she is!" Baldon said, taking a long drink from his pewter mug. Dwarven ale dribbled down his chin and beard.

"Hello, Ariel," Shaun said, offering her his wooden cup. "Thank you for seeing to my men. You should try to eat something as well."

"Aye," Baldon said. "I'll have a bit of roasted chicken brought to you."

Ariel accepted the cup from Shaun and drank the cool water it held.

"If you could spare enough for four," Ariel said. "I would be most grateful."

"Ha!" Baldon said, slapping his hands around Ariel's upper arms. "For you, we'll spare enough for a hundred! I'll see to it myself."

Baldon marched off in search of the promised food,

leaving Ariel and Shaun alone. They began to walk back to where Ariel had left the others with Jane. Her eyes darted sideways to Shaun as they walked. He was an attractive man of middle-age, tall and well-built. Yet she had the impression he was carrying a sadness in his heart.

"The years have been kind to you," Ariel said. "You look well. I was sad to hear your son had passed away. He was growing to be a fine warrior."

"Thank you. I miss him every day, but life must continue. My wife still mourns. A year later and she still mourns."

"I am sorry," Ariel said. "I wish I knew a spell that would alleviate her pain, but I do not think such a spell exists. Cassandra is a lovely person."

They walked a bit further, then Shaun spoke, "Tell me more of our new Stormlord. What kind of warrior is he?"

"He is the best kind of warrior," Ariel said, grinning. "He is athletic, decisive, and strong."

"Yes, yes," Shaun said. "But what *kind* of warrior is he?"

Ariel stopped. They were close enough to see Sawyer, Geoff, and Ishara sitting near Jane, who was still in a deep sleep. Ariel observed how close Sawyer sat to Jane, how he turned his head from time to time and looked around. He was protecting Jane, there was no doubt about that.

"As I said," Ariel looked at Shaun. "The best kind of warrior. You could not find a better student, nor a more loyal or compassionate friend."

"Hmm," Shaun said, raising his eyebrows. "You do not usually speak so highly of humans. He has left a lasting impression on you, hasn't he?"

"Each of them have," Ariel said, still watching the trio

from a distance. "Someday I will share their deeds with you. They have done the most remarkable things."

"Indeed," Shaun said, turning his head to look at them. "And the girl-druid, what is to be done with her? She is a threat that can't be ignored."

"I know. I will take her to the east, to Spirewood Forest. Perhaps the ritual of cleansing will work, but I do not know."

"Cleansing?" Shaun said. "Wouldn't it be easier to kill the vampire who bit her? Kill the bloodline and she is free again?"

"No. The vampire who bit her was the Shadowlord," Ariel said. "Even if you could kill him, the bloodline would still not be broken. You would have to kill the Scarlet Queen, too."

"I didn't know that," Shaun said.

They remained silent and watched Sawyer for a while longer.

"Don't worry," Shaun said. "I'll train him every day. He'll be as skilled in battle as any knight of Caladar. I'll look after him."

"Thank you," Ariel said. She smiled to herself. Sawyer's combat skills were already a match for Shaun and his knights. Shaun would find that out for himself soon enough.

"May I ask if you could spare a small cart and horse?" Ariel said. "It would make my journey easier."

"Of course," Shaun said. "If I can't find one for you I'll have one built, and you can choose any horse you wish."

"Again, thank you."

Shaun nodded. "I must say, I much prefer fighting with you than against you."

"As do I," Ariel said. "Those were dark times, elves and men at war with each other."

"They were. When you unhorsed me, I had never been knocked to the ground. It has not happened since. Normally, I would think I had the advantage, being mounted on a horse. You showed me how wrong I was."

Ariel smiled and looked down. "You are a brave and formidable knight in battle," she said. "I was mistaken to fight you then. Please forgive me."

"Forgive you for what? Fighting for Selra'thel? Fighting for your people?" Shaun shook his head. "There is nothing to forgive. You did as any other warrior would have done. But I've always wanted to ask why you healed me? You could've killed me at any time."

"Because you have kind eyes," she said, touching his cheek. "Now that the war is over, I can confess this to you, *I* started the conflict between men and elves."

Shaun was quiet. Ariel knew he was considering his next words. "You must've had your reasons," he said. "But I do not hold the past against you."

"Thank you," Ariel said. "One day I will tell you how I came to start that war, but for now, we must defeat the Scarlet Queen."

"Agreed," Shaun said. "You should get some rest. I'll bring the cart and horse soon."

They said their goodnights and Ariel rejoined her companions. In camp that night, there was little talk.

"Jane would've been there with you," Sawyer said to Ariel. "She would've helped with the wounded soldiers."

"I know," Ariel said. "She would not hesitate to help someone in need."

"She's still in there," Sawyer said, nodding at Jane. "I know it."

"I hope you are right," Ariel said. "I really do."

Morning came too soon as far as Ariel was concerned. But the sound of Shaun bringing a cart and horse awakened her. He had also packed enough food and supplies for two for at least a week.

"Thank you," Ariel said. "It seems I am thanking you often these days."

"No thanks needed," Shaun said. "I'll help with the girl if you wish."

They carefully picked up Jane and placed her in the back of the cart. Once Jane had been made comfortable, Shaun turned to Sawyer.

"I look forward to training with you, Stormlord," Shaun said with a smile as he clasped Sawyer's shoulder. "Ariel speaks well of your prowess in battle."

"Thanks," Sawyer said, keeping his eyes on a slumbering Jane in the back of the cart. "But Ariel is the most amazing warrior ever."

"I agree," Shaun said. He gave Sawyer's shoulder a squeeze. "She will take care of your friend, don't worry."

Sawyer didn't answer. Ariel sat her belongings in the cart and looked at them. Geoff looked sad, his blue eyes full of concern. Ishara managed a slight smile and placed her hand over her heart. Sawyer, however, looked like he had already lost Jane. Ariel climbed onto the cart and took the reins. She turned her head and looked at Sawyer.

"I will protect her with my life," Ariel said. "We will come back together or not at all. Look for us within seven days."

"Your friends will be well cared for," Shaun said. "I'll see to it."

Ariel smiled. "Until we meet again," she said.

She gave the reins a quick flip to start the horse. She looked back only once. None of them had moved. They were going to watch her until she disappeared from their sight. She waved. Geoff immediately stuck his hand up and waved back. Then Ishara and Sawyer waved.

Ariel turned back to the path in front of her. She wiped away a tear that had escaped her eyes. A sudden burst of emotion welled up and Ariel dropped her head. More tears ran down her cheeks, more than she could hope to wipe away.

Ariel missed the lone rider in the distance following her. The rider had jet black hair and steel blue eyes. An ornate gold and silver was spear slung over her back.

# CHAPTER SEVENTEEN
## CHALON, AGAIN

Geoff had mixed feelings about returning to Chalon. Of course, it would be great to see his Dad again and spend time with him, but then there was Lionel, who considered himself a king and had a dislike for Ariel. Oh, and there were two armies descending on Chalon. Geoff sighed. *Possibly another bad idea.*

He and Ishara had climbed into the back of a supply wagon while Sawyer practiced driving, after some instruction from Shaun Hammerfel. Shaun rode beside the wagon. He was doing his best to converse with Sawyer, who wasn't in a talkative mood.

Geoff admired the large war hammer Shaun carried. *Hammerfel, now that was an appropriate name.* Geoff wasn't sure which end of the hammer would hurt more, the flat, heavy looking end, or the end which curved into a wicked-looking spike. *Wait, the whole thing was made of a silvery metal. It must weigh a ton.* As Geoff studied Shaun Hammerfel, King Arthur came to mind. Yes, he looked like he could be King Arthur. And the Knights of Caladar were the Knights of the Round Table.

Ishara sat on the opposite side of the wagon. She had replenished her arrows from Trelane's supplies. Geoff noticed Trelane had always been respectful toward Ishara and denied her nothing. She sat up and rummaged through a couple sacks, emerging with two turnips.

"Here," she said, tossing one to Geoff.

"A turnip?" Geoff said.

"Would you rather eat an onion? It is all I could find."

"No apples?"

"No apples."

Geoff wiped the turnip on his tunic and took a bite. It was a little gritty, but edible.

"Do you think we'll be welcome in Chalon?" Geoff asked. "Lionel wasn't the friendliest host last time."

"I would be surprised if we even saw him this time," Ishara said. "You are the son of a great wizard. I believe you will have a better chance to gain an audience with Lionel than I would."

"No thanks. I'd much rather hang out with you."

"Hang out?" Ishara inquired, tilting her head.

"Oh, sorry. It means be together and stuff."

"Stuff?"

"Yeah," Geoff said. "Like training and maybe exploring Chalon, whatever."

Ishara smiled and bit into her turnip.

"I wonder what Dad's been up to since we left for Troll Fang Pass." Geoff said. "It seems like such a long time ago and a lot has changed."

"I am sure Maelord has been busy," Ishara said. "Your father will be happy to see you again."

"Yeah, it'll be cool."

"Cool?"

"Yeah – oh, it's the way we talk back home," Geoff said, realizing Ishara didn't know slang terms and words. "It means 'good'."

"Your language is strange to me," Ishara said. "It is so confusing."

"It is, but if you saw my world," Geoff said. "I think you'd be totally freaked out."

Ishara looked at him with wide opened eyes, shaking her head. He had done it again.

"Sorry," he said. "Yeah, you'd find my world strange."

Ishara ate some more of her turnip.

"I would very much like to see your world," she said softly. "No matter how strange and freakish it may be to me."

"I'd like to show it to you one day," Geoff said. "It's not all bad. There are some things about it I think you'll like."

Ishara smiled.

Geoff turned his attention to Sawyer and Shaun as the wagon bumped along.

"How did you come by the Stormblade?" Shaun asked.

"I fell down a hole," Sawyer said. "It was half buried in the mud. When I pulled it out, a troll attacked me."

"A troll?"

"Yeah, Ariel said it was a river troll."

"Amazing," Shaun said. "And before then you had never fought with a sword?"

"Nope. It's not as amazing as you think. I basically held the sword up and the troll impaled itself on it."

"Ha!" Shaun said. "It's always better to be lucky in battle."

"I was definitely lucky. Ariel said I had won the sword. Trial by combat or something like that."

"She's right," Shaun said. "You carry the sword of heroes."

A few moments of silence passed as they rode. Then Shaun spoke again.

"I understand you've been training with Ariel," Shaun said. "Any warrior would jump at the chance to learn from her."

"Yeah," Sawyer said. "She's fantastic."

"A warrior with the Stormblade and fighting skills learned from Ariel, now *that* is someone to be reckoned with."

"Thanks," Sawyer said. "That sounds great and all, but usually things have happened to me by accident."

"I don't think so," Shaun said, looking sideways at Sawyer. "Ariel has told me about your bravery. You saved everyone at Troll Fang Pass when the ogre tore down a wall, did you not? You faced a werewolf in battle, too, and you battled the Shadowlord for your girl."

Sawyer thought for a moment, "Yeah, I guess I did that."

"And, this is something I saw for myself, you slowed the Shadowlord's reinforcements and kept them from joining the battle yesterday. It wouldn't be a lie to say you saved us and won the battle."

Sawyer looked forward as he drove the team of horses along the path.

"I had a son about your age," Shaun said. "You remind me of him. He was also an exceptional warrior. His name was Elliot."

"Elliot," Sawyer said. "That's a good name."

"He would've been about your age. He loved sports."

"Me too. What kind of sports?"

"He was an excellent wrestler. He was also good at horseshoes and jousting."

"Wrestling, huh?" Sawyer said. "I used to wrestle until I got into football. Never played horseshoes or jousted, though."

"My guess is the two of you would've been good friends. Like you, he was very brave."

"You're probably right," Sawyer agreed.

Shaun smiled. The afternoon sun was high when Shaun pointed to the far horizon.

"Chalon," Shaun said. "The fair city lies over those hills."

"What's that?" Sawyer asked, pointing to the northern horizon. An enormous dark plume of smoke rose into the distant sky, changing its color from pale blue to gray-black.

"I'm not sure," Shaun said as he shielded his eyes from the sun and squinted. "Some hamlet or village burning, perhaps. Maybe there is a brushfire across the northeastern plains."

"It is not a brushfire," Ishara said, standing in the wagon and studying the far away spectacle. "The smoke color is wrong. A brushfire is usually lighter, more like a gray color. That fire is burning with great heat, perhaps from oil or pitch. Dragon's breath can produce that sort of smoke, too."

"Dragon?" Sawyer repeated. He looked over his shoulder at Geoff. "Good thing we have a dragon slayer. You're up, Geoff."

Geoff watched as the great blackness in the sky grew. A shiver ran down his back. The ominous smoke seemed to be a harbinger of evil.

"That would be in the Scarlet Queen's direction," Shaun mused.

"Does she have a dragon?" Sawyer asked.

"I don't know," Shaun said. "She didn't have one when she attacked us."

"It reminds me of the smoke from the pitch used in the battle yesterday," Geoff said.

"It does," Ishara said. "There are several large villages near that smoke plume."

"The Scarlet Queen is burning all before her," Shaun said bitterly. "Just as she did to Caladar."

Flames and burning ash whipped about. The black smoke hindered the sun, creating a shadowy world of gloom and destruction. Most of the screams had passed and the sounds of battle had begun to fade. The odor of death mingled with the smell of burning buildings and crops. But it was the iron-tinged scent of blood that made her senses tingle. It was exhilarating.

Upon her dark auburn hair, which was pulled back tightly into a decorative bun, rested an elegant crown of gold and gems. She closed her eyes, sweeping her arms upward, as she exalted in her latest deadly accomplishment. How she enjoyed the symphony of death with the screams, the destruction, the pain and misery. All were the tenets of her reality. She was the herald of a new world order. *Her* world order. Reality was whatever she wished it to be, for she was supreme above all living things. The rest were cattle, food for her to use, manipulate, and consume as she chose. They were dirty, weak sub-creatures. They deserved to die.

Then she caught the scent of food nearby. Her stomach growled. She heard their frightened whispers and beating hearts. To her, these sounded like booming drumbeats that rose above all other noises. She drew her sword from its scabbard and looked at the blaze ahead of her. It was a solid inferno. The village inn which had stood there was now razed to the ground.

Without hesitation, she walked into the flames. She did not fear the flames. She didn't fear anything. This was her world to conquer and feast upon. *She* was both alpha and omega. A small thing like walking through a blaze was of no consequence. A small group of armed warriors had taken refuge behind the local stables. She saw their hearts and the blood rushing through their bodies. The veins and arteries were as roadmaps to her.

Emerging from the flames behind her prey, her red eyes pulsed as she casually strode toward them. The poor, wretched things continued to whisper, plotting a way to escape. There was no escape. Not from her. One of the cowards looked over his shoulder to say something, but when he saw her, he screamed and pointed. His eyes as wide as saucers. The others turned and faced her. The first killing stroke from her sword sliced completely through the closest human-pig, halving him where he stood.

She pointed at the next warrior, who had dared to raise his axe to her. He froze in mid-stride, held in place by her will. Then she balled her fist and his body crumpled into a lump of broken bones and sinews. The next two warriors stepped forward and swung their swords at her. They were clumsy, weak, trivial attacks. They merely bounced off her skin. She smiled at the looks of fear and disbelief on their faces. Amused, she let them strike her again. The results were the same. Such pathetic creatures.

A casual backswing of her sword decapitated one, his head landing near her feet, his expression contorted with fear. She drove her fist into the chest of the second and removed his still beating heart. She took a deep breath. The scent of so much blood and gore was intoxicating. Dropping the orphaned heart to the ground, she pivoted to the final warrior. He dropped his sword and fell to his knees, begging for his miserable life.

His words were the same she had heard countless times before. His groveling annoyed her. What sort of creature would surrender and beg in such an embarrassing manner? At least the others had died as warriors. This one was a pig. A pig to be slaughtered. She sheathed her sword and looked down at him. Sheathing her weapon seemed to have given him hope. She saw it in his tearful eyes. Why did they want to live? Their lives were nothing. They were muck-dwellers.

This one continued to beg. His voice had become shrill and grating. He was wearisome and she had wasted enough time with him. Stepping forward, she grasped him by the neck and lifted him off the ground. The stark fear had returned to his eyes. He tried to pry himself free. He was weak. She twisted his head to the side, exposing one of his carotid arteries. How the delicious fluid flowed! The familiar, constant hunger within her arose from deep down.

She savaged his neck, nearly ripping his head off as she drank. The mixture of fear and blood was delectable. When she had her fill, she dropped the lifeless body and strode south to the edge of the village. Far in the distance sat a great reservoir of food and slaves. She would take her time feasting there. It would be glorious. Behind the Scarlet Queen, her Night Guard, a collection of fifty elite warriors in black and red armor assembled.

Cruel and fearless, they followed her commands without question. They always did her bidding. One warrior stepped forward. He was taller than most in the Night Guard, but it was his ruthlessness and bravery that earned him the title of Commander. Kieran was a killer. He had neither conscience nor morals and that is what she liked in him. But someday she would tire of him, and on that day he would become food.

Kieran dropped to a knee and bowed his head, as he should in her presence.

"My Queen," Kieran said, his deep voice echoing from inside his helm. "We await your command."

"South," Queen Lysis said, maintaining her gaze on the horizon. "Send word to my armies. We march to Chalon."

# CHAPTER EIGHTEEN
## REVELATIONS

The journey to Chalon went faster than Geoff had expected. The long line of troops and wagons approached the great walled city as the afternoon dipped into evening. The massive iron-bound gates of Chalon opened and they entered. The first thing Geoff noticed was the lack of guards manning positions along the walls. With two armies on the way, it seemed like there should be a sense of urgency with preparations for the coming battle.

The second thing Geoff noticed was the gloomy demeanor of the people in the streets. Nothing had changed, he thought. There wasn't enough lodging for the refugees who had flocked to Chalon for protection. He looked at the dirty, withdrawn faces. Their eyes said it all. They were miserable. Geoff watched as the peasants rushed to beg Commander Renfry's soldiers and the Knights of Caladar for food, money, anything that would help alleviate their situation, even if just for a few moments. Not many approached the elven warriors of Selra'thel, but those who did received what they asked for, and more.

Some peasants avoided the elven warriors altogether and

even cast hateful glances in their direction. Geoff longed to tell them that the elves had fought and some had died so Chalon and the rest of Alluria could be free. Shaun looked around, he gritted his teeth and Geoff heard him swear under his breath.

"How could this happen?" Shaun said. "The greatest city in Alluria and people here are starving. Damn Lionel, damn him!"

"It was bad enough when we were last here," Sawyer said. "But not as bad as *this*."

"A ruler should know better," Shaun said. "These people need help."

First, Shaun ordered his knights to give them whatever they had to spare. Then he spurred his horse into the crowd, handing out food from his own saddlebags and coins from the pouch tucked inside his belt. Every other knight followed his lead, bringing sobs and grateful tears to the eyes of the peasants.

"This is why the Knights of Caladar are loved," Ishara said. "It is not their way to let anyone suffer if they can lend aid. They are the best of humanity."

"Is that their creed?" Sawyer said, looking over his shoulder. "Is that the way they live?"

"It is," Ishara said. "They fight for those who cannot fight for themselves. They stand for good and justice. Their honor is indisputable. You have already seen their skill in battle. They are feared by the unjust, yet they are humble and compassionate."

"Hey, can one of you take over here?" Sawyer said. "I'd like to do what I can to help."

Geoff and Ishara both climbed into the front of the

wagon. Taking the reins, Ishara continued to guide the two horses along, following the column of soldiers. Sawyer held up their progress just long enough to grab any sacks containing anything that could pass for food. He even pulled out his personal rations and handed them out.

Someone in the crowd recognized the sword strapped across his back. Then people crowded around for a reason other than hunger, seeking to touch the warrior who carried the famous blade. Chants of "Stormlord! Stormlord! Stormlord!" erupted from the throng of people.

"People must have their heroes," Ishara said. "Sawyer fits that role well."

"Yeah," Geoff said as he watched Sawyer. "I've never seen him do something like that before. He's getting nicer."

"I am glad."

They followed the long line of mounted soldiers, elves, and dwarves toward Chalon Castle. As they passed through the crowds, Geoff recalled his last visit, and the little girl he'd seen by the side of the road with her family. He wanted to help them but had no means of doing so until Ishara pulled a silver ring from her finger and told him to give it to them. They were elated. Geoff imagined it must've been like winning the lottery for them. That was a good thing. Then he remembered he promised Ishara he would replace her ring. How was he ever going to accomplish that?

"Here we are," Ishara said, pulling the reins and stopping the horses. "Let's hope *King* Lionel is in a better mood these days."

"He won't be if you say it like that," Geoff said with a chuckle. "Do you want to spend another night in the dungeon?"

Ishara rolled her eyes.

"That was an awful night," she said. Then she smiled. "But I remember my favorite sneak thief risking his life to release me. You were amazing, Geoff."

"Thanks," he said. "You didn't deserve to be there. It was wrong of Lionel to put you in the dungeon. Lady Seqwil could've assassinated you."

"I believe that is exactly what she had planned," Ishara said, stepping off the wagon. "But she did not count on you coming to my rescue."

"Ariel was the one who fought her, not me."

"That is true. But who sounded the alarm?"

"I did. But I never understood why she wanted you dead in the first place."

"I am not sure," Ishara said thoughtfully. "Perhaps she saw me as a threat, or perhaps I was simply an easy target."

"That makes sense," Geoff said, jumping off the wagon and landing beside her. "There wasn't much you could do to defend yourself in the dungeon cell. Like you said, an easy target."

"Do you think he will treat us better this time?"

"I doubt it," Geoff said. "We shouldn't attract too much attention to ourselves while we're here."

"Agreed," Ishara said. "Shall we visit your father?"

"Yeah, that'd be cool," Geoff said. "I wonder if he's in the castle or his tower?"

"We can start looking for him here," Ishara said, motioning toward the massive castle. "Whom should we ask?"

At that moment they heard a familiar voice.

"Geoff!"

Turning his head toward the castle, he saw his father. His dark hair, close-cropped beard and mustache was a welcome sight.

"Dad!" Geoff dashed over and wrapped his arms around the wizard. Maelord laughed and hugged Geoff.

"It's so good to have you back, son," Maelord said looking into Geoff's eyes. "I missed you."

"I missed you too."

"How are you? Word reached us that the Troll Fang Pass garrison had fallen. How did you manage to escape?"

"We won that battle," Geoff said. "Sawyer killed an ogre that brought down a wall and kept an army of orcs from over-running us. He was awesome. He also helped defeat the Shadowlord's army yesterday, too."

"Well now, it seems Sawyer has finally stepped into his inheritance and truly become the Stormlord," Maelord said. He saw Ishara standing behind Geoff and smiled. "It's good to see you too, Ishara. How are you?"

"*Hal'inari*," Ishara said with a slight bow of her head. "Thanks to your son's heroics, I am well."

"Heroics?" Maelord looked at Geoff, raising his eyebrows.

"Oh, it wasn't much," Geoff said. "Jane tried to kill us and I threw up the shield spell you taught me, that's all."

Maelord blinked. Geoff saw that his father was mulling over what he had just heard.

"Come in, both of you," Maelord said. "Let's find you some quarters and food. I want to hear all about this. Where is Ariel? I need to speak with her."

"Ariel and Jane have journeyed to the sacred grove in Spirewood Forest," Ishara said. "Jane has fallen. She is a dark druid now. The ritual of cleansing is Jane's only hope."

Maelord stared, shocked "Jane, a dark druid? I can't believe it. Jane's always been so thoughtful of others."

"She was bitten by a vampire, the Shadowlord himself." Ishara said. "Now she does his bidding."

A deep frown fell across Maelord's face. He looked around at the soldiers and guards nearby. "Come, let's find a more private place to talk."

Sawyer had just finished giving out the last of his food when he felt an arm wrap around his shoulders.

"Well done, Stormlord," Shaun Hammerfel said with an approving grin. Behind him, he pulled his horse along by the reins. "Well done indeed."

"I was just following you," Sawyer said. "It seemed the right thing to do."

"It was," Shaun said. "I noticed you are quite popular here. They have seen the Stormlord in action, haven't they?"

"I don't know about that," Sawyer said. They walked for a few more steps. "And I'd appreciate it if you called me Sawyer, not Stormlord."

"Very well," Shaun said, removing his arm from around Sawyer's shoulders. "But you must agree to call me Shaun in return."

"That's a deal," Sawyer said.

"I think tomorrow morning would be a good time for you to start training," Shaun said. "Let's get settled in for the night. I have much to bring to Lionel's attention."

"I bet he gets an earful."

"Perhaps," Shaun said. "But I suspect King Baldon Stonemaster of Keredain will be the one to *really* bend his ear."

"The dwarves," Sawyer said. "I noticed they were better received than the elves, why is that? Does everyone still blame elves for this war?"

"Well," Shaun said, shrugging. "Not that long ago there were skirmishes between elves and humans that nearly led to an outright war between them."

"But elves had nothing to do with starting this war. They've been helping humans. I mean, Ariel, if not for *her*, I don't think we'd stand a chance."

"We know that," Shaun said. "We both know that, don't we? And for that very reason, we have to let as many people who will listen to us know the truth."

"So earlier," Sawyer began. "When we saw the smoke to the north, you said the Scarlet Queen had burned most of Caladar. What did you mean?"

"I mean just that," Shaun said. He winced and looked down for a second before answering. "Queen Lysis attacked us with orcs and barbarians, as well as infernal minions."

"But I heard you guys, the Knights of Caladar have never lost a battle, right?"

"We did manage to beat her back," Shaun admitted, "But while our forces were engaged, she attacked our cities and villages. She burned everything and killed many beloved friends."

"Sorry," Sawyer said. "That can't be easy to talk about."

"It isn't," Shaun said. "But Alluria has become a dangerous place and if Queen Lysis succeeds in spreading her evil—"

"She won't," Sawyer said firmly. He looked at Shaun. "We won't let that happen."

"No," Shaun said. "We won't."

They continued on their way to the castle, which sat above the city itself. Each time they passed guards they were acknowledged with a salute. There was a question Sawyer wanted to ask, but wasn't sure how to do so without offending Shaun, but their conversation gave him the opportunity to bring the subject up. At least, he thought it did.

"Shaun, I've been meaning to ask," Sawyer said. "Your son. How did you lose him?"

"Fighting the dark minions of the Scarlet Queen," Shaun said. "As I said, he was an excellent warrior and knight. It was his first battle and he had become separated from the rest of us. By the time I fought my way to him it was too late."

"I'm sorry," Sawyer said. "I'm sure he took a lot of his enemies with him."

"He did," Shaun said proudly. "I miss him terribly, though. I miss training with him."

"I'm looking forward to training with you," Sawyer said. "Did Ariel say I needed it?"

"Everyone needs more training," Shaun said. "But no, she didn't mention anything of the sort."

They passed a beggar sitting beside the street. She wore a dirty, patched hood which covered her face. Her slender, grimy hand extended upward while she looked down.

"Here," Sawyer said, placing a silver coin in her palm. "My last one." He gave her a gentle pat on the head. The woman clutched the coin tightly in her hand and nodded profusely in thanks. After the pair had passed, the hooded figure lifted her head. Neither Sawyer nor Shaun looked back to see the loathing in her lavender eyes.

She stood, her face contorted into a silent snarl. Dropping the coin, Lady Seqwil Ferncliff disappeared into the crowd of peasants.

# CHAPTER NINETEEN
## THE SACRED GROVE

The sun was dipping below the horizon when Ariel pulled the single-horse cart to the edge of the Spirewood Forest. Stepping off the road and seeing the trees was relaxing, like returning home after being away for a long time. She exhaled and unhooked the horse, fed it a few apples, and gave it a grooming.

"Thank you," Ariel whispered, kissing its nose. "Go now, you are free."

The horse, a dark brown mare, nuzzled her one more time before trotting off. Ariel smiled as she watched her leave. Then the hair on the back of her neck rose and she felt as if she was being watched. Ariel whirled about and scanned her surroundings and the landscape around her. Being watched wasn't the right feeling, more like *stalked*. Had she not had Jane with her, she would have investigated, but Jane was her first priority.

She lifted Jane from the back of the cart, making sure to grab the blankets as well, then hurried into the Spirewood Forest. Ariel felt safer almost immediately. Whatever was stalking her could be more easily evaded, or even dealt with while she was in her forest. Ariel looked down at a slumbering Jane. She had to be protected. As she walked, Ariel felt the forest mood, as she liked to call it. The forest was protesting Jane's presence. She heard the murmur of the trees and the thoughts of the wildlife.

A dark druid was not welcome. Still, the forest tolerated Jane because she was with Ariel, the High Druid of Alluria. Ariel looked over her shoulder. She didn't see anyone or anything trailing her into the Spirewood Forest. They would be foolish to do so. As Ariel walked, the trees moved their branches and roots out of her way.

Time was running out for Jane. If the cleansing ritual was to succeed, it should be performed as soon as possible. One thing Ariel didn't reveal to Sawyer and the others was that, if she failed, then she would die as well as Jane. But Ariel had an advantage here. A druid's powers were amplified a hundredfold in their forest. The druid's forest was an extension of the druid that watched over it. Ariel inhaled. The woodsy scents all about were comforting.

The sun had gone down completely when Ariel and Jane entered the sacred grove of the forest. Here, she could fight Jane, or rather, fight the dark druid. If a battle ensued here, Ariel would have the best chance, she was mentally prepared to do whatever must be done. And *that*, was what Ariel dreaded most.

Ariel surveyed the grove. All was as she had left it. Flowering bushes and robust fruit trees ringed and populated the area, producing a sweet aromatic mixture tantalizing to the senses.

Laying Jane down in the cool, thick grass, Ariel ascended the stone steps to a raised dais. There, a carved marble basin rested on a pedestal. Its intricate carvings of vines, leaves and flowers bathed in the early light of the moon. Ariel passed her hand over the center of the basin and a white glow began to shine from the bottom of the marble bowl. Ariel cupped her hands in the cool water and took a long drink. The water was refreshing. The magic of the water in the basin rejuvenated her weary spirit.

Ariel walked back down the steps and knelt on both knees beside Jane. She brushed Jane's hair back over her forehead and caressed her cheek.

"Jane, I hope you can hear me. We are about to embark on a dangerous journey together. So dangerous that neither one of us may survive."

Ariel took a deep breath, "I will need your help, Jane. I will do everything I can. I will muster every ounce of power within me. But you must want to live. You must want to rejoin your friends."

Ariel kissed Jane's hand and picked her up. Again Ariel ascended the stone steps. She walked past the marble basin to a shallow circular pool with glowing blue water beyond the dais. It was ringed with stones adorned with carvings like those on the basin, but at the top of each was engraved an ancient druidic rune. This was the source of Ariel's power. If she used too much of that power she would fade away and no longer exist. This, in addition to potentially unleashing the most powerful dark druid ever seen in Alluria gave Ariel pause.

There was still a part of Ariel that wished she had never met Jane. Looking at her, she was just a girl. A human girl. Why should she risk her life and risk the fate of Alluria for her? As the High Druid, she could do so much, save so many. *She* meant a great deal to Alluria, but *Jane*… Ariel sternly shook her head to clear the doubts from her mind. Jane was one of the three outlanders of prophecy, and she had always been loyal to Alluria. Indeed, it would be an honor to risk her own life for Jane. She had decided that a long time ago. Jane had earned that much from her, just as Geoff and Sawyer had.

Ariel laid Jane down beside the small pool and removed her boots. Then Ariel removed her own boots and her weapons. She placed her hand on Jane's forehead.

"Jane, I believe you can hear me. What we are about to do will be painful for both of us, but it is necessary if we are to bring you back to the light. I do not know if this will succeed. It has never been tried before, not in this fashion."

Lifting Jane up again, Ariel studied her face. She was a hardly more than a child, a human child. Yet she'd had taught Ariel so much in the time they had spent together. She would have to reveal that to Jane, if they survived. Jane's peaceful features hid a raging darkness within. Ariel sensed the enormous power growing inside her. As far as she could determine, the power Jane had was unlimited.

Ariel took a deep breath and steeled herself for what was to come, the battle for Jane's soul. Stepping into the cool, clear waters of the sacred pool, which came just up to her waist, she placed a hand under Jane's head to buoy her as she floated in the water. Closing her eyes, she recalled the spell that kept Jane in stasis, the spell she must reverse in order to release her from her magic-induced slumber.

"*Te'renar ulran valnos te'renar,*" Ariel chanted over and over.

First, Jane's head tilted slightly to the left, then Ariel saw her fingers begin to move beneath the water. Ariel's muscles tensed, timing was important. She had to keep Jane within the sacred pool while she performed the cleansing ritual. If Jane managed to escape from the pool before it was completed, all would be lost. Jane's legs shifted. Then her head began to undulate, back and forth.

With a sudden tremor, Jane's body became rigid and she awoke with a large, single gasp for air. Her eyes shot open, black as pitch. Ariel gripped the back of Jane's neck and wrapped her arm around Jane's waist as she began to thrash about. Jane squirmed and kicked desperately. Her strength surprised Ariel. It was all she could do to maintain her grasp on Jane. Her strength and agility had been enhanced by the darkness inside that fought to be released.

"*Nela'tramuul sa eridos lora'non illidas val'nar,*" Ariel spoke the first words of the ritual, Jane screamed. Abandoning her attempt to break free, Jane turned her rage on Ariel, gripping her throat. Unable to breathe, Ariel was forced to release Jane's waist, taking hold of her wrist instead. At first, she was unable to budge Jane's crushing hold from around her neck. Ariel gritted her teeth and submerged Jane under the water, holding her there.

After several seconds, Jane began to flail about under the water losing her grip on Ariel's throat. Ariel quickly caught her breath and continued, "*Ill'thayla horla'than trynor shonara!*"

As soon as Ariel completed the second half of the ritual she received a savage uppercut from Jane. The blow staggered Ariel, giving Jane time to wrench herself free from her grasp. The water around Ariel erupted as Jane surfaced. A right hook to Ariel's chin sent her sprawling backward. Ariel tasted blood. She regained her senses and saw Jane wading toward the edge of the pool.

Ariel launched herself at Jane, catching her shoulders with both hands and whipping Jane back toward the center of the pool. Jane grabbed one of Ariel's wrists, spun around, and flipped Ariel high overhead. Ariel failed to anticipate such a move and she found herself underwater, watching Jane's feet as she again made her way to the pool's edge.

Kicking as hard as she could to propelling herself underwater. When Ariel reached Jane, she had made it to the edge and begun to pull herself out of the water. Ariel grasped both of Jane's legs and pulled for all she was worth. Underwater, she heard Jane scream again as she was dragged back into the sacred waters. Ariel stood up in the glowing shallow pool. Jane tried to twist and turn her way out of Ariel's hold, but was unable to break free. Jane lifted her head above the water for a couple of seconds and sputtered, "Ariel!"

Ariel relaxed her grip, fearing Jane was in danger of drowning. As soon as she did, Jane kicked her way free and rose out of the water with a straight right jab that landed on Ariel's nose and lip. Ariel saw a blinding flash of light and again tasted her own blood. Ariel fell back into the water. She quickly got to her feet and brushed the hair from her eyes. Jane had turned and hurried to the pool's edge again. This time, Ariel leapt onto Jane's back and wrapped her legs around Jane's waist. Ariel then slid an arm under Jane's chin in a choking maneuver while applying pressure to the back of Jane's head with her other arm.

Jane screamed again and clawed at Ariel's arms. Ariel tightened her hold and squeezed Jane's sides with her legs.

"*Nela'tramuul sa eridos lora'non illidas val'nar,*" Ariel said. "*Ill'thayla horla'than trynor shonara!*"

Jane's body went rigid and then shook uncontrollably. Ariel repeated the charm of cleansing. This time Jane went limp in her arms. Ariel turned Jane around so they were facing each other. Jane's eyes were still pools of black. Ariel propped Jane's head up out of the water with a hand under her neck.

"Oh no," Ariel moaned. This was what she had most feared. The evil within Jane had remained. Ariel's eyes welled up with tears. "Jane, please hear me. Come back."

Jane continued to shake and twitch.

"Please Jane," Ariel said. "Follow my voice."

Jane's eyes closed and a long, slow exhale followed from her with a rattling sound in her throat.

"No! Jane! Stay with me! No, no, no!"

Ariel's eyes had become blurred by the tears that were beginning to flow freely. Then Jane shuddered one more time. Ariel clutched Jane close to her and closed her eyes.

"Jane," Ariel said with a quivering voice. "Please come back. I have lost so many dear friends in this war. I dare not lose you as well. My heart will never mend. Please come back to me, Jane."

Ariel looked up at the night sky. The stars flickered through her tears like blurred gems on dark velvet.

"Please do not take her," Ariel said still holding Jane close and caressing the back of her head. "This one deserves to live. Her life is important."

A moment passed and then Jane's back arched and Jane screamed again. This time her scream was more primal and a foul. A writhing, hissing black cloud escaped from her lips and floated up before dissipating near the tree tops. Jane went limp in Ariel's arms. Tilting Jane's head back, Ariel opened one of Jane's eyes with her thumb. It was blue. Ariel hugged her, sobbing like a child.

After several minutes, Ariel composed herself and carried Jane from the sacred pool. She laid Jane down on a blanket from the cart and collapsed beside her. She brushed Jane's hair back. A loud snort from behind Ariel caught her attention. She turned her head and saw the flash of a silvery-white mane in the moonlight.

"Hello, my old friend," Ariel whispered.

# CHAPTER TWENTY

## FORLORN HOPE

There had been plenty debate among the elves and King Lionel concerning whether elves should be allowed within Chalon. While many in the walled city still blamed elves for starting the war, it was becoming apparent that they too had been drawn into the conflict through no fault of their own. Geoff was glad when it was finally decided that since the elves had fought beside soldiers from Chalon and turned back the Scarlet Queen's army, they could stay. Commander Renfry had been most outspoken and insistent on the matter. Lionel reluctantly relented.

Geoff's father, Maelord, had secured two well furnished rooms in the northernmost tower of the castle. Each had a fireplace, two large beds, a table with four chairs, dressers, and an armchair. The walls were adorned with tapestries of landscapes, and large bowls of fresh fruit sat on the tables. Geoff helped himself to a juicy, red apple. Ishara did the same.

Once they had settled in, Geoff and Ishara described everything that had happened since they left Chalon. Maelord listened with great interest, especially when they disclosed the plan to attempt to release Jane from her curse.

Afterwards, he sighed, stood and went out to the balcony that faced north. Geoff and Ishara followed. Far below, the bustle of an overcrowded city went about its business. To the north, the same ominous, dark clouds they had seen the day before seemed closer.

"Should Ariel be lost," Maelord said, "then all is lost. This world will burn and there is nothing we can do to prevent it."

"We'll stop the Scarlet Queen," Geoff said. "We have to, right?"

"Together, perhaps," Maelord said with a slight smile as he placed his hand on Geoff's shoulder. "If only we could forge another alliance among the free races like before."

"What're you talking about, Dad? Men, dwarves, and elves came together and defeated the Shadowlord's eastern army. We saw it."

"I believe you," Maelord said. "However, I fear that was but one moment and the old prejudices that keep us apart will resurface soon enough. Lately, I've come to the conclusion that enemy spies are within the castle walls, working to divide us. This is the first I've spoken of it."

"Who?" Geoff said. "Who's doing that?"

Maelord shook his head, "I don't know. Best be on your guard while you're here. Stay together."

"So," Geoff said. "What exactly did you mean earlier when you said if we lost Ariel, then it was all over?"

Maelord turned and faced them, leaning on the heavy stone railing behind him. Maelord and Ishara exchanged glances. There seemed to be an unspoken understanding between them.

"Geoff," Ishara said. "When Ariel said there was a danger

neither of them would return, she did not tell you everything."

"I don't get it," Geoff said, shaking his head. "What's the problem? What *didn't* Ariel say?"

"The cleansing ritual is an extremely rare thing," Ishara said. "When the druid performs it, they are obliged to sacrifice part of their life essence in an attempt to rid the subject of whatever affliction they have. Removing such evil has never been done before. At least, I have never heard of such an occurrence. If Ariel has to use too much of her essence to save Jane, then she will die and, in her place, a terrifying dark druid will rise."

Geoff stared in shock at Ishara.

"Dad," Geoff said. "You gotta get us to the Spirewood Forest. There's a Wizard's Arch there, we've seen it. If you can port us there —"

"Geoff, Geoff," Maelord said, taking him by the shoulders. "Even if we did just as you said, there's nothing we can do. We cannot venture into the sacred grove. No one can enter except the High Druid and those with her permission. We would be of no use to either of them."

"They're my friends." Geoff said.

Maelord pulled Geoff close and hugged him. "I know, son. I know. They're my friends too. But we have to trust Ariel."

"Ariel will succeed," Ishara said. "She will. She will bring Jane back to us."

Geoff looked at Ishara. She was right, of course. While he wished Ariel had told them exactly how dangerous the cleansing was, he understood why she didn't share that information. More than likely there would've been more arguing and debate over whether or not they should accompany her and Jane. Sawyer would've insisted on going with them.

"I must go," Maelord said. He looked at Geoff and playfully brushed his hair back. "This evening we should continue your training. I'm delighted you've used the spells I taught you so far. Now, I think it's time you learned something a little more offensive in nature. Agreed?"

"Yeah. That'd be cool."

"In the meantime, I think both of you should stay put," Maelord said. "I'll have food brought to your rooms."

"Aww c'mon," Geoff said. "We were gonna explore Chalon. We haven't seen much of it yet and this is our second time here."

"Geoff, listen to your old man," Maelord said. "It's dangerous here."

"Okay, then let's go to your tower," Geoff suggested. Ishara fidgeted and looked away. She apparently was in no hurry to return to Maelord's filthy tower.

"Soon," Maelord said. He opened the door and before he left he turned back to Geoff and Ishara. "I promise. There's so much I want to show you. Now, do not open this door for anyone but me, okay?"

"Okay," Geoff said, surrendering to his father's sentence of house arrest.

Maelord closed the heavy iron-bound door behind him. A second later, they heard a sharp *click*.

"Perhaps he can show you were the broom is, too," Ishara said with a smirk. "Or perhaps teach you a spell that will make dust and dirt disappear? Now *that* would be magic."

Geoff smiled.

"His tower was really dirty," he said, wrinkling his nose.

"I don't remember seeing a broom, either."

"There was no broom," Ishara said, wrinkling her nose too. "I looked."

Geoff turned and looked to the north. The dark clouds of war seemed so far away. Ishara hugged him, resting her head on his shoulder. She slipped so easily into his arms, a perfect fit.

"Your father should know by now," she said. "That it is impossible to keep a good sneak thief under lock and key."

Geoff began laughing.

"He had a hard time keeping me out of his study."

"After dinner," Ishara said. "We shall sneak out and explore a little."

"Cool."

"Cool," Ishara repeated as she squeezed him.

Geoff returned the affectionate squeeze. For him, being with Ishara was a reward in itself.

"Geoff, where is Sawyer?" Ishara asked a moment later.

Geoff thought.

"Last time I saw him, he was with Shaun Hammerfel and the Knights of Caladar. Do you think they're still giving food and money to the poor?"

"I do not know," Ishara said. "But we should find him and let him know what your father said about it being dangerous here."

"You're right. I'll bet he's with Shaun. They seemed to be getting along well."

"I thought so."

"Should we tell him about Ariel and Jane? He might want to grab a horse and ride to Spirewood Forest alone."

"If it were you, would you want to know?"

"Yeah," Geoff said. "I would for sure."

"What spells do you think your father will teach you this time?"

"I don't know. Perhaps a spell to bring down a mountain," Geoff mused. "I'll learn whatever he's willing to show me."

"You could do it, you know," Ishara said taking her head off his shoulder and looking at him. "You have the power inside you to destroy mountains."

"Back at the battle," Geoff said. "When Jane attacked us, it looked like she had that kind of power."

"She did," Ishara said placing her head back on Geoff's shoulder. "And she may still have such power if Ariel failed."

"Hey, didn't you just say Ariel was going to succeed in helping Jane? Where's that positive elvish thinking?"

Ishara squeezed him again. "It will be dark soon. We should find Sawyer."

"Okay," Geoff said, releasing her from his embrace. "Let's ask around and find out where the Knights of Caladar are, I'm pretty sure we'll find him there."

They walked back into the room. Geoff selected another apple from the fruit bowl when he heard Ishara say, "Geoff, there is a secret door beside the fireplace." She was pointing at a spot on the wall behind a plush chair.

"I don't see anything," he said. "Are you sure?"

Ishara moved the chair aside and ran her fingers along the edge of the fireplace mantle. She stepped back and studied the wall.

"This is a human castle," Ishara said. "Humans tend to hide levers and buttons in plain sight."

"It looks like a wall to me," Geoff said. "Nothing special."

"My room is on the other side of that wall," Ishara said. "I think it is worth investigating."

"I agree, but how do we—"

"There." Ishara said, pointing at an empty sconce on the wall. She grasped its base and pushed it, pulled it, then she twisted it toward the balcony and the wall opened with a muffled *pop*.

"Wow," Geoff said, amazed. "Just like Scooby Doo."

Ishara stopped.

"Scooby who?" she said with one eyebrow raised.

"Scooby Doo. It's a cartoon on…nevermind. Sorry. I'll tell you later."

Ishara looked Geoff over. Her green eyes opened wide, searching for a reason for his seemingly insane outburst.

Ishara turned and went through the secret door into her room. Geoff followed. Her room looked identical to his.

"Hey," Geoff said in a slight whisper. "How'd you do that? How'd you see the secret door?"

"I looked," Ishara said. "And why are you whispering?"

"Oh, I thought we were sneaking and stuff. I wanted to be quiet."

"Sneaking and stuff?" Ishara turned and looked at him again. "Sometimes you say the strangest things, Geoff."

"Yeah, I guess so."

Ishara wandered around the room, her eyes perusing every inch of the walls. Geoff thought she was searching for something in particular.

"There are no other secret doors here," Ishara said at last. "I am sure of that."

"Good. In that case, let's go find Sawyer."

He walked to the door that led from Ishara's room to the

hall and tried to open it but it wouldn't budge.

"Locked," Geoff said.

"Not for long," Ishara said, producing her small leather pouch which held various tools and instruments for opening things like locked doors.

"Now," Ishara said, dropping to a knee in front of the door and opening her pouch. "Watch and pay attention."

# CHAPTER TWENTY-ONE
## CLOAK AND DAGGER

Sawyer had decided to join the Knights of Caladar and elves of Selra'thel in the great dining hall of the castle. Shaun Hammerfel shared story after exalted story of the knight's battles against impossible odds, the individual duels with fearsome opponents, and the rescuing of damsels from evil-doers. Sawyer listened to them all. Shaun was old enough to be his father, which would normally send Sawyer in the opposite direction, but Shaun also seemed to be genuinely interested in Sawyer and his friends.

Sitting across from Shaun at the long wooden table, Sawyer watched the knights eat. Most were so hungry they tore into their roast pheasant or leg of mutton like animals. The elves, on the other hand, ate quietly and kept their voices low. The obvious segregation with elves seated on one side of the great hall and the knights on the other struck Sawyer as worrisome. They had fought together and won a great battle against the Shadowlord, yet they preferred to eat apart.

Sawyer leaned closer to Shaun.

"Why are the elves sitting over there and the rest of us over here?" Sawyer asked. "Aren't we allies?"

"Allies? Ha!" A knight sitting beside Shaun snorted as he threw the remnants of his pheasant, hitting an elven warrior in the back. "After all *they've* done?"

The elven warrior stopped eating, stood up, and turned around. As he did, the loud, obnoxious knight also stood.

"Easy, Sir Reymond." Shaun said. "The Stormlord is right. They're our allies. Sit down."

The standing knight had thinning, bright red hair and wild brown eyes. He was breathing heavy and his hand rested on the pommel of his sword. Sawyer's gaze went back and forth between the elven warrior and the knight. Several other knights stood, as did an equal number of elven warriors. All eyes were on the first two as they faced off. Sawyer was sure that at any moment there would be a fight between elves and men.

"I said sit down, Sir Reymond. Now." Shaun's tone had become a command.

Reymond finally obeyed, though he kept his eyes on the elven warrior as he reached for another pheasant. Then he cut his eyes to Sawyer.

"Stormlord," Reymond said with a hint of animosity. "Since he likes wearing elven armor, maybe he should sit with them?"

Shaun's hand shot out and grabbed the front of Reymond's breastplate. A sharp tug later and Reymond was looking Shaun Hammerfel in the eyes.

"You've had too much wine. You'll apologize to the Stormlord and leave this hall or you and I will have a go at each other."

Reymond swallowed. Sawyer noticed a hint of fear in his eyes.

"Apologies, Stormlord," Reymond said. Shaun released him and Reymond left the table. Sawyer watched him leave.

"So what was that all about?" Sawyer asked, picking at his undercooked potatoes.

"Well," Shaun said, raising his eyebrows but keeping his gaze on his pheasant. "Some years ago we faced elves from Selra'thel in battle. Perhaps some of these here," Shaun motioned toward the elves. "We had the advantage in numbers, but as the battle progressed, we quickly lost that advantage. They say we Knights of Caladar have never lost a battle, but I believe we lost that one, or would've lost it had we had continued fighting."

"So you were there. What happened?"

"I was," Shaun said. "I was lucky to have survived, too."

Sawyer took a drink of water from his wooden mug and waited for Shaun to continue.

"It was there that I faced the greatest warrior I had ever encountered. Standing downhill of me, she unhorsed me with a single blow. I was younger then, stronger, more agile. But I was completely outmatched."

"Wait," Sawyer said. "You said *she*…who was she?"

"Your companion, Ariel," Shaun said without a hint of embarrassment. "She led the elves that day and she had all but won the battle when she stopped."

"Ariel?" Sawyer said. "You're kidding. I don't believe it. She wouldn't do something like that. She's working overtime to defeat the Shadowlord. Without her, we'd be done for."

Shaun put the last of his pheasant down and wiped his hands. He looked at Sawyer and motioned him to lean even closer. Sawyer did so and Shaun placed a hand on the back of his neck and leaned closer to Sawyer too.

"First," Shaun said in a steady voice. "A knight doesn't lie. He always tells the truth. A knight's word is his honor. Second, to question a knight's word is to challenge him to combat."

Sawyer was about to apologize but Shaun continued with a wink, "And thirdly, as I said, I was there. I know whose scimitar was at my throat that day. It was indeed Ariel. All she had to do was flick her wrist and I'd have died. Instead, she helped me to my feet and offered me her hand. It was she who called an end to the battle. Since then, there's been a truce between men and elves, fragile, mind you, but it still holds."

Shaun released Sawyer's neck and smiled. As Sawyer leaned back, he blinked several times. He didn't see a reason for Shaun to lie, especially since he had admitted to losing a fight to Ariel.

"So just like that, the fighting was over?"

"Not quite," Shaun said, taking a long drink of ale. "There was some dissention among the elves. Some didn't want to stop fighting. One dark haired elf in particular wanted us all dead. She opposed Ariel. She had the bluest eyes I'd ever seen."

"I bet Ariel put her in her place, too."

"No. There was something else between them," Shaun said. "I'm not sure how that played out. However, I'm proud and happy to fight *with* Selra'thel again and not against them."

Shaun stood up and looked at the elves sitting a couple tables away. He raised his mug.

"To the elves of Selra'thel! Fierce warriors with the wisdom of scholars. Together we will win this war!"

The other knights all stood and raised their mugs, "To Selra'thel!" they said in unison.

Sawyer also stood and raised his mug too. As he drank his water, he wondered if they would all be here if Ariel had killed Shaun that day. *What a difference a single decision could make for everyone.*

Next, Trelane stood and raised his goblet to Shaun.

"To the brave Knights of Caladar. It is an honor to fight by your side."

The elves all stood and drank. Trelane and Shaun exchanged nods and the mood, as well as morale, lightened. At least, from the increase in laughter it seemed that way to Sawyer. Then something else occurred to Sawyer, he arched his back and surveyed the great hall.

"Hey, where are the dwarves?"

"Knowing King Baldon," Shaun said. "He has them down in the cellars ensuring Chalon's finest wines don't spoil."

A couple knights sitting nearby laughed.

"Dwarves," Shaun said, wiping his hands again. "Have a fondness for wines and spirits. They can, and probably will, drink all night."

Sawyer smiled.

"So, tomorrow morning we begin training," Shaun said. "I'm not sure what I can show you that Ariel hasn't, but there must've been a reason for her to ask me to train you. Personally, after seeing you in action, I don't think you require training."

"Thanks. I'd still like to learn from you, though."

"Aye," Shaun said smiling. "I look forward to it."

"I better go find my friends," Sawyer said. "Thanks for everything, Shaun."

"Sleep well, Sawyer."

Sawyer stood and left the great hall. The last time he saw Geoff and Ishara, they were with Geoff's father, Maelord. More than likely, they had rooms somewhere in the castle, probably the noble's quarters or something. After all, Geoff's Dad was a big shot in Chalon. He passed two castle guards as he made his way. They gave him little notice. He needed to find someone like an officer or noble who could direct him to Geoff and Ishara.

Sawyer took a few turns and he found himself alone in a maze of dim corridors. The flickering torches cast gloomy shadows across the carpeted corridors. He kept walking, looking for a major intersection or something that indicated where he was at the moment. After another minute, he heard the sounds of someone whispering and then he thought he heard a scuffle and someone cry out in pain before it was abruptly cut off. He picked up his pace. As he ran, he was pretty sure he recognized some of the tapestries on the walls from the last time he was there.

From around the next corner he heard a dull thud, like something had fallen to the ground. Pulling his sword, Sawyer dashed ahead and rounded the corner. A hooded figure in a dark gray cloak was bending over the body of a Knight of Caladar with a blood stained blade.

"Hey!" Sawyer shouted lifting his sword. "Get away from him and turn around!"

The cloaked figure froze.

"Now!" Sawyer ordered, getting into a defensive stance.

The stranger straightened, still gripping the blade, which Sawyer recognized as elven in make. The figure advanced, then suddenly spun the opposite direction and swept

Sawyer's feet out from under him with a booted foot. Sawyer landed hard on his backside and lost his grip on his sword. The cloaked assailant was upon him immediately. Sawyer barely had time to bring his hands up and catch the wrist of the figure, which was trying to drive the elven blade into his eye.

Even with both hands wrapped around the stranger's wrist, Sawyer was losing. The blade crept closer to his eye. The wrist he grappled with was slender, yet strong, incredibly strong. He tried to twist and move his lower body to gain leverage, but the figure on top of him prevented it. He tried to force the blade to either side, but he wasn't strong enough. Everything he tried was countered with ease. These were elven moves he'd learned from Ariel, but they weren't working.

The sound of heavy footsteps on the carpet and voices approaching made Sawyer's attacker stop and glance up. Sawyer was unable to see his attackers face under the dark hood, but the distraction was just what he needed. He pushed the elven blade away. It struck the carpet beside his head, narrowly missing his ear. Sawyer grabbed the hood and flipped it back, he saw an ear, a slightly pointed ear. The cloaked figure struck him on the chin, stunning him. Next, he was rocked by an elbow smash to his face and a punch in the nose. Sawyer fought to regain his senses. Looking up, he saw the cloaked figure hoovering over him. The hood had been replaced, preventing Sawyer from identifying the mysterious figure.

Then he heard shouts and yelling. Someone was calling for guards. The cloaked figure whirled and disappeared. Sawyer's vision blurred. He heard himself breathing heavy, like he was struggling to catch his breath as the light faded. A dim torch burning caught his attention. The voices were closer now. He saw movement over him. Various shapes moved back and forth and then all went dark.

# CHAPTER TWENTY-TWO
## SOMETHING ETERNAL

There was an aroma of fresh flowers and birds were chirping. Someone's hand brushed against her cheek. Jane opened her eyes, then shut them tightly. The sun was too bright and it hurt. She saw a collage of reds, yellows, and oranges behind her eyelids. She took a deep breath.

"Wake up, Jane."

It was a voice she'd heard before, but she couldn't connect it to a face. Distorted images swam through her mind, she saw men and elves being thrown high into the air. There was a battle. *He* was there. He had commanded her to do horrible things. There was a small blond boy. He was dead now, she was sure of it. She killed him. There was another, handsome and strong. His dark hair and eyes were fabulous. She loved his smile, the way his dimples shone on each side of his face…

"Sawyer! Geoff!"

Jane's eyes shot open and she sat up suddenly, reaching out. She blinked repeatedly, the world was a whirlwind of colors, shapes, and sounds. Someone grabbed her arms.

"Jane," Ariel said. "Look at me, all is well."

Jane stopped moving and turned toward the comforting voice beside her. The emerald green eyes and dark blonde hair reminded her of someone. The smile that made her feel at ease, she'd seen it before.

"Jane," Ariel repeated. "You are fine now. I am here. Do you remember what happened?"

"Ariel…?" Jane said. "Where am I? What's going on?"

"Easy," Ariel said, taking Jane's hands in hers. "You have endured what no one has endured and lived. You are truly remarkable, Jane. Welcome back to the light."

"Sawyer and Geoff," Jane said, alarmed. "Where are they? Are they okay?"

"They are fine, Jane. They are both fine and they are safe in Chalon at this moment."

"But I killed them. I saw it!"

"You did no such thing, Jane. They were injured, but they have recovered. You need to realize it wasn't you who attacked them or the troops during the battle. Now, take your time and breathe. Here, drink this."

Ariel handed Jane a small carved wooden cup with water. Jane drank all of it, gulping down the refreshing liquid.

"Easy, Jane," Ariel said. "Try to relax."

Jane wiped her mouth with her hand and gave the cup back to Ariel. She felt much better. A calming feeling settled on her. Jane glanced about.

"I remember this place," she said. "This is your grove, isn't it? We're in the Spirewood Forest."

"Yes," Ariel said, smiling. "That is right, Jane. Tell me, do you remember what happened to you at Troll Fang Pass?"

"Troll Fang…I'm not sure. I can try."

Jane looked past Ariel and concentrated.

"It was night time," Jane said. "I think there was a slight chill in the air. We won the battle, right? We saved the garrison?"

"That is right, Jane. We did."

"There was something else…no, wait. I'm not sure. You and I…we had a conversation, didn't we? We were both tired. We had tended the wounds of so many injured soldiers…I think you left. Wait, we were on the wall of the garrison. You left but I wanted to stay."

"Yes, Jane."

"The night was beautiful…I just wanted to stay a little longer and take it in. Oh, I wasn't alone!"

"I know, Jane."

Ariel held Jane's hand in hers. Jane's eyes again opened wide.

"It was him, Ariel! The Shadowlord. He kidnapped me off the wall! I tried to fight him but he was too strong. Ariel, he flew me to his castle in the mountains!"

"Yes, the Iron Citadel," Ariel said. "Did he harm you?"

"No…he seemed kind of normal," Jane said. "He wanted me to call him Zorn."

"Yes, that is his name."

"There were times…he was kind to me," Jane said. "He…I think he's sad, Ariel. Lonely and sad. Yes, that's it. He's sad. He feels trapped, I think. Just like I was…he's suffering."

"Do not feel sorry for him, Jane. He answers to Queen Lysis, the Scarlet Queen."

"Yes. He mentioned a queen who made him do awful things," Jane's hand went to her neck and she gasped. "He's a vampire, Ariel! He bit me!"

"Yes, Jane. He is a vampire lord and he planned to turn you into a dark druid."

"Ariel, I tried to escape. I tried several times."

Jane dissolved into tears as Ariel pulled her close and wrapped her arms around her. Jane sobbed into Ariel's leather tunic. Her tears were remorseful for all that she had put Ariel and the others through. Her ordeal was over, but she sorely regretted what she had done.

"I know, Jane," Ariel said quietly. "I would expect no less from you."

"I'm a horrible person," Jane sobbed.

"No. You are not," Ariel whispered. "Your aura shines again, Jane. You shine oh so bright. You are a miracle. Your very existence is a miracle. Just think of the multitude of events that have brought us to this moment. Your parents met. You were born. Your parents raised you the best way they knew, and they did a wonderful job. How lucky Alluria is that you were friends with Sawyer and Geoff. I cannot guess the odds of the three of you being together on just the night that brought you here. What you have done is amazing. *You* are amazing. You have taught me that there are some people worth fighting for, Jane."

Ariel shook her head in amazement.

"Humans," she said. "You have so much power inside you. Nothing is beyond you. Humans are capable of so much compassion, yet they can be horribly cruel. In a life as short as yours, it must be maddening to have the power to change the world around you for the better, but not do it."

"We don't see ourselves like that," Jane said, wiping her face.

"Of course not. But even humans must know that there is something eternal in all of us. Something that continues after our time here is done."

Jane nodded and held Ariel close for several more minutes. Ariel was right about everything, of course. Finally, Ariel tapped Jane on the shoulder and pulled away. Jane looked at Ariel, her eyes were moist, but she was smiling.

"You have a friend who came to be with you," Ariel said. "Look behind you."

Jane turned her head and looked. Her heart leapt and her mouth fell open. Lying behind them in the grass, was the most beautiful creature Jane had seen. Its white mane shone in the sunlight like a thousand diamonds. Its large, luminous eyes were looking directly at her. It swished its tail in the grass and nodded its head a few times. Jane thought she saw a smile on its face, too. There, in the grove, was a unicorn. The same unicorn she, Sawyer, and Geoff had saved from goblins. Jane lost her breath. It was beyond beautiful.

Jane spun around and hugged its neck. She felt the warmth of more tears stream down her face as she stroked the magnificent mane. She felt the unicorn rest its chin on her shoulder and pull her closer. Jane was all too happy to squeeze its neck and bury herself in its fragrant white fur.

"You came back to me," she marveled. "You came to help me."

"Indeed he did," Ariel said. "A unicorn can never resist goodness and innocence when a young lady is in distress. If you ever needed proof that your heart is good and pure, you have it now."

Jane exhaled and snuggled deeper into the unicorn's fur. She wished she could stay there forever. To her, it felt like she was hugging love and it was a tangible thing.

"He stayed with us all night, Jane," Ariel said. "A unicorn never forgets the hearts of those it holds dear."

"What's his name?"

"Unicorns do not have names," Ariel said. "But I think if you chose one for him, he would be honored."

"Galahad," Jane said immediately, lifting her moist face from the unicorn's chest. "I choose Galahad."

"Galahad?" Ariel asked.

"Yes," Jane said, scratching the tuft of hair hanging from its chin. "The best and purest of all knights."

The unicorn nuzzled Jane's chin, giving its approval of the new name.

"An appropriate name for the most wonderful and magical of creatures," Ariel said. "He is the first unicorn to be named so, and he is proud to have you name him. Galahad it is."

Jane kissed his nose and the unicorn responded with another playful swish of his tail. Jane and Ariel laughed. For the first time in as long as Jane could remember, she was safe. A warm, contented feeling fell over her as she sat in the grove with Ariel and Galahad. Ariel stood and went along the fruit trees and berry bushes, picking the most delicious looking edibles. As Jane watched, she noticed every time Ariel plucked something off a branch or vine, it regrew. It was a fantastic sight.

Ariel returned with an armload of fresh, healthy goodies for them to munch on while they sat in the grove.

"You must be hungry," Ariel said. "Eat, you need to regain your strength."

Jane picked up a few strawberries and as she was about to pop one in her mouth she saw that Ariel had a small, puffy bruise and cut on her upper lip.

"What happened?" Jane said, pointing. "How did you get a fat lip?"

Ariel looked at Jane, touched her bruised lip and it healed, the discoloration and cut melted away. Jane smiled.

"I knew you were going to do that," Jane said, taking a bite out of a large, red strawberry. Ariel winked at her and picked up a handful of blackberries.

"Did you get punched in battle or something?"

"Yes," Ariel said. "You could say that."

"Ariel," Jane said, putting down the rest of her berries. "What happened?"

Ariel exhaled and looked at Jane again.

"You are a most stubborn dark druid, Jane," Ariel said with a slight smile. "Or, at least you *were* a stubborn dark druid. You did not wish to participate in the ritual last evening."

"Whoa. What? You're saying *I* did that?"

"Not you," Ariel said quickly. "It was never you. In order to try and purge the darkness from within you, there is a cleansing ritual that must be performed."

Ariel pointed to the shimmering shallow pool before them.

"It was quite a struggle," Ariel said. "But we had to have our brave Jane back."

Jane swallowed. She couldn't believe what she was hearing. Images flashed in her mind. She *did* try to kill Ariel in the sacred pool last night. As a dark druid, she and Ariel had fought. Jane suddenly realized that Ariel had refused to let her go. She'd fought for *her* life.

"I'm so sorry."

"There is nothing for you to apologize for, Jane."

"You saved me, didn't you?" You saved me from a horrible fate," Jane said, looking down. "You risked your life for me. You've always done that, Ariel. You save lives. You're always doing noble and courageous things like that. It's what you do. Thank you."

There was a moment of silence before Ariel spoke. When she did, Jane heard her voice breaking as she tried to hold back tears.

"You think too much of me, Jane," Ariel said. She had turned her head so Jane only saw her back. "I am not what you think I am."

"Yes," Jane said. "You are. You're all that and more. Without you, we'd all be dead a long time ago."

"No, Jane," Ariel said. "I am short-sighted, selfish, and cruel. When I asked for your help to save Alluria, I...I did not stop for one moment to consider how you, Sawyer, and Geoff would be affected. All I cared about was Alluria, nothing else. My foolishness has cost the three of you your childhoods. I cannot undo the evil I have done to you, Jane. There is no spell that will repair the damage...please forgive me. You see...I have so many secrets..."

"Then tell me," Jane said. "I want to know all about you."

Ariel sniffled, but kept her face turned away from Jane. She swallowed and brushed her hair out of her eyes but twirled a long braid that ended with a blue-green feather.

"No secrets," Jane said, placing a hand on Ariel's. Ariel grasped Jane's hand.

"Very well," Ariel said as she turned to Jane and wiped a tear from her cheek. "You must know that I was different. Until I met you, Sawyer, and Geoff, I was arrogant, mean, and spiteful. I hated humans."

"Why?"

"Many reasons," Ariel said. "But when they killed my parents, I gathered other elves who felt the same as I did and we went to war against humans."

"So you led Selra'thel to war?"

"No," Ariel said. "Selra'thel had nothing to do with it. *I* started a war with humans. First, we tracked down the ones responsible. They were brigands disguised as guards from Chalon, nothing more. When we were done with them, we searched for more humans to slaughter."

Jane said nothing.

"I wanted them all dead, Jane," Ariel said. "Every human, young or old. It did not matter to me. As far as I was concerned, they should all pay for the deaths of my parents. I wanted to eradicate the human plague."

Ariel paused and exhaled loudly.

"Oh, how I wanted to kill them all. We slaughtered many, many humans and burned their villages."

Jane wrapped her arms around Ariel. Her body trembled, it matched the trembling in her voice.

"No one's perfect," Jane said.

Ariel smiled at Jane's words and touched her hand.

"No," Ariel said. "I suppose not."

Another minute went by then Ariel spoke.

"I have decided," she said. "I…I must send you and the others home. It is too dangerous for you here. You must return home and I will return to Selra'thel…or perhaps stay here in this grove. In time, this evil will pass."

Ariel wriggled free from Jane's hug and stood. She paced back and forth while she continued to speak.

"Perhaps the Scarlet Queen will leave my forest be and other forests. After all, what use is a forest to her? I can assume the shape of a fox or a bird. I can hide. She will never expect that."

"Ariel," Jane said as she stood and brushed a few blades of grass off her trousers. "I'm not going anywhere. Neither is Sawyer or Geoff. We're staying."

"You cannot." Ariel said, spinning around to face Jane. "This is not your war. You must return home and live your lives."

"It's our choice," Jane said. "We're here now and we've chosen to help you. We aren't going back."

"Jane," Ariel said as she walked to her and took both her hands in hers. "Do you not understand? I almost killed you last night." Ariel's eyes became moist again. "Your dark powers had grown so much and so fast that you were more powerful than me. You would've crushed Alluria for the Scarlet Queen. How could I let that happen? How could I live with myself if I had killed you?"

Jane looked into Ariel's eyes. That choice was tearing her apart inside.

"I am weary, Jane," Ariel said. "I am so weary. I cannot continue to fight and kill those I hold dear, no matter the cost. I will send you home."

"No. I said we're staying."

Ariel shook her head.

"Jane," she said, her voice breaking again. "Why?"

"Because it's the right thing to do," Jane replied stubbornly. "Friends help friends. It's what they do."

Ariel looked at Jane for a moment and then hugged her, "It is what friends do."

# CHAPTER TWENTY-THREE
## THE SILENT ORDER

Sawyer awoke with a start, he sat up in bed with his hands attempting to fend off an attack. Geoff was relieved he hadn't been seriously injured. When Sawyer was found, he was brought to their room. Ishara had raced ahead and closed the secret door between their rooms as a precaution. In the room with Sawyer, Geoff, and Ishara were Trelane, Commander Renfry, Shaun Hammerfel, and, to Geoff's disappointment, a surly Lionel. The physician had come and gone, simply stating Sawyer was in shock and needed rest.

"Easy now, Sawyer" Shaun said. "You're fine. You aren't hurt."

Sawyer looked around. When his eyes landed on Geoff and Ishara, they waved at him and Geoff gave him a thumbs up signal.

"What happened?" Sawyer said.

"We were hoping you could tell us, *Stormlord*," Lionel sneered, leaning against the wall. He wore a deep purple robe and a heavy, gem studded crown.

Geoff cut a quick glance at Lionel. He didn't like the mocking tone in his voice.

"Can you tell us who attacked you?" Shaun said, steadying Sawyer's shoulder. "Did you see who killed my knight?"

"I'm not sure," Sawyer said as he rubbed his forehead. "Everything happened so fast."

Lionel let out a long sigh, demonstrating his disapproval of Sawyer's answer.

"Do you remember anything about the attack?" Trelane said.

Shaun handed Sawyer a mug of water. Sawyer took a sip and closed his eyes.

"Any day now," Lionel said pointedly.

"It was an elf," Sawyer opened his eyes. "I pulled their hood back and saw their ear, it was pointed."

"As I suspected," Lionel said. "More elven treachery."

Geoff noticed Lionel was glaring at Trelane, daring him to deny what Sawyer had said.

"Sawyer, is there anything else you can tell us?" Shaun said. "Anything at all."

"Not much," Sawyer said. "The killer moved so fast."

"Have you seen this before?" Shaun said, holding the blade the assassin used in their attack. Sawyer shook his head.

"No, not before tonight."

"I have seen it," Ishara spoke up. "It is an elven assassination blade. Only a small number are known to exist."

And how is it *you* know of this weapon, girl?" Lionel demanded.

Geoff frowned. He wished Ishara hadn't revealed what she knew about the weapon. He had no desire to see her hauled off to the dungeons again.

"I am an elf," she said.

"Think, Sawyer," Shaun said. "What else do you remember?"

"They reminded me of…"

"Of who, boy?" Lionel snapped.

"Lady Seqwil," Sawyer said. "The killer moved like she did when she fought Ariel."

"Oh this is nonsense," Lionel said, stepping away from the wall. "Lady Seqwil Ferncliff is dead. You're confused. You hit your head and need time to recover."

He turned to Trelane and pointed a finger at him.

"I expect all elves to leave Chalon by tomorrow evening. This is my castle and I won't have elven assassins roaming the halls."

Lionel turned to leave but he stopped and pointed a finger at Ishara.

"That goes for you too," he said. "Especially you."

Lionel left the room, followed closely by four guards who had been waiting in the corridor.

"Guys, I'm not lying and I'm not confused," Sawyer said, looking about the room. "I had the drop on the killer but they moved so fast. If someone hadn't come along when they did…"

"I believe you," Shaun said. "I owe you my gratitude for trying to save the life of one of my knights."

Shaun stood and looked at Trelane.

"So," Shaun said, holding his arms out at his sides. "What do we do now?"

Trelane shook his head and crossed his arms over his chest.

"Tell me," Trelane said scanning the room. "Did any of you *see* Lady Seqwil's body?"

Every one shook their head.

"We saw her fall from the gryphon's tower," Geoff said. "The aerie, I think it's called."

"She was a sorceress," Ishara added. "No one knew that until she fought Ariel. I think she saw a way to evade capture and took it."

"This blade that belongs to elven assassins," Shaun said, holding it up. "It's perfectly balanced. There can't be many elven smiths capable of forging such a weapon."

"There are not," Trelane said. "Only through decades of rigorous training does one earn that blade and other weapons."

"Where do they train?" Commander Renfry said. "Someone must know something about them."

"They are a secretive group," Ishara said. "Only spoken of in hushed tones in Selra'thel. No one knows who they are or where they train."

"They are called the Silent Order," Trelane said. His voice had lowered and his demeanor became grim. "And they are rumored to be everywhere."

"So why would this killer target one of your knights, Shaun? Why not kill me? Or King Lionel?" Renfry asked.

"I don't know," Shaun said. "Sir Yarric was a good man, a good knight."

"I know," Trelane said. All eyes fell on him. "Whoever killed Sir Yarric wanted to create dissention and divide us. Lionel has never trusted elves. This is just the excuse he would need to send us away."

"Just like before," Geoff said. "Lady Seqwil did this last time we were here. She assassinated a diplomat and we got blamed."

Geoff looked at Ishara.

"That's why she got thrown into the dungeons."

"So what else do we know about the Silent Order?" Renfry asked. "How many of their agents are here? Do they work alone?"

"No one knows," Trelane said. "I have heard it said they're also masters of disguise, so be alert, all of you."

"What will you do now?" Renfry asked Trelane.

"In the morning we will leave," Trelane said. "What other choice do we have?"

"Splitting our forces," Renfry said bitterly. "And with the Scarlet Queen drawing closer."

"We will not go far," Trelane said. "But we cannot defeat her unassisted, either."

"The Knights of Caladar will fight with you," Shaun said. "Lionel has lost his mind. He drinks too much. He was an average leader at best. But now, he would watch while Chalon is razed to the ground."

"Agreed," Trelane said. "I must see to my men. We have preparations to make. At least they will have one night of sleep before we are thrown out of Chalon."

Trelane turned to Geoff, Ishara, and Sawyer.

"You should keep your doors locked and barred this night," he said. "Be safe."

"And you," Renfry said. "I must also see to my men. Good night."

Shaun stood and scratched his chin as Trelane and Renfry left the room. He paused and looked at the three of them.

"I can offer you guards, if you wish," he said.

"Thanks, but we'll be okay," Sawyer said. "You should get some rest, too."

"Very well," Shaun said. He turned to leave the room but before he closed the door behind him he stopped and looked at Sawyer. "I'll see you in the morning? Training begins at sunrise."

"That early?" Sawyer groaned.

Shaun smiled and closed the door.

Geoff went to the door and opened it a little to make sure no one was in the corridor. Satisfied they were alone, he closed the door and turned to Sawyer.

"We were coming to find you," Geoff said. "We heard alarms and shouting. Do you really think it was Lady Seqwil that attacked you?"

"Dunno," Sawyer said. "But it was definitely an elf, I saw the pointed ear when I pulled their hood back. I can't even say if it was a male or female."

"If it was her, how did she survive that fall?" Geoff asked. "It must've been a few hundred feet at least."

"Have you forgotten she was also a sorceress?" Ishara said. "I suspect her magic saved her."

"Yeah," Geoff said. "Guys, if she is alive and that was her tonight, she tried to kill Sawyer. That means she's probably going to try to kill all of us, right?"

"So we gotta hunker down," Sawyer said. "I don't know, barricade the doors or something. Make a stand."

"If she wants in," Ishara said. "There is not much we can do to stop her."

Geoff walked to the door and bolted it. As he turned around, a thought occurred to him.

"How about this," he said. "What if we set a trap for her if she breaks in?"

Sawyer and Ishara looked at him like he was crazy.

"I know that sounds nuts," Geoff said. "But she's probably going to come after us regardless, right? So let's be waiting for her."

"And do what?" Sawyer said. "When she shows up, what do we do?"

"I don't know," Geoff said. "Knock her out, capture her, something."

Ishara paced the room for a minute, looking at her feet as she strode and thought.

"Geoff, she went toe to toe with Ariel, remember?" Sawyer said. "What can we do to stop her, much less capture her?"

Geoff shrugged, "It was just an idea."

"One not without merit," Ishara said. She looked at Geoff. "As you said, she will be coming for us. We must defend ourselves and perhaps if we act in concert, we can defeat her."

Sawyer stood up and began pacing, his hands clasped behind his head. He exhaled and closed his eyes.

"Look, it's a good idea," he said. "But unless we have something we *know* will work..." Sawyer shook his head. "Then we're toast."

"Toast?" Ishara inquired.

"Nevermind," Geoff said. "Maybe I can shape my shield spell around her and keep her here until help arrives."

Ishara narrowed her eyes and looked at him, suspicious of the suggestion. Sawyer also looked at him. He could see the doubt in their eyes.

"C'mon," Geoff said. "My shield kept Jane from killing us, right?" Geoff pointed at Sawyer, "And it kept us from being shot full of arrows at Troll Fang Pass. I think it'll work, guys."

No one said anything.

"Ariel said Jane was as powerful as she was when she was the dark druid," Geoff said. "Who is more powerful than Ariel? No one. I can do this."

Geoff looked at Ishara, "Trust me."

Ishara took a step toward Geoff, "I trust you."

Sawyer plopped down on one of the beds and slapped his hands on his knees.

"Okay, Geoff," he said. "You're on. But I think we need a backup plan in case things go sideways." He looked at Ishara. "I can't hang with Lady Seqwil in a fight. She's out of my league. Got any ideas?"

# Chapter Twenty-Four

## Ambush

Jane and Ariel spent the rest of the morning in the grove. They ate their fill of fruits and berries and Ariel even had some salted fish, which tasted better than Jane thought it would. Galahad stayed as well, always following Jane as she walked around the grove, seeking more kisses and snuggles. Jane even engaged Ariel in a food fight, throwing a never ending supply of berries at her. Ariel laughed and returned fire. Galahad pranced and stamped his feet while he tried to intercept the juicy missiles by catching them in his mouth. Afterwards, Galahad gave Jane an affectionate nuzzle and trotted back into the forest.

"Where is he going?"

"He is a willful creature of the woodlands," Ariel said. "Who can say? I suppose we were fortunate to have him stay with us for as long as we did."

"Oh, I'm going to miss him."

"I am sure he feels the same as you, Jane."

Jane and Ariel sat in the grass to rest and wipe away berry juice, which wasn't easy.

"You have some on your forehead," Jane said, smirking.

Ariel brushed her forehead with her fingers and looked at the red juice. She placed her fingers in her mouth and narrowed her eyes at Jane.

"You've got to admit," Jane said, laughing. "That was a good shot."

"It was," Ariel said. "Remind me to return the favor later."

"No way," Jane said as she laid back in the grass. "You're too accurate. I hope you forget."

Ariel laid back in the grass too. Jane watched as she closed her eyes. It seemed like a tremendous weight had been lifted from Ariel, she looked happy. A smile slowly crept across Ariel's face.

"Jane," she said, keeping her eyes closed. "What are you doing?"

"Nothing," Jane said with a snicker.

Ariel opened a single eye and looked at her.

"Nothing?"

"Nope. Not a thing," Jane said in her sweetest, most innocent voice.

Ariel closed her eyes and stretched her arms and legs in the sunlight. Her firm, golden limbs reminded Jane of a fitness model.

"Ariel," Jane said. "When we get back to the others…"

Ariel rolled onto her side and looked at Jane. "What is it?"

Jane thought for a moment, there had to be a good way of phrasing this, something had been troubling her and she wasn't sure she'd be able to fully say what she was thinking.

"Sawyer and Geoff," Jane said. "Do you think…I tried to kill them…do you think they'll…hate me?"

"Oh Jane. Of course not," Ariel said. "They will be so happy to see you again. I am quite sure they miss you."

"But...I tried..."

"But you did not," Ariel said. "You will be warmly welcomed by everyone. Do not think on such matters because they do you no good."

"When do we go back to the others?" Jane said. There was a new hope and anticipation in her now. She had a desire to wrap her arms around Sawyer. She planned to kiss him and apologize until he forgave her.

"I thought we might spend some time here together before we returned," Ariel said. "You have been through so much, Jane. A nice rest in a safe place might be helpful?"

"Mmmmmmmm," Jane purred as she stretched. "Sure, why not? You talked me into it."

Ariel smiled and gave Jane a nudge with her elbow.

"It was easy," she said. "Rest, Jane. Regain your strength and when you are ready, we will return to our friends."

Jane and Ariel lay in the warm sunlight, surrounded by all sorts of woodsy smells and aromas.

"If only we were on a beach on a tropical island," Jane said with a laugh. "I'm sure my strength would return much faster."

"You are the strongest person I have ever met, Jane."

Jane laughed so hard she covered her mouth and nose with both hands. Ariel looked at her.

"I did not expect that response," Ariel said.

"I was going to say the same thing about you," Jane said with a giggle. "You're my inspiration."

They lay in the sun, laughing together for a while longer, then Ariel sat up, crossed her legs, and faced Jane.

"Very well," Ariel said, motioning for Jane to sit up too. "Then let us be strong and inspiring together."

Jane sat up and Ariel took her hands in hers. Ariel studied Jane for a minute. Jane began to worry if something was wrong with her hair, or perhaps she had a berry smudge on her face.

"What?" Jane said.

"Among druids," Ariel said. "There is a link, a bonding, if you will. Would you like to join us, Jane?"

"Sure," Jane said. "How's it work? What will happen?"

"You will be able to know the thoughts of every animal, wild or domesticated, you will also be able to converse with the trees and know their feelings. You will know other druids when you see them. You will be one with nature and a daughter of Alluria."

"That sounds wonderful," Jane smiled.

"Close your eyes," Ariel said. "Clear your mind and repeat my words."

Jane closed her eyes and took a deep breath. In her mind, she saw Ariel sitting in front of her. There was a golden-white shimmer surrounding her.

"*Thel'aran mar nu bel'ara eghrol sylvae.*"

As Jane repeated the strange words, a new feeling of contentment arose in her. It was more than that, though, a feeling of happiness. A sense of belonging.

"Open your eyes, Jane."

Jane did so and she was surprised to see Ariel was still shrouded in the golden-white glow. Jane blinked to try and focus her sight.

"You are not hallucinating, Jane," Ariel said, flashing a bright smile. "You see my aura. Unless you concentrate on seeing it, it will fade. Give it time."

"Wow, why am I tingling all over?"

"It is the bond," Ariel said. "I feel it too."

Jane heard something and turned her head. There was a squirrel in the brush nearby, munching on a fragment of an apple. No, she *felt* the furry little mammal. Its tiny heart rapidly beating as it chewed a mouthful of fruit. It looked at Jane, but it wasn't afraid.

"Do you feel like this all the time?" Jane said. "This is incredible!"

"Most of the time, yes," Ariel said.

"It feels...wonderful!" Jane laughed and stretched her arms out wide. "The forest, I feel it. There's so much life here."

Ariel took Jane's hands in hers again.

"You are now a true child of Alluria," Ariel said, squeezing her hands. "We are sisters, Jane. Damsels of the forest, and protectors of the woodlands."

Jane looked at Ariel. Joy and happiness reflected in her green eyes. Jane's initiation into this new, exhilarating world made her senses tingle with heightened levels.

*Jane, can you hear me?*

"Yes, I can hear you," Jane said, what a strange question. She was sitting in front of Ariel, how could she not hear her?

*Jane .*

Suddenly, Jane realized Ariel was looking at her and speaking with her, but her lips weren't moving. How could she hear Ariel?"

"What's going on?" Jane said.

*This is part of the bonding, Jane. You and I can speak with each other using our thoughts now.*

"Wait, how can you do that? It's a druid thing, right?"

*Yes, it is a druid thing.*

"So you can read minds? Does that mean I can read minds too?"

*It is not mindreading, Jane. It is a deeper form of communication. We can speak like this even if we're surrounded by other people, no matter the distance.*

"Wow," Jane said.

*Try it, Jane. Concentrate on me and think what you want me to hear.*

Jane focused on Ariel. She was calm, yet excited and encouraged by Jane's reaction to the bonding. Jane closed her eyes and thought of something to say to Ariel.

*Ariel, can you hear me?*

*Yes, I can hear you.*

"Oh my gosh!" Jane's mouth dropped. "I did it!"

*You did, Jane. I heard you perfectly. However, you do not have to close your eyes.*

"This is awesome," Jane said. "Let me try again."

This time she didn't close her eyes.

*Ariel? Are you there?*

*Of course I am.*

*Can others hear us, too?*

*No, only druids can communicate like this. It is, as you say, a druid thing. It is called Druidspeak.*

They spent the rest of the afternoon communicating with their thoughts. Jane discovered other abilities, too. Trees and plants would move for her. They would bend their limbs and branches out of her way. She seemed to have an instinctive understanding for plants and herbs and a feeling of being one with the forest creatures was a delight. Jane kept practicing her Druidspeak. She left the sacred grove and continued their mental conversation. It was just as Ariel said, distance didn't matter.

While Jane roamed the forest, a young fawn walked up to her and greeted her with a lick of her hand and a soft nuzzle. Jane held her hand up, extending her index finger, and a blue jay landed on it. What an intoxicating sensation! She was no longer feared by animals. The birds and animals knew who she was and they sensed she meant them no harm.

Ariel joined her in the forest. Birds and squirrels took turns hopping from her shoulder to Ariel's and then back to hers again.

"They trust you, Jane," Ariel said, using her outer voice. "I think—Jane! Get down!"

As Jane dove to the grass, she heard a whistling sound over her head, and then a loud *thwack*. Ariel screamed in pain. Jane was stunned. She'd never heard such a sound from Ariel. Jane jumped to her feet and stared in horror. Ariel had been pinned to a tree by a spear. It had penetrated Ariel's shoulder, leaving the spear embedded in the tree.

"Jane!" Ariel said as she struggled with the spear. "Get back to the grove, now!"

Jane whirled and saw a figure charging toward them through the trees. She felt like prey watching a predator close in. Their attacker moved with unbelievable speed. She wore a suit of armor that reminded Jane of Sawyer's armor. From under her helm, a long mane of thick black hair flowed and her face was a twisted snarl. The black haired warrior's teeth were bared, like an animal's. She held a sword in one hand, a slim dagger in the other. But what chilled Jane was her eyes. They were a vivid blue, as hard as steel, and they were focused on her.

Jane turned back to Ariel and gripped the spear. She'd seen it before, she remembered the ornate metal shaft and the intricate etchings on the blade.

"Jane, you must get back to the grove now," Ariel said, grimacing in pain. "You will be safe there."

"Not without you," Jane said as she pulled the weapon free.

Ariel fell to the ground, her shoulder was a flooded with crimson, her tunic soaked. Taking a stand in front of Ariel, Jane faced the rushing warrior, spear at the ready.

*Jane. The trees. They will give us time.*

Ariel's thoughts sounded like a drum in her head. Jane dropped the spear and held her fists up for a second. Then, she brought her arms together in a smashing motion. The forest obeyed and every tree or shrub launched itself in the way of the dark-haired warrior. Trees wrapped their branches around her while the smaller plants attempted to pin her arms and legs or trip her. Initially, their attacker was impeded, but she slashed at the branches and shrubs with blinding accuracy, freeing herself in seconds. However, she was slowed by the continuous attempts of the trees as they moved to block her.

"Jane," Ariel said, still on the ground. "We must get to the grove. She cannot enter there."

Helping Ariel to her feet, Jane half-carried, half-pulled her toward the sacred grove. Ariel's wound was dreadful and left a trail of blood.

"Come on, Ariel," Jane said as they entered the grove. "We have to stop your bleeding."

Every bit of flora closed together, producing a thick, impenetrable dome of greenery all around them.

"Hurry, Jane," Ariel said pointing at the sacks containing their stores of food. "We need to leave."

"We're safe now, right?" Jane said in a near panic. She lowered Ariel to her knees and scooped up their sacks of food. "Like you said, she can't come in here. And who *is* that?"

Ariel closed her eyes and placed a hand over her shoulder. Jane stopped and watched. Ariel's wound slowly closed and she seemed to have regained most of her golden color. From outside their safe zone, Jane heard a primal, infuriated roar, like a raging animal. Then the distinct sound of chopping and hacking reached her ears.

"Her name is Talia Ravenmane, the Spearslayer," Ariel breathed. "And no one is safe from her."

"Ariel, what're we going do?" Jane said. "She's not giving up."

# CHAPTER TWENTY-FIVE
## VISITORS IN THE NIGHT

Moon light permeated through the thin curtains from the balcony, casting a pale glow across the floor and most of the room. Outside, several owls could be heard hooting away in the distance. The castle and everyone in it seemed to be asleep. The door to the room had been bolted and a few chairs propped against it for good measure. Two figures slumbered beneath the covers of each bed, oblivious to the hooded shadow that drifted onto the balcony.

It crouched. For several minutes the figure remained absolutely still. Then, like a wisp of smoke, it stood and made a gesture with its hand. The bolt to the balcony doors silently slid open and one of the doors popped ajar. The figure carefully opened the door wide enough for it to slip through. Once inside, it crouched again and scanned the room. Its gaze fell on the two beds and the lumps beneath the covers.

It watched. The figure slowly rose to its feet and looked around the room again. It took a step toward the bed with the smaller occupant, its hands disappeared inside the dark gray cloak. The intruder moved with surety. It withdrew a curved elven blade from beneath its cloak and prepared to strike a fatal blow.

At that moment, the secret door sprang open and Ishara stepped through, bow drawn and arrow nocked. In one fluid motion, the hooded figure spun and launched the elven weapon at her. Ishara ducked a split second before the blade whirled over her head and embedded itself in the wall behind her. Ishara loosed her arrow as she shouted "Now!"

The cloaked figure reacted instantly and caught the arrow in its hand, the tip of the arrow mere inches from penetrating the face under the hood.

The two figures pretending to sleep threw the covers off and jumped to their feet. Sawyer assumed a defensive position while Geoff held both hands up, like he was making ready to catch a ball. A golden, translucent sphere encompassed the hooded intruder.

"We got her!" Sawyer shouted.

Ishara had nocked another arrow and kept her eyes on the dark figure within the sphere. She moved closer to the others. Dropping the arrow, their prisoner watched her.

"Geoff," Ishara said. "You must maintain your concentration at all costs. The assassin must not escape."

Geoff only nodded. He was determined to do just that.

Sawyer began pulling the chairs away from the door as fast as possible.

"Yeah, we know who you are, *Sequil*," he said, looking over his shoulder as he worked.

The hooded figure stood still, facing them. Its face still hidden. Ishara was careful to keep some distance from Geoff. Sawyer unbarred the door and opened it. Sticking his head out into the corridor, he shouted, "Hey! We did it! She's trapped."

The door across the hall opened and out walked Trelane and Maelord. As soon as they entered the room, the cloaked figure clapped its hands together. A blinding flash of light exploded from its hands. Everyone had to avert their eyes, even Geoff. As soon as he did, he lost his concentration and the glowing prison evaporated.

Quick as thought, another shimmering shield appeared just in front of Geoff and Ishara. Thrown up by Maelord, it seemed thicker and more opaque than Geoff's. The blinding light faded in a few seconds. When everyone regain their sight, the figure was gone.

"No way!" Sawyer said. "We had her."

"Everyone stay put," Maelord said, stepping forward and holding them back with his hand. He stepped to the shield spell he had thrown up. It stretched across the room from wall to wall. He pointed toward the balcony and the shield began to slide in that direction. As soon as it passed the secret door, Trelane went into Ishara's room, followed by Ishara then Geoff and Sawyer.

"Geoff," Maelord said. "Careful. Stay in the doorway where I can see you, son."

Geoff did as his father said, keeping his hands at the ready to cast another spherical prison if the assassin had managed to escape into Ishara's room. Trelane and Ishara scoured the room carefully, their elven vision found no one in hiding.

"We had her," Sawyer repeated, tossing the Stormblade on the bed. "How could she get away?"

"I never saw the assassin's face," Maelord said, releasing his shield spell. "We can't be sure its Lady Seqwil Ferncliff."

"We can," Ishara said, pulling the elven dagger from the

wall the assassin had thrown at her. She looked at the etchings on the blade and handed it to Trelane. He looked at it for a second and held it up.

"This weapon carries the markings of Lady Seqwil's family crest."

The others crowded around and he pointed the house symbol out to them.

"So, it *is* Lady Seqwil after all," Maelord said, rubbing his beard as he closed and locked the doors leading to the balcony. "Lionel had said he sent her body back to Selra'thel."

A deafening horn sounded throughout the castle followed by shouts, screams, and the ringing clang of weapons.

"An alarm. The castle is under attack," Maelord said. He pointed at Geoff. "You three better stay here. An assassin or assassins in the castle this night is no coincidence."

"Dad, we can help," Geoff protested. "Seriously."

Maelord leaned closer to Geoff, "Duly noted. But until we know what we're up against, I want the three of you to stay here. Understood?"

"Okay," Geoff said.

Maelord and Trelane hurried out the room. Before he closed and locked the door again, Maelord looked at Geoff, "Your time is coming, son. Don't rush into danger. There's plenty to go around."

"Be careful," Geoff blurted out.

The door closed with another *click* a second later.

"Don't rush into danger?" Sawyer said with a laugh. "What's he talking about? Danger follows us like our own shadows."

"So, we will not rush into danger," Ishara said, producing her small leather pouch of tools and handing it to Geoff.

"But he did not say we are forbidden to sneak up on it. Your turn."

Geoff took the pouch as Ishara nodded toward the door. He had watched her every move and asked many questions. He was pretty sure he could duplicate her feat.

"What's that?" Sawyer asked. "What're you gonna do?"

"We're getting out of here," Geoff said. "Unless you want to wait for Lady Seqwil to come back?"

"No way," Sawyer hopped off the bed and looked back at the doors leading to the balcony. "Get us outta here."

Geoff knelt on one knee and pulled out the same long, thin instruments Ishara had used. Geoff thought they looked like a pick or cleaning tool a dentist would have. He glanced over his shoulder. Sawyer, fascinated, was watching him while Ishara, arrow nocked, covered the balcony. Turning his attention back to the lock, Geoff slowly maneuvered his tools and lifted the locking mechanism. *Click*.

"Whoa! Geoff, that was cool," Sawyer said with a wide-eyed look of surprise on his face. "You gotta show me how to do that."

"You are too strong," Ishara said. "You would break the tools in the lock. This requires a delicate touch."

Ishara went to the door and opened it enough so she could peek out into the corridor. Geoff replaced her tools and closed the pouch.

"Here," he said holding the pouch out to Ishara. "It wasn't as hard as I thought it would be."

"Keep it," Ishara said with a smile. "You earned it. A good sneak thief needs a good set of tools."

She opened the door and they emerged into the hall. The torches lining the walls burned and crackled, generating small streams of sooty, black smoke. The commotion seemed to be coming from the direction of the great hall and the king's chambers.

"Sounds like one hell of a fight," Sawyer said.

"Be aware," Ishara said. "A distraction like this is exactly what Lady Seqwil would use to her advantage."

Ishara took lead, followed by Sawyer, sword in hand, then Geoff, who was looking behind them as much as in front. They crept around corners and down long corridors, keeping to one side as they went. The sounds of fighting raged on, but they were closer now, much closer. Ishara held her bow higher, ready to fire in an instant. They turned down a hallway that Geoff recognized from the tapestries on the walls. It was in the noble's section of the castle.

The far end of the hall ended in a 'T' intersection. Normally, there would be at least four guards posted along this hall, but this time it was empty. The recessed, iron-bound wooden doors to each room seemed shrouded in shadows this time of night. Any number of assassins could lurk inside them.

Suddenly, two castle guards appeared from around one of the corners at the far end, slashing and parrying against an enemy or enemies still hidden around the corner. Ishara stopped and aimed. Sawyer stepped around her.

"Do not stand in front of me," she whispered.

Sawyer looked at her and moved to the other side of the hall. Suddenly a heavy hand landed on Geoff's shoulder, causing him to jump and recoil. He turned around as did Ishara and Sawyer. It was Trelane. His armor was soaked with blood, but he appeared to be unharmed.

"What are you doing here?" Trelane said.

Before any of them could answer the two castle guards at the end of the hall fell and their killers rounded the corner. They were dressed in black plate mail armor with red highlights and markings. The visors of their helms were angled and dreadful. At least eight more invaders appeared in the hall.

"Go!" Trelane ordered. "Go now!"

Ishara loosed an arrow, dropping the first one with a shot through the slit in his visor. She nocked another arrow but Trelane touched her arm.

"You, as well," he said. "I will take care of this."

"C'mon Ishara," Geoff said, grabbing her hand and pulling her away. "Let's get outta here!"

They turned to run back the way they'd come, but before Geoff and Sawyer rounded the corner, he saw more armored attackers had appeared. Trelane rushed to meet them in battle. Recalling the trail of bodies he'd left behind him on the battlefield, Geoff was pretty sure Trelane would be fine.

They dashed through the halls, turning left then right, then running down a circular flight of stone carved stairs. After a few more twists and turns, Geoff was both lost and breathless. *What a confusing maze of halls, who'd designed this place?* They turned a last corner and stopped. Standing at the other end of the hall was a living mountain. Geoff had seen him before. He had an ugly scar running the length of the left side of his disfigured face. Black, stringy patches of hair dotted his head, which sported several old wounds.

He was massive, standing nearly seven feet tall and at least half that around the middle. He wore a leather tunic and breeches, which had been mended many times. His arms were the size of small trees and his belly was big enough to hold Geoff, if the giant ever decided to make a meal out of him. When they were last in Chalon, King Lionel had plotted to have this massive warrior take the Stormblade from Sawyer by rite of combat.

"That's…" Geoff began.

"Cruelon," Sawyer said. His voice filled with awe and his mouth dropped open as he looked at the man-behemoth. "Oh no…"

A wicked grin crept across Cruelon's scarred face and he laughed hoarsely.

"Stormlord," Cruelon said, his deep, mocking laughter became louder.

He reached behind him and unslung a huge double-bladed battle axe that was as tall as Geoff. Cruelon stepped forward, Geoff thought he felt the stone floor vibrating under his feet. Sawyer raised his sword and Ishara took aim.

"Sawyer, I can—" Ishara started to say, but Sawyer cut her off.

"No, let me handle this," Sawyer said, taking a quick, deep breath. "It's me he wants. This is my fight."

Sawyer assumed a defensive stance and raised the Stormblade, ready to meet Cruelon. The wicked grin and hateful stare from his one good eye made Geoff freeze. If Sawyer lost, what would he and Ishara do? Suddenly, Cruelon stopped. The evil smile on his face changed. His eyes widened and he seemed confused. He stood in place for a few seconds, then he fell forward, his face striking the stone floor and a loud *thud*. The pommel of a dagger protruded from the base of his enormous skull, but that wasn't what drew their attention. A familiar figure wearing a dark gray cloak stood where Cruelon died.

# CHAPTER TWENTY-SIX
## FAMILIAR FACES

"You did well, Jane," Ariel said as she faced the wall of vegetation that stood between them and the spear wielding warrior. She held her hand up and closed her eyes. Then she drew a symbol in the air with her finger. Jane recognized it as one of the symbols of power that was carved into the stones surrounding the small pool. The intricate symbol floated in the air before Ariel. Small green and gold flames engulfed it and then Ariel clapped her hands.

A rush of wind shot forth from Ariel's hands and the ghostly rune exploded into a cloud of sparkling dust, its flecks falling onto the trees, bushes, and vines surrounding the grove. As the tiny flecks settled, they faded into the greenery, which grew thicker.

The warrior outside continued her venomous assault, but judging from her increasing fury, to no avail.

"What was that?" Jane said curiously. "What did that spell do?"

Ariel turned to Jane and motioned all around them with her hand.

"The rune's magic created a protective barrier around

us," Ariel said. "In time, Talia would have hacked her way through and tried to enter our grove. Now, she cannot, no matter how much time she spends. We are safe."

"Who is she, Ariel?" Jane said. "I've seen her before…at the Iron Citadel."

"Oh?" Ariel said. "Now that is interesting. Tell me what you saw."

Ariel motioned for Jane to join her as they ascended the carved steps in the grove again.

"I remember her spear," Jane said. "And her eyes. They were icy blue and when she looked at me it was like a hatred or something evil burning behind them. She met with Zorn, I think…yes, I'm sure she did."

"Do you remember the purpose of their meeting?"

"No. No, wait, I *do* remember!" Jane touched Ariel's arm. "Zorn wanted her to lead his armies, but she refused. She didn't care for him at all. Then he asked her to do something else. Ariel, he wanted us killed! That's when I tried to escape, but Zorn found me."

Ariel studied Jane for a moment, then turned to a bit of overgrowth and waved her hand. The shrubs and vines fell away, revealing an oval archway similar to the one in Geoff's house. It was covered with ornate carvings of vines and woodland creatures and large enough for a full-grown man to step through.

Ariel looked at Jane. "Talia Ravenmane is the most skilled of all warriors," Ariel said. "The name 'Spearslayer' is a name she earned through years of fighting in the arenas to the west. She is a master of all weapons and fighting techniques. Talia has never been defeated in combat. It seems our problems have grown."

"But she's an elf," Jane said. "Why would she want to kill you?"

"What you saw burning behind her eyes was indeed hatred. Hatred and a desire for vengeance."

"Vengeance?"

"Yes," Ariel said. "I had always mistreated her and I was the one who had her banished from Selra'thel."

"Banished? Why? What did she do?"

"She did not want to stop slaughtering humans. Her parents were killed in the same attack as mine. She never forgave me when I decided to halt the carnage and return to Selra'thel. But I still believe I was right."

"That's it? She was banished for that?"

"No. That was not enough to have her banished. She would have obeyed King Andurys of Selra'thel and stopped the killing."

Jane picked up their sacks of food and handed one to Ariel.

"So then why was she banished?"

"Because of me. I lied to the king," Ariel said evenly. "I convinced the king that she was a threat to him. I said if he commanded her to stop killing innocent humans, then she would seek to kill him as well."

"You lied? To the king?"

"I did. We were rivals growing up. We never liked each other. You see, in elven society, being a druid is considered the highest and most desirable of callings. Such is not the case for warriors. I was lavished upon while Talia was forsaken. There were times when she tried to be my friend, but I behaved appallingly. I was prideful and arrogant. I ridiculed her, belittled her. I was—"

"A bully," Jane said flatly. "You were a bully. You made her feel miserable because somehow it made *you* feel better."

"A bully," Ariel said. "Yes, you are right. I was different then, but that is no excuse for the way I acted."

Jane stood there looking at Ariel, dumbfounded. Her heart ached, she had been let down. Ariel looked down and then met Jane's bewildered gaze.

"I am not proud of my younger self. If I could change what I did so many years ago, I would."

She caressed Jane's cheek and sighed.

"I am sorry to be a disappointment to you, Jane. I never want to cause you pain. If you wish to return home, I will send you there now. When I find Sawyer and Geoff, I will do the same for them."

Jane shook her head.

"No," Jane said. "I may be a little disappointed, but I know you're not like that now. Everyone makes mistakes, right?"

Ariel looked at Jane for a moment.

"Such wisdom from one so young," Ariel said. "You truly are a remarkable young lady, Jane."

The warrior outside the barrier screamed again, actually, this time Jane thought it sounded more like a roar. The indignant roar of a predator that had been denied its meal. Jane pointed at the wizard's arch.

"Where to?"

"I think we should travel to a location not far from Chalon," Ariel said. "We can walk the rest of the way."

"Why not go directly to Chalon?"

"After our last visit," Ariel said. "Would you not agree that perhaps we should be a little more cautious?"

"Yeah. Good point."

Ariel held up a hand and from within the portal a swirl of gray and white mists appeared. A few moments later she nodded to Jane.

"No key?" Jane said. "It must be another druid thing."

"It is," Ariel said raising an eyebrow. "A *High* Druid thing."

Jane stepped into the portal followed by Ariel, their shapes vanishing into the mists. Seconds later, Jane found herself standing on a hillside near a patch of woods overlooking a wide valley. In the far distance, at least several leagues to the west, she saw the walled city of Chalon. Ariel appeared beside her.

"Looks like it's still there," Jane said. "It's beautiful from this distance."

"We should camp there for the night," Ariel said pointing to the copse of woods. "Tomorrow we begin our journey to Chalon."

They walked down to the small, cozy wooded area. The sun was beginning to descend when they found a suitable spot to set up camp.

Jane was unable to get Talia out of her mind. Her icy blue burning eyes, the way she moved, the spear, she threw it so accurately from such a long distance. Had Ariel not warned her, Jane would've been killed.

"Thanks for saving my life again," Jane said looking up at Ariel. I would've been dead if not for you."

Ariel bowed her head slightly. "You are welcome, Jane. However, you saved my life too. So shall we say we are even?"

"Sounds good," Jane said. "Since we have a new enemy, what can you tell me about her?"

Ariel stopped unrolling her blanket and thought for a moment.

"Jane, I want you to promise me that under no circumstances will you fight Talia. If you or the others see her again you must run. Do you understand?"

"Why?" Jane said. That was an unusual request of Ariel to make.

"Because she would kill you."

"You have lost my eastern army!" Queen Lysis said as she slapped Zorn's face. The force of the blow sent the warrior to his knees. "And you failed to kill the dark wolf that hunts us at night. Can you not do anything I command?"

Zorn's cheek bore deep scratch marks and his nose was bloodied. He bowed his head and waited for his punishment.

"My Queen," he said. "The dwarves of Keredain saved the man who is the dark wolf. King Baldon then led his forces into battle against your army. He is responsible for our loss."

Queen Lysis narrowed her eyes and looked down at him. Perhaps she had made a mistake with this one. He may well have served her better as food. They were standing on a small smoke-covered hill overlooking a burning village. As she had commanded, there were no villagers left alive. Still, the real prize lay to the south. Chalon. She had planned to attack the city from three directions, but, without the eastern army, that had been rendered impossible.

"And the girl-druid," Queen Lysis said, her voice dripping with sarcasm. "Was she not enough to tip the balance in your favor?"

"She did well. We were on the verge of winning the day," Zorn said, still looking down. "I was about to kill the Stormlord when the Knights of Caladar arrived. They ran our forces down like –"

"*My* forces," Queen Lysis shouted, striking him again, this time much harder. The blow toppled the Shadowlord to the ground. "Is this all I can expect from you now? Excuses and disappointment after disappointment?"

"No…my Queen," Zorn said, holding up a mailed hand to protect himself.

"Perhaps I should have chosen another to oversee this war," she mused, turning away from the prone warrior. She decided at that moment that when this war was over and she had conquered Alluria, Zorn would be food. She would drink him dry. His failures had become an annoyance. *He* was starting to hinder her plans. Still, until now, he had performed well enough.

"If you cannot deliver what I command," she said, looking over her shoulder. "I will feast on your soul."

"I will, my Queen," Zorn said, getting to his knees. "I am your loyal servant."

"At least you know your place," Queen Lysis said, noting he remained on his knees. "How did we lose the girl-druid? She was to be my hammer I would use to crush Chalon and Selra'thel."

"It was Ariel," Zorn said, lifting his eyes to her. "She overpowered Jane…the girl-druid."

"Ariel…" Queen Lysis said. "Every time I am set back and undone, she is involved. She has plagued me through the years. First she defeated Bhael, then my advance army, then you, and now my new dark druid."

"I turned her for you, my Queen. But now I cannot sense her. Perhaps she is dead."

"And the other elf you promised me? The one who will do what you cannot? The one who will kill Ariel and her friends? What of her?"

"The Spearslayer hunts them even now. She will not fail you."

Queen Lysis turned around.

"If she does, I will hold you responsible. I am weary of your disappointments."

She reached down and took hold of the top of Zorn's breastplate with one hand and lifted him off the ground. Her eyes became swirling pools of red and she sneered at him, revealing her fangs.

"Weary."

"Understood, my Queen."

She dangled him there, at least a foot off the ground. While he was feared, he was not unbeatable. Simply being a warrior and a vampire was not enough. Even with the infernal gifts she bestowed upon him, he was not the indomitable commander she required. However, there was something she could do.

"I will give you one more chance," Queen Lysis said. "You will take my northern army to Chalon and wait for me. When I arrive with my western army, we shall crush Chalon and I will reign over Alluria."

She opened one of her wrists with a fang and held it over Zorn's mouth. The dark red ichor dripped into his mouth. He eagerly drank.

"Now you will truly be as powerful in daylight as you are in moonlight. No one can match your strength. For the rest of Alluria, your power is undeniable."

# CHAPTER TWENTY-SEVEN
## ARCANE DUEL

The cloaked figure pulled back her hood, revealing the face beneath. The first thing Geoff noticed were her lavender eyes.

"Lady Seqwil." Geoff said.

She focused on him. Once her eyes had been warm and welcoming, now they were cold. Sawyer stepped forward and raised his sword. The corners of Seqwil's mouth curved upward.

"Why do you challenge me, Stormlord?" Seqwil motioned to Cruelon's corpse before her. "I just saved your life. You should be thanking me."

"I've taken down bigger than him," Sawyer said.

"Truly, Stormlord? If so, why do I see fear in your eyes?"

Sawyer didn't say anything, he remained ready for an attack. Seqwil stepped atop of the large body in front of her. At that moment, Ishara loosed an arrow at Seqwil, who deflected it with her hand. She glared at Ishara.

"Not today, girl," Seqwil said through clenched teeth.

Without warning, Sawyer charged Seqwil, sword high and yelling a battle cry.

"Sawyer, no!" Geoff shouted.

Sawyer sprang at Seqwil. She held up her hand and he was stopped motionless in mid-air. He wriggled and kicked with his legs, but he was stuck. Amused, Seqwil raised an eyebrow as she watched him desperately try to free himself.

"Let him go, Seqwil!" Geoff shouted.

"No," Seqwil said. Her eyes remained on Sawyer, watching him dangle like a fish on a hook.

Ishara fired two arrows in rapid succession at Seqwil. Again, Seqwil deflected the missiles with her hand. Then Seqwil closed the fist that held Sawyer captive and then pointed to the right corridor wall. He flew into it with a crash. Then she pointed to the left wall and Sawyer smashed into it with terrible speed. Sawyer went limp and dropped his sword. Geoff gasped in disbelief and his body went cold.

"No!" Geoff yelled, pointing his fists at Seqwil.

Twin bolts of magical lightning surged toward Seqwil from his fingers. She held her other hand up and reflected the bolts back toward him. Ishara grabbed the collar of Geoff's tunic and yanked him out of the way, just in time. The bolts of lightning struck the floor exactly where Geoff had been standing, although the force of the impact threw him and Ishara against the far wall. Everything went black for Geoff for a few seconds.

The grogginess made his vision blur and swirl. When his sight came into focus, he saw Ishara on all fours shaking her head and attempting to get to her feet. Geoff looked up at Seqwil. She wore a disappointed smirk on her face. She lowered her hand and released Sawyer, who fell to the floor. Seqwil stepped off Cruelon's body and sighed.

"I have no idea what she sees in you," Seqwil said in a

nonchalant tone. "You are quite weak and you have but an inkling of magical power. Oh well, best I kill you now and save you from a lifetime of disappointment and misery."

A sickly green whip formed in Seqwil's hand, tapering off at the end with a wicked looking barb. Geoff grunted as he got on one knee and held his hands up. From inside his chest he felt a familiar flow of energy and his same gold-tinted shield spell formed, filling the entire dimensions of the hall. The magical barrier separated Seqwil from them. Seqwil attacked with her conjured whip. The weapon struck Geoff's shield and then dissipated in a green flash.

Seqwil stepped back, mildly surprised.

"Well now," she said. "That is much better. It seems you have some talent after all."

"Ishara," Geoff said. "Go. Get out of here. I'm not sure how long I can keep the shield up."

Ishara crawled to his side.

"I will not leave you," she said, pulling the dagger Geoff carried from his belt.

"*That*, is my blade," Seqwil said. "What have you done to it? Is that a dragon's tooth you fitted onto the pommel? How revolting…"

"You dropped your blades the night you fell from the tower," Ishara said. "They belong to us now."

"Not for much longer," Seqwil said. Then she spun around and held her hands out. A beam of green light shot forth from her fingers and struck Geoff's shield, throwing him back. He'd only felt such an impact when Jane was the dark druid. His shield spell held. A trickle of sweat ran down his forehead. He was weakened, but determined to repel Seqwil's attacks. Again she launched a green bolt at Geoff's shield. This one was stronger than the first. The impact cracked the walls and ceiling causing bits of stone to fall.

Something inside Geoff began to hurt. His chest felt like it was on fire. His shield wavered, but he managed to regain control and keep it up. He felt Ishara clutch his arm and squeeze. Through the shimmering shield, he saw Seqwil close her eyes and extend her arms out from her sides. In each of her palms, a pulsing green glow formed and grew until her hands were engulfed in green.

Geoff braced himself. This was going to be it. Seqwil was winding up with a massive spell that would not only shatter his shield, but probably be the end of him and Ishara. A hand touched his shoulder. Geoff looked up and saw his dad, Maelord.

"Together, son," Maelord said as he held his hand up too. Geoff felt his shield strengthen, become far stronger than he thought it could ever be. His father's magical energy reinforced his perfectly. Refreshed, Geoff once again focused on the shield, which had nearly become opaque. Seqwil opened her eyes and clapped her hands, discharging a green ball of fire.

The green globe struck the shield and exploded, sending bits of ceiling and wall flying as well as throwing Seqwil backwards. The explosion was deafening.

"Well done, Geoff," Maelord said as he stood between him and Seqwil. "I'll take over now. Stay back."

This time it was Seqwil's turn to shake the grogginess from her head.

"Wizard," Seqwil sneered.

"I am," Maelord replied. "Let's see how you do against someone who knows the arcane arts as well as you."

Seqwil stood and glared at him but didn't do anything. Ishara grabbed Geoff and pulled him around the corner, out of the line of fire.

"What's the matter, *Lady* Seqwil," Maelord said. "My back isn't turned this time."

"Sorcery against wizardry," Seqwil said. "An ageless struggle. I wonder, will your son mourn for you?"

Before Maelord could answer, Seqwil conjured another barbed whip and lashed at him with it. But Maelord also conjured a whip, this one yellow in color. He attacked with it, at the moment the whips struck each other there was a loud *crack* and they became entwined. Maelord and Seqwil glared at each other, holding their magical weapons. Where the two whips had become entangled, a large sparkling and glowing popped while they hissed and crackled. Two incompatible magical energies dueling each other to the end.

Geoff peeked around the corner. He could hardly believe what he saw. The magical energy building up between the two whips began to vibrate and hum. The tone of the hum increased to an ear-splitting pitch and the glow suddenly became a blinding flash of light. Geoff had to duck back around the corner and cover his eyes. His head throbbed with pain. The high pitched hum stopped and then an explosion in the hall shook everything, knocking Geoff and Ishara to the ground.

Geoff and Ishara found themselves showered with pieces of broken stone and plastering loosed from the ceiling. He put a hand on top of his head as several pieces of stone hit him. He also pressed Ishara's head to his chest to shelter her. She buried her face in his tunic. A stifling cloud of dust from the explosion lingered, making breathing difficult. There was a ringing sound in Geoff's ears, too. He coughed while Ishara gasped for air.

"Are you okay?" Geoff asked, brushing dust and bits of stone off of her. Ishara coughed but nodded. Arm in arm, they helped each other up and made their way back into the hall where Maelord and Seqwil had been. Sawyer was lying where Seqwil had dropped him with dust and debris covering his body. Ishara knelt and examined him, looked up at Geoff and nodded. Sawyer was still breathing. His elven battle armor had protected him from harm as parts of the ceiling fell.

Geoff looked down the wrecked hall, but it was still too cloudy to see anything. He and Ishara walked in that direction. Geoff expected to find his father lying amongst the rubble.

"Geoff!" Ishara took his wrist and pointed just ahead.

His gaze followed Ishara's finger and there he saw a translucent golden sphere. Standing inside was his dad, Maelord.

Geoff rushed up to his father. Inside the spherical shield Maelord was looking at the floor and frowning.

"Dad!" Geoff called, hitting the shield with his fist.

Maelord dissolved the shield and Geoff hugged him. "Are you alright? What happened?"

"I'm fine," Maelord said, looking at him and then Ishara. "Are you two okay?"

"Yeah."

"Are you sure? You're bleeding, son," Maelord said as he wiped a trickle of blood from Geoff's forehead. Geoff felt the tender area and looked at his fingers. They were soaked red with blood.

"It doesn't hurt," Geoff said. "I'm okay."

"Lady Seqwil," Ishara said looking around. "Where is she?"

Maelord shook his head, "She's escaped again. I lost her in the explosion."

"I don't think she's gonna to stop coming after us," Geoff said. "What do we do now?"

# CHAPTER TWENTY-EIGHT
## THE WAY BACK

She'd slept well and had awoken refreshed and ready to resume their journey to Chalon. As Jane and Ariel trekked through the butterfly-strewn meadows, Jane felt her strength returning. The sun, the butterflies, and the birdsong added to her spirits as they headed due west. Ariel glided over the grassy landscape, but Jane found it difficult to keep up with Ariel.

"How do you move over things so easily?" Jane said. "Is that a druid thing?"

"No," Ariel smiled. "It is an elf thing."

"Hrmph," Jane grunted.

"There is a road used by trade caravans over the next hill," Ariel said as she stopped and waited for Jane. "From there it will be a much easier trek."

"Good," Jane said. "I'm looking forward to sleeping in a comfy bed again."

"Another couple of days," Ariel said. "And you will have your comfy bed."

"And a hot bath. I could use one."

"Agreed," Ariel said, smiling again.

Jane narrowed her eyes and glared at Ariel, but said nothing. She thought it kind of was funny, too.

"I have been meaning to ask you something," Ariel said.

"Go ahead," Jane said. "We're sisters, right? Ask me anything."

Ariel thought for a moment.

"So," Ariel said as she continued walking. "Perhaps you can tell me how you made snakes sprout from your fingers when you were the dark druid."

"What?" Jane said, following Ariel. "Snakes? What snakes?"

"You made snakes come out of your fingers," Ariel said.

"Eww," Jane said. "Gross. No way. I hate snakes."

"Nevertheless, it happened."

"No it didn't."

"Yes it did."

"I didn't do that."

"Yes you did."

"Snakes shoot from my fingers? I don't believe it."

"They did not shoot from your fingers. Your fingers turned into snakes."

"I'm going to be sick," Jane said. "I don't remember that."

"Good," Ariel said. "I am thankful that is the case."

"Why is that?"

"It means whatever evil was inside you has left."

Jane and Ariel walked for a few minutes in silence, then a troubling thought came back to Jane.

"What if Sawyer hates me now?"

"Do not be silly, Jane," Ariel said. "Why would he hate you?"

"Because I tried…to kill him."

"He knows you were not yourself."

"But—"

Ariel stopped Jane and took her hand.

"These thoughts can do you no good, Jane. Have I not said they are looking forward to seeing you again?"

"Yes."

"Then do not concern yourself with how you will be received by your friends."

"Okay," Jane said with a nod. "Thanks."

Ariel hugged Jane.

"We are sisters, Jane. Do not forget that."

"I won't."

As they crested the next hill, Jane was relieved to spot the dirt road. Suddenly, Ariel pulled her down in the tall grass and crouched beside her.

"What is it?" Jane whispered.

Ariel pointed to a location along the road a few hundred yards away. Several figures moved along the tree line, staying in the shaded areas.

"Why are there no Sentinels in the skies?" Ariel said, looking over head.

"Hmmm, what?" Jane said, only half listening as she watched the figures move closer to Chalon.

"Gryphon riders," Ariel said. "You remember, they patrol the skies around Chalon."

"Oh, yeah," Jane said as she glanced upward. The armored sky warriors were nowhere to be seen. "There used to be a lot of them flying around."

"This is troubling," Ariel said. "Strange and troubling."

"So who is that sneaking along the road to Chalon?"

"Barbarians. Advance scouts of the Scarlet Queen," Ariel said. "More than likely they will observe and report back to her. Perhaps they were also tasked with stopping supplies from reaching Chalon as well."

"Are you sure? They could be travelers staying in the shade," Jane said. "How do you know?"

"They are too well armed to be mere travelers," Ariel said. "And they are moving in a manner such that they do not wish to be detected."

"You can see all that from here? We have to do something," Jane said.

"Indeed we do," Ariel said. "Follow me."

They went back down the hill just enough to stay out of sight and made their way toward the scouts. From time to time, Ariel would crawl to the top of the hill again and peer over while Jane kept watch behind them. They moved behind the hillside until they found a position just ahead of the scouts.

"Okay," Jane breathed. "What's the plan?"

Ariel glanced about, making sure their presence had gone unnoticed.

"First, I must get closer," Ariel said. "I want to be sure who our enemies are. You stay here."

"Stay here?" Jane said. "You're kidding, right? What if something happened to you?"

"I will be fine," Ariel said. "Stay here, Jane."

Jane looked at Ariel, who was searching her eyes and waiting for her acknowledgement.

"Okay, okay," Jane relented. "I'll stay here."

With a nod, Ariel slipped over the top of the hill. She stayed low and moved like a snake through the tall grass. Jane peeked over the hill just enough to watch Ariel slip closer to the enemy scouts. Ariel's skill at approaching them with stealth was amazing. She blended in with her surroundings and the speed at which she moved was much faster than Jane could've managed. Jane didn't dare take her eyes off Ariel because if she did, she'd probably lose her.

Then, to Jane's surprise, Ariel abruptly turned around and made her way back. Was something wrong? A minute later Ariel crawled back over the hill and was beside Jane.

"What did you see?" Jane said. "Why did you come back so soon?"

"They have a spellcaster among them," Ariel said. "I am not sure if it is a wizard, sorcerer, witch, or what. Here take these, they are all I have."

Jane held out her hand and Ariel placed three acorns in it.

I believe you remember what to do with them?"

"I do."

"Very well," Ariel said. "We shall approach them directly from the south. That way we will have a better chance of surprising them. I will entangle as many as I can while you stay back and, if necessary, cast your acorns at them."

"Okay," Jane said and then they made a wide circle to the south, turned west for a bit, and then headed north. Jane was concerned about the spellcaster which Ariel was unsure of, it could be anything, but most certainly was dangerous. As they approached the wooded section which held the scouts, Ariel and Jane lay flat on their stomachs and began to crawl. Jane heard their voices, but was unable to make out what they were saying. She looked at Ariel.

Ariel was listening, almost hanging on every word she heard. She leaned close to Jane.

"Barbarians from Uln," she whispered. "Ten at least.

They are disguised as farmers and laborers."

"Why the disguises?"

Ariel held a finger up while she continued to listen.

"They wish to gain entry into Chalon," Ariel said. "There are other agents who will assist them once they are inside the city walls."

"Assist them with what?"

"I do not know," Ariel said. "Perhaps we can convince one of them to tell us."

They lay in the grass at the edge of the trees, waiting for an opportunity to attack. Jane managed to catch sight of a few of the scouts. They were not as large as the barbarian warriors she'd seen before, but they looked formidable enough. She watched as they mocked each other's new appearances, making coarse jokes about each other's transition from warriors to farmers and laborers.

"Jane," Ariel said as she grabbed her arm. "They mean to release a plague within Chalon when the time comes."

The heinous plan made Jane clench her fists.

"What an awful thing to do," Jane said. "Who'd want do that? Chalon is crowded with refugees and people seeking help, trying to survive the war. A plague there could kill thousands."

"Not if we stop it first," Ariel said. She pointed out a barbarian wearing a worn brown peasant's hat.

"That one there, he is the spellcaster and leader. Be wary of him."

"Got it." Jane zeroed in on him. He could easily pass for a farmer, or even just a peasant. Chances were the guards at the gates to Chalon would let them enter with no difficulty.

"Keep an eye on him," Ariel said, unsheathing her

scimitars. "I will begin. If he should free himself from my entanglement spell, you will need to cast one yourself. Do not let him finish uttering a spell. Do you understand?"

"Yeah," Jane said. "But what if he gets loose anyway?"

"That is why I gave you my last acorns," Ariel said. "Do not hesitate to throw them. And please, do not hit me."

Jane looked at Ariel. She was smirking at her last remark.

"Okay," Jane said.

Ariel crouched low, ran to the nearest tree, and hid behind it. Balancing both scimitars in one hand, she used the other to cast her spell. There was an immediate commotion among the scouts as the trees came alive and scooped them up, wrapping their branches around them and securing them fast. Ariel jumped from behind the tree and dashed at them, scimitars flashing in the sunlight.

Jane crawled closer, never taking her eyes off their leader. He'd been lifted at least ten feet off the ground. His arms and legs were stretched out from his body and his waist was encompassed by tree limbs. Four scouts, however, had been out of range of Ariel's spell. Two drew their swords and rushed toward her, yelling obscenities as they swung their weapons.

Ariel dodged both attacks with ease and followed with a series of spinning slashes that dropped her opponents where they stood. The remaining pair unaffected by Ariel's spell had begun to hack the others free, but when they saw Ariel they turned to attack her. Jane crept a little closer, her gaze never left the leader. He closed his eyes and uttered a single word in a language she didn't recognize.

The tree branches that had been suspending him froze and broke, shattered into tiny glasslike shards on the ground.

The leader landed on his feet behind Ariel and held up both hands.

"Ariel! Look out!" Jane shouted and then she stood and commanded the nearest trees to once again entangle him. Before he was again clasped and captured, he uttered another syllable and crossed his hands in front of him. Two scythe-like blades appeared and flew at Ariel in a swift, crisscrossing motion. Alerted by Jane's shout, she looked over her shoulder just in time to see the twisting blades heading in her direction.

Ariel stepped forward to meet the oncoming attack from the other two scouts, then dropped to the ground at the last second. The whirling blades passed harmlessly over her, but went through them and through another two scouts. The grisly results splattered blood over everything near, including Ariel. The scout leader turned his head and glared at Jane with hate-filled eyes.

"*Ka-tha!*"

This time Jane heard the spell as the second tree's branches instantly froze and splintered, releasing their prisoner. The barbarian landed, furious. He pointed a finger at Jane, but before he could utter a word, Ariel threw one of her scimitars at him. He spun and brought his hands together in a clapping motion, catching the weapon in mid-air. He let Ariel's scimitar drop to the ground and grinned at her.

Ariel began to move in a zig-zag fashion toward him and pointed at the ground near his feet. Grass and leafy plants grew and entwined his feet, holding him in place. The barbarian leader motioned with his hand again and another scythe appeared and spun toward Ariel. This time, Jane noticed that he was controlling it with his mind. Ariel sidestepped the attack, but the scythe spun through another scout.

In that moment, Jane decided that she had to do something.

Jane threw an acorn and shouted the druidic charm, *"Ana'thel!"*

Jane's acorn flew wide, sailing past the spellcaster. It struck a large tree behind him and exploded. The impact of the explosion splintered the oak, causing the rest of the tree to fall. Seeing his peril, the barbarian abandoned his attack on Ariel, put both hands up, and created a thick ice-barrier above him. The tree struck the barrier. Several chunks of ice chipped and broke away.

The spellcaster tried to step out from under the shield, but Ariel pointed a scimitar at him. When he looked behind, he saw that Jane had another acorn poised and ready. Sweat began to trickle down his forehead, as the strain of maintaining the ice spell took its toll.

"Surrender and you will be unharmed," Ariel said firmly. "You may even see your homeland again."

The other three confined barbarians continued to struggle and shout obscenities in their native tongue. Their leader made a sudden movement from under the tree and toward Ariel. As soon as he did, the ice barrier fractured and the splintered tree struck the ground with a booming crash. Before Ariel or Jane could react, he placed something in his mouth. Ariel sprang at him, but as she did, he blew a cone of freezing air at her.

Ariel twisted sideways and landed on her back. Missing her, he sprayed the other scouts with his arctic breath. To

Jane's horror, they were frozen alive. The leader turned his head to blow his freezing cone at Ariel again, but she had rolled and moved to his side. A well placed thrust of her scimitar ended his spell. Jane saw him drop to his knees and topple over.

Jane rushed over. "Ariel, are you okay?"

Ariel calmly retrieved her second scimitar.

"Yes," she said. "And you, Jane, are you unharmed?"

"I'm fine," Jane said. "What was he? I've never seen magic like that before."

"He was a shaman from Norland," Ariel said. "More than likely from the upper Dragonscale Mountain range. I have never seen one in battle. His skills were impressive."

"Why did he freeze the others?" Jane said, pointing at the icy bodies suspended in the air.

"Perhaps they were not to be captured," Ariel said, looking over her shoulder at them.

Jane averted her eyes from the other carnage wrought by the spinning scythes. She didn't need to see that. The air around them smelled like a frosty morning tinged with the sickening smell of blood. Ariel searched the pockets and belongings of the shaman. In a small pouch under his belt she found a small glass globe which contained a black ichor, in which small brown and orange worms swam.

"What is it?" Jane asked.

"I believe it is the plague meant to decimate the people of Chalon," Ariel said. "Jane, this confirms the arrival of a terrifying new enemy. A necromancer."

# CHAPTER TWENTY-NINE
## LIMITS

Geoff and Ishara helped Sawyer sit up. Propping him against the wall, Geoff removed his helm, which undoubtedly saved him from falling debris. Ishara poured some water from her flask into her hand and wiped the dust from his face.

Sawyer groaned.

"Sawyer," Geoff said, "are you okay? Is anything broken?"

Sawyer blinked his eyes open.

"Yeah, I'm okay…I think. What happened?"

"You were very brave," Ishara said. "You faced Lady Seqwil in battle."

Sawyer grunted as he shifted his weight. He held his side and gritted his teeth.

"Doesn't feel like I was brave," he said, "feels more like stupid."

"Can you stand up?" Geoff asked, offering his hand. Sawyer took it and with Ishara helping on the other side, they got him to his feet. Sawyer slid his helm off and rubbed the side of his head. At that moment, Maelord returned from checking the hall and handed him the Stormblade.

"Well done, Sawyer." Maelord said, placing a hand behind Sawyer's neck and giving him a gentle squeeze. "Thank you for defending Geoff and Ishara. How are you?"

"Yeah, no problem," Sawyer said. "I'm okay. Just a little banged up."

Shouts and the sound of armored feet getting closer let them know the castle guards would soon arrive.

"Did we get her?" Sawyer said. "Is Lady Seqwil dead?"

"No," Maelord said, looking back down the corridor where their arcane battle. "She escaped. It won't happen again."

"Come, Sawyer," Ishara said. "You should lie down. We need to get you to your room."

"You aren't going anywhere."

The voice was that of Lionel Naram, self-proclaimed king of Chalon. They turned and looked at him. Geoff saw the same contemptuous glare from Lionel that he always seemed to have etched on his face. *This probably wasn't going to go well.* Lionel walked past them, surveying the significant damage to the corridor.

"What has happened here?" Lionel demanded. "What have you children done to my castle?"

"They did nothing," Maelord said, "except defend themselves from harm."

"Harm?" Lionel scoffed. "The only harm I see is the near destruction of my castle."

Placing his hands on his hips, Lionel walked over to Sawyer, Geoff, and Ishara and glowered at them.

"Why is it that every time you show up," Lionel said, "the tranquility of my surroundings is shattered by chaos and murder?"

"Perhaps," Maelord said, "you should be asking someone else exactly how a group of the Scarlet Queen's elite warriors managed to enter your tranquil surroundings and attack us."

Lionel spun around and walked to Maelord. The two looked each other in the eye.

"And whom should I ask?"

"You can start with Lady Seqwil," Maelord said without hesitation.

"Lady Seqwil is dead," Lionel countered.

Maelord looked around the hallway, then returned Lionel's gaze.

"Really? How interesting. She was alive a moment ago."

Maelord stepped around Lionel and motioned for Geoff, Sawyer, and Ishara to leave with him.

"Be careful, Maelord," Lionel said. "Do not question my word. My patience and generosity has its limits."

Maelord, who was following the others out of the hallway, stopped and looked back at Lionel.

"As do mine, King Lionel."

Maelord bowed his head and followed the others. Geoff was waiting for him a few paces away.

"Dad," Geoff said in a hushed tone. "Why do you bow to him? You know he's lying."

"I know, son," Maelord wrapped an arm around Geoff's shoulders, "but it's best for now if we don't anger him or make him suspicious."

"Do you think he's working with the Scarlet Queen?"

"I don't know. I just don't know. In the morning, I want all three of you to move into my tower with me. It's safer there."

Ishara looked mournfully at Geoff. He smiled. He knew

that was not a place Ishara cared to revisit. She didn't care for the dust and clutter. Their first kiss drifted into his mind. How beautiful she looked standing by the window in his father's tower, sunlight reflecting off the dust that swirled around her, making her look like an angel.

Ishara had refused to leave his side in their confrontation with Lady Seqwil, not even when he was weakening and his shield spell began to falter. No one had ever done that for him before, he wasn't used to it, but the feeling he got inside when he looked at her always made him smile.

"Where to, Dad?"

"Back to your room for now," Maelord said. "We stay together this night. Tomorrow morning we get out of this death trap."

"I heard that," Sawyer said. "The sooner the better as far as I'm concerned."

Once back at their rooms, Maelord went in first. At the doorway, he made a few gestures with his fingers and went to the center of the room. There, he stood and concentrated with his hands out at his sides. Ishara had readied another arrow and was prepared to fire in an instant. Geoff and Sawyer stayed in the corridor, looking both ways.

"Clear," Maelord said. "Try and get some rest, all of you. It'll be light soon."

"Ariel always said that to us," Sawyer said, removing his armor.

"Ariel was always right, too," Maelord said. "I'll stay up and keep watch."

Geoff helped Sawyer with his armor. He was about to remove his tunic when he saw Ishara making a bed for herself on the floor.

"Hey," Geoff said to Ishara. "Take the bed. I'll grab a comfy chair."

Ishara smiled at him, "Thank you."

Geoff grabbed a pillow and an extra blanket and pulled two big, plush reading chairs together. *If he curled his knees a bit, it would be a nice substitute for a bed*. Maelord had pulled a chair against the far wall and sat there, facing their beds.

"Goodnight, Dad," Geoff said as he climbed into his makeshift bed. "Goodnight Ishara, Sawyer."

Everyone said goodnight and Geoff closed his eyes. Finally, he felt safe. With his dad watching over them, not even Lady Seqwil wouldn't dare show her face again.

Morning came sooner than expected for Geoff. He was shaken awake by Ishara.

"Time to get up," Ishara said with a cheery tone.

Geoff lifted his head, the side of his cheek was moist, as was his pillow. Even Sawyer was awake and dressed before him, which was probably a first. There was a knock at the door. Geoff heard at least two voices speaking in the corridor on the other side of the door.

"Geoff," Maelord said as he tossed a ripe apple in his direction. Geoff caught it with both hands and took a bite as his father answered the door. Trelane, Shaun Hammerfel, King Baldon, and Commander Renfry were on the other side of the door. Geoff kept his attention on the group at the door while he munched on the red fruit.

"We lost twenty good men last night," Renfry reported. "At least a dozen more may not see tomorrow."

"How did the enemy get in?" Baldon demanded. "I tell you there are agents of the Scarlet Queen within these walls."

"Agreed," Maelord said. "I fought one last night, but she escaped."

"She? Who?" Baldon said, leaning on his large battle axe.

"Lady Seqwil," Maelord answered. "She attacked my son and his friends."

"I had heard she died," Trelane said with a touch of surprise in his voice. "How is it she still lives?"

"She has her ways. She is a sorcerous assassin," Maelord said. "A very powerful one at that. I'm sure she had a hand in last night's attack on the castle."

"So what're we gonna do about it?" Baldon growled. "I don't like being cooped up waiting to be slaughtered."

"Whatever she tried to accomplish last night," Maelord said, "she failed. But she is sure to make another attempt on their lives."

"Sawyer Stormlord is to begin training with myself and my knights this morning," Shaun said. "I will look after his well-being."

"The elves of Selra'thel must leave Chalon," Trelane said. "By order of the king."

"King?" Baldon said. "He's no king. He's a mouse. Always has been."

"Where will you go?" Renfry said, looking at Trelane. "We need your army if we're to stand against the Scarlet Queen."

"Not far," Trelane said. "We intend to make camp to the north. Lionel may have ordered us out of the castle, but he said nothing of our camping within Chalon's borders."

"We'll accompany you," Baldon said. "No one will dare attack an army of elves *and* dwarves."

"As will the Knights of Caladar, but I think it's best if I

keep some of my knights here for the time being," Shaun said. "They can offer aid in guarding the castle, perhaps help patrol the streets of Chalon."

"When I receive my daily orders," Commander Renfry said, looking at Shaun. "I'll attempt to convince the king that any aid from the Knights of Caladar would be most welcome."

"This would be so much easier if Alex were here," Baldon said. "A part of me feels like we're plotting behind another king's back. Even wounded, I'd wager he'd be a far better leader than the one Chalon has now."

"When did you last see Alex?" Maelord said as all eyes turned to the dwarven king.

"Before the battle with the Shadowlord and the Scarlet Queen's eastern army," Baldon said. "We saved him from being carved up like a roast goose by Zorn."

"How is he?" Shaun asked.

"Not as well as I'd hoped," Baldon said. "We dressed his wounds as best we could and fed him, but I think he's losing hope. I could see it in his eyes."

There was a moment of silence. Geoff noticed Sawyer and Ishara were also listening.

"I propose we meet each evening," Trelane said. "We can share any news or rumors then."

"Agreed," Shaun said. "But where should we meet?"

Maelord looked at Commander Renfry, "Do you think you could leave the castle after dark without being observed?"

"Aye. I can manage that."

"Good," Maelord said. "Then come to my tower after dark and we'll travel to Trelane's encampment together."

Renfry nodded.

"We meet tonight, then," Trelane said, clapping a hand on Baldon's shoulder. "My tent."

Each nodded their agreement and then Shaun stepped into the doorway.

"Sawyer," Shaun said. "Let's begin your training. Come." He motioned for Sawyer to get up and follow him. Sawyer stopped at the door before putting on his helm and looked back at Geoff and Ishara.

"Be careful, you two."

"Thanks," Geoff said.

"You be careful too, Stormlord," Ishara said. "Stay alert."

Sawyer turned and left the room with Shaun and the others. Geoff wasn't sure splitting everyone up was a good idea. Trouble always seemed to show when they split up. Maelord turned around and clapped his hands.

"Are we ready?" Maelord said.

Ishara had already packed her belongings and stood by, patiently waiting for Maelord to conclude his conversation. Geoff, on the other hand, still had half an apple to finish and couldn't find his boots. With some help from the others, he managed to get himself sorted. His father led them out of the castle and into the city. Geoff on his left and Ishara on his right.

Maelord put an arm around both of them as they walked.

"I think this is going to be a good day," he said, looking at Ishara then Geoff. "I have a present waiting for you, son."

"What kind of present?" Geoff asked.

"My first spell book," Maelord said. "It may be old and worn at the edges, but the spells within are useful and well worth brushing away a little dust."

Geoff looked at Ishara. Her frowning expression said it all, she dreaded going back to his dad's old tower. Geoff smiled to himself.

"Dad," Geoff said, putting an arm on his back as they walked. "I didn't know you had spell books."

"Of course I do," Maelord said. "Spell books, scrolls, magic gemstones...how do you think a wizard ever learns new spells?"

"How many spell books do you have?" Geoff said.

"I lost count a long time ago," Maelord said. "Perhaps the two of you could help me organize them?"

Ishara groaned.

# CHAPTER THIRTY
## MORE TRAINING

Sawyer accompanied Shaun to the training area, which included several barracks, stables, and armories. Activity was abundant with most of the participants being knights from Caladar. Some knights were sparring in a corral of sorts. A large round area surrounded by a wooden fence that most spectators sat on or leaned on while watching the match-ups. The smell of fires burning in the armories mingled with that of hay and manure.

Two fully armored knights were sparring with wooden swords, which had been chalked for the purpose of practice. A crowd of people had gathered and watched. Sawyer took it all in, impressed. Though their swords were wooden, neither gave any quarter to the other.

"We train every day," Shaun told him. "It's a way of life for us."

"Does anyone ever get hurt?"

"My son asked the same question when he first saw us spar," Shaun said. "No. Perhaps a bruise here or there, but rarely anything serious."

Several knights rode by on horseback, churning up dirt

and a few small stones. A couple knights saluted Shaun as they passed in tight formation and moved in near perfect concert.

"Maneuvers," Shaun said. "We are heavy cavalry, first and foremost, so we must act as one unit in battle. Can you ride?"

"Not like that," Sawyer said, watching them stop, turn, and charge in unison. "They're awesome."

"Would you like to learn to ride a heavy warhorse like that?"

"Definitely."

"Someday, when this war is over, you'll have to visit Caladar and I'll show you," Shaun said. He looked Sawyer over. "You look like the right size for my horse."

A rowdy cheer arose from the spectators watching the sparring match, which had just ended. Sawyer watched as the victor helped the loser up. The knights lifted their visors and both were laughing and smiling as they recanted their match.

"Would you like to watch for a bit?" Shaun asked.

"Yeah, looks like fun."

"For us it's fun," Shaun said, "but most people are afraid to set foot in the arena because they don't wish to get hurt."

They walked up and found a good place to lean on the wooden fence. The next match featured Sir Reymond, the loud, obnoxious knight from dinner in the great hall the other night. He was paired with a younger, slimmer knight who looked close to Sawyer's age. Both knights faced each other and waited for the judge, more than likely another knight, to drop a flag.

The instant the flag was dropped, Sir Reymond charged

the younger knight, sword swinging in all directions. This tactic served to confuse the younger knight and Sir Reymond struck him three consecutive times, knocking him to the ground and ending the match in seconds. Another cheer went up from the crowd. Turning his back on his fallen sparring partner, Sir Reymond opened his visor and raised his hands while yelling in celebration. Sawyer watched the other knight get up, the three strikes from Reymond's wooden sword had left him all but covered in white chalk.

As Sir Reymond turned around in the arena, he shouted, "Who's next?"

Then his gaze settled on Sawyer. *Uh oh*.

Sawyer knew from the glint in his eyes that Sir Reymond wanted to give him the same treatment.

"Stormlord!" Called Sir Reymond, pointing his wooden sword at Sawyer. "I challenge the Stormlord!"

The bystanders watching the matches exploded with cheers and whistles. Sawyer looked at their faces. They were smiling and nodding. Shaun leaned closer to Sawyer.

"You do not have to accept," he said. "There is no dishonor in refusing. Reymond likes to knock smaller knights down so he can feel better about himself. Come, let's get started with your training."

"No, wait," Sawyer said. "I'll give it a try."

"Sawyer," Shaun said. "Sir Reymond is a seasoned veteran. I do not doubt your abilities, but he has been through many campaigns and battles."

"Let me try," Sawyer said, looking at Shaun.

"Very well," Shaun said throwing up his hands and motioning for Sawyer to enter.

As soon as Sawyer entered, he noticed the surrounding

crowd had grown. Many more knights were watching and it looked like some of them were placing bets. Sawyer removed his sword and handed it to Shaun for safe keeping. The judge handed Sawyer and Sir Reymond freshly chalked wooden swords. Sawyer took it and tested its weight and feel in his grasp.

"Stormlord," Sir Reymond said, grinning while he mocked Sawyer's movements.

Then Sawyer realized how small he must look in his elven battle armor compared to the full plate armor worn by Sir Reymond. *He must be the favorite in the betting.* He looked around and noticed some of the dwarves from Keredain had found spots from which to observe the sparring match. Though from the looks of Sir Reymond, who looked like a hungry wolf licking his chops, this wasn't going to be a friendly spar.

"Take him on, Stormlord!"

The shout, which came from King Baldon, was followed by cheers, retorts, and lots of laughter. Yet, something clicked in Sawyer's head. A lesson Ariel had taught him a while back. A larger, slow moving opponent will always be an easy target. Sawyer's smaller, lighter armor provided him with full mobility and ease of speed. While Sir Reymond's armor was beautiful and fully encompassed him, it would slow him down, too. This was no time to be defensive, Sawyer remembered a specific series of offensive moves he had learned from Ariel.

Sir Reymond slammed his visor shut as the judge held the sparring flag between them. The instant the flag dropped, Sawyer feinted left, drawing a long looping swing from his opponent. Then he spun swiftly to his right, putting him in a perfect position to attack. Sawyer's first two blows landed on the knight's breastplate and side of his helm, respectively. Before he could recover, Sawyer kicked his legs out from under him and again struck Sir Reymond's chest as his legs flew up in the air. He landed hard on the ground and his wooden practice sword flew out of his hand.

The arena exploded with cheers. The raucous crowd began chanting "Stormlord! Stormlord!"

Before acknowledging the crowd, Sawyer offered his hand to Sir Reymond, who was still on the ground.

"Get away from me!" Sir Reymond shouted, slapping Sawyer's hand away. He lifted his visor and Sawyer saw his gritted teeth, red rimmed eyes, and a vein bulging on his forehead. Sawyer stepped back and Sir Reymond got to his feet and took a step toward Sawyer before he was stopped by Shaun Hammerfel restraining him on one side and another knight on the other side.

"You fight like an elf!" Sir Reymond yelled, then spat on the ground.

"That's right," Shaun said, pulling Reymond's arm so he would look at him. "He does fight like an elf. He put you on your backside quick enough, didn't he?"

Reymond struggled to free himself, but Shaun and the other knight held him fast.

"You go and cool off," Shaun said. "Now."

He glared at Shaun, then at Sawyer. Then Sir Reymond wrenched his arms free and left the arena. Baldon laughed so hard he nearly fell over. Shaun handed the Stormblade back to Sawyer.

"Impressive. You've been well taught by Ariel," Shaun said. "I recognized that combat maneuver."

"How's that?" Sawyer said, strapping the Stormblade on. "Did Ariel train you too?"

"No," Shaun said, putting an arm around Sawyer's shoulders as they walked toward the exit. "That's the same move she used on me, with the same result. Well done, Sawyer. Sir Reymond needed to have his ego and buttocks bruised. However, I think for now, it may be best if you and I find a quieter place to train."

Geoff thought his father's tower looked just as he'd remembered, a little roughhewn, but solid. Three stories high, it leaned a little to one side, and it was the coolest place he'd ever seen. They passed through the metal gate, which squeaked when they opened and closed it. The iron-bound front door to the tower, however, opened for them before they had walked up to it. Geoff grinned as he followed his dad into the tower. This was a wondrous place for him.

Ishara, the last to enter, paused at the doorway and coughed. Glancing around, Geoff noticed the layer of dust that still covered everything. The dingy windows allowed only a small portion of sunlight in. The room itself became a swirl of dust as Maelord passed through.

"Now, then," he said. "Make yourselves at home while I find that spell book."

Geoff went to the nearest chair and brushed the seat with his hand. A large cloud of dust arose, making him sneeze. He looked at Ishara. She appeared to be on the verge of tears.

"Maelord," Ishara said. "Is there no spell that will rid you of this dirt and dust? Perhaps one that will organize your…work as well?"

"Hmm? Oh no," Maelord said. "That's what brooms are for."

"Then where is your broom?" Ishara asked.

"Never had one."

Ishara frowned and shook her head. Geoff snickered, he couldn't help himself. Ishara's misery over being in such a filthy place was pretty funny.

"Hey Dad, why don't you get a maid to clean up around here?"

"Why?" Maelord said as he walked to one of many bookshelves in the room. "A little dust never hurt anyone, right?"

"I guess not," Geoff said, "but this is more than a little dust."

Maelord stopped looking through his books and scanned the room.

"Perhaps," he shrugged. "Ishara, would you be kind enough to close the door? We don't want any eavesdroppers, do we?"

"A little fresh air never hurt anyone either," Ishara said grumpily as she went to the door. She took a deep breath and then closed it. Geoff wondered how long elves could hold their breath. She turned around and Geoff laughed out loud. The indignant glare on her face was priceless. She began to move closer to him. Her tight lipped expression was a clear indication that she was not amused.

"Ah! Here it is!" Maelord said, holding up a small, well-thumbed book the size of an index card.

"That's a spell book?" Geoff said. "I thought it'd be bigger, like those tomes in your study."

"Oh no," Maelord said as he walked to Geoff and Ishara.

"A spell book must be able to be carried easily. It must be light and…" Maelord blew a layer of dust off the cover, which sent Ishara back-peddling toward the door, finger under her nose. "It must be studied."

Maelord handed the thin book to Geoff. It was bound in light brown leather with dark leather bindings. There was a strange symbol etched on the cover.

"What's that symbol?" Geoff asked.

"A wizard's mark," Maelord said. "It simply means the book is a wizard's book."

"And it serves as a warning to others not to open it," Ishara added. Then she narrowed her eyes a little at Maelord, "Once you blow the dust off so they can see it."

"Now son, consider this an intermediate-level spell book, but I assure you there are many good and useful spells inside. Some I still use myself."

"Oh this is cool," Geoff said as he opened the cover. "Thanks."

"The first thing to remember," Maelord said as he sat across from Geoff, "is to start from the beginning and learn each spell in order because the next spell builds upon the previous spell. Got it?"

"Yeah, yeah," Geoff said, flipping through the pages. "So what sorts of spells are in here? I can't read this. It looks like gibberish."

"That's because it's written with magic. The first spell will enable you to read any magical glyphs or writing, then you should be able to understand the rest. You should start with that one, of course."

Geoff looked at the first page. It was torn and missing its corners, but it had a diagram indicating the placement of the index and middle fingers of a hand on the page. There were some runes or symbols inscribed at the top of the page. Maelord pointed to the first rune, "*Sylla*," he said. Then he pointed to the second rune, "*Arcanum*."

"*Sylla Arcanum*," Geoff said. He looked at the first page. Nothing had changed.

"You must perform the gestures as well. They are just as important as the words."

Geoff repeated the new words while placing his index and middle finger on the page. This time, the strange writing re-arranged itself and he was looking at a spell that would enable him to read magical writings.

"Cool! This is awesome."

"Isn't it?" Maelord smiled. "Now, the next spell will allow you to search for items of magical nature. I've found it to be very useful at times."

"Will this work on any sort of magic?"

"Yes, but only on items and *only* items enchanted with enough magic to be distinguished from others."

"Like Sawyer's sword," Geoff said.

"Of course, but keep in mind that not all magical items are as magnificent as Sawyer's sword and armor. Some can appear to be fairly mundane. In fact, some of the most powerful items may appear to be no more than a small piece of junk."

Geoff flipped the page, the next spell showed a different configuration for his fingers and an illustration of a man floating in the air.

"Levitation," Maelord said. "But do not try that when you're learning unless you're over water. Trust me on that."

"Are there any words for this spell?"

"No, keep in mind a wizard's advantage is the ability to visualize the spell in his mind and then make it a reality. Hence, the pictures."

"Dad, this is the best present, really."

"Listen carefully, the secret is your concentration and practice. Be patient. Don't attempt to levitate yourself too high, for example, understand?"

"So will I be able to fly, too?"

"Goodness no," Maelord said. "But, if you should find yourself falling a great distance, you can slow your fall. Also, toward the back of the book are a few spells to use on your enemies. "I'll be happy to demonstrate them after you've mastered the others, okay?"

"Okay."

"And you can levitate other objects, too."

"Really? Even people?"

"Sure," Maelord said, "if you so choose."

Geoff glanced at Ishara. Her arms were folded in front of her.

"Do not," Ishara said through clenched teeth, "even think about it."

"She's right. If you wanted to make a rock float or a gold coin, for example, that would be fine. However, do not use that spell on anything alive unless there is a dire need."

Turning the page, Geoff saw a drawing of a man using inanimate objects as missiles against his enemies.

"We'll save that one for later," Maelord said. "First, practice levitation and then we'll explore that telekinetic spell."

Geoff leafed through the rest of the pages. Some had burn marks on them while others were all but falling out of the book. The last few pages looked interesting to Geoff. They were more complicated with their hand gestures and some even had verbal components associated with them.

"Are there any spells where we *have* to speak, Dad?"

"Only a few," Maelord said. "And those tend to be the most powerful and the most dangerous."

"Is there anything in here that will help if Lady Seqwil attacks us again?"

"Of course," Maelord said. "Why do you think we're doing this? The day will come when you must embrace your true inheritance as a wizard…and you must be ready."

# CHAPTER THIRTY-ONE
## ROADSIDE ENCOUNTERS

"Are you sure it's a good idea to bring that plague with us?" Jane asked, looking over her shoulder as they resumed their journey.

"I have no safe way of dispelling the plague. Perhaps Maelord will be able to help us," Ariel said, "and why do you keep watch behind us as we walk? You have been doing that far too often today."

"I'm just…how far from Spirewood Forest are we?"

"Several days at least. What are you afraid of, Jane?"

"That Spearslayer woman, Talia."

"She will not catch up to us before we reach Chalon, and do not let her hear you call her that," Ariel said. "She would take exception to being called a 'woman'."

"She's the first I've seen to *rush* into battle with you," Jane said. "Not even the Shadowlord did that."

"True, she has great confidence in her skills."

They walked along the dirt road for a while longer, with Jane enjoying the slight breeze and glowing sunshine. Then she remembered what Ariel had said a moment ago.

"Hey, wait a minute. You said you had no safe way of

*dispelling* the plague. Are you saying it's magical, then?"

"It is," Ariel said. "Although I do not know its exact magical nature, I alone do not have the means to rid us of it."

"Can't we just bury it?"

"No. The contents would eventually leak from the glass globe, which is fragile, and into the surrounding environment."

"Yeah, but what if it breaks while you're carrying it?"

Ariel stopped and looked at Jane. "Then we die."

Jane searched Ariel's eyes for a sign she was joking, but Ariel rarely joked. Especially about something as serious as this.

"You don't have a spell to stop the plague or cure someone who has it?"

"I do not know."

"None of the spells you taught me would work?"

"Again, I do not know. The orb contains a combination of sorcerous and necromantic enchantments. I must consult Maelord."

"Then I'm glad you wrapped it in lots of cloth before putting it back in its pouch."

"As am I."

A disturbing thought occurred to Jane.

"What if another team of scouts has already managed to get into Chalon and unleash the plague? What if the others have already been infected?"

"Best not to dwell on such things, Jane. We must hope we stopped the only plague from entering Chalon. It is such an evil, heinous plan."

Ariel cast her eyes skyward and scanned the clouds. She frowned and shook her head.

"Something is wrong in Chalon," Ariel said. "Still no Sentinels in the skies. This has never happened before, we should hurry."

They picked up their pace and began jogging. Jane wasn't sure how long she would be able to keep up with Ariel, who had already started to pull away, but she was going to run until she dropped. *Why couldn't those barbarians have left us a few horses?*

After a while, Ariel had outdistanced her and was waiting up ahead beside a small thicket with lots of trees for shade. As Jane drew near, she noticed a small pond, too.

"We need to rest," Ariel said, though as far as Jane could tell, she hadn't so much as broken a sweat.

"Okay," Jane joked, holding her side. "If you need to stop, I'll wait."

Ariel smiled and walked off the road into a camp that looked like it had been used regularly by travelers either coming from or going to Chalon. A ring of stones sat at the center of a small clearing. Within the ring was the charred remains of a campfire. A small bundle of kindling lay beside the campfire. Along the edge of the camp lay several other, larger stones connected to each other by either long pieces of wood or tree branches that had been tied and bundled together.

Jane was about to have a seat and take a drink of water from her flask when Ariel suddenly unsheathed her scimitars and stepped in front of her.

"Are you mad?" Ariel said sharply. "What are you doing here?"

Jane peered from behind Ariel and gasped. Sitting against a tree, holding his side with his hands was the man in tattered animal skins, Alex. The werewolf which had hunted them and tried to kill them several times.

"Answer! Why are you so close to Chalon? And evening is so near," Ariel said. "You have endangered many people by venturing this close to Chalon."

"I mean you no harm," Alex said, his voice raspier than ever.

"And the wolf?" Ariel said. "Can you say the same for the beast that will soon visit us this night?"

Alex said nothing. He was breathing heavy and Jane noticed his hands were stained red. He looked pale, too.

"You're hurt," Jane said.

Ariel lowered her weapons. Alex only nodded and then collapsed. Jane and Ariel went to him. His breathing was labored. Ariel moved his hands aside and saw he had been wounded with a long blade and he'd lost a great deal of blood. He had also been slashed across the chest.

"We need to help him," Jane said. "He's in terrible shape."

Ariel pulled some small bandages from her backpack and wetted them with water from her flask.

"I am curious as to what sort of foe could do this to Alex," Ariel said. "Man or beast, Alex is formidable in battle."

After she cleaned his wounds, Jane removed some oak leaves from the pouch that Ariel had given her and crushed them in her hands. She sprinkled the bits of leaf over his wounds and placed her hands over his wounds.

"*Ilinara tae ullnara taethos,*" Jane said. Suddenly she fell back.

"Ariel! The Shadowlord did this," Jane gasped. "It's the same darkness that prevented me from healing you when you fought the Shadowlord."

"Are you sure, Jane?"

"Yes, I'm sure." Jane looked around. A shiver ran down her back. "Ariel, what if *he's* here too?"

"I doubt it. These wounds are two or three days old," Ariel said. "He will need to rest, just as I did."

Ariel tore some strips of fresh cloth and laid them over his wounds. Jane wiped the grime from his face. He smelled like an animal, the same musky odor mixed with sweat and blood was almost overpowering. It made her feel a little nauseous.

"Start a small fire, Jane," Ariel said. "I will do what I can for him, but he should try to eat, too."

Jane watched Ariel while she got the fire going. She closed her eyes and kept her hands on his wounds. As Jane prepared some vegetables, she noticed Alex had regained some of his color and his breathing had become more even. After several more minutes, Ariel removed her hands and looked down at him.

"He looks better," Jane said. "Whatever you did, it helped."

Ariel sat beside Jane at the fire and leaned forward to smell the stew.

"He needs time to heal," Ariel said. "Jane, we cannot stay here and watch over him."

"But if we leave him, he might die."

"There are two excellent reasons for us to leave him," Ariel said. "First, we must get to Chalon, find our friends, and seek help or a plague may befall the city. Second, tonight Alex will become a werewolf. You have seen it for yourself. Do you really wish to stay?"

Before Jane could answer Alex spoke.

"She's right," he said, sitting up on an elbow. "You can't stay here. You two need to get as far away from me as you can."

"How do you feel?" Ariel asked.

"Better, thank you."

"What are you doing, Alex?" Ariel demanded. "Why are you here?"

He grunted and winced as he sat up. He kept one hand on his wounded side. Jane spooned a bit of stew into a small bowl and handed it to him.

"I don't know," he said, taking a spoonful of stew into his mouth. "I can't say. All I can tell you is, every day when I wake up, I'm further west than I was the day before. The beast within is drawn to something."

"The Shadow...Zorn," Jane said. "Did you kill him?"

"No," Alex said as he swallowed and coughed. "He nearly killed me." He looked at Ariel. "But Baldon and his army showed up just in time."

Ariel nodded. "The dwarves fought well a few days ago. It was good to see Baldon again."

Alex quickly finished his stew and sat the bowl down.

"The darkness from the north is coming," Alex said. "I'm sure of it. You must rally Chalon. They need to join Selra'thel and Keredain if the Scarlet Queen is to be defeated."

"Do you think Lionel will listen to me?"

"Who *will* he listen to, then?" Jane said, looking at Alex and then Ariel. "There has to be someone he'll listen to, right?"

"I don't know," Alex said, as his body was racked by another terrible cough. "Perhaps Maelord, but I just don't know."

Alex pointed to the bloodstained hole in Ariel's leather tunic.

"What happened?"

"Talia," Ariel said in a low tone.

Alex lifted an eyebrow.

"It appears you've done what they say cannot be done. You have faced the Spearslayer in battle and survived."

"I did not face her in battle," Ariel said. "She hurled her spear from a distance and wounded me. We retreated to my grove in the Spirewood Forest."

A moment of silence passed, then Alex looked at Ariel and Jane.

"I'll rest for a little longer," Alex said, "Then I'll head south. But now you both need to go. Get as far away from here as you can. After dark, it won't be safe outside Chalon. I thank you for your aid and for feeding me. Now please go."

"Why do you hunt us?" Jane asked suddenly.

"Jane, now is not the time..." Ariel said.

"No, I really want to know," Jane looked at Alex. "Why can't the werewolf leave us alone?"

"I'm not sure," Alex murmured. "But there is something that draws it, me, to you and your friends. I think perhaps it's your auras."

"It can see our auras?" Jane said.

Alex nodded. "All supernatural creatures can see your aura. I see it now."

Jane shook her head. "How is that possible?"

"A bit of the beast is always with me," Alex said. "Your aura is astonishingly bright again. Please go. You have the rest of the day...to run for your lives."

Ariel stood and gathered up her belongings. Jane did the

same. Before they left camp, Ariel turned around and looked at Alex.

"Do you need anything else?"

Alex shook his head. "You better hurry," he said. "It'll be dark before you know."

Ariel nodded. "Farewell."

Then Ariel and Jane turned and began to run along the road toward Chalon.

"Shadowlord, Spearslayer, and now werewolf," Jane puffed as they sped up. "Ariel, how're we going to beat all of them?"

"Faster, Jane," Ariel said. "If we do not travel far enough today, we will never again see Chalon."

# CHAPTER THIRTY-TWO
## WHAT IT MEANS TO BE A KNIGHT

Once Sawyer and Shaun left the sparring arena, they collected two horses from the stables.

"Don't concern yourself with Sir Reymond," Shaun said, "he always lets his temper get the best of him. I suppose it will cost him dearly one day."

"I'm not worried," Sawyer said, "I've seen lots of guys like him. They talk a lot but when you put them in their place, they shut up."

"You did exactly that," Shaun said. "Ariel has been an excellent teacher for you. Imagine, the Stormlord with the fighting abilities of an elven warrior. That is a tough combination to beat."

"Ariel's not a warrior," Sawyer said, mounting his horse. "She's a druid."

"Oh, I know what she is," Shaun said, "she's definitely a warrior. She may be a druid as well, but I assure you she's also a warrior."

Shaun and Sawyer rode their horses out of the castle grounds and into the city. They made a striking pair, the Stormlord in his ornate elven battle armor and Shaun

Hammerfel, Commander of the Knights of Caladar in his shining plate armor. Crowds swarmed around them as they walked their horses along. Sawyer noticed their dirty faces and ragged clothes, especially the children. Some appeared to have been sleeping in the streets, but when they came up and touched Sawyer, or shook his hand, the looks of despair turned into smiles of hope and joy.

"They love you," Shaun murmured.

"I don't see why. I haven't done anything."

"It's not what you've done. It's what you mean to them, what you symbolize. To them, you're a hero, and heroes are in short supply these days. You bring them hope."

"If I could do more for them I would," Sawyer said. "Some of them look like they haven't eaten for days."

"Aye, that's true," Shaun said as he glanced around. "They look desperate."

"Can we do anything for them?"

"That," Shaun said shaking his head, "is the duty of a ruler. The well-being of their people should always come first."

"I don't think that's going to work out for them."

"If I had wagons of food," Shaun said, "I'd give it all away."

"I'd help."

They rode through the gates, some peasantry in tow, mostly adoring children. Sawyer was sure to give every one of his young fans a smile and a handshake. A few of the older ones begged to be his squire.

"I'm not a knight," Sawyer replied. "I'm no different from you."

His answer was met with puzzled looks, but nonetheless,

they continued to ask if they could accompany him on his next adventure.

"They're persistent," Shaun said. "Come, let's find a good spot to train in private."

He spurred his horse and headed south, leaving the adoring youngsters and Sawyer behind.

"I gotta go," Sawyer said, waving. "Bye!"

Sawyer wasn't able to ride as fast as Shaun, but he managed to catch up with him a mile outside of Chalon. Shaun had slowed his horse to a walk on the dirt road.

"Where are we going?" Sawyer asked.

"We're too obvious," Shaun said. "We need to find somewhere hidden from sight."

"A barn," Sawyer said. "Ariel and I used to train in a barn."

Shaun looked at him and smiled. "An excellent idea. I'm sure we can find one around here. Perhaps a farmer will be kind enough to let the Stormlord and his companion use it?"

Sawyer rolled his eyes at Shaun, which made him laugh. Soon, they came upon a small farm which had a barn of suitable size. The old farmer was only too happy to allow them the use of his barn. When they asked about his family, he mentioned that he was alone. His wife was long dead, and he had sent his two sons to join Chalon's army.

"Are you concerned about the Shadowlord?" Shaun asked, as he dismounted. "Rumor has it that he leads an army this way from the north."

"Aye, I'm worried for my sons," the farmer said. "They're strong but they've no experience fighting a war. As for me, I'll start to worry if Chalon falls."

Sawyer dismounted as well and the farmer led them into

the barn. It needed some patching in the roof and the doors looked like they were about to fall off, but there was a sizeable area in the middle that could be used as a sparring arena – once the manure was shoveled away. They thanked the farmer and began shoveling.

"So you're not a knight of Chalon?" Shaun inquired. Scooping up a hefty pile.

"No, just a regular guy."

"Would you accept a knighthood if Lionel asked you? It's quite an honor, you know."

"I guess it's a big honor," Sawyer said. "But I don't know the first thing about being a knight. And, I'm not sure I'd ever want to be *his* knight, either."

"True, I suppose you need to know whom you serve," Shaun agreed. "But I think you know more about being a knight than you realize."

"Only what I've seen in movies."

Shaun stopped shoveling.

"Movies?"

Well, where I'm from we have movies. They're like books with moving pictures…kinda."

"How interesting," Shaun said, returning to his shoveling. "And how far are you from home?"

"A long way," Sawyer said, laughing. "We came through a Wizard's Arch, I think that's what it's called."

"A Wizard's Arch? So Ariel was telling the truth, wasn't she? You and your companions are the three outlanders the prophecy speaks of, aren't you?"

"I don't know about that," Sawyer said. "But Ariel seems to think so."

"If Ariel thinks so then that's good enough for me,"

Shaun put his shovel aside and surveyed the area. "Looks safe to me. Ready to train?"

"Yes sir," Sawyer said, putting his shovel down too. "Plenty of room here."

"I wonder what those young admirers of yours would think if they'd seen us shoveling manure," Shaun said, tossing a wooden sword to Sawyer. "Not quite 'hero work' eh?"

Sawyer laughed, "No. I don't think so."

He walked to the center area they had just cleared and tested the balance of his sparring weapon. It was heavy on the back end.

"What's it like being a knight?" Sawyer asked, turning to Shaun. "I mean, what do you do?"

Shaun raised his eyebrows at his question, "Well, first off a knight must be honorable and true. When he gives his word it is a bond he cannot break. Defend yourself, Sawyer."

Shaun quickly swung his sword in a diagonal slashing motion, which Sawyer dodged, then he followed with a backhanded swing that almost caught him across the midsection. Sawyer jumped back and landed an overhead strike on Shaun's shoulder, which left a white mark. Shaun stopped and looked at his white-streaked pauldron.

"Very nice," Shaun said. "You're difficult to hit. That's good."

"The way you're swinging that wooden sword," Sawyer said, "I better be hard to hit."

"Hmm," Shaun said, stepping forward and swinging his sword in rapid succession. Each time Sawyer parried his attack and then spun out of Shaun's way, landing a strike to Shaun's back and side.

"If you keep this up," Shaun said, grinning, "I'll be white as a ghost by the time we get back."

"That's the plan," Sawyer said, giving Shaun a wide grin.

"Oh? Well then, let's continue, shall we?"

"Just let me know when you get tired," Sawyer laughed.

This time Shaun went straight at Sawyer, then feinted to his right and swung at Sawyer's knees. Sawyer sidestepped low attack, landing two quick overhead strikes to Shaun's back, which was becoming completely white by now. Shaun walked over and leaned on the wall, setting his wooden sword against a haystack.

"Remind me, just what did Ariel want me to teach you?" Shaun said.

"Dunno," Sawyer said, giving his sword a twirl. "How to take a hit?"

"Oh you're cocky for a young one," Shaun said. "I'll have to teach you humility. I'm sure that's what Ariel wanted you to learn."

"Bring it, old man."

Shaun laughed and picked up his sword.

"Humility," Shaun said as he lunged at Sawyer, "is a knight's greatest virtue."

"I thought you said honor was," Sawyer said, blocking the lunge. "What about strength and bravery and all that stuff?"

"They're all good to have, of course," Shaun said, "but what is honor, strength, and bravery without humility? A true knight fights for those who can't fight for themselves."

Shaun tried to land an overhead attack, but Sawyer blocked and held it. They stood close together, eyes locked for a second. Then Shaun slammed his shoulder into Sawyer, knocking him on his backside in the dirt.

"Hey," Sawyer protested, "That's not fair. That's dirty fighting."

"Aye," Shaun stepped back and twirled his sword. "It is. Are you happy lying there in the muck or do you want some more?"

"Oh it's on," Sawyer said, getting to his feet.

They spent the rest of the afternoon sparring, with Sawyer attempting to dodge and sidestep his way out of trouble whenever Shaun moved in close. If Sawyer maintained his distance, it usually meant a new white mark on Shaun's armor. However, once Shaun closed in he was able to use his strength to send Sawyer to the ground. At intervals, the old farmer brought buckets of cool water to drink.

"You're an excellent warrior," Shaun said. "When you find yourself in close combat you must maintain your balance. Move your feet."

Sawyer finished gulping down some water and looked at Shaun, "You could've told me that hours ago. Look at how muddy I am."

"I'll wager some of that isn't mud," Shaun said. "Let's have one more bout, shall we?"

"Okay," Sawyer grabbed his sword and walked to the center of the barn again. He turned and raised his sword. This time, Shaun let out a loud battle cry and charged, swinging his sword wildly. First, he knocked Sawyer's sword away with a disarming move, then hit Sawyer two times before he reacted by sweeping Shaun's feet out from under him. Shaun fell to the ground with a crash.

Sawyer laughed and bent over to help him up but was

met with a wooden sword at his neck. Sawyer swallowed. Shaun's expression was grim. He shook his head and got to a knee while pulling Sawyer down to take a knee beside him.

"Have you ever killed a man?"

"No," Sawyer said.

"Listen carefully," Shaun said with a grunt, he placed a mailed hand on Sawyer's shoulder. "In battle, expect no quarter from your enemy, be it man or beast. They will do anything to end your life, do you understand?"

"I...I don't think I could kill someone," Sawyer said. "It's murder."

"In battle, its kill or be killed. *This* is what Ariel wanted me to teach you," Shaun's gaze never left Sawyer's eyes. "It isn't murder, its war. The armies that are marching toward us are comprised of men, orcs, and various foul creatures. You need to know that if you join the battle, you will be sought out because you are the Stormlord. Your death would be a blow to the morale of many."

Sawyer blinked then shook his head.

"I still don't think I could do it," he said. "Maybe I'm not the Stormlord after all."

"Would you fight to save your life? The lives of your friends?"

"Yeah, I've done that already," Sawyer said.

"You have," Shaun agreed. "Now, would you kill to stay alive?"

Sawyer said nothing. It was a hard question to answer. He was just a teenager, how could he answer a question like that? He realized at that moment that he'd been 'playing' at being a hero. Was it time for him to grow up? If so, he needed to grow up fast.

"But killing a man..." Sawyer's voice trailed off. "I didn't sign up for that."

"In battle," Shaun said, "its self-preservation. The barbarians from the north will come straight for you. They'll bite, throw dirt in your eyes, and attack you from behind if they can. There's no such thing as a fair fight, remember that."

Shaun stood up and helped Sawyer to his feet. "When battle comes, stay close to me."

"It was an excellent day's training, Sawyer. You worked hard, with great discipline. And, I hope you learned something that may save your life one day. Now, let's get back to Chalon before it gets dark."

Sawyer took one last drink of water before they left the barn. Outside, Shaun pressed a gold coin into the farmer's calloused hand. Then they mounted their horses and cantered off, while the farmer was still stammering out his thanks.

They failed to notice a hooded figure in a gray cloak at the far edge of the farmer's field.

# CHAPTER THIRTY-THREE
## WIZARD TRAINING

Geoff spent most of the afternoon grilling his father about how wizardry stuff worked. He learned a few more spells as well as which schools of magic were diametrically opposed to each other, such as wizardry and sorcery. It was an important concept for him to learn. Since wizards and sorcerers generally detested each other, they tended to clash.

"So which is more powerful, a wizard or a sorcerer?"

"Neither," Maelord said. "They're equally powerful. Each is armed with a deadly array of spells."

"Why do wizards and sorcerers hate each other?"

"Most don't hate like that," Maelord said. "But you need to know there is a certain animosity between them because they're competing schools of magic."

"Competing for what?" Geoff asked.

"Power, of course."

"So are wizardry and sorcery the most powerful schools of magic?"

"Oh no," Maelord said. "Two of the most powerful, but not *the* most powerful."

"Really? So what is the most powerful school of magic, then?"

"The druidic arts, in my opinion," Maelord said. "Because their magic centers around life and seeks to preserve a natural balance with all living things."

Ishara nodded in agreement.

"Well," Geoff said, "that makes sense. You should see what Ariel can do. She's awesome."

"I've seen her in action," Maelord said, "yes, she is awesome. Now, I think you've learned enough to begin practicing your spells, don't you?"

"Yeah," Geoff began leafing through his spell book again.

"Not here," Maelord added. "There isn't enough room and you could break something. Instead, I recommend you go to the same place I go when I practice. There is a small pond beside a hill to the west of Chalon—"

Ishara jumped to her feet, which started another swirl of dust, "I know exactly where that pond is," Ishara said, "I can take him there and observe his progress."

"Excellent!" Maelord said, clapping his hands. "I'll see you back here before nightfall, then. Tonight, we sleep here."

Ishara frowned. Geoff saw a definite downturn in her demeanor. This was probably the last place in the world she wanted to spend the night. She stood, pulled on her cloak and strode to the front door, a trail of dust floated up in her wake. She turned and looked at Geoff, waiting. He looked at his father.

"Go, yes, go," Maelord said. "Remember what you've just learned and you'll be fine."

"Okay," Geoff said, springing to his feet. "We'll be back before it gets dark."

Before he could turn around, Ishara had opened the door and dashed out of the tower, taking time breathe in fresh air. Geoff followed her out the door. Ishara pulled her hood over her head, concealing her elvish features. Geoff opened his mouth to say something, but Ishara held up a finger for silence.

"Not a single word," she said. "We are buying a broom, mop, bucket, and other cleaning supplies before we return."

Geoff smiled. There was no getting around it, they were going to be cleaning his father's tower tonight. They walked along the cobbled street, the smell of animal and human waste was appalling. Peasants begged for scraps of food and gangs of ruffians kept an eye out for easy targets. Geoff was glad Ishara had pulled her hood up because elves were still considered to be the source of all troubles in Chalon. It wasn't true, of course, but Geoff wasn't sure how to remedy the situation. After exiting the city through the front gates, they headed toward the site Maelord had recommended, a pretty hillside overlooking a small pond, ringed with trees and tall reeds.

"How'd you know about this place, anyway?"

"I know most of Chalon and the surrounding areas well," Ishara said. "This is the only nearby location that matches your father's description."

"Seems peaceful here," Geoff said, observing a few dragonflies skimming across the surface of the pond. There was a slight breeze.

"It does," Ishara said. "I feel more relaxed here than in such an overcrowded city."

"I imagine all elves feel that way, right?" Geoff asked as he pulled out his spell book.

"You are right," Ishara said. "Selra'thel is as large as Chalon, but we do not have the same troubles humans seem to have, we care for one another. You will not find a homeless elf in Selra'thel."

"Wow. That sounds like a great place to live."

"It is," Ishara said proudly, "elves are known to be generous, especially toward our own kind."

"Didn't you say you were going to show me around Selra'thel someday?"

"I did," Ishara said. "I think you will like what you see."

"I know I will," Geoff said. "Your home must be the best place in Alluria."

Geoff flipped through a few pages and then a page near the back of the book caught his eye.

"This looks interesting," he said, "I'm not sure what it is…some kind of explosion…an incendiary burst, maybe?"

Ishara looked at the page he was referring to and placed her hand over it.

"Geoff, no," she said firmly. "Have you forgotten your father's advice? You must start at the beginning and work your way to the end."

"No really, I think I can do it," Geoff said. "It doesn't look that hard."

"Geoff, you never attempt to cast a spell unless you are sure of the outcome."

"I can do it," Geoff said. He looked at Ishara. There was concern in her eyes. "I can."

Ishara's eyes searched his for a moment. Then she shook her head and sighed.

"Fine," she said, "if you will not listen to others then you must learn for yourself."

Ishara turned and began marching up the hill behind Geoff.

"Hey, where're you going?"

"Since you have decided to attempt that spell against my counsel *and* your father's advice," Ishara said as she sat down and rested her arms on her knees. "I am keeping a safe distance."

Geoff looked at her. She was perched a good fifty feet away watching him with a stoic look on her face.

"Continue if you must," Ishara said, then she pointed straight ahead. "That direction, please."

Geoff turned away and faced the pond. He looked at the page again. He wasn't sure how to pronounce a couple words, but he was pretty sure he'd get it right.

From behind him, up on the hill, he heard Ishara mutter, "Wizards…yet another term for lunacy."

Ignoring Ishara's comment, Geoff practiced the pictured hand movements a few times. Then he cleared his throat. He glanced over his shoulder. Ishara had retreated further up the hill. Geoff turned back around. How cool would it be if he showed his father he could cast a spell like this? Though he'd never tried one with words that must be precisely coordinated with gestures, Geoff wasn't worried.

Holding the book in one hand, Geoff waved his other hand and moved his fingers in exactly the same fashion pictured in the book. Then he uttered the phrase beneath the illustration, "*Igna thol ehran.*"

Nothing happened.

"What?" Geoff said. "I know I got it right."

He scratched his head and flipped the page, thinking maybe he missed more instructions, but the next page was blank. He'd have to ask his dad what went wrong. He turned around and looked at Ishara.

"It didn't work."

As soon as he finished speaking, a massive bright explosion erupted behind him. Geoff felt a rush of hot air behind him as he was catapulted through the air. He landed hard on the hill several feet below Ishara. One of his boots went flying in a different direction and his spell book flew over Ishara's head.

"Geoff!" Ishara shouted as she bounded downhill, sliding to a stop beside him. "Are you injured? Can you move?"

Geoff blinked and looked at Ishara. He felt the back of his head, a sizeable bump had begun to form.

"Ouch," he said, "yeah, I'm okay. I thought it didn't work."

Ishara began laughing so hard she had to grab her stomach. He smiled and then started laughing too. Soon, they'd both exhausted themselves laughing and were relaxing on their backs in the lush grass. Ishara placed a hand on his chest.

"Next time, *Nu Tel'mor*," Ishara said, "you will listen to me, yes?"

Geoff nodded. Then Ishara leaned over and kissed him on the lips. Geoff put his hand over hers. They kissed over and over, the softness and warmth of her lips made him tingle all over. Ishara raised her head and smiled as she looked into his eyes.

"More," Geoff urged. Ishara raised an eyebrow, but he was rewarded with another long kiss. *If he knew this was going to happen, he'd have blown himself up sooner. Wow, she liked him. She really liked him.*

After a couple more kisses, Ishara helped him to his feet and began brushing off the mud and dirt that had hit him during the explosion.

"I lost my boot," Geoff said, looking around, "and my book."

"Wizards," Ishara grumbled, "your book is on the other side of the hill and your missing boot is floating in the pond."

Geoff looked back at the pond and sure enough, his brown leather boot was bobbing in the middle.

"I wonder what went wrong." Geoff inquired. "I'm pretty sure I managed to get it right."

Ishara looked at him in disbelief.

"Are you serious? You did not 'get it right' as you say, and you should not even think about that spell again until you are ready."

"Yeah," Geoff said. "I guess you're right."

"Guess?"

Geoff looked at Ishara. Her hands were on her hips and she was glaring at him.

"I mean, yeah," he said quickly. "You're right. I'll leave that spell alone for now."

Ishara went and retrieved Geoff's spell book. When she handed it to him he noticed it was opened to the first page.

"Thanks," he said. "Now to get my boot."

They walked down the hill and to the edge of the pond. His boot was floating lower in the water, far outside his reach.

"Let's try this levitation spell," Geoff said, glancing at Ishara. She said nothing. Geoff noticed she didn't retreat to the safety of the hillside either. He flipped the pages to the third spell. Geoff pointed to his soaked boot and made the appropriate movement with his fingers. The boot rose three feet out of the water.

"Excellent," Ishara said, "nicely done."

"Thanks, so how do I get it? It's still out of reach."

"If you are careful," Ishara said, "perhaps the telekinetic spell on the next page will help."

"Okay," Geoff turned to the next page. The spell looked exceedingly simple. The only difference was a minor change in the way he moved his fingers. Other than that, he only needed to think where he wanted the boot to go and it would float in that direction. Easy. Geoff bid his boot to return with a gesture of his fingers. However, instead of floating over to him, the boot shot toward him with blinding speed. It was coming straight for his nose!

Geoff's eyes shot wide open. He didn't have time to react. A split second before his nose was to be flattened, Ishara's hand darted in front of his face, catching hold of the oncoming projectile, splashing them both with grimy pond water that was inside the soggy boot.

"Geoff!" Ishara said as she glared at him. "Are you *trying* to hurt yourself? Where is your concentration?"

"I...I..." Geoff stammered, shaking a little from the near impact.

Ishara rolled her eyes, "Here," she said, slapping the wet boot against Geoff's chest and further dousing him with pond water. "Stick to levitation. You are far too dangerous for your own good."

"Yeah," Geoff said. "Levitation it is."

Ishara grunted as she turned and stomped back up the side of the hill and sat down again. She was not amused by his miscasting antics. So, for the next few hours, Geoff did nothing but practice levitating objects. First, he levitated his boot up and down, attempting different heights, then he moved on to other objects, like stones. The heavier the stone the more effort it took for him to lift it off the ground. He managed to get to where he could levitate two or more small objects at the same time if he cleared his mind and focused on them.

As the afternoon wore on into evening, it was time to stop and return to Chalon. They walked along a tiny path, Ishara strolling beside Geoff. She took his hand in hers.

"You did well," she said, giving him an encouraging smile. "I think your father will be proud of your progress."

"Thanks. You aren't going to tell him about the other stuff are you? You know, the explosion and flying boot and all that?"

"I may," Ishara said. "Unless you help me clean your father's filthy tower."

"Deal," Geoff said with a smile.

Ishara pulled him to a stop and kissed him.

"You are a far better sneak thief than a wizard," she said, "But I think in time, you will be a wonderful wizard...and much less dangerous to be around."

"Thanks," Geoff said. "I can be both, right?"

"Perhaps."

"A sneak thieving wizard," Geoff mused. "I wonder what the possibilities are."

"We shall explore them," Ishara said, "after you demonstrate your house cleaning abilities."

Geoff laughed. *Wow, she's beautiful, tough, and has a great sense of humor.* Ishara pulled her hood over her head before they returned to Chalon. As they walked the crowded streets, Geoff heard hushed rumors of a fire breathing dragon to the north that burned whole villages to the ground.

Geoff leaned close to Ishara and whispered, "Is that—"

"Yes," she replied.

They stopped in front of a humble shop. Ishara pulled out a small black leather bag whose contents clinked and jingled.

"We shall worry about dragons later," she said. "Tonight, we have the daunting task of cleaning a wizard's tower."

# CHAPTER THIRTY-FOUR
## EXPERIENCE AND DELIBERATIONS

Sawyer and Shaun arrived in Chalon before the gates were closed and torches lit for the evening. In the alleys and doorways Sawyer saw huddled forms of peasants preparing for another night on the streets. He lowered his head and sighed.

"I agree," Shaun said, "this is a pitiful sight and it shouldn't be happening, especially not in Chalon."

"Can't we do anything?"

"We've given all we can for now, you and I," Shaun said glancing at Sawyer from the corner of his eye. "They need help from their ruler."

"That isn't gonna happen," Sawyer said. "He's delusional, or just plain nuts."

"Lionel is my friend," Shaun said, "he wasn't always like he is now. He's changed a great deal."

"Then maybe you can talk to him," Sawyer said. "I dunno, maybe persuade him to give out food and create shelters. Something, anything."

"I believe I will do that," Shaun said. "Would you care to accompany me when I have my talk with Lionel?"

"Me?" Sawyer laughed. "You don't want me there, I don't have a good history with that guy. None of us do. He hates Ariel, imprisoned Ishara, and plotted to have that big guy, Cruelon, kill me. He wants the Stormblade for himself."

"I've known about his animosity toward Ariel," Shaun said, "but I've never known him to make such a plot against someone for what they carried. Did you say he imprisoned Ishara? The young elf-girl?"

"Yep. That's when Lady Seqwil first attacked us. I think she was trying to kill Ishara first because she was in a prison cell, then she was going to come after the rest of us."

"Did he have a reason to imprison Ishara?

"Not much of a reason," Sawyer said. "He suspected Ishara had assassinated some foreign diplomat from Khorthos."

"How did you stop Lady Seqwil?"

"I didn't," Sawyer said. "Ariel did. Lady Seqwil fell from that tower," Sawyer pointed up, "the highest one with the gryphons."

"And yet Lady Seqwil lived," Shaun said. "She's very resourceful."

"Yeah," Sawyer said. "She kicked my butt yesterday in the castle. Geoff and his Dad saved me."

"Yes, the boy wizard," Shaun said, nodding. "Is he as powerful as I've heard?"

"Oh yeah," Sawyer said. "I've seen him fry a cavern of carrion mite-things, kill a bog drake, and he even stopped a hail of arrows from turning me into a pin cushion. He's for real. He's legit."

"A bog drake?" Shaun said with some surprise in his

voice. "A boy his age killed a bog drake?"

"Fried it," Sawyer said. "With a bolt of lightning."

"That would make him a—"

"Dragonslayer," Sawyer finished Shaun's sentence and looked at him. "Yes. He is."

They rode on to the stables beside the castle. Only a few knights were still training. Sawyer noticed the young knight Sir Reymond had embarrassed earlier was among them. An older knight with a gray beard and bushy mustache, was berating him for not following directions. Sawyer stopped and watched. Some memories flooded back into his mind, memories he would rather have forgotten forever.

"Why do you frown so," Shaun said. "It's only training, not unlike our day today."

"Does he have to yell at him like that?" Sawyer said, his voice bitter.

"Perhaps you have not trained with a knight like Lord Jorrin," Shaun said. "He's an effective teacher."

"He's a jerk," Sawyer said. His eyes flashed as he looked at Shaun. "And yes, I've been taught by a jerk like that. My dad. No matter how well I do, it's never good enough."

Sawyer rode over to arena, leaving Shaun contemplating his words. He stopped and watched for a moment longer. Lord Jorrin was still yelling at the young knight.

"Hey!" Sawyer shouted.

The young knight looked up at him and Lord Jorrin whirled about, his face red from either yelling or angry from being interrupted. Sawyer pointed at the young knight and gave him a thumbs up. His gesture brought a wide grin across the young knight's face. As Sawyer turned his horse toward the stables, he glared at Lord Jorrin. A challenging glare that dared him to do or say anything. Lord Jorrin opened his mouth but before he said anything he looked at Shaun, who held up a hand and shook his head.

The knights in the arena returned to their training, Lord Jorrin's voice was quieter as he continued to instruct the younger knight. In the stables, Sawyer dismounted and grabbed the Stormblade before giving his horse a pat and letting a squire take it away. Shaun dismounted beside him.

"I'd wager that was the first time Lord Jorrin has been interrupted," Shaun said.

Sawyer said nothing.

"Sawyer, you should understand that a knight's training is difficult and there are times when a knight must—"

"Yeah, I've heard it all before," Sawyer said. "To be the best you have to train harder than anyone else, be willing to go the extra mile, sacrifice more, blah, blah, blah."

Sawyer began removing his armor, as did Shaun.

"I see you do have some experience with that sort of thing," Shaun said. "We're only trying to help that knight so he won't fall in battle."

"I bet yelling at him does the trick," Sawyer said, removing his boots.

"Sometimes it does."

"And sometimes it doesn't," Sawyer replied as he stood up, nearly nose to nose with Shaun. The same cold glare he'd given to Lord Jorrin was now directed at Shaun. Sawyer turned away to go, but Shaun caught his arm and spun him back around.

"What's gotten into you?"

"The same crap that I have to take at home from my father," Sawyer said. He rolled up his tunic and revealed a long scar on his back. "No pain no gain!" He turned to his right side and pointed to a few burn marks. "This is what happens when you lose a game in the final minute!" Sawyer then rolled up his left sleeve, revealing a scar along his forearm, "This is what you get when you talk back, a broken arm!"

Shaun released Sawyer.

"Experience?" Sawyer said. "Yeah, I got lots of experience with that. You should see what my dad does when he's drunk. That's when he really gets nasty. Mom always tried to cheer me up and say he's only doing it because he loves me and wants me to succeed. What a load of crap."

Sawyer stormed out of the stables, carrying his dirty armor and sword. He didn't want Shaun to see tears in his eyes. It wasn't until Sawyer found his way to his room and flopped on his bed that he realized what he'd said to Shaun. He regretted behaving like a jerk to the one man who seemed to actually care about him in this world or any other. The day had started out to be a pretty good day, too. Sawyer took a deep breath. After so many beatings and scoldings from his father when he didn't 'measure up', he'd simply lost it when he saw someone else getting the same treatment.

He wondered if in the morning Shaun would let him apologize. Sawyer shook his head and said with a long sigh, "Not likely."

He looked over at Geoff's empty bed. He was glad Geoff wasn't in the room. He needed some time to chill, being alone tonight seemed like a good situation. Then he thought of Jane, how could he have not thought about her for most of the day? Sawyer hoped she and Ariel were okay and on their way back. He really wanted to see Jane again. He missed her. It struck him as strange, but when he recalled all the girlfriends he'd had in the past, Jane was the only one he'd ever really *missed*. He needed to see her again.

Several minutes later there was a knock at his door. Sawyer got up to see who it was. He was shocked to see Shaun Hammerfel, trim, washed and clean, wearing a tunic bearing a family crest, a stag on one side and a lion on the other. There was a squire standing behind him in the corridor.

"You are not ready yet?" Shaun asked.

"Ready? For what?"

"We're to meet Lionel in his war room," Shaun replied. "Have you forgotten? I have some questions for him and I think your presence would help."

"Me? What can I do?"

"Quite a lot," Shaun said, putting a hand on his shoulder. He looked at the filthy armor on the floor in the room and turned to the squire.

"Would you please take the Stormlord's armor and have it cleaned for tomorrow?"

"Yes, my lord," the squire squeezed past Sawyer, gathered up his armor, and left the room.

"Thank you," Shaun said as the squire left with Sawyer's armor.

"That's special armor," Sawyer said to Shaun, watching after the squire. "It's—"

"Elven battle armor," Shaun said. "Magical and priceless. Don't worry, it will be well cared for and not a single piece will go missing."

Sawyer nodded and let Shaun in the room. "Thanks."

"These are better quarters than my own," Shaun said.

"You must have good friends here."

"Maelord got it for us."

"Very good friends," Shaun said.

"Hey, I'm sorry about what I said earlier," Sawyer said. "I over-reacted. I just hate seeing that sort of thing."

"No apology needed, Sawyer," Shaun walked over to the fruit bowl, which had been replenished earlier in the day. "Most fathers do want the best for their children. I can see now that with your father...well, it's something else. Drinking too much, perhaps."

Sawyer nodded.

Shaun plucked an orange from the bowl and began peeling it with his fingers.

"I think you should be there tonight," he said, looking at Sawyer. "According to Ariel, you and your friends have already contributed so much to this war."

Sawyer went to his belongings and pulled out a fresh tunic and breeches. As he changed he thought of a question for Shaun.

"Do you think we're the three travelers of prophecy? Are we really making a difference here?"

Shaun took a large bite of the orange and wiped the juice from his lips. As he chewed he studied Sawyer.

"I do," he said finally. "I had my doubts until today, but no longer. I believe you're destined to save Alluria."

Sawyer finished dressing, put on a fresh pair of boots, and strapped on his sword. They left his room and made their way to the king's war room. Along the way, Sawyer felt the need to say more to Shaun.

"You have a point about my dad," he said, keeping his eyes straight ahead. "He keeps pushing me to be the best, but it's like he's making up for something in his life, I dunno. I get tired of being yelled at all the time. I can't make even one damn mistake. He embarrasses me at my games. I wish he'd stop coming to watch me if he's going to act like that."

"Do you think your father loves you?"

"No."

Shaun glanced at Sawyer.

"Do you love your father?"

Sawyer was silent for a few moments as they walked.

"I don't know," Sawyer said. "Sometimes, I guess."

They approached the war room, four well-armed guards stood at each side of the double doors. Shaun opened the doors and entered as Sawyer followed. The room itself was luxurious and well-lit, with a long wooden table and thick carpeting on the floor. Sawyer had seen it before, he recognized the embroidered tapestries on the walls. The smell of burning torches lingered in the room.

Those present in the room were Geoff and Ishara, Maelord, Trelane, King Lionel, wearing his crown and sitting on a throne above everyone else, Commander Renfry, and King Baldon of Keredain. Sawyer had hoped to see Ariel and Jane in the meeting too. However, they had entered the war room at a moment of contention.

"Why do you refuse to join us?" Trelane asked. "Elves and dwarves are spilling their blood for the safety of your kingdom."

"I don't recall asking for your help," Lionel said. "Nor do I remember giving your armies leave to enter my kingdom. You may remove yourselves at any time."

"You may try to remove us," Baldon said, glaring at Lionel, "anytime."

Geoff turned and smiled at Sawyer as he and Shaun entered. It didn't go unnoticed by Lionel.

"Lord Hammerfel," Lionel said in a loud voice, "why do you bring this boy into my war room? Is it not enough that two other children are here as well? Did they bring their toys?"

"The Stormblade is this one's toy," Shaun replied. "His name is Sawyer."

"It matters not," Lionel said.

"I think it does," Shaun said in a challenging tone that was ignored by Lionel.

"*I* choose to send my army where I want," Lionel said, addressing Trelane again. "At the moment, I see no need to send them beyond my walls."

"Your walls will not protect you forever," Trelane said. "I came here in good faith at the request of King Andurys to ask you one more time to join us against the Scarlet Queen."

"No," Lionel said.

Trelane's jaw clenched. "Then we are all doomed."

Baldon stood up and stomped out of the room, saying nothing.

"My King," Commander Renfry said, bowing low, "we've proven we can defeat her armies. Why not join with our allies and beat back this invasion?"

"The only invasions I see," Lionel snapped, "are the dwarves and elves from the east."

"And do you not see the dark clouds approaching?" Maelord said, pointing northward. "Those are not dwarves. The Scarlet Queen has assembled vast armies. She will not stop until all of Alluria is laid waste."

"The Scarlet Queen doesn't exist!" Lionel pounded on

the arm of his throne. "She's just a fairy tale made up by elves to distract us from whatever it is they're trying to accomplish."

"She is not a fairy tale," Ishara said, stepping forward. "I saw her at the Iron Citadel, with the Shadowlord. I assure you, she is real."

"I don't believe you," Lionel said, looking down at her.

"Then perhaps you can answer these questions," Maelord said, stepping forward, arms crossed. "Where is Lady Seqwil Ferncliff? And why do the Sentinels not fly overhead?"

Lionel's nostrils flared and he stood up. It looked to Sawyer like he was going to have another emotional outburst, or maybe a mental breakdown.

"I'm the King and you aren't," Lionel said. "I don't answer to you. However, if you must know, I sent her body back to Selra'thel. As for the Sentinels, the gryphons have become ill and cannot fly."

"Then you have a ghost wandering the halls of your castle," Maelord said. "You may want to investigate that. As for myself, I'll be joining Trelane and Baldon on the field of battle. We leave in the morning."

# Chapter Thirty-Five
## A Plan of Attack

Geoff and Ishara followed Maelord out of the war room. He'd seen his father angry before, but what he'd just witnessed was something beyond anger. In the corridor outside the war room, King Baldon stood. He appeared to be waiting.

"Dad," Geoff asked, "what's gonna happen now?"

"We go to war," Maelord said. He looked at Baldon and nodded.

"It's about time," Baldon grumbled. He turned and walked away.

Trelane, Shaun, and Sawyer joined them. Trelane was tight-lipped and his fists were clenched.

"So," Shaun said. "Shall we consider that a successful war council? We no longer need to meet this evening."

"I am not sure anything is successful as far as Lionel is concerned," Trelane said. "He behaves strangely, even for a fool like him."

"Agreed," Maelord said. He scratched his thin beard for a second. "The old Lionel would've wanted to join us. Wait here, I'll be right back."

"Dad," Geoff said, "what're you gonna do?"

"Wait here," Maelord said.

Maelord turned and walked back into the war room. Geoff, ever the curious type, followed several steps behind. He didn't trust Lionel. He was worried his father would say or do something and wind up in a prison cell. Geoff stopped outside the war room, under the watchful gaze of the guards. Maelord, however, strode in as usual.

Lionel had just given Commander Renfry orders. Judging by the disapproving expression on Renfry's face, they were orders he didn't agree with, but he had to obey. He walked out past Maelord and Geoff, giving each a nod. Geoff watched his father approach Lionel, who was yawning on his carved throne.

"Yes," Lionel said grumpily. "What is it now?"

"You and I go back a long way, wouldn't you agree?" Maelord said.

"Of course."

"If I have done or said anything to offend you, then I apologize," Maelord said, bowing low. "But I beg you, in the name of our friendship, please help us. We can't win without the might of Chalon."

"I've already given you my answer," Lionel said. "That is it."

Lionel looked around the room, searching for something.

"Where is my royal goblet? I'm thirsty."

"Permit me to get your drink for you, Your Majesty," Maelord said, moving behind the throne to a table which held Lionel's goblet and wines. *What was Dad doing? Calling Lionel 'your majesty'? He was up to something.* Geoff's heart began to beat faster. While Lionel waited for his wine, Geoff saw his father make a few gestures with his hands. *Dad's casting spells on the King!* Geoff gulped.

"You there! Boy!" Lionel shouted at Geoff. "Get away from that door."

Geoff bowed and hurried back to the others.

"So what's your Dad up to?" Sawyer wanted to know. "Did he turn Lionel into a pile of ashes?"

"No," Geoff said. "I'm not sure what he did."

A moment later Maelord returned, frowning. He took Geoff by the arm and looked him in the eye. "This is not the time to be sneaky. Next time I tell you to stay put, you need to do so. You nearly ruined everything."

"Sorry," Geoff said. "What did you do?"

Maelord looked around.

"We can't talk here," he said. He looked at Trelane, Shaun, and Baldon. "We'll meet you in the morning at the elven encampment."

"You might want to do that sooner," Commander Renfry said, walking up to the group.

"Why is that?" Trelane asked.

"I've just been given orders to mobilize the army of Chalon and get them ready for battle."

"That's great," Shaun said. "Finally some movement from Lionel."

"Not exactly," Renfry said in a hushed tone. He looked at Trelane. "Tomorrow we're to attack the elves and drive them back to Selra'thel."

Everyone stood in silence, too stunned to speak. Geoff looked at Trelane, who had a typical elven stoic look on his face.

"Come, let's talk elsewhere," Maelord said.

As a group, they walked outside the castle and around back to the training grounds. Once there, everyone looked in all directions for potential eavesdroppers, but they were alone. There, Maelord asked Renfry, "What size force will you be taking against the elves tomorrow?"

"Everything," Renfry said. "I've been instructed to bring the entire might of Chalon against Selra'thel."

"Good," Maelord said. "Bring everything you can, every man, every catapult, every weapon in the armories of Chalon."

"What're you planning?" Shaun asked.

"If this is the only way we can get Chalon in the war, then this is what we must do," Maelord said. He looked at Renfry. "You know the elves are not the true enemy here."

"Aye," Renfry said.

"We will be waiting with the elves, dwarves, and Knights of Caladar. I hope it will be enough."

"Maelord," Renfry said. "If I disobey my King, I will be executed."

"And if you obey your king," Maelord replied, "then all of Alluria will fall beneath the boot of the Scarlet Queen."

Shaun put his hand on Renfry's shoulder.

"It is not an easy thing for men such as us," Shaun said. "All our lives we've been conditioned to obey without question. Now, the only way to save Alluria is with disobedience."

"These are indeed strange times," Trelane said. He nodded at Renfry. "It will be an honor to fight by your side again."

"There are two armies advancing," Trelane said. "If they should meet and combine their numbers they would be too much for us – even with Chalon's army."

"So we attack as soon as we can," Shaun said.

"Exactly," Trelane said. "We attack the northern army and crush them before the Scarlet Queen's western army can arrive."

"I only hope we can defeat that army first," Shaun said. "The Shadowlord leads it."

"We defeated him last time," Trelane said, "did we not?"

"Has anyone seen or heard from Ariel?" Maelord said.

Everyone fell silent and shook their heads.

"Pity," Trelane said, "Having the High Druid of Alluria fighting with us might be just the difference we need."

"We can't worry about Ariel," Maelord said. "If she and Jane can be there, they will."

"You must know," Renfry said, "that rumors have spread throughout the troops of Chalon since the last battle. Some say the girl, Jane, is a witch."

"No she isn't," Sawyer said. "You know that's not true."

"We do," Maelord said. "And know this, if Ariel and Jane return, all will be well and we'll have two druids standing with us in battle."

"And the Stormlord," Sawyer said.

"And another wizard," Geoff said, determined not to be left out of the conversation.

"Well then," Trelane said. "It appears we have our plan. I will see most of you tomorrow."

Trelane looked at Renfry and shook his hand.

"I will see you when you arrive. Be careful, the hour approaches, my friend."

"Aye," Renfry said. "I say let the dread Queen come. We'll be ready."

"Then it's settled," Maelord said. "We'll meet tomorrow. Trelane, do you have scouts you can send out to locate the enemy's northern army?"

"I have already done so," Trelane acknowledged.

"Good. Until tomorrow, then," Maelord said.

They went their separate ways with Sawyer electing to go with Shaun while Geoff and Ishara followed Maelord. After they exited the castle grounds and entered the darkened city, Geoff leaned close to his father and whispered, "What spell did you cast on Lionel?"

"Spells, son, spells," Maelord said in a low tone. "First, I detected a charm on Lionel, then, I disenchanted it, or at least I tried to disenchant it."

"You mean he's under someone's control?"

"Yes," Maelord said. "He was, but I'm not sure my disenchant spell worked, so he may be still."

"Lady Seqwil," Ishara said. "She could exert her influence over Lionel and make him believe things that are not true, or send his army to attack an ally. It would be far easier for the Scarlet Queen to march into Chalon and Selra'thel after they had weakened each other."

"Correct," Maelord said. "Come on, you two. We must gather our things and make for Trelane's camp."

"Dad, we bought brooms, mops, buckets and soap," Geoff said.

Geoff's statement drew a bewildered look from his father.

"What on earth for? Why would you do such a thing?"

"We thought we were going to be staying with you tonight," Geoff said. "And maybe we could clean some."

"What nonsense," Maelord said, waving him off. "We travel to the elven encampment tonight."

A long, soulful howl rang out from somewhere outside the city walls. Everyone who heard it paused. Geoff shivered a little. It was a sound he'd heard before. The werewolf was prowling the countryside.

"Perhaps we should leave first thing in the morning," Maelord said.

# CHAPTER THIRTY-SIX
## A MUCH NEEDED REST

Jane could barely breathe as she stumbled after Ariel down the road. The previous night was a race to live. The werewolf had gained on them during the night despite Ariel's efforts to mask their trail. They hadn't even dared stop. By morning they had come within sight of Chalon. The first thing Jane noticed was a long column of soldiers heading north. Some were mounted and wore shining silvery armor while others marched on foot.

Ariel pointed to the walled city in the distance, "We will be there this afternoon. Come, eat something and rest."

Jane followed Ariel off the road to a large oak tree. Both sat, leaning against the tree and enjoyed the welcomed shade. Ariel offered her water flask to Jane, who took a big swallow. Then she leaned back and shut her eyes.

"How are you, Jane?"

Jane laughed at the question. She was exhausted, scared, and miserable.

"At least we didn't get eaten by the werewolf," Jane said.

"You drank all of your water last night," Ariel said. "That slowed you down."

"I couldn't help it," Jane coughed.

They sat in the shade for a few more minutes. Ariel ate a handful of berries. Jane wasn't hungry.

"Was that the army of Chalon we saw leaving?" Jane asked.

"No, they were the Knights of Caladar and dwarves from Keredain. Lord Shaun Hammerfel and King Baldon must be riding to meet the northern army of Queen Lysis."

"That's a good thing, right?"

"It is," Ariel said, "if Lionel has sent the army of Chalon to join the battle."

"What about the others," Jane said, glancing at Ariel. "Sawyer, Geoff, and Ishara, do you think they're still in Chalon?"

"I do not know," Ariel said. "It is possible."

Jane leaned her head back and closed her eyes. They must've run, or sometimes, in her case, walked swiftly throughout the night. A sharp pain shot through her left calf, causing her to cry out and grab at it. Ariel rolled Jane onto her side and started expertly massaging the cramped calf, digging deep with her thumb and fingers. After a few minutes of Ariel's treatment, the pain subsided.

The cool, shaded grass felt so inviting that Jane closed her eyes again. She could easily have fallen asleep, but Ariel nudged her awake.

"I know how tired you are," she said, "but we need to get to Chalon. If you wish, I will carry you, Jane."

Jane rolled onto her back and groaned.

"Just five minutes, please."

"I am sorry, Jane. Let me help you up."

They resumed walking, as Jane watched the last of the

long column of knights and dwarves disappear over a hill. The sun glinted on their armor, but they were heading into a dark and cloudy horizon. Ariel put her arm around Jane and propped her up as they walked.

"You're so strong," Jane said. "You never sleep, you eat like a bird, and you never seem to tire. How do you do it?"

"It is an elf thing," Ariel said.

They arrived in Chalon in the early afternoon. They stopped briefly so Ariel could pull on her cloak and cover her head as well as her weapons. Jane smelled the refuse and waste before they walked through the gates. Her stomach churned.

"Ariel, I'm going to be sick. For real."

"I may be sick as well," Ariel said. "I cannot believe no one is helping these people. They are barely surviving in the streets."

Worn and dusty from the travels, the pair were largely ignored by the peasants and beggars. Ariel steered them away from a potential encounter with street ruffians on their way toward the castle. At the gates to the castle, Ariel revealed her identity but the guards refused to allow them inside stating that King Lionel had ordered all elves from the castle. Ariel said nothing in protest. She pulled her hood up again and helped Jane back down the cobbled path to the city.

"That was unexpected," Jane observed, wincing at the blisters on her feet as she limped along.

"Indeed," Ariel said. "Unexpected and troublesome. I know a safe place for us. It is in the noble's sector."

They wove their way through various alleyways toward a warm-lit stone home with smoke coming from the chimney. Ariel's knock was answered by an older man with broad shoulders. He had a full head of black and gray hair, yet his sunken eyes and stern expression made Jane nervous. She half expected to have the large wooden door slammed in their faces.

"*Hal'inari*," Ariel said, removing her hood. "Sir Andrew, we need help."

The large man's features softened the instant he saw Ariel's face.

"Not any longer," he said as he opened the door wide. "Come in, come in."

The house was well-furnished. Two plush reading chairs faced a large fireplace that Jane thought she could stand in. Mounted over the fireplace was a sword that must've been six feet long at least. There were thick rugs on the floor, oil portraits hanging on the walls, and a long wooden table on the far end of the room, leading to the kitchen area. There wasn't much of a smell, which Jane thought was odd since a large man lived there.

Ariel sat Jane on one of the chairs in front of the fireplace and hugged the old man. He wrapped his large arms around her and held her close.

"It is good to see you again," Ariel said. "I have missed you, Andrew."

"I've missed you as well," he said softly. "It's been too many years."

"My friend, Jane, needs time to rest," Ariel said. "We are not welcome in the castle. May we rest here for the day?"

"I insist on it," Andrew said, looking into Ariel's eyes. "You haven't changed at all in fifty years. My how these old eyes are grateful to see you again."

Ariel smiled. Andrew walked to Jane and offered his

hand, "Welcome, Jane," he said. "My name is Sir Andrew Ingram. I will see to your needs, whatever you require."

"Thank you," Jane said. "Nice to meet you."

Andrew stood up and looked at them, putting his hands on his hips.

"You both look exhausted," he said. "There are comfortable beds upstairs and I'll bring you food once you're settled in."

He showed them to what had to be the master bedroom because the bed was large enough for five people at least. There, Ariel removed Jane's boots and healed her blisters with a quick spell. Andrew bade them rest and went downstairs. Jane crawled into the comfy bed, closed her eyes, and sighed. *This was heavenly!* She felt movement on the other side of the bed. Jane opened her eyes and saw Ariel had lain down and was preparing to get some rest herself.

"We are safe here, Jane. Sir Andrew will care for us."

"I like him," Jane said, closing her eyes again.

"As do I," Ariel said. "He is a wonderful man."

Jane was in the process of drifting off, so she wasn't sure if she heard Ariel's last remarks or dreamed them. It didn't matter.

Jane awoke as the sun was setting. While she'd been asleep, someone had opened the bedroom window just enough to admit a slight breeze. She could hear a horse or two clopping by, a wagon creaking, and voices of passersby.

Then she heard Ariel laugh from downstairs. Jane sat up and rubbed her eyes. *What time is it? Wait, nevermind. Something smells good.* She climbed out of bed and went downstairs, still fully dressed but barefoot, with hair that appeared to have been attacked by a hurricane.

She found Ariel and Andrew cutting and chopping

vegetables side by side, while retelling shared stories of their pasts. She couldn't help noticing that they seemed very relaxed and comfortable together.

As Jane entered, Ariel welcomed her with a smile.

"How are you, Jane? Did you get enough rest?"

Jane nodded, her eyes going from Ariel to Andrew and back to Ariel again. Andrew bowed, "I hope the bed was comfortable enough for you. Are you hungry?"

"Starving," Jane said. "Something smells delicious."

"It's an old recipe for roasted chicken," Andrew said, returning to his chopping duties. "I haven't made it in years. I'm surprised I still remember it. Have a seat, Jane."

Jane took a seat by the fire while Ariel brought her a cup of water. Jane took the cup and looked at Ariel, raising an eyebrow. Ariel returned the gesture.

*Who is he?* Jane communicated to Ariel mentally through Druidspeak.

*Sir Andrew is an old friend from days long ago. He was a great knight in his day,* Ariel replied with her thoughts.

*Mmmhmm, seems like he's more than a friend.*

*Jane, you are too suspicious.*

*He's handsome.*

*Jane…*

*Okay, okay. Just saying.*

At dinner Jane listened to Andrew and Ariel go on about their earlier adventures. Andrew had been considered the strongest warrior of his day. Ariel remembered some details of his stories that he had conveniently forgotten, like how many times a dwarven thief had disarmed him in battle. It got to the point that the thief kept kicking his two handed sword back to him while he called Andrew names.

"I never could maintain a grip on that damn sword," Andrew said. "I even tried tying it to my wrist but that didn't work, either. So, I retired from adventuring."

Ariel and Jane laughed. Andrew's charm and hospitality was both disarming and refreshing. After the meal, they sat together by the fireplace.

"Andrew, you may want to leave Chalon," Ariel said. Her voice was low. "Two armies approach and I am not sure we can defeat them."

"I may want to pick up my sword and join the fight," Andrew said.

"Jane and I must to follow the dwarves and the Knights of Caladar north," Ariel said. "The Scarlet Queen herself is coming."

"I've heard rumors of the like," Andrew said. "Would you like me to come with you?"

"No," Ariel said. "Your sword will be needed here if we fail to stop her. We must leave as soon as possible."

"I can't advise you leaving tonight," Andrew said, watching the fire in the fireplace. "There is a beast roaming the countryside at night. A werewolf that can't be killed. Stay here tonight and leave at first light tomorrow morning."

"We've seen it," Jane said. "I think it followed us here."

"Does it hunt you?" Andrew asked.

"In some strange way, our fates seem intertwined," Ariel said. "It has a part in this story that I cannot yet see. Thank you for your offer."

The next morning when Jane awakened the house was abuzz with several servants. Baths had been prepared for Jane and Ariel and new clothes had been laid out for them. Ariel was quite fond of her new leather vest and breeches. Their packs had been packed with fresh supplies and linen. Outside, in the early morning light, Andrew stood, holding the reins of two magnificent horses.

"These are the best horses I could find," he said. "May they carry you swiftly to your destination. Be safe."

Without a word, Ariel wrapped her arms around his neck and kissed him passionately. Jane blinked, stunned to see Ariel display such affection.

"I placed some coins in your saddlebags as well," Andrew said. "If you should need them."

"You have done more for us than I could have asked for," Ariel said, "thank you."

Andrew took a deep breath, his eyes were moist.

"You best go," he said. "There is an elven army camped to the north. That's where the Caladarian knights and dwarves have gone."

Ariel and Jane mounted their horses.

"While I was getting these horses for you, I heard a rumor that troubles me," Andrew said in a low tone. "Later today Chalon will send her entire might against the elves. Even the wizard Maelord and his apprentice will join the fight. They travel with Lord Shaun Hammerfel and the Knights of Caladar."

Jane shot a look at Ariel.

"Apprentice? Geoff?" Jane said.

"I don't know the boy's name," Andrew said.

"Again," Ariel said, pulling her hood up. "Thank you. I hope to see you again."

They waved their goodbyes to Andrew and led their horses through the nearest gate. Once they had cleared the gate and passed beyond earshot of the guards, Jane asked,

"Ariel, if Chalon attacks the elves, what's going to happen?"

"I do not think that will be the case," Ariel said. "I do not think Lionel would want a war with Selra'thel *and* the Scarlet Queen."

They rode for a while, until Jane couldn't keep to herself any longer.

"So you and Sir Andrew…"

Ariel kept looking forward and didn't reply. Jane cleared her throat, which brought a raised eyebrow from Ariel.

"So you and Sir Andrew…"

"What do you wish to know, Jane?"

"Do you want to tell me about that kiss? Hmm?"

"Jane…"

"Come on, Ariel," Jane said. "I know there's something between you two. Let's have some girl talk."

"Elves do not 'girl talk'," Ariel said stoically. "Andrew was and is, an unusually kind human."

"And nothing more?"

"We need more men like him."

"Of course," Jane said.

"Alluria would be a better place if we had more people like Andrew."

"I agree."

"We have had our adventures together and he is a dear friend."

"Mmmhmm," Jane said.

"He was a young elf's fantasy many years ago. Nothing more."

"Mmmhmm."

Ariel smiled.

"And, if he had asked…I would have been his."

Ariel spurred her horse into a full gallop while Jane sat, her eyes popped open and her jaw dropped. Jane covered her mouth and giggled.

"Oh! Ariel! You little flirt!"

Jane laughed and urged her horse to speed up. They raced north, following the wagon tracks and footprints of the two armies they had seen the previous day. The sky to the north and west roiled and churned. A final battle approached that would probably change Alluria forever. Jane shuddered. It seemed that all their struggles had led them here, and there was no avoiding their fate.

# CHAPTER THIRTY-SEVEN
## A HEART FULL OF LOVE

They raced along the trail, stopping only to water their horses. They had made good time, Jane thought. However, the humor and frivolity Jane had felt while they were in Andrew's house was long gone. She hoped they would catch up with Geoff and his dad later in the day, and if they were traveling with the Knights of Caladar, then it was a good bet Sawyer and Ishara would be there, too.

Ariel slowed her mount to a walk as they rounded a bend in the trail. Jane guided her horse alongside. It was mid-afternoon, by Jane's guess. The sun was still high, but beginning to drift lower. Here and there they passed patches of green woodland, but the plains grew less lush and far rockier the further north they traveled. In the distance, Jane could just make out smoke plumes from many campfires.

"Is that them?" Jane asked.

"I believe it is," Ariel said. "It will be good to see familiar faces."

"This would be a beautiful area if it hadn't been trampled over," Jane said, looking around. "I'd even say peaceful."

"Agreed," Ariel said. "War takes away so much.

Sometimes the cost cannot be measured in lives alone."

"I'm nervous," Jane confessed.

"Of what, Jane?"

"Everything," Jane said. She looked at her hands on the reins, and willed them to stop trembling. "I'm worried we may lose, I'm worried some of us will die, I'm worried Sawyer…"

"How can a girl like you worry so much after all you have done?"

"I don't know," Jane said. "It's a human thing, I guess."

Ariel smiled.

"I am afraid as well," Ariel looked at Jane. "If we lose, Alluria will be plunged into an age of darkness." Ariel gave her horse a pat and neck rub, which was well received.

"But if these are to be my last days," Ariel said, "I am grateful to have shared them with you."

"You can't say that," Jane said. "Ever. Don't even joke about it because it isn't going to happen."

"Very well," Ariel said. "Shall we go find our friends?"

Jane nodded and they trotted toward the encampment. Jane's heart was pounding in her chest again. How would Sawyer react to her after she had almost killed him? What about Geoff? Jane exhaled loudly as they rode and shook her hands in an effort to stop them from trembling. There was a sense in the back of her mind that everything was going to change, and that frightened her more than anything.

After several minutes, they came upon a few elven sentries keeping watch. When they recognized Ariel, they greeted the two of them and let them pass. They rode into camp, which was full of activity. Dwarves and elves worked together to construct catapults and ballistae. The ringing of blacksmith hammers echoed throughout the clearing as weapons were repaired, armor fitted together, and horseshoes as well as ammunition were created.

Thanks to the lines of campfires and the furious fires in the makeshift smithies, a smoky haze covered the area. Several knights in exquisite armor were practicing maneuvers until they moved as one unit. Jane thought they looked like they had jumped out of the pages of a fairy tale.

"Who are they?" Jane asked.

"Knights from Caladar," Ariel said. "Heavy cavalry from the west. They are chivalrous and brave. I am glad they are here."

They rode through the camp and made their way to a small hill dotted with tents. Ariel and Jane dismounted and left their horses with two squires, who led them away. Ariel pointed to a green banner which bore an oak leaf and a pair of antlers in its center, flanked by a rampaging white unicorn and a golden dragon.

"Selra'thel", Ariel said.

"It's beautiful. I've never seen anything like it," Jane said.

They were about to enter the elven tent when someone behind them shouted.

"Jane!"

Spinning about, Jane saw Geoff and Ishara running toward her, wide smiles on both their faces. Jane rushed to meet them. She all but ran into Geoff and they hugged each other tightly. Jane felt tears running down her face.

"Oh Geoff!"

"We were worried about you and Ariel! So much has happened since you left, Jane. You'll freak out when you hear what's been going on."

"I'm sure I will," Jane said with a laugh. "I want to hear all about it. Everything."

"*Hal'inari,*" Ishara said. "Welcome back, Jane."

Jane grabbed Ishara and hugged her too. The move seemed to have caught her unawares, but Ishara smiled and wrapped her arms around Jane.

"This is awesome!" Geoff said. "Everyone's here now."

Jane glanced about. "Where's—"

"Sawyer?" Geoff blurted out. "He's over there, in the next clearing. C'mon, I'll take you."

Geoff grabbed Jane's wrist and pulled her behind him as he ran. Jane looked over her shoulder. Ariel and Ishara were following with smiles beaming across their faces.

"Hang on," Jane said, trying to pull back and slow him down. "Let's wait for Ariel and Ishara."

"They'll catch up," Geoff said. "C'mon, Jane."

Jane's heart was pounding again and there was a different kind of pain deep inside her. It was a longing, a pang, a need. They reached the edge of the tree line and Ariel called out for them to stop. Geoff pointed to the far side of the clearing. Sawyer was sitting on top of a moss-covered boulder, sword beside him. He was dressed in his elven battle armor, but didn't have his helm on. Even from that distance, Jane was struck by how handsome he was.

"Sawyer's just over there," Geoff said, as Ariel reached them. "Let's go surprise him."

"I think," Ariel said, freeing Jane's wrist from his grasp. "It would be better if we wait here for a while."

"Huh? But Sawyer is right there," Geoff protested.

"I can see that," Ariel said. "Go back to camp, Geoff. We will be along soon. You can tell us all about your adventures."

Geoff blinked and shook his head, "Really? Okay. I'll stand over there."

He walked over to Ishara, who took his hand and kissed his cheek.

Jane stood there, watching Sawyer from afar. Her heart skipped a beat and there was a heavy feeling inside her chest. Ariel brushed off Jane's clothes and brushed her hair with her fingers.

"You know, Jane," she said while she kept her eyes on Jane's hair. "When you were taken from us, Sawyer wanted to find you that very night. He would have gone off to rescue you by himself."

Ariel picked up a small flower that had been trampled. She blew on it and the damaged bloom expanded and became full again.

"And between us girls," Ariel said, "I believe he would have succeeded."

Ariel tucked the flower behind Jane's left ear and stepped back to admire her work.

"There, now," she said smiling, "beautiful."

Jane couldn't move. The fear of Sawyer rejecting her was paralyzing. She found it hard to breathe.

"Such devotion is a rare thing, Jane," Ariel said. "In any world."

Jane forced herself to take a deep breath and exhaled through her mouth. Her palms were moist. Ariel leaned closer.

"Go to him, Jane."

The first step was hardest. Jane's feet rebelled and refused to move, but she forced herself step out from the shadows of the trees and into the sunlit meadow. As the sun touched her, Jane felt as if she'd been long encased in ice, and that, suddenly, all the ice was beginning to melt away. She couldn't take her eyes off Sawyer. He was absently tossing pebbles from his perch on the boulder. He hadn't noticed her yet, she was still far away.

"It's great to have her back," Geoff said from behind Jane.

"Indeed it is," Ariel said.

Jane took another step. She no longer felt like she was trudging through mud, with each step she took her feet felt lighter. The pace of her walking quickened, then she was running, then she felt like she was floating on air. At that moment Sawyer turned his head and looked at her. Jane stopped, as the longing from deep within became still more acute. She clutched her chest. Yet, her heart raced. Sawyer hopped off the boulder and looked at her. Jane took another step toward him. To her delight, he began walking toward her.

"Sawyer!" Jane burst into tears and reached a hand out as she ran to him. She flew over the meadow. The only thing she could see was Sawyer running toward her as fast as he could, nothing else mattered.

She crashed into him, wrapping her arms around his neck. His arms closed around her, holding Jane close. She heard herself crying and laughing at the same time. *How was that even possible?* He squeezed her tighter. *Closer. She wanted him closer.*

"Oh Jane," Sawyer said, his face buried in her neck. "You're back, you're really back!"

He lifted her off the ground, but Jane was already flying. Her heart soared above the clouds. She was exactly where she was meant to be, she knew that. Sawyer set her down and Jane looked into his deep brown eyes. His wonderful smile, the gorgeous dimples in his cheeks, the feeling of being held by him was overwhelming for Jane.

Sawyer opened his mouth to speak but Jane lunged and kissed him. She ran her fingers through his thick hair as his hands slid to her waist and pulled her close again. *Ask me. Just ask.* She kept thinking over and over. Sawyer spun her around as they maintained their passionate kiss. Hugging his neck as she kissed him, Jane let her feet fly out, kicking excitedly.

Sawyer set Jane down and laughed.

"Wow," he said. "That was awesome."

Jane couldn't say anything, words escaped her for the moment. She laughed and kept looking into his eyes.

"I missed you, Jane," Sawyer said. "I thought about you every day."

Jane felt her lower lip quiver. Sawyer touched her cheek and wiped away her tears. His touch made her skin grow warm. Inside, she felt like she was on fire.

*Ask me.*

"Hey, this is a nice touch," Sawyer said, tapping the flower behind Jane's ear.

Jane removed it and offered it to him. Sawyer took the flower in his hand, but Jane didn't let go. Their eyes met. With her other hand, she caressed his cheek and the area above his eye she had injured that horrible night.

"I'll never hurt you again."

Sawyer took her hand and kissed it.

"I'll never let anything happen to you ever again," he said.

Jane knew in that second, everything in her life had been leading up to this moment. The tingling feeling inside, the way her arms got goosebumps when he touched her, how special she felt when he smiled at her, there was no denying it. Jane was completely and absolutely in love with Sawyer. She grabbed both sides of Sawyer's head and kissed him. *Ask me.*

A breeze swept through the meadow, the tall grass and wildflowers waved back in forth in unison.

"Cool," Geoff said as he watched Sawyer and Jane embrace in the picturesque setting.

"Cool," Ariel repeated.

Geoff shot an amazed look at her. He'd never heard her use slang before, she was always so proper and exact when she spoke. Ariel glanced at him from the corner of her eyes and winked. He turned his attention back to the two figures in the meadow.

"Thanks for bringing Jane back," he said. "It wasn't the same without her."

"You are most welcome," Ariel said, placing a hand on his shoulder. "Although, I think Jane brought me back as well."

"Really? How's that?"

"I will tell you about it later," Ariel said. "Come. Let them have this moment to themselves."

Ariel patted his shoulder, turned around, and headed back to camp. Ishara appeared on the other side of Geoff.

"They are a romantic couple, would you agree?" Ishara said.

"Yeah," Geoff said. "It's good to see them together again."

"It is," Ishara said. She took his hand and squeezed it. Then, she turned and left.

Geoff turned his attention back to Sawyer and Jane. They hadn't stopped kissing for a few minutes at least. How did they do that? Geoff took a couple steps forward, squinted his eyes and tilted his head for a better view.

"Geoff," Ariel said. "Come along."

Geoff looked back and saw Ariel and Ishara waiting for him to join them.

"Yeah, okay," Geoff said. "On my way."

He started to turn and leave, but he caught another glimpse of Sawyer and Jane. *How much longer are they going to kiss? That has to be a world record or something.*

"Geoff," Ariel said in a louder tone.

"Sorry," Geoff said as he turned to join Ariel and Ishara. When he caught up with them he looked back at the sunny meadow one more time. They were still at it.

"I think they're going to miss dinner," Geoff said.

# CHAPTER THIRTY-EIGHT
## THE WAR COUNCIL

B ack at camp, Geoff and Ishara prepared the evening's meal, which consisted of a pork stew with grains, potatoes, and carrots mixed with cooked strips of pork. Geoff had read about food in the middle ages, so having meat, any kind of meat, was a bit of a luxury. Still, a juicy hamburger and french fries would hit the spot at the moment, he thought.

Ariel had gone and retrieved some bread from a nearby supply wagon. After twenty minutes of making out in the meadow, Sawyer and Jane finally showed up, smiling with arms wrapped around each other. Sawyer pumped his fist into the air.

"We got the band back together!"

Geoff laughed. He looked at Ariel and Ishara. They were staring at Sawyer as if he had spoken a different language.

"It's great to be back with you again," Jane said, tearing off a small piece of bread. "I missed you guys so much."

"We missed you too, Jane," Geoff said. "We thought you had gone all dark side on us forever."

"I'm sorry about all that," Jane said.

"It wasn't you, babe," Sawyer said putting an arm around her shoulders. "We know that."

"That's true, it wasn't." Geoff said. Then he turned to Ariel. "Hey, how'd you get Jane back anyway?"

"It was not easy," Ariel said. "Light or dark, our Jane is a fighter."

"You guys are the best," Jane said, tears welled up in her eyes. "If anything had happened to any of you…if I had… you know…"

"We feel the same about you, Jane," Ishara said earnestly.

"And you came for me, all of you. You came to rescue me," Jane wiped a few tears away. "I can't tell you how much that means."

"You would have done the same for any of us," Ariel said. "It was never a question of whether or not we should *try* to rescue you, but rather how could we bring you back. There was never any doubt."

"That's right," Geoff said. "We had to have you back."

"Thank you," Jane said, sniffling.

"So Jane, did it hurt when your fingers turned into snakes?" Geoff asked.

Jane's moist eyes popped open and she looked at Ariel.

"I said nothing," Ariel said, shaking her head slowly. "They were present during the battle and saw for themselves."

"I don't remember," Jane said with a small laugh. "Thankfully, I must've blacked out during that fight."

"Really?" Geoff said. "You don't remember blowing me and Sawyer up?"

"What?" Jane looked at Sawyer, appalled.

"It's true, babe," he said. "You sent us flying."

"Wow, I only remember small bits here and there," Jane

said. "But I'm glad I can't remember that…and the snakes."

The sounds of horns and approaching hoof beats interrupted the conversation. They looked up. Trelane and Shaun Hammerfel were riding toward their camp. Ariel and Sawyer stood up. Behind them, Geoff clearly saw their troops forming into ranks, facing south. Trelane and Shaun saluted Ariel as they rode up.

"*Hal'inari,*" Trelane said. "The army from Chalon approaches."

"Who is leading it?" Ariel asked.

"Lionel," Trelane answered.

"Aww great," Sawyer said, looking down and shaking his head. "There goes the neighborhood."

"Are they in battle formation?" Ariel said. "How many troops from Chalon approach?"

"Perhaps fifteen thousand," Shaun told her. "They are not in battle formation."

"We plan to meet Lionel," Trelane said. "And determine his intent, will you join us?"

"Yes," Ariel said.

"Then we'll meet you at the front lines," Shaun said.

They turned and rode off to join their soldiers.

Ariel turned to the others. "Stay here. I will return soon."

Before anyone could speak up, she had gone.

"Since we have our orders," Sawyer said. "How about some of that stew? It smells good."

They ate and waited for any news or even an attack from the army of Chalon. The sun was nearly down by the time Ariel returned.

"There is to be a meeting," she said, "in Trelane's tent. I think we should all be there."

"So Lionel isn't going to attack us?" Sawyer asked, standing up.

"Not yet," Ariel said. "But we shall see."

They followed Ariel across the encampment to the large tent with the Selra'thel banner. Wind chimes dangled from the corners of a small awning over the front of the tent. There were two elven guards who opened the tent flap for them. Inside they found Shaun Hammerfel, Trelane, Maelord, Baldon, and Commander Renfry already seated in a semi-circle. A large, empty wooden chair sat in the middle of the semi-circle.

There was a long wooden table in the middle of the tent with an ornate map of Alluria on it. The inside of the tent was lit by dozens of candles. Most eyes in the room fell on Jane as she entered. Sawyer took her hand in his.

"Jane is no longer a threat to us," Ariel said. "In fact, I believe you will be grateful to have her aid at this time."

"You vouch for her," Renfry said. "That's good enough for me."

"I do," Ariel said. "I vouch for her."

"*Hal'inari*," Trelane said, standing and bowing his head. "Lionel will be here shortly."

"Ha!" Baldon said. "I'll wager he keeps us waiting half the night."

"He's done it before," Maelord said, standing up and going over to Geoff. He ruffled Geoff's hair and gave him a wink and a smile.

"We have received reports from our scouts that the Scarlet Queen's northern army is close," Trelane said. "By this time tomorrow we will be in a battle."

"Perhaps sooner," Ariel said. "If Lionel chooses to fight us instead."

"Well I say bring it on," Baldon growled. He stood up and walked around the room. Geoff was amazed to see that he was a little taller than the king of the dwarves. However, Baldon was perhaps twice as wide as him.

Lionel arrived an hour later, dressed in his royal purple robe and wearing a golden crown. Baldon guffawed and shook his head as he returned to his seat. Lionel looked about the meeting area of the tent. He grunted and seemed to be mildly insulted that his chair was no larger than anyone else's. He sat in the middle chair.

"Let us waste no more time," he said. "It is immensely tedious, especially as we're just going over and over old ground. First, I told you I will not tolerate an invading army, why are the elves still here in my domain?"

"They fight for you, you sheep-biting dandy," Baldon said.

Lionel slammed his hands on the arms of his chair and shot up.

"I will not be spoken to like this," Lionel said, pointing at Baldon. "One word from me and my army will ride over everyone here."

"Dead men don't speak," Baldon said. "One swing of my axe and we'll have nothing to worry about."

"The invading armies are what we need to worry about," Trelane said, holding up his hand for calm. "They come from the north and from the west. Our bickering could cost us valuable time which we cannot afford to waste."

"Yes, yes," Lionel said as he sat back down. "The Scarlet Queen and the Shadowlord. I know all about them. However, the army encamped on my soil is comprised of elves, dwarves, and, to my surprise, knights from Caladar."

Lionel glared at Shaun, who remained stoic.

"They're coming," Jane blurted out as she stepped forward. "I know, I've seen the northern army and I've been a prisoner of the Shadowlord. You must know the threat is real. If you don't join together, then Alluria is doomed."

"How kind of you to state what Ariel has told you to say," Lionel said. "Now silence, girl."

"Jane speaks her own mind," Ariel said, standing beside Jane. "I did not tell her what to say here."

"Jane?" Lionel said. "The one who nearly cost us the battle against the eastern army of the Shadowlord?"

"Us?" Sawyer retorted. "I didn't see you there."

Lionel looked at Sawyer. His upper lip curled into a sneer. "Careful, boy."

Sawyer tensed at being called 'boy' by Lionel. Geoff wasn't sure what was going to happen in this meeting, but if Lionel kept insulting everyone, the outcome wouldn't be pleasant.

"Jane is no longer controlled by the Shadowlord," Ariel said. "Whatever hold he had over her is gone."

"And we're supposed to believe you?" Lionel said with a chuckle. "You travel with mere children. You've filled their heads with stories. Why are they here? They should be tossed from this meeting this very moment."

"Who else would you believe?" Ariel asked. "These three 'children' as you call them have earned the right to be here. Many times they have faced our enemies and terrible creatures for our sakes, not theirs." Ariel walked to the table and looked at Geoff, Jane, and Sawyer. "They are here because I asked them to help save Alluria. They could have refused and stayed safe in their homes. No one would blame them for that choice." Ariel walked to the semi-circle of chairs and addressed Baldon, Shaun, Trelane, Renfry, Maelord, and Lionel.

"Yet they chose to come back to Alluria. They chose to help. We owe so much to these three whom we know so little about, but I would gladly spend my lifetime learning everything about them."

Ariel walked over to Geoff and caressed his cheek, she did the same with Sawyer and Jane.

"Did you know I had given up?" Ariel whirled and looked at the seated leaders. Her eyes were moist. "It is true. I despaired. Does that surprise any of you? Hmm?"

"Aye," Baldon said softly, nodding his head. Shaun and Maelord also nodded.

"I was ready to let Alluria burn," Ariel said. "I planned to assume the form of a hawk and simply fly away."

"But this one," Ariel said, turning to face Jane. "This one would not let me. She lifted me up, shared her strength with me – and she is so very strong. She refused to let me flee and hide." Ariel moved to Sawyer and put a hand on his shoulder.

"Throughout the ages of Alluria we have had many who carried the mantle of 'Stormlord'. None more deserving than Sawyer. Many times he has risked his life for others. He can turn the tide of a battle," Ariel turned to Commander Renfry. "You have seen this for yourself at Troll Fang Pass."

Renfry nodded.

"Several days ago, he singlehandedly prevented the Shadowlord's reinforcements from decimating our ranks. Indeed, I have seen him battle the Shadowlord himself. His courage is extraordinary." Ariel looked at Geoff and smiled.

"Geoff, the son of Maelord," Ariel said. "Has there ever been one so young to earn the title 'Dragonslayer'?" Geoff swallowed as all eyes fell on him. "He has incinerated caverns of carrion mites with a single spell. I have seen it with my own eyes. The power this young wizard can summon may save us all someday."

Ariel looked at the seated men.

"Yes, they are the three outlanders of prophecy," Ariel said. "I know this. They stand between us and the coming darkness and with their actions they say, 'we will not let you fall, we are here'."

Ariel looked at Lionel. "You call them children but they are so much more. They bring us hope, and hope is an ally we sorely need now."

Ariel looked at Geoff, Jane, and Sawyer. She smiled. "It has been a privilege to walk at their side. I am honored to have faced our common enemies together."

Ariel turned back around. "And not once have they asked for a reward. Not even so much as a single coin. If you were to ask them why they do this for us, your answer would simply be 'because it is the right thing to do'." Ariel held her arms out at her sides. "Children, Lionel? Oh no. They are heroes. They are my heroes." Ariel walked over and stood beside Jane. "They are here to fight for us and I stand with them."

Trelane got up and walked over to them. "Selra'thel stands with the High Druid of Alluria," he said, then he looked at Geoff, Jane, and Sawyer. "And any friend of Ariel's is a friend of Selra'thel."

Baldon and Shaun stood and walked to them. Baldon looked Geoff in the face, eye to eye, and squinted.

"I can see they have the heart of warriors," Baldon growled. He slapped Geoff on the shoulder, nearly causing him to lose his balance. "That's good enough for any dwarf. Keredain fights with these three."

Shaun stood in front of Sawyer and looked him over. "There is no denying your bravery, or your great deeds. The Knights of Caladar proudly fight with the Stormlord and his friends."

Maelord, a wide grin across his face, walked behind Geoff and wrapped an arm around his shoulders and hugged him.

"King Lionel," Renfry said. "I've witnessed some of what Ariel has spoken of and I tell you she speaks the truth. You rule Chalon. But if you still think elves are our enemies and wish to attack this army, then you will do so without me."

Renfry stood beside Trelane. "I make my stand with them."

"This is treason," Lionel said, glaring at Renfry. "I'll have your head for this."

"Or," Ariel said. "You can join us and save Chalon. And in so doing, you will help save Alluria."

"Did you do this?" Lionel yelled as he pointed at Ariel. "Have you bewitched my commander?"

"I am not bewitched," Renfry said. "Nor am I a traitor. I seek only to defend Chalon."

"Join us, Lionel," Maelord said. "We're stronger with you than without you."

"And if I refuse?" Lionel mused. "If I take my army back to Chalon?"

"Then we all die," Shaun said. "You will die behind your walls knowing you could've made all the difference in the world."

Geoff watched Lionel closely. The look of loathing on his face as he glared at them eventually softened. He sighed and slumped back in his chair.

"Very well," he sighed, "what is your plan?"

"First," Ariel said as she gently extracted a small pouch from inside her tunic and opened it. "We must decide what to do with this." She unfolded a few bits of cloth and held up the small glass orb that contained the plague meant for Chalon.

Jane put her hand to her mouth, "I forgot you still had that."

# Chapter Thirty-Nine
## The Wind in the Chimes

"What," Lionel said, "is that?"

"A plague orb," Maelord answered, his tone low and serious.

"A plague orb meant for the people of Chalon," Ariel added. "Jane and I encountered a small scouting party of barbarians dressed as peasants. They were going to release this plague in Chalon."

"Insidious," Maelord said.

Ariel walked over to the table and placed the nest of cloths and orb on it. The thick dark ichor still writhed with small brown worm-like creatures. Lionel got up and stepped back.

"You brought that here?" he said. "How do we know you don't mean to unleash that on us now?"

"Because," Ariel said, narrowing her eyes at Lionel, "if I had wished to unleash it on you, I could have done so two days ago while you were still in Chalon."

"You mean, you brought that *thing* into my city?" Lionel said.

"Chalon is not your city," Ariel said. "I had no choice. I

did not dare leave it unattended."

"I've heard of those damn things," Baldon breathed. "If they are powerful enough, they can wipe out entire populations, killing everything alive wherever the plague goes. Livestock, animals, everything would die."

A silence descended on the room. Everyone stared at the ominous small globe on the table.

"So what're we gonna do?" Sawyer inquired.

"Can we launch this orb at the armies of the Scarlet Queen? Decimate her ranks and perhaps kill her too?" Shaun suggested.

"No," Ariel shook her head. "The plague would not stop after killing the barbarians and orcs. It would spread to all corners of Alluria. I am not sure if the Shadowlord or Queen Lysis would be affected."

"Can we not dispose of it? Bury it, perhaps?" Baldon said.

"We could, but for how long," Maelord said. "Eventually the glass will weaken and break and then it will seep into the ground."

"We'll put it in a box," Baldon said. "Yes, a box of steel and bury it so deep in a mountain that no one will ever find it."

"Again, even after a thousand years the glass and the steel box will fail," Maelord said, shaking his head. "The plague must be neutralized."

"How?" Renfry said. "And who would create such a weapon?"

"The Scarlet Queen, of course," Lionel said. "Her sorcery is legendary."

"No," Maelord said. "This was created by dark magics far more dangerous than sorcery. A necromancer did this."

"A necromancer?" Trelane said. He looked at Ariel. "Who?"

Ariel shook her head, "I do not know. It seems we have another enemy we have yet to see."

"Necromancers are pure evil," Maelord said. "They have no redeeming qualities whatsoever. Some are neither living nor dead. They have traded their lives for power. The dark magics they dabble in are not meant for mortals. The necromancer who created this is no dabbler. He is a master."

"There must be a way to deal with this," Trelane said. "We cannot have such a thing among us on the eve of a battle."

"No," Maelord said. "We cannot."

"The solution may prove to be as dangerous," Ariel said. "Druidic arts are life giving, the opposite of necromancy. I will need help, but there *is* a chance we can destroy this device."

Maelord nodded.

"Everyone should leave this tent," Ariel said. "Maelord and I must work in close tandem."

"Can't we help?" Jane asked.

"No Jane," Ariel said. "Please go outside. It is too dangerous and I will not risk losing you again."

Sawyer took Jane's hand, "C'mon," he said. "Let the experts work."

Everyone left the tent except for Geoff, Jane, Sawyer, and Ishara. Geoff gave his dad a long hug and turned to leave.

"Just a second, son," Maelord said, "How long can you maintain your shield spell?"

"I don't know," he said. "If it's getting pounded on, not very long."

"When you go outside, I want you to shield the entire

tent, understand? Completely encircle it from top to bottom," Maelord said. "Keep it up for as long as you can, or until you see the two of us come out."

"How exactly are you going to destroy it?" Jane asked. "It's such an evil thing."

"I will begin infusing the orb with life-enhancing spells in an effort to counter the necromantic magic," Ariel said, "while Maelord continuously tries to disenchant it and remove the protective magic keeping the plague within."

"Good luck," Geoff said. "Let me know when to begin, okay?"

"Thanks, son," Maelord said, "I will."

Geoff and Ishara left the tent. Then Jane and Sawyer, still holding hands. Once outside, Jane noticed everyone standing nearby, even Lionel.

"Okay Geoff," Maelord called. "Begin."

Geoff held his hands up like he was holding a ball. A glowing sphere encompassed the tent.

"Pity," Baldon said. "I liked the idea of using it on the Shadowlord."

Trelane turned to the two guards by the tent, "Your task is to protect the boy wizard," he said, "Much may depend on him."

"Geoff, if you need anything just let us know," Sawyer said.

"Sawyer, I think Geoff needs to concentrate," Jane said. "We better leave him alone for now."

"Okay," Sawyer said. "Sorry Geoff. Keep concentrating."

Jane noticed that a dull red glow had begun to pulse from inside the tent. There was an occasional line of oily blackness that rippled through it, but the virulent tinge was unmistakable, and there was something about it that unnerved her. Anything that looked like that can't be good.

Sawyer noticed it too. "Hey, that doesn't look good."

"No, it doesn't," Jane said nervously.

Then there was a flash of vivid green, then liquid white, then the lurid crimson again. Could it be that their spells were fighting the dark magic of the necromantic plague? Jane and Sawyer stepped back. She thought she heard Ariel and Maelord casting spells at the same time, but she didn't recognize any of the chants coming from Ariel. The battle of three different magics went on for another hour longer. Jane became worried Geoff would become tired and let his shield lapse.

"Geoff, how're you holding up?" she said. "All good? It's been a while."

"I'm good," Geoff said. He didn't take his eyes off the tent. Jane noticed a bead of sweat running down the side of his face.

"Okay. If you need anything, just let us know," Jane said.

Renfry marveled, "How could anyone even *attempt* to dismantle a magical plague?"

"Aye," Baldon said. "It sounds mental. But Maelord's done strange and wonderful things before now."

"As has Ariel," said Trelane swiftly. "The answer to your question is, they can only try."

Jane noticed Lionel, though he remained, said nothing.

Then there was a sharp *crack* and another flash of red, this one larger and lasting longer than the first glow. The guards by Geoff put their hands on their weapons and more warriors approached the tent, having seen the flash.

Sawyer unsheathed the Stormblade and took Jane's wrist,

"Get behind me," he said.

Jane did so, but she was worried about Ariel. She wanted to use the druid speak Ariel had taught her to ask if everything was okay inside the tent, but didn't dare risk breaking her concentration. Suddenly a brilliant flash of forest green followed by gold scintillated from inside the tent.

"What's going on in there?" Sawyer said. "Geoff, can you see anything?"

A few moments later the tent flap opened. Ariel and Maelord emerged. They leaned against each other and looked exhausted. Maelord could hardly walk, and Ariel looked ghostly, as if every drop of blood and energy had been drained from her.

"It is done," Ariel said quietly.

She looked very ill. However, it was Geoff who collapsed. The strain of securing the shield and sustaining it for far longer than he'd ever done before had been too much for him.

Jane and Ishara ran to Geoff.

"Are you okay?" Jane said. "Geoff, can you hear me?"

Maelord knelt and examined him. "He's exhausted. Let's get him into the tent."

"I got him," Sawyer said to Maelord. "Looks like you need rest, too."

"How're you feeling?" Jane asked Ariel.

"I am fine, Jane." Ariel said. "But we still need to plan for tomorrow's battle. However, I could use some water, if you don't mind."

"No, I don't mind at all," Jane said, looking around for a source of water. Trelane pointed to a nearby barrel.

Ariel, Maelord, and the others returned to the tent,

where Jane and Ishara ministered to them, and to Geoff. The others, however, were awestruck at what awaited them there.

On the table, sitting on the nest of cloth Ariel had prepared, was the remains of the plague orb, still hissing and smoking, but twisted into a black-ashed husk. Not a fragment of the putrid liquid or its oozing worms remained.

Once they cleared the broken glass orb out of the way, Shaun unrolled a map of Alluria on the table and they began to go over strategies and contingencies. Jane took a seat and did her best to stay tuned in, but they may as well have been speaking a different language.

Sawyer had taken a seat beside her and fallen asleep. Jane got up, kissed Sawyer on the head, and walked outside. It was late. The moon was beginning to rise and a breeze had begun to blow. Jane passed the two elven guards and took a seat in the grass. As she sat there, a wondrous harmony rose up from the chimes behind her. It was the most amazing sound she'd heard. The chimes sounded as if an entire orchestra was playing.

Curious, Jane walked over to investigate. The elven chime was beautiful. Made of all sorts of metals, some of which looked like gold, and different types of wood with multi-colored feathers dangling from the bottom of each chime.

"You should hear the sacred chimes at the royal court of Selra'thel."

Jane turned around and saw Trelane standing behind her. He was smiling. He placed a hand over his heart in greeting, "*Hal'inari*," he said. "Do you like them? How they form a melody?"

"I love them," Jane said. "How do they do that?"

"No one knows," Trelane said. "Only the wind."

Jane smiled and watched the chimes as they continued their symphony.

"In Selra'thel, we have a saying," Trelane said. "When one seeks help and guidance, the wind in the chimes answer their prayers. That is how one knows they have been heard by the higher powers."

"That's beautiful."

The tent flap opened and Lionel emerged, frowning. He was rubbing his forehead. He nodded at them, got on his horse, and rode away with four well-armed guards.

"Is the meeting over?" Jane asked.

"I do not know," Trelane said, "I must go back inside."

Jane watched Trelane go back inside, then turned her attention back to the chimes. She began to formulate a prayer. With the coming battle, they would need one.

The troops of Chalon had formed a defensive camp just to the south. Lionel dismounted outside his regal tent, which dominated the middle of the camp. Tossing the reins of his horse to his servant, he stalked irritably inside. Six guards roused themselves to salute as he entered. Lionel removed his cloak and tossed it onto a cushioned chair. Next, he poured himself a goblet of wine and sat at a long table that was similar to the one in Trelane's tent.

A breeze blew the flap of his tent open for a second.

"Close the tent," Lionel shouted to the guards outside. "I don't wish to be disturbed tonight."

Lionel took a long drink of wine. As soon as he swallowed, he felt a sharp pain in the back of his neck. His first thought was a bite from an insect, but when he tried to slap the thing away his arm failed to respond. He tried to move his head but with the same result. Alarmed, he tried to call for help, but all he could manage was a wheezy cough. A slender hand appeared and removed the goblet from his hand. Its elegant features looked familiar.

"No need to struggle," A female voice assured him. "You are already dead."

A figure wearing a gray cloak lay across the table on her stomach, facing him. She removed her hood and smiled. The lavender eyes looked into his.

"Men are such idiots," Lady Seqwil said, bending her knees and playfully twirling and flexing her feet in the air. "I imagine you never thought you would die like this."

Lionel tasted blood. His heart was beating so fast, but he was barely able to breath. He felt like he was being smothered.

"This venom," Lady Seqwil held up a forefinger with a metallic tip which had a small needle at the end, "is that of a Tunneling Cave Spider from the Crystal Peak Mountains to the south of Chalon."

Seqwil rested her chin on her wrists. "They are small but quite aggressive. I admire them because the toxin in their fangs not only paralyzes its prey, but also causes excruciating pain, which, while unnecessary for the spider to feed, is entertaining to watch." Seqwil nodded. "I shall enjoy watching you die."

Lionel coughed, his body felt like he was on fire. He was burning alive from the inside. He desperately tried to scream or move any part of his body, but nothing responded. Seqwil raised both eyebrows and tilted her head as she grinned.

"You were a poor ruler," Seqwil said, shrugging. "It was too easy to manipulate you." Seqwil placed a hand over his and caressed it with her thumb. "Still, you were useful…for a while. But now that you have thrown your lot in with Selra'thel, Keredain, and Caladar, what good are you? I thought my spell was unbreakable, it made you mine to control. Oh well. I have been meaning to ask you something. Have you ever accomplished anything for yourself? All your life you have leeched off better men, taken some of the glory intended for others more deserving, lied and schemed to profit yourself at the expense of others. Now you are here. Was it worth all the deceit?"

Lionel began to gurgle. A trickle of blood ran from the corner of his mouth.

"Uh oh," Seqwil said. "The end is near. Such a pity you cannot answer me, I would have liked to hear your thoughts on the topic. I will, however, tell you one thing before you die. The Silent Order is real. We are everywhere. There is no court, no kingdom in all Alluria where we do not have influence." Seqwil sighed in relief and giggled. "I feel so much better now that I have said that out loud."

Lionel gurgled again, then began to spasm as he slumped forward.

"There we go," Seqwil said, wrinkling her nose. "The last agonizing moments of Lionel the First, the fool who thought he was a king."

Seqwil slid off the table and took hold of Lionel's head with both hands as his body went limp. She forced his eyes open with her thumbs and bent closer so she could watch the light leave him.

"Good riddance," she said, letting his body drop to the

ground. Looking around the room, she noticed a lockbox with a key in it. Seqwil looked down at Lionel, "Seriously? I cannot overlook a gift. I may as well take something for my trouble." Seqwil turned the key and opened the lockbox. It was filled with gems, coins, and jewelry.

"My," she said. "This *is* a treasure. Whatever did you intend to do with it during a battle?"

Seqwil removed a few choice bits of jewelry and several gems before closing the box and re-locking it. She turned to go but stopped and held up a finger.

"I almost forgot," she said, removing an elven dagger from her belt. She walked over to Lionel's body. "This is the most important part." Seqwil buried the weapon in Lionel's heart and stood over him. Satisfied with her handiwork, she pulled on her hood and quietly slipped out. No one noticed the shadow that stole into the night.

# CHAPTER FORTY
## THE KEEP

The alarm in the camp sounded before sunrise. The troops of Chalon assembled in defensive positions. Commander Renfry, wearing a worried look on his face, arrived soon thereafter. Jane and the others watched him ride up. He looked at Ariel.

"Will you please come with me? Lionel is dead. He was assassinated after our war council."

"Of course. Do you know who killed him?" Ariel said as she swiftly gathered her things.

"No," Renfry said. Then he held up an elven dagger. "But this was in his chest."

Ariel stopped and examined the weapon. It was a typical elven blade. Every soldier from Selra'thel had one.

"Did anyone see what happened? Anything at all? Anything strange?"

"No," Renfry said as Trelane and Maelord rode up. Maelord was pulling an extra horse for Ariel. "The assassin left no trace except the elven dagger."

"Who will lead Chalon's Army now?" Trelane asked.

"For now, it must be Commander Renfry," Maelord said.

"I don't know," Renfry said, shaking his head. "The troops are restless and divided. Many soldiers speak of attacking this encampment. There's talk of declaring war on Selra'thel."

"Then you must take command," Trelane urged. "Without a strong leader, your army will fall apart."

"You don't think anyone in this camp killed Lionel, do you?" Maelord asked.

"No," Renfry said. "Of course not. But the men believe it, or some of them do."

"The men will follow their leader," Trelane said. "That is you, my friend."

"Maelord," Renfry said. "As the designated wizard of Chalon, you have claim to lead as well."

"The soldiers will be more inclined to follow one of their own," Maelord said. "Trelane is right. This is your time to lead."

"This does nothing to change our battle plans," Trelane said. "All is as we decided last night."

"Aye," Renfry said. "It is."

Ariel mounted her horse, "I assume you wish for Maelord and myself to investigate Lionel's death. I wonder, will elves be safe in your camp, today?"

"No one will harm you, or even try to harm you," Renfry said. "And you're right, a keen eye is what we need now."

Ariel looked at Jane, Sawyer, Geoff, and Ishara.

"I will not be long."

"Ariel," Jane said. "Are you sure?"

Ariel nodded, then held out her hand, "Come Jane. You may be needed."

"What about us?" Sawyer asked.

"Bring your sword," Renfry said, offering Sawyer a hand up.

Geoff rode with his father while Ishara rode with Trelane. It was a shorter distance to the camp than Jane had expected. As the troops noticed them, Jane heard mutterings and murmurings of discontent. The faces of some of the men looked hard and angry. They glared at Ariel, Trelane, and Ishara.

"Ariel," Jane whispered. "They look like they want to kill us. What do we do if they attack?"

"There is not much we can do," Ariel said, "but I doubt that will happen."

They rode up to Lionel's tent, which was guarded by at least a dozen soldiers. Before entering, Renfry addressed the guards, "Stay here and keep a sharp eye out," he said.

Inside, they saw Lionel lying on his back, his face contorted in anguish. Ariel moved instantly to examine the body while Trelane, Maelord, and Ishara searched the rest of the room for clues.

"That looks like the dagger Lady Seqwil tried to put in my eye," Sawyer said. "I remember it."

"While I do not doubt you, nor the source of the blade," Ariel said. "We must keep in mind that it is a common elven weapon."

"There are no signs of a struggle," Ishara said, looking around the body.

Maelord opened the chest and pulled out some gems. He held them up. "Obviously robbery wasn't a motive," he said as he replaced the gems. "Killing Lionel was the objective."

"But why?" Sawyer said, looking around. "Why now? He could've been killed in his castle any time."

"So what changed?" Geoff asked. "Sawyer's right. Why kill him now?"

"Because," Maelord said, "Last night Chalon joined the war. Good thinking, you two."

"The assassin might've been sent to make sure Chalon *didn't* enter the war," Renfry said. "When that failed, Lionel was no longer needed."

"What do we do now?" Sawyer said.

"We follow our battle plan," Ariel replied. "There is nothing else to do."

The tent flap opened and a ranking guard stepped inside. He was younger than Commander Renfry, but just as tall. He was clean shaven and his blond locks were pulled back into a pony tail. His skin was tanned from many days in the sun.

"Commander Renfry," he said. "Forgive the intrusion, but this is urgent. We haven't had any reports from our forward scouting position at the old northern keep since early yesterday. Riders were sent to investigate, but they haven't returned. Other scouts have reported back, the Shadowlord's northern army could arrive an hour sooner than anticipated."

"What, none have returned?" Renfry asked.

"None, sir. Shall I send another patrol?"

"No," Renfry said. "Start battle formations. We need to be ready."

"Against whom, sir?" The blond lieutenant glanced at Trelane for a second.

"Against the Shadowlord and the Scarlet Queen, of course," Renfry said impatiently. "Elves are not our enemies. It'll be best if you pass that along to the men."

"Aye sir," The lieutenant turned and left the tent.

"That position," Renfry said. "Is vitally important. From there, we can see the Scarlet Queen's army coming long before they arrive."

"You should take it back if it has been compromised," Trelane said. "I can send a patrol."

"A patrol will be seen," Ariel said. "Perhaps ambushed. I will go."

"We will go," Jane said, looking at her.

"That's right," Sawyer said. "Let's go check it out."

"It will be dangerous," Ariel said. "I do not know what we will find."

"We are stronger together," Ishara said.

"Very well, it is settled," Ariel said. "We leave now."

Maelord locked eyes with his son, "Remember your spells and listen to Ariel."

"I will," Geoff said.

Outside a horn sounded, then it was followed by shouts of "Battle formations!"

They stepped outside to a huge commotion as the soldiers hurried to their positions. There was so much movement in all directions, Jane wasn't sure what they were trying to accomplish.

"Dad," Geoff said. "What will you be doing?"

"I'll be fighting a war, son."

"This is an opportune time to slip away," Ariel suggested. "If there are spies here, we will be more difficult to spot."

"Should we get horses?" Sawyer asked.

"No," Ariel said. "We need to be as stealthy as possible, for we do not know what we will find."

"How far is the keep?" Jane asked.

"Nearly half a day by foot," Ariel said. "Come, follow me."

They moved among the soldiers quickly, leaving the camp as several groups of soldiers from Chalon and horses pulled and pushed numerous catapults and ballistae into battle positions. They crouched low until they reached a small section of woods. Ariel stopped and turned around.

"Once beyond this small copse of trees," she said, "The landscape changes and becomes rough and craggy. The old keep sits on the edge of a small cliff. I doubt we will escape detection as there will be nowhere for us to conceal ourselves."

The terrain past the woods was just as Ariel had described, rocky and uneven. This made for more difficult footing for Jane and Geoff. Even Sawyer almost lost his balance. Ariel and Ishara, however, had no trouble navigating the rocky hills and ridges.

To their right was Troll Fang Pass and Gholaran. A tall, jagged set of peaks jutted upward from the horizon to the left. Ariel stopped and pointed.

"There," she said. "That keep has stood for over a hundred years."

"Yeah," Sawyer said. "Looks like it's been around that long. It's pretty beat up."

Jane followed the line of Ariel's finger and saw a three-story structure built from dark, heavy stone. She thought it like a tower, but it was in such a desolate location. No greenery, no water source, nothing beyond a small path to the front of the keep. A suspension bridge stretched from the keep over a steep gorge. The bridge looked like it might collapse at any moment.

"It's crumbling," Geoff said, "falling apart. I wonder who built it."

"Dwarves," Ariel said. "Dwarves and men from a bygone age."

"I see horses," Ishara said, nocking an arrow. "Just inside the front entrance. Their saddles bear the crest of Chalon. I do not see any other movement."

"There is smoke as well," Ariel said. "Someone is in the keep."

"How do you see that far?" Sawyer said, squinting. "Anyway, sounds like a trap to me."

"You have good instincts," Ariel nodded at him. "It is indeed a trap. Someone wants us to think it is safe to approach. Keep as low as you can."

Behind them, to the south, several horns blared. Beyond the hills they had just traversed, a multitude of fireballs filled the sky.

"They have engaged the northern army," Ariel said. "We can do nothing for them now. It is their battle."

Geoff looked back at the fireballs flying north and south.

"I hope Dad's okay," Geoff said. "More than likely those are containers of flaming tar launched from catapults."

"Do not worry," Ariel said. "Your father has seen his share of battle. He will be fine."

Ariel crouched and moved toward the lonely keep. The others followed. Every now and then Ariel would stop and study the keep for signs of danger before continuing. Ishara did the same. A few minutes later they found themselves just outside the keep, their backs against the walls as they crept toward the front entrance.

Ariel signaled for Jane, Geoff, and Sawyer to stay put while she and Ishara went in first. Jane looked around. This was an awful place. It was gloomy, ugly, and lonely. The hair on the back of her neck stood up. Jane moved along the rough stone wall of the keep. Sawyer grabbed her hand when she was a few feet from the entrance. Jane looked back, Sawyer was shaking his head.

A few minutes later Ishara emerged and pressed a finger to her lips and motioned for them to come inside. Jane and Sawyer entered with Geoff close behind. The first thing they saw were the bodies of scouts from Chalon lying everywhere. Ariel had knelt on one knee and was examining a body. The horses were still tied and had been fed and watered, they didn't appear to have any wounds. Jane noticed they didn't seem skittish or afraid, either.

The lower chamber was about forty feet in diameter. The remnants of a smoldering fire still endured in the middle of the room, which had been a barracks at some point in the past. Several rotted cots lay among the debris. Bits of stone and rocks had been broken off or were worn away with time.

"Ishara," Ariel whispered, beckoning her over. "Look at this."

Jane and the others followed Ishara over. Ariel pointed to the soldier before her, then the others. Each one bore almost identical wounds in their chests.

"Ambush?" Ishara asked.

"No," Ariel said. "They died in combat. Their weapons were drawn and they had fought together."

"These wounds," Jane said, "are in nearly the same location on every soldier. What could do that?"

"Some sort of monster, maybe?" Geoff said, looking up toward the second level.

"The footprints indicate a single attacker," Ishara said, pointing to a boot print that looked different from the others. "An assassin of great skill did this. They wore elven boots."

"I am not sure it was an assassin," Ariel said. "Nor am I sure whoever did this is gone. Be on your guard."

As Ariel moved toward the stairs leading to the second level, Ishara followed, ready to release an arrow in an instant. Sawyer was next in line with his sword drawn. Jane was behind him, and Geoff last. The decrepit wooden stairs leading to the second level groaned under Sawyer's weight. Ariel waved him back as she and Ishara silently climbed to the second floor of the tower.

Sawyer looked at Jane with a disgruntled expression, indicating the steps with his sword. Jane mouthed the words 'elf thing'. She noticed part of the roof of the second floor had decayed and collapsed, exposing the roof of the third floor. They could both see Ishara, arrow nocked, at the top of the stairs. She had positioned herself so she could pivot in any direction if an attack came.

Jane couldn't see Ariel, partly because Sawyer was standing in front of her, and partly because Ishara blocked much of her line of sight. She was about to turn her head and check on Geoff when a shadow moved on the third floor. She looked up just in time to see a figure in elven battle armor drop through the hole in the ceiling.

The elven warrior landed in front of Ishara, sliced her bow in two with the edge of a long, wicked-looking spearhead, and swiftly sidekicked her in the chest. The attacker's speed was terrifying. Ishara grunted in pain as she flew backward, crashing into Sawyer, who tumbled back into Jane and Geoff. They all fell back into the black stone wall at the base of the steps. Geoff's head hit the wall hard, knocking him unconscious. Sawyer winced as he rubbed his head, momentarily dazed from the impact. Ishara was clutching her ribs and Jane had the wind knocked out of her. A single, stunning attack had momentarily incapacitated all four.

All she could do for the moment was watch as she gasped for air. Their attacker glanced down at them and Jane's heart froze.

Those icy blue eyes glared at her.

A sinking feeling washed over Jane, she watched as the ornate metal spear the blue-eyed warrior carried magically shrank to the length of a long sword. The others didn't know, but Jane knew. She'd seen those eyes before.

# CHAPTER FORTY-ONE

## TALIA SPEARSLAYER

"**M**y, my," Talia said mockingly. "You brought your friends. When I am done with you, I will kill them too."

Ariel assumed her defensive stance, scimitars ready to parry and strike. Talia slowly approached, dragging the blade of her spear against the stone walls, sending tiny sparks flying. Talia stopped. Her brilliant blues eyes surveyed about the room from under her helm.

"I see no trees," she said, again in a sweet tone. "I see no shrubbery, not even a blade of grass."

Talia lowered her gaze at Ariel and playfully wagged a finger. "Poor Ariel. It looks like you will have to fight for yourself, for once."

Talia mimicked a sad frown, pushing her lower lip out. Ariel opened her mouth to say something but Talia launched a small throwing knife at her head. Ariel barely managed to duck the blade as it imbedded itself in the wall. As she rose, Talia slammed against her, immobilizing both hands while expertly shoving her elbow under Ariel's chin.

As Ariel struggled to breathe, Talia applied more pressure to her neck.

"You are pitiful," Talia mocked as she gritted her teeth. "I have waited so long for this."

Summoning her strength, Ariel jammed a knee into Talia's midsection while she spun out of her grasp. There were only two ways out of this room; the steps, which led to her friends, or the window that was now behind Talia. Ariel stepped back, not daring to take her eyes off of her assailant for a moment.

She would need every ounce of energy, strength, cunning, and focus or they would all die in this keep. Snarling, Talia again charged, spinning her sword dizzyingly and producing a long slender knife from her belt that could pass for a short sword.

Ariel blocked the attack but at the cost of being pushed hard against the wall, her skin scraped against the crumbling stones. She glimpsed her friends down the steps, at least they had survived that fall.

"Ariel!" Jane shouted as she struggled to get up.

"No!" Ariel ordered, "Stay back, all of you! She—"

A swift punch in the mouth from Talia ended Ariel's sentence.

"By all means," Talia called out derisively, "Come and try to save her."

Ariel slashed at Talia with both scimitars, spinning and attacking from two different directions. Talia casually dodged each attack and closed to grapple with Ariel, first pulling her off-balance and then tossing her across the room. Ariel's head hit the edge of the window. In that blinding flash of pain, it dawned on her that Talia was humiliating her, toying with her, like a cat playing with its prey. Talia wanted her to suffer, but she intended to kill them all. Could she possibly get under Talia's skin, enrage her, perhaps even cause her to miscalculate? It might just be their only chance.

"Very well," Ariel sneered. "Come, let us finally dance, *ravenspawn*."

Ariel turned and leapt out the window, trusting the old childhood insult she had directed at Talia would work. It was a short drop to the ground. Ariel landed lightly, facing the suspension bridge, which spanned fifty feet across the gorge. Behind her, as anticipated, Talia had jumped through the window. Ariel dashed across the bridge, conscious that Talia was gaining.

Once on the other side, Ariel turned to face her. Talia stopped and slipped her long knife back into its sheath while her spear elongated to a length of over six feet. With one fluid stroke, Talia severed the ropes sustaining the rotting bridge. It collapsed and swung to the far side of the gorge. This was exactly what Ariel wanted, now the others could no longer interfere. They might even be safe.

"You think fighting me here will provide you any advantage?" Talia said as she began to walk to Ariel. "You are mistaken, *druid*."

Ariel sprang at Talia, this time she had room to maneuver and her attacks would be varied, but on target. However, Talia's spear proved to be an effective defensive weapon. She blocked Ariel's first multiple attacks and stepped neatly away of the rest.

Then, Talia attacked with a spinning slash at the back of Ariel's neck, meaning to sever her head from her shoulders. At the last second, Ariel crisscrossed both scimitars behind

MITCH REINHARDT

her head, saving her life. Both combatants spun away and looked at each other. Ariel saw the hatred in Talia's icy blue eyes.

"Today is the end of your days," Talia said as she began to circle Ariel.

From back across the gorge, Ariel heard Jane cry out her name from the second story window. Ariel saw the concerned look on her face.

"Is she your pet?" Talia questioned. "I saw her before, at the Iron Citadel. Had I known she was dear to you I would have killed her."

"Have you never had anyone dear to your cold heart?" Ariel retorted. They closed on each other again, Talia's spear had shrunk to three feet in length and her attacks were lightning fast. First a thrust followed by a spinning slash, then an overhead strike. Ariel dodged the first two and blocked the overhead attack with her weapons. As soon as she had blocked, Talia kicked her chest, knocking Ariel backward. The force of the kick was enough to break ribs. Ariel winced.

She had time for nothing else as Talia immediately followed with a dual-wielding attack with her long knife and sword length spear. Ariel faced multiple attacks from every direction. She blocked and parried the ferocious barrage, but was forced to give ground. Talia used her forward momentum to press her advantage. The next instant Ariel was slashed across her upper arm. Ariel grunted and backed away. Talia smiled and raised her chin.

"I have only begun to make you bleed," Talia said, twirling her long knife. "For everything you have ever done to me and my family, I will make you pay."

"I did nothing to your family," Ariel said. "You were my rival, no one else."

Talia screamed and lunged at Ariel. This time her spear elongated past Ariel's defenses and buried the razor-sharp tip in her shoulder. Biting her lip, Ariel knocked the spear away with a scimitar. Talia sneered. Ariel's nostrils flared. *No. She was not going to die like this. She was not going to die being slowly cut to pieces.* Gathering her wits, Ariel attacked Talia with some of her own ferocity. This time, she went straight at her, knocking Talia's long spear aside and slashing her chest and arm, which left a mark on her elven battle armor, as well as a cut on her forearm. Ariel's last attack was an uppercut that flung Talia's head back, sending her helm flying.

Talia responded by spinning around and sweeping Ariel's legs out from under her. Ariel hit the ground hard, then rolled left just as Talia stabbed the ground at exactly the spot where she had landed.

Ariel rose to her feet and raised her scimitars while Talia brushed her hand under her chin and looked at her own blood. Then she quickly glanced at the wound on her forearm. Ariel knew it was a deep cut, but Talia would never stop coming. The sight of her own blood made her snarl and roar at Ariel.

"Is that the best you can do?" Talia said. "A punch and a cut? Seems like so much work for a small wound."

"I can do more," Ariel assured her.

"I am the more powerful warrior," Talia raged. "I *will* have your head on my spear!"

"Careful," Ariel advised. "You need to defeat me before you gloat."

Meanwhile, Jane rushed downstairs and outside the keep. Sawyer had helped Ishara up, then she and Sawyer pulled Geoff to his feet. Geoff was still groggy and far from lucid. Sawyer and Ishara each took a side and helped Geoff walk to where the sounds of battle resounded from the other side of the keep. Jane rushed there as fast as she could, coming to a sudden stop at the edge of the gorge, where the chopped suspension bridge dangled uselessly before her. Ariel and Talia were fighting in plain sight, not seventy feet away, but there was no way she could get close enough to help.

Talia charged Ariel again, teeth bared like a tiger's. Her spear shrank back to sword length as she struck with her long knife. Ariel responded with her dual scimitars, just managing to defend, but rarely capable of attacking. Both combatants danced around each other, their slashes and thrusts so swift they were barely believable. To Jane, they appeared like two blurred figures weaving, dashing, and lunging. Talia's spear expanded or shrank back effortlessly in a stunning display of skill. Jane began to feel frantic as she noticed Ariel was far more often the defensive warrior. She turned wildly to the others as they arrived.

"Sawyer, do something!" Jane shouted.

"What? What do you want me to do? Ariel can take care of herself. No one can beat her."

"No, Sawyer!" Jane said. "Help her! She's losing!"

"What can I do?" Sawyer said. "Look at them, I wouldn't last two seconds over there."

Ariel heard their voices, though she couldn't distinguish the words, over the clashing of weapons. It had the effect of bolstering her determination. If she failed, Talia would kill them simply because they were her friends. Suddenly, she felt a sharp pain in her left side as Talia's long knife found its mark. Then Talia's spear flashed past Ariel's head. Something flew up in the air.

Ariel watched as her beloved braid with her blue and green feathers drifted down. Talia snatched the braid out of the air and held it up triumphantly.

Ignoring the pain, Ariel slashed Talia's shoulder and midsection, which caused Talia to momentarily back away. A trickle of blood began to run from beneath her pauldron. Talia winced and looked confused as she rotated her shoulder.

"Does it hurt?" Ariel said.

"Oh, I will show you pain," Talia said. "I will not let a weak human lover best me."

"And if you do win, who do you think the Scarlet Queen will attack when she is done with the humans?" Ariel said. "Do you think she will stop when Chalon falls? No, she will come for Selra'thel."

"Let her! I do not care! Selra'thel is no longer my home! Let it burn to the ground! Every tree, every leaf, every flower!"

"Then you fight for no one," Ariel said with as much disdain as she could muster.

Talia again attacked. This time, she opened with a sweeping shot to Ariel's legs, which nearly succeeded due to Ariel's wound. Then she kicked Ariel in the side, this time, Ariel felt something crack.

The others watched in horror as Ariel and Talia sliced and stabbed at each other. They were having their own private war and only one was going to walk away. In all respects, Ariel had the worse of every exchange. Jane's heart was racing, she had to do something.

"Sawyer, can't you do something with your sword?" Jane begged. "I don't know, hit Talia with a lightning bolt or something."

"It doesn't work that way. Geoff's our resident bolt-lobber."

Jane turned and looked at Geoff, he was sitting, miserably dizzy, still holding his aching head. He needed more time, but Ariel didn't have time.

"Tell me," Talia said. "Who do you fight for? *Them*?" She thrust her spear contemptuously in the direction of Ariel's friends.

"For them," Ariel said. "And for all of Alluria."

Talia shook her head, and came for Ariel with a distasteful look on her face, "Oh you must die."

She thrust her spear at Ariel's chest, but Ariel stepped back, batting it away with her scimitar. Then she kicked the shaft of the spear, sending it spiraling from Talia's hand. In retaliation, Talia brought her knife down on Ariel's arm, leaving a deep slash just below the elbow. Ariel responded with a hard slash from her second scimitar across the top of Talia's hand. Had Talia not been wearing armor, she would've lost her hand. However, the force of Ariel's blow was enough to make her drop her knife.

Infuriated, Talia spun around and kicked a scimitar from Ariel's hand, then grabbed Ariel's other wrist and brought that arm down hard on her knee. The moment Ariel's second scimitar hit the ground Talia kicked both scimitars away. They stood looking at each other, weaponless, two opponents determined to win at all costs. Ariel vaguely heard the others screaming, but she had to force herself to ignore them if she were to have even the slightest chance.

Ishara had been exploring. Finding what she sought, she rushed back. "Jane, look there," Ishara said, pointing into the gorge. "There is a ledge we can use to cross, if we are careful."

"You gotta be kidding," Sawyer said. "Hell no. That's barely big enough for a kid."

"It is the only way," Ishara urged. "If we took horses and rode around, we may be too late to help Ariel."

"I vote horses," Sawyer said, looking down into the gorge. "Geoff's in no shape to try something that risky anyway." As Jane watched, Ariel was rocked back by a barrage of attacks. Her heart sank. The frustration and despair she felt over being powerless to help Ariel was maddening.

"No!" Jane shouted furiously. "Leave her alone!"

"You are powerful," Ariel admitted, gasping, "But with all that power, you have not the wisdom that must accompany it. Your passion is undeniable, but you have lost the capacity to love. There is a hole where your heart was."

Talia threw a jab at Ariel's nose. Ariel blocked it but was struck by a jarring punch to her left cheek. Ariel stepped back, the blow had made her legs wobble. Was she imagining it, or could she hear Jane's voice? Perhaps it was only the ringing in her ears. Talia stepped forward and threw a spinning back fist at Ariel's head. Ariel ducked the blow and her face met Talia's knee. This time Ariel stumbled back and blinked. Her surroundings began to swim about and her vision blurred. Ariel shook her head in an effort to clear her thoughts.

Talia moved in again, her steel blue eyes burning like fire. She swung at Ariel's head. Ariel, clear-headed again, grabbed her arm, turned, and threw Talia over her shoulder. Talia landed hard on her back. Ariel twisted her arm, wrapping a leg around it to force Talia to yield, or have her arm broken. Talia responded with a shocking kick to Ariel's face.

Ariel released Talia's arm and staggered back, barely able to keep her balance. Talia rolled to her feet and took a few steps toward her. Ariel attempted a spinning back kick but Talia easily blocked it with her arm. Next, Ariel threw a left jab, which Talia also blocked, but then she hit Talia with a forearm smash to the face. Talia stepped back and wiped the blood from her nose. The sight of more of her own blood seemed to infuriate her. She came straight at Ariel and hit her with a palm smash to the face.

Talia drove a straight right punch into Ariel's face. It felt like a mountain had fallen on her head. Ariel dropped to her knees. Again Talia hit her with a straight right. Then another, and another. Ariel's vision began to fade and she fell. Talia walked over and picked up her enchanted spear.

*No way. This can't happen. Not like this.* Jane felt her pockets and found the last two acorns she had left. Ariel had given them to her before they attacked the barbarian scouting party outside Chalon. Jane reared back and threw an acorn as hard as she could.

"*Ana'thel!*" She shouted as she pointed at the acorn. However, it exploded harmlessly over the gorge. Jane didn't have the arm strength to get the necessary distance. Talia glanced in their direction for only a second. Jane handed the last acorn to Sawyer.

"Here, throw this as hard as you can at Talia," Jane said. "Jane, you're crazy," Sawyer said. "This could kill Ariel."

"Just do it, Sawyer!"

Sawyer took a couple steps back and then stepped

forward, heaving the acorn at Talia. Jane watched it leave his hand and never took her eyes off the tiny projectile. She waited until it was halfway over the gorge.

"*Ana'thel!*" This time, thanks to Sawyer's accurate throwing arm, the acorn went directly at Talia. Unfortunately, she was close to Ariel as well. Talia batted the acorn with her spear as it neared. The resulting greenish explosion knocked the spear from Talia's hands and sent her flying over a cliff on the far side of the gorge.

"Yes! Great throw, Sawyer," Jane said. Then she looked across the gorge at Ariel. "What's she doing? We gotta get over there!"

Jane's acorn had hit its mark. Ariel saw the explosion as it was struck by Talia's spear. The impact was such that Ariel received only minor cuts from rocks and other debris. Talia, however, was thrown off the plateau on which they had fought. She heard scrambling sounds and grunts from over the edge. Ariel crawled over and looked down. There was Talia, trying to hold on and gain a foothold as piece after piece of the dark cliffside broke off, each one threatening to send her to her death. There was a desperate look in Talia's eyes.

Ariel reached out and grasped Talia's wrist as the last piece of rock she held onto broke away. Talia looked up, her eyes wide with astonishment.

"What are you doing?"

Ariel didn't answer. She wasn't sure if her wounded shoulder would allow her to pull Talia to safety. Nevertheless, she had to try. Gritting her teeth and summoning what strength she had left, Ariel pulled. Talia reached the top and finished pulling herself up. Ariel rolled over onto her back, breathing more hoarsely than ever. She heard Talia growl and get to her feet. Ariel wanted to stand and meet her end fighting. However, she had only enough strength to roll onto her side. Talia had retrieved her spear and was marching toward her.

Talia grabbed the collar of Ariel's leather tunic and roughly jerked her to her knees. Ariel managed to stay there. She lowered her head, she was too tired to lift her chin. Then she felt the cold metal from Talia's spear on her throat, lifting her chin so she was forced to look at Talia. Her face was twisted with rage and her lower lip quivered. Streaks of tears ran from the corners of her eyes. Her teeth were clenched.

"Why?" Talia screamed.

Ariel blinked and closed her eyes. She needed rest. As the sharp edge of Talia's spear began to slide along her neck, Ariel felt the cut. Then she felt Talia grab her hair and pull her head back.

"Why?" Talia repeated.

Ariel blinked and opened her eyes. The rage in Talia's face was still there.

"You are the greatest warrior in the history of Alluria," Ariel finally said. "Never again will there be a warrior the likes of you. I do not think falling to your death will be your fate."

"Do not beg for your life," Talia hissed. "*I* am the victor."

"Oh Talia," Ariel coughed. "Now you know what I have known since we were children. I could never defeat you in battle. Not without using my magic."

"You knew you were going to lose," Talia said, "and *still* you fought?"

"There are some things worth fighting for," Ariel said. "And some people. I have learned this recently."

Ariel closed her eyes but was shaken awake by Talia pulling on her hair again.

"I will not beg for my life," Ariel said. "Nor will I ask your forgiveness, I do not deserve it."

Ariel felt Talia's hand tremble through the vibrations of the edge of her spear. She looked into Talia's eyes and wondered what might have been if she hadn't been so cruel to her.

"Take your revenge," Ariel said. "All I ask is that you spare my friends."

Talia roared as she lifted her spear high in the air. Ariel closed her eyes and waited for the killing stroke.

# CHAPTER FORTY-TWO
## ONE DAY...

Jane scrambled along the ledge in the gorge, keeping as close to the wall as she could. Behind her was Ishara and then Sawyer, a distant third. Geoff's head injury was such that he couldn't attempt walking along the ledge. Sawyer was sweating as he stepped lightly, testing every foothold before trusting his weight on it. Jane had forgotten how heights terrified Sawyer, but right now they needed to get to Ariel as quickly as possible. Talia was sure to kill her. Jane hoped they would make it in time.

She reached the other side and as she crested the top of the ledge, her heart stopped. Ariel was on her knees before Talia, who had her spear at Ariel's throat. Then Talia screamed and raised her spear high in the air.

"No!" Jane shouted.

Suddenly, Talia turned and walked away. Her head down and her steps slow. Ariel fell back, motionless. Jane climbed onto the plateau and struggled to her feet. She ran and stumbled to Ariel, falling to the ground as she reached her. Ishara appeared at her side. The first thing Jane noticed was all the blood. Ariel had so many wounds that Jane didn't know where to begin. Ariel's eyes began to roll up in her head. The left side of her face resembled a bloodied, bruised pulp.

"Oh no, no, no," Jane cried, bursting into tears. "Oh Ariel…no."

"Jane," Ishara said, her voice cracking, "can you help her? Please."

Jane nodded as tears ran down the length of her nose and dropped to the ground.

"I'll try," Jane said, sniffling and half-blinded by tears. "Even if it kills me, I'll try."

Sawyer thundered past, his sword raised. He seemed determined to run Talia down.

"Sawyer, no!" Ishara shouted. The tone in her voice was a command. "She will kill you!"

He stopped and looked at Ishara and Jane, then he looked back at the figure of Talia as she became smaller and smaller in the distance. He put his sword away and joined them beside Ariel.

"Oh wow," he muttered, "so much blood…"

Jane had emptied her pouch and crumpled the leaves in her shaking hands.

"Where is she hurt worse?" Jane asked.

Ishara looked at Ariel's myriad of wounds and pointed to a deep gash in her side, "Here," she said.

Jane cast her healing spell as Ishara and Sawyer worked to staunch and wipe away the blood from Ariel's wounds. Her next spell centered on Ariel's battered face, which returned to its usual size and beauty.

"Guys," Geoff yelled from the other side of the gorge. "How is she?"

Sawyer and Ishara looked at Jane, awaiting her opinion. Ariel seemed to be responding well to her healing charms, and she was breathing easier. Jane smiled and nodded.

"Yeah," Sawyer shouted. "She's gonna be okay!"

Geoff responded with a thumbs up gesture. Jane continued to keep her hands on Ariel as she cast every druidic healing charm she knew.

"I will go and bring horses," Ishara said. "Keep safe, and keep Ariel safe."

After she had gone back to the ledge and started her trek back to the other side, Sawyer put a hand on Jane's.

"You're awesome, Jane," he said. "What would we've done if you hadn't come back?"

Jane sighed and looked at Ariel, "Thanks," she said. "But Ariel is the awesome one. What would we do if we ever lost her?"

"Well, I think you're gonna make a great doctor someday."

Jane smiled. "Actually, I was thinking veterinarian," Jane replied, "but maybe I can do a little of both, at least for a while."

Ariel turned her head and moaned. Though this was an encouraging sign, she was still far from being able to function. Sawyer collected her scimitars and they waited for Ishara to return with horses. When she did, she had Geoff in tow as well. They lifted Ariel onto a horse. She wasn't completely recovered after Jane's healing, but she was able to remain in the saddle with help. They had to round the northern most part of the gorge in order to turn south, that's when they saw a great black mass appear on the northwest horizon.

"Oh no," Jane said. "Is that…?"

"Yes, Ishara said. "The Scarlet Queen's western army, led by Queen Lysis herself."

"You mean all of *that* is her army?" Sawyer asked, pointing along the entire horizon.

"It is," Ishara said. "All forty thousand at least."

"Forty thousand? There's no way…" Jane's voice trailed off.

"Come," Ishara said. "We must get back and let Trelane and Commander Renfry know what we have seen."

"Yeah, okay," Sawyer said.

They traveled on the road south as fast as they could, keeping Ariel's condition in mind. Jane was glad to see trees and grass again. They kept looking to the east, but saw no signs of battle.

"It must be over," Sawyer said. "Who won?"

Just after dark, they stopped for a rest and hastily made camp. Jane stayed with Ariel while the others went out searching for firewood. Jane had wetted a bit of cloth she had torn from her tunic and placed it on Ariel's forehead.

"How is she?"

Startled, Jane whirled around. Then she froze. Standing only ten feet away was Talia. Jane's first thought was to scream, but that would only mean the others would die, too. Grabbing one of Ariel's scimitars, she assumed a defensive position between Ariel and Talia.

"What do you want?" Jane said hotly. There was no way she was going to let Ariel be slaughtered in her sleep. Jane swung the scimitar a couple times and pointed it at Talia, who never flinched. "If you've come to finish the job, you're going to have to get past me first."

"Easy, girl," Talia said, raising a hand. "If I had wished

to kill either of you, then you would already be dead."

Jane was trembling so much her knees were weak. She knew she was looking at her own death.

"Why are you here?" Jane said, lowering her weapon.

Talia walked to Jane and looked her over. Jane felt as if she were under a microscope with those icy blue eyes staring at her.

"How is Ariel?" Talia asked.

"She'll live," Jane swallowed.

Talia walked past Jane and knelt on one knee beside Ariel. She caressed the side of Ariel's face that had been beaten.

"So you are the human," Talia said. "The girl druid."

"Jane. My name is Jane."

Talia looked up at her and then stood. She sighed.

"Ariel chose her friends well," Talia said. "She has always done so. I hated her throughout childhood. She was always everyone's favorite, the special one destined to become the High Druid. She was the light and I was the dark, a cast-off, the forsaken one."

"I know," Jane said softly. Talia looked at her. "She told me. She regrets the way she treated you and what she did to you."

Talia studied Jane for a moment. Apparently, she was surprised a human knew about her childhood. Talia turned her attention back to Ariel.

"Until today, the thought of defeat had never entered my mind during battle," Talia said. "She was by far the best opponent I had ever faced. She could have defeated me with a single spell. Instead, she fought like a true warrior, she fought with honor and saved my life."

Jane noticed an injury on her arm was bleeding through its bandage. She also saw that Ariel had done a good bit of damage to Talia before falling. Jane pulled out the last of her leaves and crumpled them. She reached for Talia's arm, but Talia jerked it away and Jane found herself facing the steel blue eyes of a predator.

"Sorry," Jane said, she pointed at the bleeding wound. "May I?"

Talia glared at her for a few seconds. Jane wondered how hard her life must've been to not have anyone to help her, perhaps no one to speak with and no one to trust. Talia nodded and removed the military dressing. Jane carefully took her arm and sprinkled the leaf bits on the wound.

"*Ilinara tae ullnara taethos*," Jane murmured as she placed her hand over the wound. She felt some of her energy rise up from deep inside and pass into Talia, healing all her wounds. Talia tilted her head, this time her face was soft. Jane noticed that she was as beautiful as Ariel or Ishara. She was stunning.

Talia looked back at Ariel, "Perhaps one day I will be able to call her 'friend'."

Jane said nothing.

"And perhaps you as well…Jane," Talia said softly.

Jane looked at Talia and smiled.

"I'd like that."

Talia looked her over again and then abruptly turned and began walking away. She stopped and with one fluid motion, pulled her spear, and fully extended it toward the Misty Cliff Mountains. She kept her back to Jane.

"The Scarlet Queen will be camped on the lower part of the eastern-most peak," Talia said. "She will have no fewer than fifty of her elite Night Guard with her. Do not concern yourself with them. If you wish to win this war, you must first slay Queen Lysis. Without her, the army she has assembled will fall apart."

Then Talia disappeared into the darkness, leaving Jane still shaking. She had faced the most dangerous warrior ever and lived. She must be the luckiest person in Alluria. Jane exhaled and held out a quivering hand. It took her several minutes to calm herself. When the others returned, Jane told them everything that had happened, emphasizing precisely what Talia had told her about the Scarlet Queen. They were all amazed that Jane was still alive. After a brief rest, they got back on their horses and continued their journey south to the elven encampment. The sound of a terrifying wolf's howl made them ride faster.

Upon reaching the encampment, they were admitted by the sole guard on duty. They were less surprised by this once they noticed that, everywhere they looked, they saw wounded warriors – dwarves, elves and humans. Physicians and caregivers circulated among the wounded and tried to ease their pain and suffering. Their mood was subdued as they rode up to Trelane's tent and dismounted.

"Sawyer!"

Turning around, they saw Shaun Hammerfel. He wasn't wearing his armor, only a red tunic and black breeches. His right arm was in a makeshift sling.

"Shaun, what happened? Did we win?" Sawyer said as he and Shaun embraced. "Are you okay?"

"Aye and aye," Shaun said with a sigh. "We won, but at a terrible price. We lost many good warriors. What news from the old northern tower?"

"It's not good," Sawyer admitted. "We saw the Scarlet Queen's army. Forty thousand at least."

"Forty...thousand?"

He looked at Ishara, who nodded confirmation.

"Also, the scouts from Chalon were already dead. Talia Spearslayer killed them before we arrived. Then she nearly killed Ariel."

Shaun noticed Ariel was leaning on Ishara while seated on her horse. He frowned and went to help Ariel down.

"You should all rest," Shaun said.

He and Sawyer carried Ariel inside Trelane's tent. Geoff and Ishara were close behind. Trelane and Baldon were standing at his table, studying the map of Alluria. When Trelane saw them, he stopped and went to Ariel.

"What happened to her?" Baldon said as he rounded the corner of the table.

"Talia Ravenmane, the Spearslayer," Ishara said.

Baldon blinked and exhaled, he recognized the name.

Trelane laid Ariel on his cot and covered her with his blanket. Standing up, Trelane looked over his shoulder at the others.

"She is lucky to have survived," Trelane said, then he looked at Jane. "Would that be your doing?"

"Ariel fought like a true hero," Jane said, nodding. "She gave Talia everything she had."

"And Maelord?" Trelane said. "Where is the wizard Maelord?"

# CHAPTER FORTY-THREE
## A KNIGHT'S NIGHT

"What do you mean?" Geoff said. "Dad's here. He was here to help with the battle."

"He was," Shaun said. "He disappeared before the battle. We could've used the services of a wizard today."

"Wait, Dad was getting ready for the battle," Geoff said. "He was right here, in this tent."

"Yes, he was," Trelane said. "He was last seen leaving this tent. No one knows where he is now."

Geoff sat down and put his head in his hands and shook his head. This was unbelievable. Ishara put a hand on his shoulder.

"Do not worry," she said, "We will find your father. We did so before, did we not?"

"Lady Seqwil," Geoff said, looking up at her. "I bet she kidnapped him again."

"That sounds like something she'd do," Sawyer said. "Maybe she wanted revenge for losing that magical fight in the castle."

Commander Renfry entered the tent. His face was grim.

"After today's battle," he said, "we can muster a little less than ten thousand. We lost over half our number."

"Ten thousand?" Shaun said. "Against forty thousand? That's not enough, not nearly enough."

"Forty thousand?" Renfry asked, having missed the earlier conversation.

"Aye," Shaun said. "Ariel and her friends have seen the Scarlet Queen's western army and it numbers forty thousand at least."

Renfry looked at Shaun, "We can't repel an army that strong. Especially with the Scarlet Queen leading it and our wizard missing."

"What would you have us do?" Baldon retorted. "Turn and run?"

"No, of course not," Renfry said. "But we can't defeat an army that size."

"There might be another way," Jane said. All eyes turned to her. "I know where the Scarlet Queen will be in two days. If we can slay her then her army will…disband or whatever, stop fighting."

"What are you talking about, girl?" Baldon said. "The western army will be here by then."

"How do you know where Queen Lysis will be?" Trelane asked.

"Talia told me," Jane said, "and I believe her."

"Talia?" Shaun said. "The Spearslayer? You said she nearly killed Ariel. Why would you trust her?"

"Earlier this evening I was alone with Ariel. I was watching over her while everyone else was gathering firewood. Talia visited the camp," Jane said. "She surprised me. She could've killed us in a second, but she didn't."

"It's a trap," Baldon said. "Just like the northern tower.

She wants us to send our best so she can slaughter them."

"It's out of the question," Shaun said. "We can't trust her. She's made a name for herself killing others. She enjoys it. In the west, there is a saying about her; 'Death is an exquisite elven beauty with cold blue eyes'."

"Hold on…is that Ariel?" Renfry said, just now noticing she was in Trelane's cot.

"It is," Trelane said. "She is resting after her battle with Talia."

"I'll wager *that* was a battle to see," Shaun said.

"It was," Jane said.

"How did it end?" Trelane asked.

"Talia won, but walked away," Jane replied.

"Walked away? I do not think Talia has ever behaved like that," Trelane said. "She and Ariel have always had a deep animosity toward each other, I would have expected her to finish Ariel."

Geoff had listened to as much as he could bear. They said his father was missing, but he didn't feel they had a sense of urgency in finding him.

"I'm gonna go find my dad," Geoff said standing up, almost bitterly adding, "If anyone wants to help, that'd be great."

"We've already searched everywhere," Baldon said. "We don't know where he is, young wizard. He wasn't at the battle and he isn't in this camp."

"Then it would not hurt if Geoff and I searched too," Ishara said. She turned to Trelane, "My bow was broken by Talia. May I take one from your armory?"

"Take what you wish," Trelane said with a nod.

"Jane, if you're not too tired," Renfry said, "We have wounded who need your help."

"Of course," Jane said.

"Stormlord, since you have seen the western army of the Scarlet Queen," Trelane said, "your strategic insight could be invaluable."

"Sure," Sawyer said. "I'll be happy to help."

With that, Geoff left the tent with Ishara and Jane while the others began to pour over the map of Alluria.

"Dad wouldn't just leave like that," Geoff said. "He would've joined the fight and helped."

"From what I hear about your dad," Jane said. "He would've won the battle by himself."

"Yes," Ishara said. "Maelord would have made a difference in battle."

They walked toward the wounded soldiers. The chorus of groans and pain-filled yells made Geoff want to cover his ears. Jane stopped.

"There's so many," she said. "I can't heal this many."

"Do what you can, Jane," Ishara said. "Even if you can save one life, it will be enough."

Jane took a deep breath. Geoff noticed the familiar look of determination on Jane's face as she stepped into the mass of wounded soldiers. Then he turned to Ishara.

"Where would Dad have gone?" he said. "Did he have his own tent?"

"Yes. It is likely," Ishara said. "He would have gathered whatever he needed to fight a battle."

"I don't suppose you can track him?"

"No," Ishara said. "There has been too much movement, too many footprints everywhere. It would be impossible."

"Let's go find his tent, then," Geoff said, "Maybe we can find a clue."

Geoff and Ishara had little trouble discovering which tent was Maelord's. It seemed everyone knew where the wizard resided in camp except them. It was a small brown tent near Trelane's. Geoff ran to it and opened the flap. Stepping inside, he noticed a cot in the corner and a small table on the opposite side of the tent. A single candle no longer burned on the table, beside an open, thick, leather-bound book. Geoff crossed to it and instantly saw the book contained spells.

"I don't recognize this spell," he said, "it looks complicated."

"Geoff," Ishara warned.

"Don't worry. I'm not going to try to cast it, but maybe if I use the spell Dad taught me so I could at least *read* it…"

Geoff gestured with his fingers and closed his eyes.

"*Sylla Arcanum.*"

When he opened them the runes and writing on the page began to re-arrange themselves. They formed words he recognized. He studied the page for a minute then gasped and stepped back.

"Geoff, what is it?" Ishara was at his side in an instant.

"It's a spell of porting," Geoff said. He looked at Ishara. "I think Dad teleported out of camp. But why would he do that with a battle coming?"

"I do not know," Ishara said, "his courage is beyond doubt."

Geoff glanced around the small tent. Under the cot was a small knapsack. He removed it and emptied the contents on the cot.

"I don't see anything unusual," Geoff said, "more clothes and stuff like that. He was beginning to stuff his father's belongings back into the knapsack when something fell onto the grass. It was his Dad's wallet.

"That's weird," Geoff said. "Why would he even bring his wallet here?"

Geoff opened it. There was a bit of money and some credit cards, nothing useful in Alluria. Then he began browsing through the pictures. Suddenly, it occurred to Geoff that there were no pictures of him in his dad's wallet! His father had kept several pictures in his wallet, but they were missing.

"What is it?" Ishara said, running her fingers over the smooth leather. "I have never seen this sort of thing."

"It's a wallet," Geoff said. "Back home, we carry our money in it when we go out."

"Would your father normally have it here?"

"No," Geoff said. "I doubt it."

"Let's go find Jane," Geoff finished repacking his dad's belongings, then stuffed the spell book inside too. "Probably not a good idea to leave this behind," he said.

"It is not," Ishara agreed. "So, why would a great wizard like your father depart and not take such valuable things with him?"

"I don't know. It doesn't make sense. Let's go get Jane and Sawyer."

Geoff slung his father's knapsack over his shoulder, and they returned to the hospital area. Jane had already helped many, several of whom were even getting up and walking around. Geoff and Ishara rushed over to her.

"Jane, you gotta see this," Geoff said, opening the knapsack. "Look here, Dad's spell book and wallet. He'd never leave these behind on purpose."

"A spell book is far too precious a thing to leave behind," Ishara added.

"Yeah, and there aren't any pictures in his wallet," Geoff said.

Jane looked at the book and wallet Geoff held, "Why would he remove all of his pictures? They were pictures of you, right?"

"Yeah, and other relatives," Geoff said. "And his spell book was open to a spell of porting. I think Dad teleported away before the battle."

"That doesn't add up," Jane said. "Why would your dad do that?"

"I dunno," Geoff said.

"You better get back to Trelane's tent and stay with the others," Jane said. "I'll be there as soon as I can."

Geoff and Ishara went to Trelane's tent, stopping only to find a replacement bow for Ishara. Though it was of elven manufacture, she said it wasn't as good as the one Talia had sliced apart. Still, she felt better having a bow at all. They opened the flap to Trelane's tent and walked in. Sawyer and the others were still looking over the map on the table. From their expressions and the tone in their voices, they hadn't discovered a way to defeat the Scarlet Queen's army.

Geoff and Ishara went over to Ariel, who was still resting on the cot. She hadn't moved since they left.

"I wish she were better," Geoff said.

"She needs rest," Ishara said.

An hour later, Jane joined them, looking pale and exhausted from her efforts. Sawyer glanced up from the table and smiled at her.

"Very well," Shaun said loudly. "Now that your friends are assembled, Stormlord, there is something that must be done." Everyone stepped away from the table except Sawyer, whose eyes darted around. A dozen Knights of Caladar entered, all wearing their shining plate armor and formed two perfect lines.

"What's going on?" Sawyer asked.

"With these knights and heroes as witnesses, the time has come to recognize a true champion," Shaun said. He accepted a gem encrusted sword from one of the knights, then turned to Sawyer. "Stormlord, with your deeds you have more than earned this. Is there anyone among this court who will second my choice that you join our ranks?"

All of the knights as well as Trelane, Ishara, Baldon, and Renfry cried, "Aye!" Then Geoff said the word after everyone else.

"Stormlord," Shaun said as he nodded at the ground in front of him. "Take a knee."

Sawyer blinked a few times. His mouth was open and he hesitated to move closer. He glanced over at Jane, who smiled encouragingly. Sawyer gulped and walked over to the gauntlet of knights, who all stood at attention and placed a mailed fist across their chests. Shaun Hammerfel nodded at Sawyer.

As he strode forward, the knights beat their chests in rhythm with every step he took. Sawyer kneeled before Shaun, his heart pounding.

"Sawyer Collins, Stormlord, warrior, hero. On this day of victory, it has been deemed necessary to bestow upon you the honor and rank of Knight of Caladar."

Shaun took the ornate sword and touched Sawyer's right shoulder, "Will you always be honest and true. Never lie or break a promise and never mislead another?"

"I will," Sawyer said.

Shaun lifted the sword over Sawyer's head, and rested the blade on his other shoulder, "Will you remain courteous to others, always remembering that humility is a knight's greatest virtue?"

"I will."

Shaun lifted the sword and again placed it on Sawyer's right shoulder, "Will you always remain brave and defend those who cannot fight for themselves?"

"I will."

Shaun removed the sword and stood at attention.

"Arise, Sir Sawyer Collins, Stormlord, Knight of Caladar, and protector of Alluria."

As soon as Sawyer stood up, the other knights began to applaud. Jane, overwhelmed, rushed past the knights and launched herself into Sawyer's arms, kissing his lips the moment they touched. A loud cheer rose from the knights. Geoff and Ishara congratulated Sawyer, who was grinning from ear to ear. Sawyer shook their hands as his fellow knights patted him on the back and saluted him. Shaun Hammerfel embraced Sawyer. Then, from the other side of the tent, they heard Ariel's voice.

"How can one be expected to rest during a knighting ceremony?"

"Ariel!" Sawyer called out and ran over to her. Jane, Geoff, and Ishara close behind. She had sat up on the cot and watched the entire ceremony. She extended her hand as they approached and Sawyer took it while he knelt beside her.

"I am so proud of you," Ariel said quietly. "Becoming a Knight of Caladar is no easy feat. Congratulations, Sir Sawyer."

"Thanks, Sawyer said. "I had no idea. They sprung this on me with no warning."

"After everything you have done," Ariel said. "You should have expected it."

"How are you, Ariel?" Jane asked. "Is there anything I can get for you?"

"You have saved me yet again," Ariel said. "For now, I will rest. Tonight, Alluria celebrates her newest protector."

# Chapter Forty-Four

## Fireside Chat

The next morning, Ariel seemed renewed. She even insisted on joining Jane among the wounded, attempting to heal as best as she could. Her magical strength was returning, but she tired very quickly and was forced to return to her seclusion.

Commander Renfry, while overjoyed to see the return of so many soldiers, was still troubled by the numbers they would face.

"Hey Sawyer, Congrats on the knighthood, seriously," Geoff said. He was eating an apple on the top railing of a makeshift corral. Ishara sat beside him, restringing her bow.

"Thanks Geoff," Sawyer said as he practiced an attack maneuver Ariel had shown him a while back. "But I think all of you should be knighted, too."

"You deserve it, Stormlord," Ishara said. "I overheard many knights discussing you as I walked around the camp. They are honored to count you among their number."

"You know," Geoff said, taking another bite from his apple, "In some history books, knights were pretty much thugs and picked on people because they could. But these guys, these Knights of Caladar, they're different. They're the real thing."

"What do you mean?" Sawyer asked.

"Look at how they take care of their own wounded," Geoff turned around and pointed with his apple. Two knights were helping one of their own walk. He had a leg wound that neither Ariel nor Jane had attended yet. "And I saw a few knights help an old peasant couple with their wagon. The wheel had broken off or something so they got off their horses and fixed their wagon. It was cool to see them doing what they pledged to do."

"Yeah?" Sawyer said as he leaned against the wooden rail Geoff and Ishara sat on. "So real knights were thugs and mean? Just like…"

"Bullies," Geoff said, lowering his voice. "Sometimes they were considered to be bullies."

"Just like me…"

"Well, that's back in our world," Geoff said with a gulp. "And…well…things are kinda different here."

Sawyer gave Geoff a gentle nudge with his elbow, "Relax," he said. "I was a bully and a jerk. I know that now. I'm sorry."

Geoff patted him on the shoulder, "It's cool."

"Knights in your world do not sound like knights at all," Ishara said. "They sound like villains."

"Maybe some were," Geoff said. "But I wouldn't say that about these Knights of Caladar."

"Nor would I," Ishara said.

"So, Sir Sawyer," Geoff said. "What's the plan? What did you, Trelane and the others decide yesterday?"

"I don't think I'll ever get used to being called 'Sir',"

Sawyer said. "But, they're going to meet the Scarlet Queen's main army. The idea is to inflict as much damage as possible and slow her advance to Chalon."

"How's that gonna work?" Geoff asked.

"Harassment, hit and run tactics," Sawyer said. "If they can weaken her forces enough, they may try a frontal attack."

"Guys, are we gonna be able to pull this off?"

"We have no choice," Ishara said. "We must."

"Hey, any word about your father?" Sawyer asked.

"No," Geoff said. "I don't understand why he took off. He would be here, I know it."

"He would," Sawyer agreed. "Don't worry. We'll find him."

"Gather your things," came a voice from behind them.

Looking around, Geoff saw Ariel, with Jane. Sawyer vaulted over the fence while Geoff and Ishara swung themselves off the top rail. Sawyer hugged Jane.

"How're you doing? Not tired yet?" Sawyer asked.

"Maybe a little," Jane replied. "But I can ride."

"When do we leave?" Geoff inquired.

"As soon as we can," Ariel answered. "From what Jane has shared with me, we must try to be at the Misty Cliff Mountains by tomorrow night."

"What if the Scarlet Queen isn't there?" Sawyer pressed. "And what if it's a trap?"

"We should be far more concerned if she *is* there," Ariel said. "She will not be an easy enemy to overcome."

"Ariel, we need to find my dad, too," Geoff said. "I think he ported away for some reason."

"We will, Geoff. We will," Ariel said. "For now, we must have faith that Maelord knows what he is doing and is unharmed."

Her words made Geoff feel hopeful. They were going to succeed.

"Now hurry, all of you," Ariel said. "I will pick out the five freshest horses. Come back when you are packed and ready."

Geoff, Jane, Sawyer, and Ishara dashed off. Geoff wondered when they would have time to look for his father. Rather, how would they look for him? *If he ported away, how could they track him? Where would they start looking?*

They returned to the corral to find Ariel sitting atop a beautiful white mare. Four other horses had been prepared for the journey. As they mounted their horses, Trelane appeared with a small wooden box. He handed it to Jane.

"Here," he said. "In hopes that all your prayers will be answered."

Jane opened the plain, small box and gasped. Inside were all of the elven wind chimes that always hung around his tent.

"Oh my! Oh no!" Jane said, trying to hand the box back to Trelane, but he refused. "This is too much…"

"A gift like this is to be appreciated, not declined," Trelane said, placing a hand over his heart. "Good luck to you. Good luck to you all."

"Thank you," Jane said, bowing her head.

They rode out of camp, following hundreds of elven archers toward the large mountain range to the west. They had been tasked with the initial harassing. The archers were an elite force designed to fire multiple volleys of arrows from a long range, then move quickly to another spot and attack again. Geoff felt safe travelling with them. He looked over at Ishara, who was riding beside him.

"You'd be with them if not for us," Geoff said. "Do you want to join them?"

"Of course not," Ishara gave him a terse glare. "We have come too far together."

As they drew closer, Geoff became more impressed with the Misty Cliff Mountains. They were a majestic, vaguely forbidding mountain range, its peaks seemed to almost disappear into the clouds. Jane had pointed to the peak that Talia had indicated where the Scarlet Queen would be tomorrow. Ariel said that would be the ideal location from which to direct a battle. The combined armies of Keredain, Selra'thel, Chalon, and Caladar would probably meet her western army in a narrow valley just below.

The day's travel passed by without any incident, which Geoff appreciated. They stopped for the evening but the elven archers continued riding. As they unpacked their blankets, Geoff started to gather stones to ring a campfire.

"Just a small fire tonight," Ariel advised. "Too dangerous."

They sat around the fire without saying much. Then Sawyer spoke up, "If all goes well, this'll all be over tomorrow night."

"I hope so," Jane said. "I miss my parents. I feel like I haven't seen them for years. I miss my dog, Lucy, too."

"Yeah, but remember when we get back," Sawyer said, "It'll be like no time has passed at all."

"What were we doing when we left?" Jane laughed. "I can't remember."

"I was taking out the garbage," Geoff said. "That's when the skeletal assassin attacked me. Do you remember, Ariel?"

"I do."

"Chocolate," Jane blurted out, "I miss chocolate."

Geoff and Sawyer snickered.

"What? Don't laugh," Jane said. "I could really use some right now."

"What is chocolate?" Ishara asked.

"Oh, it's the yummiest, most fabulous, delicious, sensual, heavenly food ever."

"I don't think it's considered a 'food', Jane," Geoff said, laughing.

"Well it should be," Jane insisted. "It's like 'edible happiness'."

"My, that does sound fabulous," Ariel said. "I would like to try this chocolate from your world one day."

"As would I," Ishara said. "Your world is most interesting."

Geoff laid back on his blanket. *Funny how Ariel and Ishara thought their world was interesting when they were lucky enough to live here in Alluria. If not for the war, this would be paradise.*

"What else do you guys miss about home?" Geoff said.

Jane and Sawyer started to speak at once, then stopped.

"Go ahead," Sawyer said as he rolled onto his side and propped his head on his hand.

"I miss so much," Jane said. "My phone and texting with my friends, shopping for new clothes at the mall, my spin class and working out, I really miss that, cooking, oh and music. I so miss music and dancing, too!"

"What about you, Sawyer," Geoff asked. "I bet you miss playing football, right?"

"Yeah," Sawyer agreed. "We have a good team this year, which helps. I miss working out too. But I think I miss hanging out with my friends most, like Robbie Mac."

"Oh yeah, Robbie MacLean," Jane said. "His sister, Elayne, is one of my best friends. I just call her 'Layne'. We study together all the time."

"Yep, they're cool," Sawyer said.

"That whole family is cool," Jane said. "You know their mom is a super smart computer analyst at a major firm."

"What does their dad do?" Sawyer asked.

Jane thought for a minute, then shrugged, "I don't know. I think he's a spy or a secret agent – something like that."

"Ha! Wouldn't surprise me at all," Sawyer said. "I'll have to ask Robbie what his dad does for a living when we get back. Hey Geoff, their younger brother, Ray, is a year behind you in school."

"Is he like Robbie and Layne?" Geoff asked.

"Yeah, I think so," Jane said. "He's nice and smart. You'd like him."

"I'm sure I would. They've always been nice to me, Robbie and Layne," Geoff said. "Layne always smiles and says 'hi', and I remember one time when some guys knocked my books out of my hands in the hall at school, everyone laughed until Robbie stopped and helped me pick them up."

"That's because he's a black belt in Karate," Sawyer said.

"Really? I didn't know that," Geoff said.

"Layne's a black belt too," Jane said.

"What is a black belt?" Ariel asked.

"That's the highest level of achievement in martial arts," Sawyer said. "Hand to hand combat, self-defense, and stuff."

"They certainly are an impressive family," Ariel said.

"Geoff," Jane said, "I'm just curious. Who knocked your books out of your hands that day?"

"Just some guys," Geoff said, fidgeting.

There was a moment of uncomfortable silence, then Sawyer sighed.

"It was me, wasn't it?" Sawyer said. "I knocked your books out of your hands that day, didn't I?"

"Don't worry about it," Geoff said shaking his head. "It was a long time ago."

"No, I am worried about it," Sawyer said. "I did a lot of things to you and others that I'm not proud of, and it stops right now. I'm sorry, Geoff. It won't happen again, I promise."

"It's okay," Geoff said. "You're not the only…you know. Lots of other guys do it too."

"Are you serious?" Jane asked.

"Yeah," Geoff answered. "And I'm not the only one who gets picked on, either. There's lots of us."

"What are we going to *do* about that, Sawyer?" Jane asked firmly.

"Well," Sawyer said, thinking. "I dunno. Maybe we can start a student organization against bullying or something? We can call it 'JAB', 'Jocks Against Bullying', what do you think?"

"It's a start," Jane said. "But make it more inclusive, like 'SAB', 'Students Against Bullying'."

"Yeah," Sawyer said, rolling onto his back. "I like that. Let's work on it when we get back, okay?"

"Sounds great," Jane said. "That includes you too, Geoff."

Geoff raised his head, a bit surprised anything included him back in their world.

"We're going to need your input, too," Jane said.

"And pizza," Sawyer said. "Bring pizza."

"Oh I would *kill* for a slice of pizza," Jane said.

Geoff, Sawyer, and Jane all laughed. When they were done, Sawyer rolled back onto his side.

"It just occurred to me," Sawyer said. "This might be our last night together. Who knows what we're gonna run into tomorrow? If the Scarlet Queen is as powerful as they say, we're in for a big fight."

"Don't think like that," Jane said. "If we stick together we can win."

"I agree with Jane," Ariel said. "While we do not know what we will face tomorrow, we will face it together."

Geoff swallowed and laid back on his blanket. He opened and closed his fists numerous times. It was okay for the others to be so brave and upbeat, but he was scared.

# CHAPTER FORTY-FIVE
## COURAGE AND SACRIFICE

They reached the base of the Misty Cliff Mountains mid-afternoon of the next day. Ariel had found a safe place in a thicket from where they should be able to observe the combined armies approaching from the south. Occasionally, they heard distant thunderous bursts from the north and west, which reminded Geoff of drums or explosions.

They stayed among the trees for the rest of the afternoon. As soon as the sun began to skim lower on the horizon, Ariel slipped away to find a path leading to the lowest ridge of the mountain. After about an hour, she returned.

"The Night Guard are indeed there," Ariel said. "That means Talia spoke the truth."

"How many?" Sawyer asked.

"At least fifty."

"She said we shouldn't worry," Jane said. "Talia said not to be concerned with them."

"If it was just a few, I wouldn't be too worried," Sawyer said. "But fifty? How're we gonna get past them?"

"I believe I may have found a small deer trail, and, if we are lucky, perhaps they have no knowledge of it," Ariel said.

"If we can reach it after nightfall, we may be able to slip past undetected."

"Yeah, okay," Sawyer said. "But what if when we find the Scarlet Queen she sounds the alarm and then all fifty of them come running?"

"Sawyer," Jane said.

"Hey, I'm just being realistic here," Sawyer said. "I wanna go home and eat pizza and chocolate too, but first we gotta deal with this."

"If that should happen," Ariel said, "then we will need the services of a wizard and the Stormlord."

"I was hoping this was gonna be easier," Sawyer said.

"I saw the armies coming from the south while I was scouting," Ariel said. "If they arrive at the mountain valley first, there is a chance they could delay the Scarlet Queen's advance."

"Then Trelane, Shaun, Baldon, and Commander Renfry must be informed," Ishara observed.

"Agreed," Ariel said. "Come, we must warn them."

They rode south as fast as their horses would carry them. When they met with Trelane and explained the situation, he instantly ordered the troops to accelerate their march northward. Then he requested a meeting of the other leaders. Standing in an open field, the leaders of the combined southern army discussed the plan.

"So this narrow mountain valley," Shaun said, "You say we can wedge the dark army in there and slow their advance?"

"That is correct," Ariel said. "If we have time, suitable defenses can be prepared and, if the information we have is correct, we may be able to slay the Scarlet Queen."

"How do you know your information is correct?" Renfry asked. "This is a dire gamble."

"Talia told Jane there would be fifty of the Scarlet Queen's personal guard camped on the lower ridge of that mountain," Ariel said. "I have seen them with my own eyes."

"Do we trust that it isn't a trap?" Shaun asked. "Treachery is the norm these days."

"Yes," Ariel said, glancing at Jane. "This time I trust Talia."

"Very well. We're still outnumbered badly," Renfry said. "How do we succeed in slowing so large a host?"

"I believe the archers sent earlier are already slowing them," Ariel said. "But it will not be enough. If we can force them to fight in the valley, their greater numbers should prove less of an advantage."

Shaun asked, "And as for the Queen? How much time will you need?"

"As much time as you can give us." Ariel said.

"When we arrive at the mountain valley, the Knights of Caladar will assume the forward position," Shaun said. He looked at the other commanders. "Let fly with every catapult and every arrow you have, then we will ride into the Scarlet Queen's army."

"What?" Sawyer said, startled. "That's crazy. You'll die."

Shaun glanced at Sawyer and then the others, "In order for this plan to work, someone must take that risk and slow them. We lost many good knights when the Scarlet Queen ambushed us, but her army lost four times as many warriors. She will again learn that the Knights of Caladar do not easily die."

"We'll throw everything we have at them," Renfry said.

"Aye," Baldon said heavily. "Then it's settled."

As everyone mounted their horses, Sawyer spoke to Ariel in hushed tones, "What's he doing? Does Shaun want to die?"

"Of course not," Ariel whispered. "But he is an honorable man and a Knight of Caladar. Ask yourself, what is the price you would pay to save your world and your loved ones?"

"There has to be another way," Sawyer said.

"I have seen you demonstrate similar acts of bravery," Ariel said. "You have faced the werewolf, the ogre at Troll Fang Pass, and even the Shadowlord. How is this different?"

"That was the sword," Sawyer said. "It did everything."

"No, Sawyer," Ariel said, lowering her eyes at him. "It was the man, the hero I see before me."

They accompanied the southern army to the mountain valley, arriving just before sundown. Geoff and the others noticed Sawyer was quiet the whole way. Geoff paced back and forth as he flipped through the pages of the spell book his dad had given him, memorizing hand and finger movements. Ishara had collected two additional quivers of arrows in preparation for the upcoming battle. Shaun Hammerfel walked past looking for Sawyer, who was nearby watching the knights form their ranks.

"Sir Sawyer," Shaun said. "A word with you, please."

Sawyer turned and looked at him, "I can guess what you're going to say, but I'm coming with you."

"No," Shaun said. "I understand your disappointment, but I am the Lord Commander of the Knights of Caladar and I command you to accompany your friends."

"But I can fight," Sawyer said, "if you're worried whether or not I can kill to save lives…"

"I know you can fight," Shaun said. "Fight alongside your friends. And I am not worried about you in any regard. Here, I have something for you."

Shaun removed a gold chain with a milky, dark red polished stone from around his neck and placed it over Sawyer's head.

"This belonged to my son," Shaun said. "Keep it with you."

"Thanks," Sawyer said. He took the stone in his hand and looked at it.

Shaun placed a hand behind Sawyer's neck and pulled him closer so their foreheads touched.

"Always remember your knightly pledge," Shaun said quietly. "You're a knight. In any world, you are a knight. No one can take that away from you."

"I will," Sawyer said, wishing that he had the words to do his feelings justice.

Shaun patted Sawyer's shoulder and then walked away. The sounds of horns both in camp and in the distance almost caused Geoff to drop his spell book. Ishara came running up to him.

"It is time," she said. "We must go."

She led Geoff over to the spot where Ariel and Trelane stood. Soon they were joined by Baldon and Renfry. Before them, two thousand knights had assembled, their silvery armor glistening like mirrors in the yellow-orange light from the torches. Sawyer appeared beside Geoff as Shaun mounted his horse and rode to the front of the line to address his knights.

"Knights of Caladar," Shaun called out. "This is our time. Today we fulfill the pledge we took when we became knights. You have trained, fought, and bled every day in preparation for this moment. Let all of Alluria remember us. Let history remember us, and let the enemy fear us. Together with our brothers from Selra'thel, from Keredain, from Chalon, we stand here and fight. We fight against an evil tyranny that threatens all of Alluria. But this tyranny will not prevail. Not today. My fellow knights, it is our duty to stop the darkness here. I am proud to ride into battle with you."

Geoff's arms were covered with goosebumps. He'd never heard such a speech. Shaun lifted up his large war hammer and shouted, "For Alluria!"

An explosion of cheers ebbed into war chants echoed from men, elves, and dwarves as the ranks began to move. Ariel drew a scimitar and Ishara drew her dagger and hoisted them high overhead. Geoff drew his dagger and followed their example, as did Jane. Sawyer, however, turned away and wiped his face again.

"Do not look away," Ariel commanded. "Watch them and honor them. Their courage will not be forgotten, nor will their sacrifice."

Sawyer spun back around and unsheathed the Stormblade. He thrust it into the air and shouted "For Alluria!" Perhaps this was the sign some of them had been watching for, because a great roar came from the men, as they returned the salute of the Stormlord.

As the knights rode past, Geoff was in awe of the size of both horses and men. They looked like shining silver tanks as they passed. A moment later, Shaun Hammerfel cantered up to Ariel and said, "You will have the time you need. I give you my word."

"Thank you," Ariel said. "All Alluria will know what you do

here today. The Knights of Caladar will never be forgotten."

Ariel placed a hand over her heart and bowed her head. Ishara and Trelane did the same. Shaun nodded and turned his horse to ride away, but he stopped when he saw Sawyer and Jane.

"Sir Sawyer," he said. "After today, you will be the last of us. I'm counting on you to see this through to the end. I know you want to join this battle, but your task is far more important. You are to live. Tell everyone what happens here and, above all, live a long, joyful life. These are my final orders to you."

Sawyer's eyes were moist. He was doing his best to hold back a torrent of tears, but he managed to give Shaun a tight-lipped nod.

"If you ever find yourself in Caladar," Shaun said, pulling a sealed, crumpled envelope from inside his gauntlet and handing it to Sawyer. "I'd be grateful if you could find my wife. This letter is for her."

"I will," Sawyer said as a single tear escaped the corner of his eye. "I promise."

"And Sawyer," he said as he leaned forward in his saddle and smiled, "If I were your father…how proud I'd be."

"Me too," Sawyer said, his voice breaking and tears streaming down his face.

Then Shaun wheeled his horse around and rode away to join his men, and to join other legends of Alluria.

Jane suddenly wrapped her arms around Sawyer and began to weep. Geoff grabbed Ishara's hand. He looked into her emerald green eyes. He wanted to tell her what she meant to him, but the words didn't come. Instead, he squeezed her hand.

"Okay," Sawyer said, his voice loud and commanding, "we have a job to do. Let's get on it."

Sawyer took the lead, followed by Ariel and Jane. Geoff and Ishara, still holding hands, brought up the rear.

The Night Guard. Known and feared in Uln and in battlefields far beyond, they were the most ruthless of warriors. The Scarlet Queen valued them for their cruelty and their unquestioned loyalty. Whenever she traveled throughout Alluria, they always went first and were always by her side. They were fifty in number. That was all the queen required. To them, the Scarlet Queen was a goddess and they followed her commands without hesitation. That was their single purpose for living.

They had made camp on the lower ridge, just below where their Queen would be soon. They had scouted the area and found no one. Some ate and drank, while others sharpened their weapons in anticipation of the coming battle. If their Queen was pleased with them, they were allowed to join the attack. They looked forward to those chances.

Kieran, the leader of the Night Guard, was a large brute who had filed his teeth into sharp fangs. He was the first to notice a figure approaching. The setting sun was behind her, but there was no mistaking her hourglass figure as she casually walked toward them. She carried a helm and shook her head from side to side, letting her long hair fly free. He nudged his lieutenant, sitting beside him at the campfire.

"Who's that?" grunted the lieutenant as he chewed on a greasy piece of mutton.

"That," Kieran said with a lewd grin, wiping his mouth with the back of his hand, "is my reward for a job well done."

Several Night Guard sitting nearby laughed.

"Save some for the rest of us," the lieutenant said.

Kieran walked toward the shapely female, meeting her several yards outside of camp. His eyes roamed over her form and he grinned.

"Why are you here?" He growled.

Her bright blue eyes shone like a cloudless sky. She ran her fingers through his thick, unkempt hair, and placed her soft cheek against his. A sudden, sharp pain in his chest made him gasp. Looked down, he and saw he had been impaled by a sword-length spear.

"I am repaying a debt," Talia whispered.

She let the leader's corpse drop to the ground by her feet. Then, she fully extended the blood-soaked spear she had used to kill him. Several Night Guard shouted and swore as they jumped to their feet, weapons drawn. Talia calmly placed her helmet on her head. *This will not take long.*

# CHAPTER FORTY-SIX
## AGAINST THE SHADOWLORD

The night sky behind them lit up with fiery missiles as the southern army under Trelane and Renfry opened fire with catapults and flaming missiles. As the projectiles struck the ground, huge explosions erupted, sending flaming liquid everywhere. The massive army of the Scarlet Queen stopped to regroup after the first two volleys. Then Geoff saw a river of silver flooding forward. The Knights of Caladar resembled a silver spear as they cleaved into the dark horde, driving a wedge deep into their ranks.

Sawyer had also stopped to watch. He fingered the dragon's eye necklace Shaun had given him. Geoff thought he'd never seen Sawyer's face grimmer, or more resolute. With a heavy sigh, Sawyer turned back to the trail. As they neared the lower ridge, Ariel placed a hand on his shoulder and stopped Sawyer.

"Wait," Ariel said. "Let Ishara have a look first."

Ishara let Geoff's hand go and crept up to the crest of the ridge. Peering over, she stopped, motionless. Geoff briefly worried that she'd seen something terrifying, something that they'd have to fight. After a moment, she returned, moving as silently as ever.

"They are dead," Ishara said. "The Night Guard are all dead."

"All dead?" Ariel asked.

"Yes."

"How can they be dead already?" Sawyer asked.

One by one, they crept up to the ridge, but their care was wasted. It was just as Ishara had reported. The Night Guard lay strewn about, some of them headless. They had been slaughtered.

"Who could've done this?" Jane asked, looking around.

Ishara had been inspecting the area. Just then she motioned for everyone to come and see something. In the dark brown soil, she outlined a footprint. It was slender and smaller than the other prints.

"Talia," Ariel said.

"You mean she did this?" Jane said. "One person did this?"

"Talia is not a 'person'," Ariel said. "She is the perfect warrior, and yes, she did this."

"Okay, cool," Sawyer said. "So now she's on our side, right?"

"I would not count her as an ally yet," Ariel said, "but at least for the time being, she is not an enemy, and I will take that."

"She did say we shouldn't be concerned with the Night Guard," Jane said. "Now we know what she meant."

"So where's the Queen?" Sawyer said. "All of this is for nothing if we can't find her."

Ishara pointed to the far side of the ridge. There was the small path Ariel had discovered earlier. Geoff's heart was suddenly pounding again.

"Guys, this is too easy," Geoff said. "It feels like a trap."

"He's right," Jane said. "I don't like it."

"Be alert," said Ariel. "I do not like it either."

They ascended the trail, Geoff noticed it got steeper the higher they went. Soon, they arrived at another ridge surrounded by craggy outcroppings. The ridge provided a good view of the battle. Geoff peeked. The silver wedge of knights had grown smaller but held their ground. Catapults on both sides loosed their deadly armaments. There was a constant barrage of arrows from the elven archers.

Then Jane screamed. Spinning around, they saw the Shadowlord. He was fully armored in his black and silver plate mail and held a wicked looking sword with glowing red hot runes. His face was concealed beneath a wicked looking spiked helm.

"Spread out!" Ariel shouted.

Ishara fired three arrows at the Shadowlord in rapid succession. They shattered as they bounced off his armor. Sawyer's sword began to glow with small, blue-white arcs of lightning running along the length of the blade. Ariel and Sawyer rushed the Shadowlord. Ariel on the left and Sawyer on the right. They attacked in coordination, forcing the Shadowlord to step back or be flanked. Geoff and Jane maneuvered around the fight, toward the small trail leading higher up the mountain.

Ariel landed two consecutive blows to the Shadowlord's breast plate, staggering him momentarily. However, her attacks and her movements seemed slower, less sure. Geoff thought she still looked tired from her fight with Talia and she was more defensive, perhaps protecting her wounded side.

Sawyer followed up with a slash across his lower leg,

which dropped him to one knee. As Sawyer raised his sword for another strike, the Shadowlord suddenly stood and punched him in the face as he fended Ariel off with his sword. Sawyer fell backward, landing on the ground and lay motionless.

Ariel slashed the Shadowlord's sword arm, which drew a grunt of pain. Then, she made a thrusting attack with a scimitar. The Shadowlord reached out with uncanny speed and grabbed Ariel's wrist, stopping her in mid thrust. Geoff saw the puzzled look on her face as Ariel tried to free herself. The Shadowlord swung Ariel against the rough stone outcropping, slamming her against it with incredible force. The impact knocked the scimitar from her free hand.

The Shadowlord held Ariel's other hand up by the wrist and began to tighten his grip until Ariel cried out and let her second scimitar drop to the ground. Then he slammed her head against the rocky surface.

"No!" Jane screamed, rushing forward with her dagger. But the Shadowlord had seen her. The Shadowlord's cloak began to move and writhe, sending black, smoky tentacles toward Jane. Before she could react, her feet and legs had been ensnared and yanked out from under her. Jane fell backward, dizzy and disoriented. Turning his attention back to Ariel, the Shadowlord lifted her off the ground.

"This is where you all die," his voice resonating from under his helmet. "You were never strong enough to defeat me. So much for the prophecy of the three outlanders."

"I will not…let you…harm them," Ariel vowed through her teeth, as she struggled to fight back. "They…"

Geoff watched in horror as a smoky black tentacle slithered around Ariel's neck. Geoff saw that it was tightening, squeezing the life from her. She went limp. He pointed to a large rock on the ground and gestured toward the Shadowlord. The stone obediently levitated and propelled itself, striking him hard on the side of the head and removing his helmet. The Shadowlord swirled and snarled, revealing a malicious set of fangs. He looked different, too. His skin was paler and Geoff noticed tiny purple veins on his face and neck.

Another tentacle whipped at Geoff, striking him across the chest and sending him tumbling a few feet back down the trail. Just then two arrows struck and penetrated the Shadowlord's side. Spinning around, he received two more arrows in his neck. These stopped him in his tracks. He glared at Ishara as he pulled the arrow shafts free. Two more arrows flew toward his face, one for each eye. He deflected these with his fist.

He walked toward Ishara, grinning as he knocked away arrow after arrow.

"I will twist your head from your shoulders, little one."

Ishara backed up to the edge of the ridge. They were at least a couple of hundred feet from the ground. The Shadowlord had hemmed her in with his writhing cloak, she had nowhere to go. As he reached for her, Ariel appeared and slashed his hamstrings with her scimitars. The damage she dealt would've ended the fight with any other warrior, but his vampiric powers were such that the wounds began to heal immediately. Meanwhile, Ishara had taken her chance, dodging the tentacles as she sprinted away to a safer location on the other side of the ridge.

"You will pay for that!"

The Shadowlord sprang to his feet and grabbed Ariel's

neck and ran her into the rocky crag. More arrows flew through the air, only to be whipped away by the smoky tentacles. The Shadowlord pushed Ariel's head back, exposing her arteries. But before he could sink his fangs into her, Sawyer struck him across the back with the Stormblade. Writhing with pain, his body wracked by hundreds of tiny arcs of lightning, the predator dropped his prey.

Another arrow penetrated a weak point in the Shadowlord's armor, striking him in the armpit. He spun on Ishara.

"Enough!" He shouted as two tentacles swiped at her. She ducked the first, but the second struck her midsection and sent her sprawling back toward the rocky-strewn trail.

The Shadowlord turned to deal with Sawyer.

"You don't stand a chance, boy. You aren't strong enough."

Sawyer wiped a bit of blood from his lip and locked gazes with the Shadowlord, "Yeah, today I am."

The Stormblade flashed as Sawyer charged the Shadowlord. This time, he chose the same move he had used on Sir Reymond in the sparring arena. It briefly caught the Shadowlord off-guard. The Stormblade hummed with every strike, sending arcs of lightning over his opponent's entire body, causing him to shudder and drop his sword. Sawyer did not tire. He kept up his attack, swinging with precision, recalling all that Ariel had taught him. And when he remembered Shaun, he found enough fury to cleave the blade into the Shadowlord's side, causing him to cry out.

Evading the writhing cape, Sawyer spun round, aiming a blow at his neck, but he ran into a mailed fist, which knocked him over. The Shadowlord knelt beside Sawyer.

"A nice move, boy, but not good enough."

He raised a mailed fist, intending to batter Sawyer's head to a pulp.

"No!" Jane appeared behind the Shadowlord with one of Ariel's scimitars, swinging with total abandon. "You won't hurt him! I won't let you hurt anyone ever again!"

The first stroke bit deep into the Shadowlord's armor and flesh. The second still deeper. As the Shadowlord grunted in pain and grasped at his wounds. The third struck the side of his neck, emitting purple ichor from the gaping wound. Jane was preparing to bring the scimitar down on top of his head when the Shadowlord grabbed her ankle and slammed her to the ground. Jane lay there, dazed, but she had done considerable damage to the Shadowlord. Blood was pouring from the gaping wound in his neck as he rasped, "What a disappointment you always were. I shall enjoy draining your life."

As he reached for Jane, someone grabbed his hair from behind and pulled his head back. It was Ariel, holding her second scimitar high. His eyes flew wide open. The next instant, Ariel thrust her scimitar into his heart and dropped to her knees beside him. Jane and Sawyer began to stir. They saw the Shadowlord twitching uncontrollably, but he managed to grasp Ariel's scimitar.

"Ariel...p...please," he said as he tried to pull it deeper into his heart. His eyes reflected sadness and guilt.

"I have...much to answer for."

Ariel placed a trembling hand gently on his cheek.

"I will remember you...as you were. A good man and a brave knight." Then she wrapped her arm around his shoulders and shoved the scimitar through his quivering body.

Geoff and Ishara arrived at Ariel's side as she delivered the killing blow. The Shadowlord crumbled into dust, leaving only his armor, sword, and what appeared to be just an ordinary black cloak. *What an awful way to go*, Geoff thought. *But he got what he deserved.*

"Are you okay, Ariel?" Geoff asked. "How's Jane and Sawyer?"

"Fine," Ariel said as she tried to catch her breath. A trickle of blood ran down the side of her face. "We will be fine."

Ishara raised Jane's head and held a flask of water to her lips. Ariel pressed her hands on Sawyer's chest and closed her eyes. Sawyer began to groan and slowly turn his head.

"He was a lot stronger than before," Sawyer said under his breath.

"Agreed," Ariel said, looking at Sawyer "He was."

"Ariel, I lost my bow," Ishara said. "When the Shadowlord hit me, I lost my grip."

"Oh, I saw it back there, on the path," Geoff said, "I'll get it."

Geoff ran back to the trail, rubbing his aching chest. The black tentacles really hurt when they hit. He picked up Ishara's bow and walked up the trail to the ridge where they had defeated the Shadowlord, then someone caught his eye. He dropped the bow and started running up to the next ridge.

"Dad!"

# CHAPTER FORTY-SEVEN
## THE FINAL CONFRONTATION

Geoff rubbed his eyes to make sure he wasn't imagining. His back was to Geoff, but Geoff was sure it was his dad. *Yes, it was him. He was here!*

"Dad!" Geoff called as he scrambled up the trail. "Dad, where've you been?"

He reached the ridge and stopped. Someone else was there. Geoff's skin began to crawl and his heart raced. He stepped to the right, away from the trail to get a better look. *Something just wasn't right. Something was horribly wrong.*

"Dad?"

Maelord turned around. Geoff smiled. His dad, however, didn't seem to recognize him. Instead, he stood there, arms folded looking at Geoff with no emotion on his face.

"What happened?" Geoff asked, "What're you doing here?"

"Because *I* wish it," said the other figure behind Maelord. Her back was still to Geoff, but there was something about her that seemed familiar. It wasn't the scarlet cloak, the long and elegant dress, or the longsword she carried, nor was it the ornate breastplate or pauldrons. But that dark auburn hair, the rigor with which it was pulled back, *that voice…*

Geoff stepped forward. The figure in the scarlet cloak turned around.

"Mom?"

"Of course I'm not your mother," the scarlet cloaked figure snapped, baring her teeth. "I could never spawn a worthless runt like you. I should have killed you when I first entered your world."

"But…you and Dad…you're married…"

"You're simple," the Scarlet Queen said with contempt. "Your father was easy enough to beguile. He's been my eyes and ears since before you stumbled onto the portal."

"No…this isn't happening…" Geoff said, shaking his head in disbelief. "Why?"

"Why what?"

"Why are you doing this?" Geoff said.

"Because I can, you little toad. Alluria is mine by destiny," the Scarlet Queen told him. "I am above all others."

As Geoff stepped back in horror, she ran her fingers through Maelord's hair.

"So imagine my surprise when I detected *your* presence, a boy with vast reservoirs of magical energy. Perhaps with sufficient power to rival *me* one day. So, I traveled across the realms to your world only to find you, a sniveling, pathetic, puny weakling."

"So you did *all* this," Geoff said, shaking his head, "but you're my stepmom…"

The Scarlet Queen sneered. "I knew you were nothing when I first saw you. Just a weak little boy, all alone. No friends. Unloved. Had I killed you then, it would have been a mercy killing, but I detest mercy."

Geoff crouched and put up his hands and a shiver ran down his back. Hope began to ebb. He was hopeless. He was nothing. But suddenly, he heard another voice.

"You are wrong," Ariel said, stepping onto the ridge and positioning herself between Geoff and the Scarlet Queen. "He is not alone."

"He does have friends," Jane added, standing beside Ariel.

"And he is dearly loved," Ishara said as she stood beside him and nocked an arrow.

Sawyer walked past Geoff and patted him on the shoulder, "Hang back, Geoff. We got this."

"You've got nothing!" the Scarlet Queen snapped through clenched teeth as she glared at Sawyer. "You're just a boy with a sword."

"Whatever," Sawyer said. "It's time to end this."

"Sawyer, that's Geoff's stepmother," Jane said in a low tone.

Sawyer looked in disbelief at Maelord, who looked back with a blank expression.

"No way," Sawyer said, "I don't get it. Why would you marry *her?*"

"Even a wizard can be charmed, you witless idiot."

"You cannot win, Lysis," Ariel said as she stepped forward. "Alluria will not be yours."

"*Queen* Lysis," she said, lowering her gaze at Ariel. "Do you think your paltry alliance can stand against me?" She gestured behind her at the battle below. "See? Your armies are about to be annihilated."

Geoff glanced at the struggle in the valley. He no longer saw the silvery sheen from the armor of the Knights of

Caladar. Instead, the dwarven infantry, combined with soldiers from Chalon, were engaging the black army of the Scarlet Queen. Elven archers continued to fire volley after volley of flaming arrows into the invading army.

"You are never going to be our queen," Ishara said.

The Scarlet Queen rolled her eyes and turned away. As she walked past Maelord she said disdainfully, "They bore me. Kill them." In a split second, Maelord had thrown up a shield spell that was wide enough to provide him with full cover. The next moment, he gestured toward Sawyer and a white whip shot forth from his hand, wrapping around Sawyer's legs. As Maelord pulled the whip, Sawyer fell back, hitting his head on the ground and disorienting him. Ishara fired at least eight arrows at him while he attacked Sawyer, all of them bouncing off his shield. She darted left and right in an attempt to get a clear shot, but Maelord's shield was perfect.

Then Jane stepped forward and crossed her arms in front of her, crying, "*Tae'nalara!*"

Maelord was propelled backward through the air toward the rocky outcropping behind him. Before he struck it, he held up a hand and his momentum stopped. He hovered there, four feet off the ground. He did this while maintaining his shield spell.

Next, Ariel held her hands up. A green glow sprang forth from her palms and then she clasped her hands together, sending a green orb at Maelord. The orb struck his shield and obliterated it. The impact slammed the wizard against the craggy outcropping behind him.

Maelord dropped to the ground and landed on his feet. Then he cried out in pain as an arrow from Ishara struck his leg. Ariel rushed forward while Jane went to Sawyer. Ishara continued to fire arrows at Maelord. This time, they were aimed such that he had to either duck his head and stay low or be killed. He noticed Ariel bearing down on him and did a circular motion with his hands.

A gust of wind blew outward from his hand, encircling him and stopping Ariel's advance while causing Ishara's arrows to veer off target. Next, he made a sweeping gesture with his hand and Ariel, Ishara, Jane, and Sawyer were thrown against the outcropping.

"Dad!" Geoff shouted, "Stop this!"

"Kill the boy," the Scarlet Queen ordered, still concentrating on the battle below. "And do it with your bare hands."

Geoff glanced at his friends. None of them were even moving. It was all up to him. Nobody else. Just him and his father. Maelord limped badly as he walked toward Geoff. His face was void of expression. Geoff pointed to a large stone on the ground and gestured toward his dad's uninjured leg. The stone flew at him, but Maelord waved it off and the stone flew off over the cliff. And his father continued to advance.

Geoff tried to scramble away, but slipped on some loose stones. Maelord grasped him by the collar and pushed him against the outcropping. Geoff felt his dad's hands close around his throat.

"Dad...what're you doing?"

Geoff coughed and tried to pry his father's hands from his neck, but Maelord was too strong.

"It's me...Dad. Geoff...I'm your son."

For a second, Maelord's grip loosened and Geoff saw a

glimpse of recognition in his eyes.

"Dad…fight it. You…gotta fight it."

Maelord's face became blank again and Geoff felt his Dad renew his attempt to strangle him.

"No, it's me…Geoff…your son…"

Maelord suddenly blinked and released Geoff. He looked confused at first by his surroundings, then by what he was trying to do to his son.

"Geoff?" Maelord said. "What's happening? Argh! My leg!"

Maelord grasped his injured leg and looked down at the arrow protruding from it.

"Oh?" the Scarlet Queen said, turning her head. "A father's love for his son…it *would* take a bond that strong to break my spell. How annoying. I will not make that mistake again."

Queen Lysis turned around and faced Geoff and Maelord. The same sneer and contemptuous look on her face belied the evil behind her dark eyes.

"You! Stay away from my son!" Maelord thundered, throwing a glowing ball of fire at her.

The ball struck the Scarlet Queen and exploded. Geoff stepped back, he felt the heat surge from the explosion. A second later, the flames disappeared and the Scarlet Queen still stood, unaffected. She sighed.

"This is no way to treat your wife, dear husband."

"Now I remember what you did to me," Maelord said, gesturing. "Consider this a divorce."

Maelord pointed at her and launched a huge arc of lightning at her. This time, when it struck her she cried out in shock and pain. She recovered and screamed at Maelord.

It was a harsh, primal, rage-filled scream. She clenched her fists and snarled.

"So, you are not a god after all, are you?" Maelord mused. "You can be hurt, and that means you can be killed."

"Insignificant wizard!" Queen Lysis pointed at Maelord and a thin yellow beam of energy struck him in the chest. Maelord grunted as he clutched his chest and was thrown back against the rocky mountain side.

"Dad!" Geoff yelled as he rushed to Maelord's side. He was barely breathing.

Geoff heard the sound of several arrows being fired in rapid succession, then Ariel raced past, scimitars in hand. The Scarlet Queen was struck twice by Ishara's arrows, which seemed to cause her more discomfort than pain. Ariel was a far more serious threat, spinning and slashing, forcing Queen Lysis to the edge of the ridge. Then Ariel crossed her scimitars in front of her and shouted, "*Tae'nalara!*"

Queen Lysis was violently expelled from the ridge, catapulted into the night air with tremendous velocity. She screamed as she spun and twirled through the air. Ishara continued to fire arrow after arrow, each striking the Scarlet Queen in mid-flight. Suddenly, the Queen's trajectory stopped and Geoff saw her begin to change. Her arms transformed into leathery wings, her fingers into claws, while her face became as elongated as a serpent's.

The Scarlet Queen glided back to the ridge, still in mid-transformation. Her eyes glowed red and she bared her fangs again. "I'll rip you to pieces!"

Ariel sheathed her scimitars and crouched, getting on all fours, and lowering her gaze, "You are not the only one with powers, great Queen."

Then Ariel's body began to change too. She also became more serpent-like and spines grew from her back, horns from her forehead. Her fingers became long claws that dug deep into the ground. She turned to Geoff and Ishara, "Stay back!"

Her voice was deeper, growling, more animal-like, and it reverberated all around. Ishara and Geoff looked on in shock as Ariel and Queen Lysis altered their forms. They grew into thirty foot long dragons. Ariel's form was green with gold edges on her scales and wings, while Queen Lysis' dragon form was a deep red, dappled with black highlights.

Both dragons roared at each other, revealing impressive maws lined with sharp teeth. The entire ridge shook as they charged each other, colliding with a thunderous crash. They ripped and tore at each other with frightening viciousness. Ariel whipped her spiked tail and struck Queen Lysis on the side of her head. The Queen responded by raking Ariel's neck with long claws.

Both dragons stepped back and inhaled. Then they breathed massive streams of fire toward each other. Their fiery breaths collided, with neither dragon able to force the other back. When their breaths came to an end, Ariel took flight, exploding off the ground with one great flap of her wings. The Queen followed closely behind.

Geoff's mouth dropped. He couldn't take his eyes off the two majestic creatures as they battled overhead. Streams of fire flashed and faded in the night sky as the dragons launched their fiery breaths at each other. Then the Queen flew into Ariel, hooking her claws into her spine. They began to plummet as they bit and clawed furiously at each other. When they separated, Ariel flew away, zigzagging to avoid the Queen's fiery breath.

Sawyer and Jane appeared next to Geoff and Ishara.

"What's going on?" Sawyer asked, captured by the colossal battle. "Where did the dragons come from?"

"They turned into dragons! Look!" Geoff managed to blurt out as he pointed up.

"Dragons?" Jane said. "I didn't know Ariel could do that."

"The High Druid of Alluria can assume almost any form she chooses," Ishara said. "But I do not believe any druid has ever taken the form of a dragon."

"Look at them," Sawyer said. His tone was one of awe. "They're incredible."

They huddled around Maelord. Ishara removed her arrow from Maelord's leg and Jane healed the wound with a healing charm.

"He's going to be okay, Geoff," Jane said.

Geoff exhaled. Having his dad back was great, but if Ariel lost the battle in the skies, they were all in trouble. They watched as the green dragon, which was smaller than the scarlet one but much faster, fly in uneven circles around the scarlet dragon. The green dragon swiped with its claws or snapped with its long fangs as it darted past. The scarlet dragon tried to snap at or breathe fire on the green dragon, but she was too slow.

"Is there anything we can do to help her?" Jane asked.

"I don't see what," Sawyer said. "Anything we send at the scarlet dragon might hit Ariel instead."

Then, the green dragon flew past, its scarlet rival in close pursuit. The gust of air from their wings pushing them back against the rocks. As they watched, the green dragon soared into a few clouds, causing the scarlet dragon to lose sight of her. The scarlet dragon hovered in place, breathing fire impatiently all around. Without warning, the green dragon dropped on her from above, digging her scimitar-like claws into the scarlet dragon's neck and breathing fire directly on top of the scarlet dragon's head. It looked like an explosion in the sky as the scarlet dragon screeched and twisted in every direction in an attempt to free itself.

The scarlet dragon's head caught fire and they plummeted from the sky, still clawing and snapping at each other. As they neared the ground, the scarlet dragon swung itself over the green dragon.

"Lookout!" Sawyer shouted. He pulled Jane to him as the dragons crashed into the ridge. The resulting shockwave from the impact slammed them to the ground. Geoff clearly saw both dragons crash, the scarlet dragon was thrown against the outcropping while the green dragon flipped over and over before coming to a rest. The dust and debris thrown into the air from the impact was stifling.

Through the haze of dust, Geoff saw the green dragon shape changed back into Ariel. The moonlight shown down on her prone body. The scarlet dragon also changed back into the shape of Queen Lysis. Coughing and trying to catch a breath of fresh air, Geoff looked for Ishara, Sawyer, Jane, and his dad.

They were strewn nearby, unconscious, but all appeared to be okay. Geoff rushed to Ariel. She had taken a tremendous blow from crashing into the ground.

"Ariel," Geoff said urgently, shaking her shoulder. He saw several claw marks and scratches on her body, but she was still breathing. "Are you okay? Get up!"

"She isn't okay," the Scarlet Queen said from behind Geoff. "I'm going to rip her to pieces."

Geoff whirled around. Limping toward him was Queen Lysis, at least, what was left of her. The entire left side of her face had been badly burned and she sported deep wounds from Ariel's claws. She also appeared to be in mid-transition between dragon and human. Her arms were still wings and the part of her skin that hadn't been burned away was still partially covered in scales.

"First, I'm going to drain your soul," she said. "Then I'm going to feast on your friends."

Geoff gulped. The fearsome and grotesque *thing* coming toward him looked like one of his nightmares. Geoff stood up and gestured toward a large stone. Before he could finish the spell, he himself was hurtled through the air and slammed against a large boulder. The wind was knocked from him as he struck the rough surface. Geoff sat up, a little dazed. Watching her come for him was chilling. He was unable to move. There was nothing he could do.

Then an arrow slammed into the Scarlet Queen's side, then another, and another. Ishara moved between Geoff and Queen Lysis, loosing arrow after arrow. Some were deflected by her wings while others penetrated the Scarlet Queen's armor. Annoyed, she lashed out, throwing Ishara as hard as she could into the side of the mountain with a sickening *thud*. Ishara's body slid down the surface, leaving a trail of blood behind it. The horrific sight made his heart sink, but it also galvanized Geoff.

"Ishara! No!"

He reached out to her, but she didn't move. She lay in a contorted position as he began to crawl toward her.

"Ishara!" he called.

"She's dead," the Scarlet Queen cackled. "What a shame, I so wanted to taste highborn elf blood again. Look around you, they're all dead or dying because you're weak. You should have died first, but now you can watch everyone you care about die."

Even as a half-dragon, he could sense her smile. Tears flowed down his cheeks and his heart began to beat like a jackhammer in his chest. Suddenly, Geoff felt a slow rage rising inside his chest. All those years he'd spent being picked on in school, laughed at by everyone who called him names, all the embarrassing moments he experienced when others had played cruel pranks on him, every lonely moment he had, they came together and formed a white hot rage deep inside.

Geoff didn't scream at the Scarlet Queen, he roared. It didn't matter what happened to him anymore. This was it. Trembling with fury, his hands became encompassed with white balls of electrical energy. Everything, every fiber of his being was being called upon to create the most devastating spell he had ever cast. Queen Lysis stopped and blinked, seemingly not believing what she was seeing.

"No!" Geoff screamed as he launched two bolts of lightning at her. "Noooooooo!"

Both bolts struck Queen Lysis and this time, Geoff heard her scream like a wounded animal. Geoff kept throwing bolt after bolt at her. They were far more potent than anything he had cast before, each bolt of lightning had the power to shatter keeps and burn entire fields of crops. The Scarlet Queen began to smolder and caught fire as she dropped to her knees. Geoff pointed his hands at her, causing two continuous lightning bursts to spring forth and scorch Queen Lysis.

Geoff couldn't stop. He didn't want to stop. She was a smoking pile of charred remains but he was still blasting away. Gradually, he felt his head and chest beginning to ache. He found it hard to breathe. If he was going to die, he was going to take the Scarlet Queen with him. His arms felt like lead weights and everything began to spin. Geoff slumped against the outcropping. He'd used too much of himself, but he didn't regret it. The only regret he had involved Ishara. He looked at her with a deep longing. She hadn't moved. He wanted to hold her again. He needed to tell her how he felt, but it was too late.

From the corner of his eye, he saw Ariel crawling toward Ishara.

"Help her," he croaked, "please…help her, Ariel."

Then a harsh laughter arose behind him. Geoff looked over his shoulder and saw the still smoldering, burned form of Scarlet Queen rise from the ash pile, reassembling itself, still half-dragon and half-human.

"Impressive," she said through clenched teeth. "I knew you had power. Power to kill. All you needed was a reason. You'll make a fine slave."

He couldn't even talk anymore. As he began to fade in and out of consciousness, a deep growl came from a ledge above him. All he saw were moist fangs and two hate-filled, yellow eyes glaring at him from the darkness. Again, the werewolf had followed them. Its claws dug into the rock face as it lowered itself to the ground only a few feet away from Geoff. All Geoff could do was look at the beast. His mind was filled with one thought. Ishara.

Then the werewolf snapped in Geoff's direction, its massive jaws strong enough to shred him in an instant. However, it turned its head and faced the Scarlet Queen. She hissed at the beast, her own set of fangs showing in the moonlight. In an instant the werewolf launched itself at Queen Lysis, who had become more dragon-like. The werewolf crashed into her and they fell to the ground in a tangled mass, rolling over and over. They began raking at each other with their claws. The werewolf started to savage the Scarlet Queen, her hisses and snarls mixed with the werewolf's growls.

In a wild effort to free herself, Queen Lysis kicked the werewolf away with her dragon's legs. Then, flapping what remained of her wings, lifted herself off the ground. She started to fly away, leaving the ridge behind, but the werewolf had recovered and sprang onto her back. It renewed its attack, sinking its fangs deep into her neck. As they tumbled downward they missed the ridge and fell to the rocky ground far below. Sawyer and Jane had gathered themselves and staggered to the edge of the cliff. Sawyer had a noticeable limp. Jane had wrapped an arm around his waist to support him. Holding each other tightly, they watched the epic clash unfold between two mortal enemies below.

Sawyer let the Stormblade drop to the ground and grunted as he and Jane fell to their knees. Jane held him close, her shaking arms forming a tight circle around his waist.

"They're still ripping each other to pieces." She gasped.

The Scarlet Queen had continued her transformation

into a dragon, but was unable to complete the process. She was pinned on her back by the werewolf, her neck still in the beast's jaws. This time, she had absorbed the brunt of the fall. She clawed at the werewolf's back and arms in an effort to free herself. They were a blurred mass of black fur and deep red scales.

Sawyer turned his attention to the battle in the valley. He saw only a few knights standing against an ocean of darkness. The elves and dwarves had formed ranks and fought valiantly to reach the remaining Knights of Caladar. He saw Trelane and Baldon at the forefront of the push. As he watched, Sawyer saw only two knights left, then one. The last one standing was swinging a large war hammer, battering orc and barbarian alike. A moment later he was gone.

"Oh Sawyer, I'm so sorry," Jane said, who had followed his gaze.

Sawyer's chest heaved as he fought back tears. *It's not fair. The bravest man ever. It just wasn't fair.*

A sudden commotion from directly below drew Sawyer's attention. The werewolf had begun to shake its head, its jaws ripping through scale and flesh. And then they heard it, the unearthly death-cry of the Scarlet Queen.

"He did it," Sawyer said, taking a deep breath. "She's gone."

As he and Jane looked on, the black form of the werewolf threw its head back and let out a long savage howl. Then, it turned and limped away on all fours, sometimes half-falling, heading west.

"Sawyer, look," Jane said, pointing at the battlefield.

As Talia had predicted, the army of the Scarlet Queen,

having heard her echoing death scream, broke and ran. The allied army of dwarves, elves and humans pursued them.

Geoff lay against the rock face watching Ariel work on Ishara. He hoped she would survive. She was the first girl to accept him for who he was and he'd never forget her. He hoped Ariel had enough magic left to save Ishara. A sudden, deafening shriek echoed through the night, drowning out the sounds of battle. It was followed by a chilling, aching howl. He took one more breath.

"Ishara."

Then his vision dimmed until it became a sea of black.

# EPILOGUE

His mind drifted for what seemed like an eternity. There was something about the darkness he found comforting. He was floating. Or maybe he was flying. Geoff didn't care because it was an exhilarating feeling. He didn't have a care anymore. His worries and the pain of life were over now. He could go. He didn't mind, it all seemed to be okay. Everything was okay. He was going to be okay. He wasn't afraid. There was an acceptance he felt, he resigned himself to go wherever he was going.

*Wait. Was that bacon? Do they have bacon in heaven? And did he hear voices? Were they having a bacon party in heaven?* He liked bacon. Everything started to become gray. The voices became louder, too. Then the light gray became brighter. Geoff blinked. He found himself in a camp at the base of the mountain. Ishara was sitting next to him, smiling into his eyes. Her bright smile filled his heart.

"Ishara, are you in heaven too?" Geoff asked. Before she could answer, he pulled her close and kissed her.

"I am now," Ishara said, caressing the bridge of his nose with a finger. "I am now."

"Yo!" Sawyer said. "Geoff's awake!"

The next moment, he was surrounded by Ariel, Sawyer, Jane, and his father.

"Welcome back," Maelord said, tousling his hair. "Well done!"

"It's over, Geoff," Jane said. "The Scarlet Queen is dead. We won!"

"Yeah," Sawyer said. "The werewolf finished her off."

"How do you feel, Geoff?" Ariel asked.

He looked at the smiling faces around him, "Good," he said. "Tired, but I feel good. Can I have some bacon?"

"Of course," Ishara said. She walked to the campfire and prepared a plate of food for Geoff, stacked high with bacon.

"I'm sorry I attacked you, son," Maelord said.

Geoff tried to sit up, his back was sore and stiff. His father helped prop him up and kissed the top of his head.

"It's okay. You couldn't help yourself," Geoff said. "I know you were under the Scarlet Queen's spell."

Geoff made short work of his meal. The he stretched, wobbling a little. Ishara placed a hand on his back and steadied him. After a minute or two, the dizziness began to subside.

"So what happened with the battle?" Geoff asked.

"After the Scarlet Queen died," Jane said. "Her army turned and ran. Just as Talia said."

"I wish I could've seen that." Geoff said. "What about the others? The dwarves and elves?"

"We lost many brave knights and warriors," Ishara said. "Trelane, Renfry, and King Baldon are fine. The elves and dwarves were fearless, as were Commander Renfry's forces from Chalon."

"And the Knights of Caladar?" Geoff said hopefully.

Ariel shook her head and lowered her gaze. "Shaun…"

A sadness fell over the camp. Geoff regretted his question. He walked over to Sawyer, who was sitting under a tree.

"I'm sorry, Sawyer," Geoff said. "It's because of him and the Knights of Caladar that we won."

"Indeed," Ariel said. "I believe we have a chance for a bright new era in Alluria. We paid dearly for that opportunity."

"So what happens now?" Geoff said. "It's over, right? Do we go home?"

"You two can go back," Sawyer said. "I'm going to Caladar. I have a letter to deliver. And I'm sure his wife would want that, too." Sawyer turned and pointed to Shaun's war hammer, which was leaning against a tree.

"I'm coming with you," Jane said, resting her head on Sawyer's shoulder.

"Me too," Geoff said. He put his hand in Ishara's. "Together, right?"

Ishara squeezed his hand, "Together."

"Somewhere out there is a necromancer of horrifying power," Ariel said. "And a good man who has suffered far too long. Alex deserves a second chance. Without a king, Chalon will begin to break apart and the nobles will fight each other for power. What do you say, is the adventure over or do we help him?"

"We're going to help Alex," Geoff said firmly. "Then we're going to find the necromancer, and we're going to finish the adventure."

## THE END

# BOOKS BY
# MITCH REINHARDT

## Wizard's Key
Book One of the Darkwolf Saga

Winner: 2017 Young Adult Book of the Year – NYC Big
Book Awards
2017 Finalist: The Wishing Shelf Awards
2020 Reader's Favorite Book Awards: Silver Medal Winner
– Young Adult - Adventure

## The Iron Citadel
Book Two of the Darkwolf Saga

Winner: 2018 Young Adult Book of the Year – NYC Big
Book Awards
Winner: 2019 International Book Awards Fiction: Fantasy
2018 Finalist: The Wishing Shelf Awards
2020 Finalist: Book Excellence Awards

## The Scarlet Queen
Book Three of the Darkwolf Saga

**Coming soon by Mitch Reinhardt:**
Blood Moon
Book Four of the Darkwolf Saga


Authors love to connect with readers.
Please drop by and say hello! Visit
www.mitchreinhardt.com

www.ingramcontent.com/pod-product-compliance
Lightning Source LLC
Chambersburg PA
CBHW051511250626
47156CB00001B/51